THE LIGHTHOUSE
AT THE EDGE
OF THE WORLD

THE LIGHTHOUSE AT THE EDGE OF THE WORLD

J.R. DAWSON

TOR

Tor Publishing Group

NEW YORK

THE LIGHTHOUSE AT THE EDGE OF THE WORLD

Copyright © 2025 by J.R. Dawson

Interior art by J.R. Dawson
Lighthouse art by Shutterstock.com

A Tor Book
Published by Tom Doherty Associates / Tor Publishing Group
120 Broadway
New York, NY 10271

www.torpublishinggroup.com

Tor® is a registered trademark of Macmillan Publishing Group, LLC.

EU Representative: Macmillan Publishers Ireland Ltd, 1st Floor, The Liffey Trust Centre, 117–126 Sheriff Street Upper, Dublin 1, DO1 YC43

The Library of Congress Cataloging-in-Publication Data is available upon request.

ISBN 978-1-250-80558-4 (hardcover)
ISBN 978-1-250-80560-7 (ebook)

Our books may be purchased in bulk for specialty retail/wholesale, literacy, corporate/premium, educational, and subscription box use. Please contact MacmillanSpecialMarkets@macmillan.com.

First Edition: 2025

Printed in the United States of America

10 9 8 7 6 5 4 3 2 1

To Jessie,
All my stories are for you.

To Cerberus,
Better known as Toby, Stitch, and Paddington.
Now you'll live forever.

And finally,
To who I was.
The girl who ran after L trains
slept on couches
and walked through snowstorms
alone
because Chicago held her brave, young heart.

AUTHOR'S NOTE

While this book holds many hopes, it also comes with some difficult passages, including an active shooter situation, death, self-harm, suicidal ideation and suicide, endangerment of an animal, and estrangement from a parent.

If you are struggling, as someone who has struggled herself, I can say there is hope even when it very much does not look like it. Please reach out to someone, text 988, or call the National Suicide Prevention Lifeline at 1-800-273-8255.

If you are a survivor like Charlie or her parents, there are resources and people who understand. A good place to start is Survivors Empowered at survivorsempowered.org, an organization run by Jessi Ghawi's family that provides resources and self-empowerment for those whose lives have been affected by gun violence.

For Chicago residents specifically, there is chicagosurvivors.org, which is a wonderful nonprofit that provides services to the families of Chicago homicide victims.

And these are only three organizations in a long list of groups that offer support and help. You're not alone.

"Love doesn't die, people do."

—*Merrit Malloy, "Epitaph"*

REMNANTS

Here is your story, written down. Above all, remember this.

Your name is Harosen. You are the ferryman. You built the Station. You protect the city from the Haunts and the demon beyond. He started the Great Fire. You locked him away in a tower.

You must keep your Station's light burning.

Do not let him out.

—*Excerpt from a letter to the ferryman*

1

NERA

Nera Harosen lived in a ferry station for the dead, between the city and the lake.

But living, for Nera, was living in a forever. Each day in the Station passed like the last, each night like the one to come.

But Nera did not yet know that tonight, forever would end.

Nera stood at the edge of the ethereal Station, her back straight and her eyes glassy, a specter with lantern in hand. The little basset hound named Elbee stood by her side.

The Haunts are getting closer, he said to her.

Nera saw the Haunts, frightening static and smoke, an amalgamation of lost souls, reaching out from the darkened sides of the path that led to the Station, clawing at the stones. But they still hissed and shrank back when the great light from above swung their way, like a sword from the sky.

Her father's lighthouse.

The lighthouse still holds them back, Nera said. But then the light flickered. Something wasn't right. It hadn't been right for some time.

Your father is getting older, Elbee said. *The lighthouse gets dimmer. Nera, I am afraid what will happen if things don't change.*

The lighthouse flickered again.

Before Nera could say anything else, they saw tonight's guests cross under the long bridge that separated the lake and the Station from the city. Nera raised her lantern higher. *Here!* she called to the dogs that led the souls down the stone path. She would guide them past the Haunts and into the Station, where her father waited to ferry them to the world-to-come.

As her father's apprentice, it was her great duty to keep the Haunts from devouring the new souls, to protect their guests from harm.

The ghosts who arrived did not look like the corrupted Haunts. These souls were small whispers, feelings, remnants of someones who used to be. She could not see them properly; they weren't corporeal any longer, more like wisps of clouds moving alongside one another. Guiding them were many, *many* dogs. They protected the ghosts that had not been consumed by the Haunts. They led them to the lake and beyond.

Between the bridge's underpass and Nera, on the stone path, was a fountain. A plume of water sprayed down through the crowds far beyond its circular basin, sprinkling the souls and the stones. As every dog and ghost crossed through its mist, Nera saw the spirits' bodies reappear. Not alive, but the memories of faces, hands, feet, hair. In gray scale, rather than in color, but visible all the same.

The soul remembering the body.

Nera raised her lantern, and the crowd followed her light past the four main pillars and into the massive Station. Her father said it resembled a train station. The dogs said it was grand and gorgeous. It was all Nera had known.

You are safe now. This is your resting point, Elbee sounded out to the crowd behind them, in the voice and language of the dead. Nera did not speak to the dead. Only the dogs did. *It is between the world-that-was and the world-to-come. You are welcome here. Take your time. And when you are ready, the ferry leaves every night for the Veil.*

Everything about the Station's marble, glass, and iron frame spoke strength. As Nera turned around and headed past the large pillars into the Station, the atrium ahead gleamed with the lighthouse above the glass dome and the stars beyond it. The perfectly polished floors were immaculate. Two long curved staircases stood opposite one another on either side of her, curling upward to the balconied second floor. All of this, the glass and the polished floor and the golden staircases, reflected the lighthouse's lamp that shone courtesy of her father's magic.

The dogs weaved around, guiding all the ghosts through the atrium, up to the mezzanine, and down carpeted halls that snaked off this main marble hub. Nera knew these hallways led to many rooms full of things ghosts missed from the city. An echo of life, but something safer: nostalgia.

Nera never used these rooms, because what use did she have for nostalgia?

Nera did not remember life outside. She had been found by the Station Master as a baby, her fingers grasping onto the shores of Chicago, her feet kicking in the waters of Lake Michigan. She had been raised inside the Station's walls. She was not dead, but her life was lived among the dead. Years passed in the way summers do when one is young: time marches, and there are days and nights, all uncounted. But Nera enjoyed the feeling of forever. Even when she had decided to become an adult, her life had been here, in these unmeasured echoes of others.

The souls came from the city. They would leave through the lake. And Nera would stay here as their anchor, their guide, their protector. The same scene, over and over again, an eternal welcome and goodbye. She was the sinew between here and there. Someday, when Father left through the Veil and entered the world-to-come, he would trust her own magic to light the Station. And she would give everything to this home.

She hoped she would be enough.

This existence was safe. This home was shelter, knowing no breath, but also no pain. Their staff was small, only Nera and her father and the dogs. How grateful Nera was, to not know the city's pain.

This is what she told herself.

Elbee, the leader of the dogs, stayed by Nera's side in the atrium. He had tired, doleful eyes that always seemed to know more than he told her. He nudged her side. She wondered, if they were in the city, would his touch be something more than a way of saying, "Hi, I'm here." Nera didn't feel, didn't smell, didn't taste. She sensed pressure, numbly, and saw, clearly, that her friend Elbee was beside her. But what would the fur of a dog feel like?

No. She shook the idea from her thoughts. It was enough to know Elbee existed. Sometimes these ideas of being alive would rise, but Father always said it was too easy to get caught up in life, in the world-that-was. *Don't look the guests in the eyes,* he often said. *Don't see their faces. They are a crowd to be guided. Stay in this moment, don't get distracted.*

At the stroke of midnight, her father appeared at the top of the staircase.

The Station Master's name was Harosen. He had once been a mortal man, had once lived in the city over a hundred years ago. Then, after the Great Fire that almost destroyed the city, the Haunts had risen. So, he'd built the lighthouse, became its keeper and protector. He'd held the line for over a century, forging himself into something more than a mortal. He now stood like an old white statue, tired and chipping away, but still thick and broad and confident.

He was his own kind of specter, with color in his cheeks and pepper gray in his thick, combed hair. He wore an old black vest and occasionally hooked his thumbs in its pockets. A red bow tie hugged his neck, but he did not breathe or speak aloud.

If she could, Nera would keep him here like this, forever.

Then again, forever was all she knew.

But she saw the lighthouse above him, still flickering. Still dimmer than it should be. Elbee was right.

All aboard, Father announced to the dogs in the voice of the dead. Then he looked to Nera, his hazel eyes sparkling with affection.

Nera, he said as they met at the bottom of the stairs. *You are my greatest wonder of light in this Station.*

For all the magic the Station held, it still grew very solemn when it was time to gather for the ferry. Some souls departed for the hotel wing, not yet prepared to leave, but most followed the dogs onward through the atrium to the eastern side's docks, facing the waters. They were ready. Nera and Harosen followed the souls and the dogs like two shepherds.

The colorful pair brought up the rear of this monochrome parade, passing under the red wooden archway that marked their path into the waters of Lake Michigan and the ferry that waited for them. The dogs flanked their procession, one for each spirit, and led the guests aboard. The ferry always held as many people as it needed to. The souls, their guide dogs, the Station Master, and Nera.

The boat wasn't a gondola, and it wasn't a fantastical galleon. For as long as Nera could remember, it had taken the form of a motorized double-decker ferry. Instead of architecture tours, though, this boat ferried its guests to the world-to-come.

Harosen started up the engine while his daughter dutifully stepped onto the rocking boat. Nera looked to Elbee, and Elbee reported, *Everyone is safely aboard.*

The passengers took seats on the wooden benches, or stood at the railings. Like most nights, the majority were older, but there were a few children. The souls pointed around at the dock, at the outside of the Station, and some craned their necks to see the city skyline. Others looked away, like they'd already said their goodbyes. Or maybe they didn't know how to say goodbye.

If it were Nera's final time seeing the skyline, she supposed she would watch it until it disappeared. She stole a glance now, eyeing the large buildings that glistened like the stars; lights dancing on and off from the faces of those behemoths. She did not know any of the names of the buildings. Chicago was a foreign land, too distant to see the living, but too close to ignore.

Harosen kept the helm steady, and the ferry's engine puttered. It never gave out, and Harosen never guided them astray.

As the ferry pulled away from the shore and the Station, Elbee came to nudge her again.

You always watch the city, he muttered. *I see you. Every night.*

Nera didn't say anything. Perhaps not every night.

During the day, in the Station, there were chores and halls and lighthouses and dogs and Father. A melted mosaic of memory she could dive into, as if the Station was the whole world. But out here, she could see the breadth of the universe. Or at least the city.

Your father hasn't looked out to the city since he left it, Elbee said.

Because the city is a dangerous, painful place, Nera said.

Elbee sighed, that big gruff of a sigh that only dogs can do. *Well, if I am to forever live on the edge of a city, I am glad it is Chicago.*

It was an unknown kingdom, the place they all were leaving. The place where the ferryman's daughter would never go.

Never.

And what was the point of having an opinion on such a fact? It would not change. She was never to leave the Station and the lake. If she *was* to have an opinion, surely her opinion would be the same as her father's: they were blessed to stand in the in-between, in a dream.

Elbee wandered to a quiet corner for a nap, so Nera turned from the city lights and looked ahead into the dark black lake. To the breaker, where the ferry would head deeper into the night, and the city would disappear behind them, receding into a fog.

As they passed into open waters, and the sky and the lake both glimmered with stars, there was no going back. Only forward into an unknown. All the souls around Harosen and Nera melted from gray to glowing bright gold and green and purple and blue . . . unique hues, running together like watercolors.

Then the boat arrived at the Veil.

Wide, a void in the air stretching from the lake to the stars. A glossy iridescence rippled through the dark night, catching the eye and then disappearing and then reappearing. Like an aurora borealis gleaming out from the mouth of a cave.

It led somewhere beyond. No one knew what was on the other side, but her father said it was a world-to-come. This was a portal leading beyond the lake, beyond the Station, beyond anything anyone on this side of the Veil had ever seen.

The Veil hummed quietly. The ferry puttered closer. Nera climbed the stairs, taking her place at her father's side.

The dogs stayed by the sides of their appointed souls, some nuzzling, others happily chatting.

Keep your eyes on the waters, Father murmured.

She should have stopped watching the dead. Each of their faces turning to look at their final stop, expressions of peace, anger, hope, fear, all the things she imagined a human would feel in a lifetime, now settled into this one last moment.

This was the dance of the dead performed every night. But tonight, something was different, out of step.

There, in the middle of the kaleidoscope of color, was something solid. Bold. Clear.

As clear as Nera and Harosen.

It was a woman with a messy chopped haircut: thick, unwashed dirty blonde hair with a haphazardly cut fringe. Her pale nose had little freckles. She wore a green hooded sweater, a black skirt, and bangles of silicone bracelets around her wrists. She was not glowing. She was tangible and solid, a physical body, not something bigger, not something dead. And she didn't have a dog.

She looked alive. She *was* alive.

Nera stared at her. How could she have missed this woman back at the dock? She wasn't supposed to look too closely at the crowd, but how could she have missed this?

This woman was stuck in flesh, bones, blood, schedules and deadlines and anxieties and identities.

Nera looked to her father, who had not noticed the woman. Instead, he looked to the void of the Veil. Nera couldn't see past it; only small shades of purple as the edge of the world hummed through the surface.

The glowing souls leaned forward.

But the woman, she stumbled backward, and she fell, and she gave a small hiss.

With her voice.

Not a memory of a voice, but a true voice. One that still had vocal cords, still made vibrations in the physical realm.

Nera moved closer. Harosen was readying the plank. He didn't even register Nera approaching the terrified woman with the brown eyes.

"It's alright," Nera tried. And Nera heard her voice.

I heard *my* voice.

"It's alright," I said again. Something separate from my father, from the ferry, from the dead and the lake and the Veil. It was a voice that only came from me, from a throat and a tongue and a mouth . . . *my* mouth. *My* body.

The woman shot backward. She shook her head. "It's not alright," she said. And I reached out, brushing the top of her hand. She was solid.

She really was alive.

I couldn't feel my own breath. Did I have breath?

"Who are you?" I asked her.

"Charlie," she said. Her name touched her lips, in a small inflection that only belonged to her. Her mouth turned just the slightest bit, as if she was hiding a smile . . . or perhaps a sadness. Her eye narrowed, just one, auburn specks imperfectly placed in the dark brown iris.

"You're not dead," I said.

She stared at me. "No, I'm not. And neither are you."

I suppose that is when it moved from a fairy tale to my story. My life. My death. My time in between.

When I saw Charlie, I woke up.

2

CHARLIE

Chicago was made of ghost stories.

And I could see every one of them.

I stood on the back porch of Marco's apartment in Pilsen, looking out to the alley and the other old brownstones. I'd known this city my whole life, and now it featured an extra layer of memory placed on top like an animation cell. The dead, faint little clouds, faces and limbs, shuttered in and out. Reflections.

I shouldn't have come here tonight.

The last time I saw Marco was back in April. We had been trying this whole rigmarole of finding peace in each other. It was fucking pointless.

Sam had already been dead a whole month at that point. Dad and Marco had already exploded at each other. But Mom hadn't left yet, and I still had the slightest sliver of hope that my best friend would be there for me.

"Something weird happened in the hospital that night," I had finally told him, sitting in that diner. "I was waiting for a room out in the hall of the ICU. The doctor pulled Dad into a private room to tell him about Sam. And he screamed. I could hear it in the hall."

"I heard it from the waiting room," Marco'd said, his curly black hair hiding his boyish face. Even though he was in his mid-twenties, his soft brown cheeks and big puppy dog eyes always made him look young and sweet. I felt safe to keep going, because there was no distance between us. We grew up together. He'd loved my sister, so much that he was going to marry her. He'd sat shiva with the family as one of us. He wanted to talk about her. He wanted us to say her name. He was a survivor in this hellscape with me. "I remember," he had said, as if he was here for the good, and the bad.

Well, what a fucking lie that turned out to be.

"Okay, so I'm sitting on the gurney, Dad's screaming, and I close my eyes," I'd said. "And I don't know what the hell I did, but I just begged whoever could hear me to let me see her one more time. Maybe it came out as a prayer or a spell or maybe I'm just fucking crazy but . . . Marco, I opened my eyes and saw this . . . ghost."

Marco had just stared at me. That softness was frozen. I got nervous.

"Well," I continued, "not just *a* ghost. A lot of ghosts. Everywhere. All around."

"What?" is all he'd offered me.

A very dead woman sat in the booth behind him, fuzzy and without the lower half of her body, like a frayed projection. She wore an old hat over finger-curled hair.

"You know how when music plays," I started, "you know it's all around you? You can't touch it, but you can feel it. You know?"

"Okay," Marco tried slowly. "And did you see Sam?"

"No," I said. "But I've spent the last month trying to find her. I looked around the house, the hospital, the mall—"

"Charlie," Marco interrupted. Like he was saying "stop." His hand came up, his palm in a weak plea. "Charlie, you need to tell your doctor about this."

"This isn't the concussion, Marco."

Marco's hand went limp. And he looked out the window. His eyes were welling. "Charlie, you don't fuck around with head injuries."

"You don't believe me."

He had said nothing.

Rage. I threw down my change on the table and scraped out of the booth. "You know, I really thought that if I could trust one person it would be you."

"Charlie—"

"Sam would have believed me."

I hurt him with those words. But he hurt me with his. And Dad had gutted him, and Mom gutted me. And Sam left us all with bloody gashes across our hearts. When death happens, people get hurt. And sometimes, there's no knowing how to stop it.

So now why the *fuck,* nearly six months later, was I back here at Marco's like it was gonna help *anything*?

Tonight, I stood on Marco Ramirez's back porch, the new apartment of an old friend Sam and I had known better than we'd known ourselves. Marco always threw a Halloween party, and I had never missed a single one. Neither had Sam. So I thought she might be here. She wasn't.

Everyone else stayed inside and warm, dressed up as Ashton Kutcher or Paris Hilton or George Bush. I saw at least four Spider-Men . . . I guess 2005 was the year of Spider-Men.

Marco was dressed as Bob Dylan. I cobbled together a low-effort Daria. Bob Dylan and Daria kept glancing at each other over a crowded room of spider-people and Playboy Bunnies, before I decided it was too much and headed for the porch.

The idea of enjoying a costume party seemed so normal.

But Marco and I weren't normal anymore.

We loved a dead girl. Just because she was dead didn't make us love her any less. It just meant it hurt more.

So here I was, at a party, alone on the porch, empty-handed because Sam was in fact not there. "I know you wanted me to go as Phoebe," I said to her, wherever she was. She would have gone as a pirate, for the fourteen-hundredth time. "But I found your music, and you better show up."

I pulled out some loose papers of sheet music and held them to my chest. I'd tried so many different trinkets of hers, like bait on the end of a fishing line. Old notes, birthday cards, her car keys with a silver Elphaba hat charm dangling from them. I'd tried so many places, all around the city, but she wasn't there.

But I'd found this last week, in a box I didn't like to open. This sheet music felt the most like her, a small remnant that had frayed off before the murder. Untouched by what had happened. Still Sam.

An unfinished song.

I felt someone watching me. "Sam?" I snapped around.

Nope. Just the ghost of a pale man, standing in the corner of the porch. He was *in* the corner, half of his face obscured by the brick. Like his house had been torn down and this brownstone built just a bit off-center. He looked like a glitch in the Matrix.

He just stared at me, politely. *Dobry wieczór,* he said in my head.

I turned my back. I closed my eyes. I breathed in and out. "Not today," I hissed at him. "Please get out of here."

Sam would have been kinder to him. But I wasn't Sam.

The porch door smacked open. I jumped a little. Marco stepped out, and I felt both relief and dread.

"Hey," he said. His voice sounded hoarse. Lower. Slower. But it was still him. And I wanted to hug him and say, "We'll figure this out." But I didn't. I just nodded.

Marco leaned on the railing next to me, nursing a beer. I saw him as the little boy who had grown up next door, then my roommate along with Sam, and now between us, we held a future we would never see.

"I didn't think you'd come," Marco said.

"I came," was all I could manage. If I tried to tell him about the ghosts again, he'd get that face. Like he was scared for me. Or *of* me. Like he couldn't take me losing my mind.

I clenched the sheet music in my fingers. He saw it.

"Ah," he said. I knew he wanted to look at it, but I didn't hand it over. I had a death grip. The awkward moment passed between us. "You know, for a musician, Sammy really hates to write shit down."

"Yeah," I said. "I'm glad I found this much. It's uh . . . from the Rapunzel musical she'd just started."

"Do you still have her recordings?"

I shook my head. "They got lost in the move. Along with the desktop." We had lost her all over again. Dad was crushed. He smashed a bunch of his own vinyls when we found out. I knew he blamed himself even more than he blamed me.

But I didn't want to mention Dad in front of Marco.

"Nice new apartment," I said, weakly.

"Yeah," he said, and then, like I'd finally given him an open door, he added, "Did you guys find a place? Did the house sell okay? Do you need any money? I can—"

"We're fine," I said. "We made enough to live on for a little while by selling the house and other stuff."

Like her piano. Where did you put a piano when you didn't have a home? After Sammy died, Mom said she needed to start over, and Dad didn't want to stay there all alone. The house had become a crypt anyway. So, Mom left, Dad checked out, and I was ghost-hunting when I wasn't taking care of him. Everything changed in so little time.

"You eating?"

"Yup," I lied.

"Okay. Hey, uh . . . just a heads up." He shifted his weight to his arms, resting on the wooden railing. "Some TV people contacted me about an interview, *which I didn't do*, but . . . there's probably gonna be coverage again. It's not the anniversary yet, I don't know why—"

"Yeah." The word was a shield, a barrier, a "stop now."

He didn't stop. "Do they still call Pops?"

"We changed his number and the apartment is under my name," I said. "I blocked who I could."

When someone dies, it's pain. But when strangers find fascination in your tragedy, it's uncanny and vulnerable as the world replays your grief and gives it a name and infographics. The only thing to do is keep the television off and the phone unanswered. I didn't feel like seeing it happen again. And again. With the catchy title underneath. I hated it. I didn't want it to be some official thing. Like if I refused to give it a name, it couldn't constantly haunt me.

It was a fluke, people liked to say. *These things don't happen every day. That's why it hurts so much.*

No, it hurt because my sister was fucking dead.

These things don't happen, but the century kicked off with the towers falling, Baghdad was bombed on live TV, and now New Orleans was underwater. Maybe this was just how the world was now. Every time you and your sister left your house, only one of you was coming home alive.

I felt sick. I turned away from him.

Marco looked at his bottle, and then he gave a small snort of a laugh. "You know," he said, "I tried talking to Pops a few weeks after. I asked him what we were gonna do. You know what he said?" I knew, but I didn't say anything. He took another sip, scowling. "*There is no we.*"

"I'm sorry, Dad's not been—" I started.

"But I just meant like . . . I meant how were we gonna bring her back." He shook his head, like he was disgusted with his childishness. "Like in Pops' song about that guy who walks down into hell and grabs his wife right out of the river Styx . . . Hercules?"

"Orpheus," I said. The name of Dad's song was "Orpheus." "But it didn't work out for him."

Bringing someone back from the dead, that was impossible.

But finding their ghost? I could do that. I *would* do that.

Marco nodded. "Right, duh." And then he added, "Yeah, I miss you." He squinted at me, like he was seeing me from a million miles away. "You always know a lot, and you always know what I'm talking about."

I missed him, too.

I wanted nothing more than to be back in our apartment with him and Sam, the Three Musketeers, clueless assholes in our mid-twenties trying to find our way. Getting ready for a wedding. Putting in job applications while I subbed at a middle school off the Red Line and Marco worked as a clerk and Sam wrote music. Once upon a time, we were family.

"I wonder if Orpheus would fall in love with her . . . if he knew how it was going to end . . ." Marco muttered, and then he raised his beer. "I would." And he finished the bottle.

Oh, he was drunk.

Then silence. Because what the fuck are the survivors supposed to talk about?

She wasn't here. And in that way, neither were we.

Something pulled at my stomach. I looked down to the alley, where there were lines of factory workers from the 1800s, still walking back and forth from the assembly lines and slaughterhouses. The Polish ghost was now trying to light the memory of a cigarette, his fuzzy cloud of an outline leaning on a fire escape.

Something hissed from the alley.

It was going to happen again.

Usually, ghosts went about their business. But sometimes, the smoke would come.

And eat them.

Consume them.

Boil them down, until they became part of this mass of static.

The ghosts never reemerged.

I didn't know what to call it, the static cloud of smoke. But I did not like it.

"Okay, and how are you—?" Marco began.

"I should get going," I said quickly, before I could see the Polish man be eaten.

"Charlie," Marco said as I pulled away. "Please, just look at me—"

But Daria left Bob Dylan on the porch. Alone.

I shouldn't have gone to Marco's. It was a fool's errand that led to nothing. I knew that I'd just feel like shit if I saw him, but she could have been there. She *should* have been there.

I gripped the edges of my coat, sitting frozen on the bus as it rocked and jolted down the street. Marco, she'd loved Marco . . . fine, leave me, but I couldn't believe she had abandoned Marco.

So either you're a selfish prick in the afterlife, I muttered to her in my head, *or you're in that static.*

No. That's not how this ended.

It rained the whole time I was on the bus.

The 21 bus was full of Chicago, both alive and dead, existing on top of one another. Like I'd forgotten to wind my camera before taking the next picture and all of a sudden it was photograph on top of photograph.

The living held shopping bags, wore scarves covering thinning hair, and wrapped big thick Carhartt coats around bodies that smelled like cigarettes. An older man unwrapped a CVS bag, revealing some sort of gooey leftovers he scooped up with his hands and gulped down with an underbite.

The dead looked like memories flickering through projectors. Floaters in my eye, there but not there. Although they were only parts of a memory, I could see the story of the city splayed out on their clothes: pioneer shirts, flapper dresses, Victorian skirts, Edwardian hats, T-shirts bemoaning elections thirty years ago. Honestly, when I started seeing ghosts, I only had about a week of sheer panic before I weirdly grew accustomed to it. Ghosts were, for the most part, not scary; they were just people.

It was like everyone was listening to their own soundtrack. Some of the ghosts looped, doing one action over and over again, like a gouged CD, always restarting a song twenty seconds in. I called them Loopers.

Some of them diligently watched over someone alive on the bus, their mist curling on the person's shoulder. I called them Clingers.

Others looked out the window, still trying to grasp onto life. Maybe pretending it was still a nice rainy day in 1926, and they were heading home for dinner. I just called them sad.

What if Sam was stuck somewhere?

I clutched the music sheet tighter in my sweaty palms.

You asshole, I whispered to her. *I am still here. I'm waiting for you. Come back. Come home. Find me.*

One of the ghosts must have heard me. An old white woman. I could barely make out her mist, but I saw her hair poofed like my mom's in her graduation photos. I couldn't see her legs, and barely saw her arms.

She started to come over—no, started to *float* over. It could have been a horror movie, but I knew she was just a person and not a monster.

Not like the static in the alleys.

Hello, she said. *You can see me.*

I nodded.

I have a daughter. She pointed to another old white woman sitting half-asleep in her bus seat. *Can you please let her know . . .* And she stopped. . . . *How long has it been? She's older . . . how long . . .*

Sam would have helped her. And Charlie Before All This would have never hesitated to be kind.

But I just said, *I'll let her know,* with my dull face and my dull eyes reflecting back to me in the window behind her. I was a stranger to myself.

How long had this ghost been following that woman, trying to talk to the living? And Sam couldn't even be bothered.

The bus stopped. I stood up, pressed my skirt down, put my hood up, and leaned over to the woman stirring in her seat. Her eyes fluttered open, and I said, "Your mom had some cool hair. She wants me to let you know she's with you."

Before the woman or the dead mom could say anything else, I stepped off the bus and back into the world.

Little puddles reflected the city on the ground, the lights and Chinatown archway in a mirrored universe I wished I could just sink into. I kept the sheet music close to my heart under my hoodie.

I should have been making sure Dad ate dinner. I tried to imagine him in our apartment, staying up for me. Cooking some pasta, texting me, u ok kid? But it's harder to conjure imaginary ghosts when you know real ones exist.

If I could find Sammy, maybe I could find Dad. And Mom. And Marco would stop talking about Orpheus, and we could all cobble ourselves back together into a life.

"If you don't come back for me," I muttered to her, "come back for them."

I stepped under a store's awning to get out of the drizzle. I took out the music. I ran my fingers over her notes. Touching a dead person's handwriting. Every little swoop she made, every quarter note she filled in—she'd been here. An echo of her life, still pulsing in this world that she'd broken away from. She was not here, but her notes were.

I touched the opening words: *adagio.*

"Patient," she had told me when she wrote it down. "It means be patient."

Sam was good at patience. She was quiet, thoughtful, and the only time she wasn't calmly sitting somewhere, she was running like lightning, training for whatever marathon. Either adagio—slow—or vivace—bright and full of life. Me, I was never adagio. I was presto (extremely lively), fortissimo (the loudest), with a crescendo (getting louder) for good measure. Or that's what she always said.

Not so true anymore.

Sam, I squeezed the music, closing my eyes. *I don't know who I am and I need them, and I need you. Please, Sam. Please just show yourself.*

A rain-soaked prayer to the once-living; a useless plea to someone who had only been human and now was probably just dust. Something so powerful going out into the ether, only aimed at a hope of a ghost.

But then I heard a rushing.

A percussion.

I took a sharp breath. I opened my eyes . . .

And the Red Line rushed above the street into the Chinatown station. I was gonna miss the train.

Just the train.

I felt tears hot on my flushed, burning face.

I trudged forward, slipping the sheets back under my hoodie, carefully cradling them. I kept moving, my hair wet. My cheeks red.

The streets full of people, the air full of ghosts. I walked through the dead like Marco's Disney version of Hercules swimming after Megara in the river Styx. I felt their feelings, just waves and washes like passing fish in the ocean. They disappeared, moved out of the way, screamed in my ear.

Dead people all around us, all the time. Filling up the air like ash.

God, let them drown me.

I walked faster, trying to outpace my thoughts. Then I ran. Fuck adagio.

But I couldn't outrun the memory of my sister. The constant empty spot where she should be. Grief never fucking leaves. People leave, cars and houses are sold, clothes and shoes given away, music is lost, plans destroyed . . . but grief, never. Grief was steadfast and merciless.

I tripped. I fell. The music sheets flew all over the place.

"Are you fucking kidding me?" I screamed.

I watched, helplessly, as the sheets fluttered like will-o'-the-wisps in the air, swinging in the cool rainy wind. As they scattered, landing in puddles, flying across the street, shooting under passing car tires.

I stared in utter disbelief.

Then I burst into tears. *I can't remember that song forever, Sam, I'm going to forget it . . .*

Why did I trip?

Why did we split up in the mall?

Why had we been there at all? A thousand little notations that had to happen in the perfect order to kill my sister.

The train clacked its last car above. The rails sparked and screeched. Now only ghosts remained on the platform, looking down at the tracks. Dead people who had jumped.

In a city like Chicago, sometimes the only way to scream out and be sure anyone could hear you was to fuck up the evening commute.

But even then, Dad still wouldn't notice.

I could do it. I could climb up there and jump.

Hey, a scruffy voice sounded behind me. *Are you alright there?*

I wiped my eyes. I shoved it all back in. I stood up, the papers fully scattered and ruined. "Yeah, I . . ." I turned around to face the Good Samaritan.

But the only person there wasn't a person. It was a dog.

A big black scraggly dog, part giant wolfhound, part poodle, part Muppet. He cocked his head. *You sure you're okay?* he said.

He spoke like a ghost. The *dog* spoke *like a ghost.*

I stared at him.

Oh, the Muppet dog said. *You're alive. Whoops. Uh . . . Woof.* And he kept on down the road like nothing had happened. Except he hummed under his breath. He *spoke.* Now he *hummed.*

It was a small tune, notes settled beside each other in a graceful slide of up and down and quarter note . . . rest . . . a major key sitting so close to a minor key. It sounded like a flower blooming at the end of the world.

It was Sammy's song.

My heart seized. I ran forward. "Hey! You!"

The dog stopped. He swung his head around to look back at me, a question mark in his raised brows.

"Where did you hear that song?" I demanded. "Do you know Sam?"

The dog's ears pulled back. And then he ran.

"Wait!" I shot forward into the rain, grabbing out for his fur to stop him, but I missed and stumbled under the bridge . . .

I caught my footing and looked up. The dog was gone.

But something was very wrong.

I wasn't in Chinatown anymore.

The big dragon mural, the green and red of the buildings and gray cracks in the concrete, they had given way to grass and trees. There should be buildings upon buildings, I should be in the heart of a busy neighborhood. Instead, I was at the end of a long street in a park. And beyond the trees changing colors lay the North Side, old condo buildings standing in lines like the Queen's guards.

In the dark, I saw the smokestacks of the Lincoln Park Zoo. The Conservatory. And the bridge with the L train had been replaced with the long highway of Lake Shore Drive.

"What the fuck," I muttered.

Somehow I was on the other side of the city. I had gone under the train's bridge, but there was no bridge above me now, just the overpass ahead of me.

The Lake Shore Drive overpass greeted me with cars flashing in bright lines through the rain. Sam's music whispered on the wind and pulled me from the city. A flute. Violins. It sounded like it came from underneath the overpass.

The overpass was brick, covered in vines that climbed up its side. But then the vines shook. They grew. Like Jack and the Beanstalk, they curled around an entrance, softly, matter-of-factly. They made a waterfall of green. And the vines seemed to sing, hum something . . . no, from *behind* the vines I heard the song . . .

I knew what was on the other side. Lake Michigan.

Sammy and I came here right before I moved for college. She'd dropped out a couple of years earlier. That was a hard night, not knowing what being sisters looked like when you didn't live in the same childhood home anymore. I mean, we had nothing to worry about; the future would bring us together before it tore us apart. But in that moment, we sat together at the edge of the city. The chaos of Chicago stopped in its tracks by the night sky and the black water.

She'd looked at me. "The edge of the world," she'd said in her breathy, steady calmness. Somewhere between a flute and a clarinet. I knew her voice like a favorite song. I knew her music like I knew her heart.

And now that music swelled from behind the ivy. After a few measures, it looped back around and started over. Her last song. Unfinished.

"Sam?" I whispered. I walked into the ivy, under the bridge, and . . .

On the other side of Lake Shore Drive stood a massive building made of light and glass.

It looked like a gigantic greenhouse, or train station, or Crystal Palace at Disney World, King's Cross in London, a Van Gogh painting underwater, a glissando with the damper pedal slammed down. Echoes of sound and life. A massive dome with a flickering lighthouse for a crown.

At its feet I saw a fountain and a sea of ghosts following . . . dogs? I trailed them as they forged ahead through the spraying water. I could see the ghosts now, so much clearer. No longer floaters in my eyes; just folks in black and white, walking and wheeling instead of floating. Actual full bodies. Not wisps of what was.

The current of souls pressed around me like I was stuck in a stream. I closed my eyes. There was so much to see, but I wanted to hear.

Yes, underneath the rushing whistling of the march of souls, under the dogs and the waves of the lake . . . the song played on.

This city kept stories of my sister in all its corners. And here, that story sang.

If I was going crazy, I didn't want to be sane. If I was asleep, I didn't want to wake up. My sister was here, in this dream.

I turned to face the Station. The crowd pulled me forward to the pillars. And I crossed the threshold into the light.

REMNANTS

—*From Sam Connor's notes, "maybe Rapunzel's motif? maybe violin to start. adagio."*

3

NERA

Alive.

The woman in front of me—the *live* woman on the boat for the *dead*—was neither a memory nor an ending. She breathed air. Her voice spoke through the wind, pushing out from lungs and a rib cage. Her cheeks were pink. Her death was not written—she still traveled the tracks of her unfinished timeline, aging and breathing and moving forward.

I held out my hand. "You're not supposed to be here."

Then my father started down the ferry's grated stairs, coming toward me. I realized when my father walked, he did not breathe. His boots made no sound on the stairs. And this girl, she did make noise: gasps, her boots squeaking . . . wherever she existed, life surrounded her, reaching out like vines and roots and making the world breathe.

So I breathed, too.

I had never . . . I stepped back. My eyes focused on her face, with so much detail, so much more than the souls ever had. I seemed to be seeing for the first time. Freckles. Frayed ends of her hair. The stitching in her clothing, the softness of her fingers.

The magnitude of one person was overwhelmingly beautiful.

The souls began to stare, still glowing. They whispered to each other, spitting off their emotions and their lights in all different directions.

Alright, alright, everyone just calm down, Father gruffed, batting them away unceremoniously like fireflies. *Get ready for debarkation. I'll take care of this.* His eyes shot to me.

He spoke like the dead. A soundless prayer on the wind made of words spun invisible.

He pulled me back from the living girl, huddling close like a conspirator. *Keep your distance, Nera.*

But the girl was not well; she shook and fell to her knees.

Don't worry, he assured me, seeing my face, his mouth raising in that half-smile half-grimace, still not breathing. *No one died from being close to death. We'll figure this out later.* He patted my shoulder and went to work on the upper deck.

No one died from being close to death. But could they live?

I returned to her side, offering my hand. "Follow me," I said. Out loud. Again.

Her teeth chattered, cold. I felt something I'd never known . . . the anticipation of something wonderful about to happen.

I could admit now that it had been stirring inside me for so long. A curiosity hidden underneath all the routines and habits that I took for granted. Now that curiosity bloomed like a fire, enveloping me . . . warming me.

"I c-can't . . . move . . ." she whispered. Faintly. "The curtain thing . . . it's so loud . . . it feels like I'm gonna vomit . . . it hurts, I can't—"

"Then we'll move together," I said. And I got closer.

I touched her hand. It was solid, fingers with shape, a wrist with bones, moving and compact in a physical form. No one but my father, the dogs, and I existed in a real body here, with the light of our souls tucked away behind our ribs. A thing made of the real world, dirt and dust and earth, that I now understood existed so one spirit could touch another. A gateway made of millions of impossible things so we could feel one another.

Bodies were miracles.

I was never going to be able to step back into my fairy tale.

I helped her to the bench on the other side of the boat. She wasn't going to make it to the second floor.

I set her down, my arm around her. She leaned into me, and I felt her vibrating. "My name is Nera," I told her.

A sound like a whale singing came from beyond the nose of the boat. I looked up. The Veil was calling.

On this main deck, the dogs broke off into their formation, and the angry ball of fluff named Happy yipped at everyone to get in line. They made two rows, leading up to the plank.

Go on! Happy barked in a sort of caw screech. *Our friends did not come all this way to not get a good sendoff! Chop chop, Penny! Don't give me that look.*

After the dogs lined up, they raised their heads. They closed their eyes. They glowed, lighting the way to the final step of the plank.

The souls on the ship stood single file, each one different, but bustled together. They shifted, collided, all unique colors, like fireworks. The dogs each took turns leaving their lines to rejoin their person as they passed through the corridor of guardians. The dogs whispered final goodbyes and reassurances.

Father's distant expression dimly looked toward the Veil as this process unfolded.

In a long line of reds and greens and blues and purples, the spirits moved slowly to the Veil as the dogs shepherded the dead to the plank. Each color pressed against the curtain like a drop in water, a ripple, and with a shimmer they were gone. They passed one by one into the world-to-come, until eventually there was nothing but the night sky, the rocking boat, and twin lines of soundless dogs. Father and me and the living girl felt so separate from all this.

Then came the stretching silence. The dogs stood solemn, alone in the dark. It was an abrupt end.

I'd seen this every night I could remember. But tonight, I found myself wondering if the dogs ever felt sad to let go of the people. A goodbye must be sad, right?

How could I not know this; I was the daughter of goodbyes.

Alright, Happy said. *Good show everyone. Now get out of my way and don't talk to me.*

There was something eerily callous about waving a thousand colors into the black and then yawning, stretching, and just turning around. But it would happen again tomorrow, and the day after tomorrow. Always culminating in the silence after the Void.

The only person who seemed to still be moved by the display was the girl named Charlie. She stared where the lights had vanished through the curtain, her teeth no longer chattering but her mouth gaping open.

She sat, looking with reverence. Her eyes watched the spectacle with a crisp spark behind them, aware and sharp and still so alive after whatever had brought her here.

The world I'd flown through in monotones was actually a cacophony of un-explored colors. There was more to me than I knew.

"You said your name was Charlie?" I asked softly, feeling the sound of my words in my throat come out with assigned pitches and inflections and . . . life.

Life.

She looked at me, as if seeing me for the first time. Blinking and in shock. "Yeah," she whispered, hoarse, "I'm Charlie."

And I'm tired, Father said, storming toward us. *How in the world did you get here?* he shot at Charlie.

Somehow, Charlie heard him. Charlie knew the way ghosts spoke. She found the ferry and rode it to the end of the living world.

Charlie pointed to the Veil. "What is that?" she asked.

"It's the Veil that leads to the world-to-come," I answered.

But Father said, *How did you get on this boat?*

She paused, her eyes not leaving the Veil. "I followed the music." She sounded so far away and small.

Father blinked. *The music,* he muttered. *What music?*

Charlie just continued staring at the Veil. Something softened in Father's eyes.

She's not supposed to see these things. Father loomed over us. *We need to get her back to the Station. Now.*

He offered nothing more, but swaggered to the helm where he turned the boat back to the shore. He was full of unrest, like the waters during a blizzard.

Did he hear my voice change? Did he see that my whole soul felt upside down, dizzy, electric? Not my soul . . . my body.

I always knew I wasn't dead. But it hadn't ever mattered if I was alive.

I shook my head. Right now, I needed to focus on the living girl and caring for her.

As we cut back through the waves, I saw the lighthouse cresting the horizon.

"See that?" I pointed. "That's the lighthouse on top of the Station. We're almost back home."

Charlie swallowed something back, like she was trying not to cry.

I held her closer. "Hey," I offered, "I know all of this is different. But I've got you."

She looked at me, shaking. "You're at altitude," she mumbled numbly, "you're used to all this."

"What?"

"Let me see her."

I shook my head again. "I don't . . ." Then I understood. She came here because there was someone she was missing. Someone had died, and now she had crawled her way in to find them. But that wasn't supposed to be possible. We dealt in the dead, not in the grieving.

"Let me see her," she said again, weaker.

I squeezed her shoulder into me. "I'm sorry."

Her eyes fluttered closed, then her heavy head fell into my lap. I scrambled to keep her from falling onto the floor as I held all of the weight that comes with a body.

"Oh dear," I said. "Uhm . . . er . . . Charlie?"

She was bony. Her head was so heavy. But I cradled her like a baby, wrapped up in my arms with her legs splayed over the bench, as we neared the Station and the lighthouse.

Happy looked to her, jumped up onto her lap, and kept her warm with her fur.

Charlie didn't stir as we docked and Elbee yawned, waking up from his nap in the corner. Happy shot off the boat, shouting behind her, *We're on land now, they're yours, Elbee! I'm out!*

Why is there someone left? Elbee yawned.

Why is there a live person on my boat, Elbee? Father snapped.

Elbee shrank back a little, and Father relented, kneeling down to offer his hand to the hound. Elbee apparently didn't feel like taking it and gave him a whale eye as he slunk closer to me indignantly.

She's alive, Father's words were so small, realizing the girl was sleeping in my arms. *How did she find us? How did she even step inside?*

"We won't know how anything happened until she wakes." I sat up straighter. "We should take her somewhere safe in the Station and let her rest as she gets her bearings back."

"No, we can't wait that long." Father wrung his hands, as if preparing to fix something. "Nothing good comes from the living being this close to the edge. We should take her out past the fountain." But then he looked at me. And he clutched his throat. "No." He'd spoken with his throat and voice and mouth. "No no no. No. No."

"We are speaking out loud," I said. "You hear it, as well!"

"This is why she cannot stay here!" he panicked. "This place is for the dead. There is a divide between here and there!"

Respectfully sir, Elbee cut in, *you're not exactly dead yourself.*

"I am the Station Master," Father retorted. "And we are the purveyors of the in-between. We are servants. Is she here to serve, Elbee?" He seemed so tired.

"Father, we cannot just throw her on the street."

He looked me right in the eyes then. Something struck me about his face. It wasn't like the ghosts; a memory of something lost. It was vibrant, really present. Lines and wrinkles and stubble and sad eyes that looked out to me as if he was strong *enough,* but for how long he couldn't promise. He was indeed human.

Was this the first time we had truly looked at each other? Of course we'd seen one another's faces, but now there was a consciousness to it. This was my *father.* This face was like no one else's. Now I saw how much there was to see.

He was afraid for me.

"You have seen the Haunts outside." Father straightened his bow tie nervously, pulled on his cuffs. "You know the lighthouse is dimming. A live person made her way to the ferry tonight, and that should not be possible. Something is very wrong. *Nothing* but the dead and the dogs and the Station Masters should be able to get to the Station."

"So maybe she knows something," I offered.

Father growled, throwing his hands against his face, like if he couldn't see the live girl, she wasn't there. In that wordless voice, he instructed, *You can wait until she wakes. We will ask her how she found us so we may prevent it from happening again, and then we will need to say goodbye to her.* He looked to the lighthouse. *I need to check on some things, I need to think.*

In a storm of thought, he took off down the dock.

I looked above my father's head as he marched into the atrium and up a staircase. The lighthouse flickered again.

You speak out loud, Elbee said, coming closer to me. I became very aware of my breathing. Elbee cocked his head, his floppy ears slightly lifting. *Something has changed in your scent.*

"Do the living realize they're alive?" I asked.

My favorite ones do, Elbee pondered. *Why?*

"I believe I'm paying attention now."

Elbee eyed me. But then he changed course as he went to nuzzle the girl. *Can we keep her?* A big hopeful grin panted its way across his gray muzzle.

I knew Elbee could smell everything on Charlie; not just what she'd eaten for dinner, but where she lived, how she felt, maybe even what great wishes sat lodged in her mind. Elbee's tail wagged as he sniffed, and in the pit of my stomach I knew I was right: Charlie could be trusted.

I wondered, though, what did *I* smell like now?

"We'll take her to my room," I said. "I'll sit with her. And in the morning, we'll help her leave."

I'll guide her back out, if you're certain she's to go, Elbee conceded.

"Why wouldn't I be certain?"

Elbee ducked his head down below his shoulders, a dog's shrug. *I don't know,* he said, *sometimes new people bring new things. New thoughts? New possibilities?* And before I could respond, he shouted *Hey!* over his shoulder to a passing dachshund. *Get Gurty out here. He can help move her up to the room.*

The passing dog stared at him, narrow tail drooping. *Oh God, Gurty.*

I know, Elbee said. *But he's the biggest one of us.*

It was now the dachshund's turn to give a whale eye to Elbee, before taking his leave.

Gurty was a giant black dog. He did not know he was giant. His curly long locks bounced up and down, and his nose and sparkly eyes were the only part of his face I could see as he bumbled down the dock to meet Elbee, Charlie, and me.

He stopped, frozen in his tracks. His little eyes widened to saucers as he saw Charlie.

W–Wasn't my fault! he blurted. *I've never seen her ever before!*

I narrowed my eyes as Elbee asked, *Gurty, do you know why this living person is here?*

She saw me. She asked me about some song. I ran. I hopped across town and I lost her. She's . . . not my fault. Please, Elbee, please forgive me!

What song? Elbee asked.

I don't know where I picked it up, it was just some song and she wanted to know where I'd heard it and I just thought it was pretty, that's all! Elbee? Elbee, do you still like me?

But Elbee was looking back at Charlie.

I don't know who this is, or what's going on. Elbee sniffed again. *But I think it was a good idea to not throw her out.*

4

NERA

Gurty found someone's memory of a beautiful wagon, painted with flowers and vines. We set the sleeping Charlie into its cushioned bed, and Gurty galumphed his way down the main curved hallway, towing her along. I didn't know why she was still asleep. Maybe she was hurt, or maybe she hadn't slept for a while and finally could.

I had never slept before. The idea that a body could get so tired it just shut off—it made no sense. I existed for decades and had never collapsed.

We could have taken her to the Station's hotel wing. But with her asleep, and also with her being very not-dead, would a room even open for her? Best to head to my bedroom to let her rest.

So then I said to your dad, Gurty panted as we entered the beautiful elevator just past the atrium, and he pushed the fourth-floor button with his nose. *I said, "Look, sir, I have waited all day for you to come here and play with me, and you're just walking past me. That's not gonna do." And then he had the audacity, the absolute gall, to pass over me and give a good scritch to that bastard Chestnut. Can you imagine? I'm sitting right there! So then I go to sir and I didn't push Chestnut, no matter what he's telling you, I didn't push him. I just sort of knocked him out of my way. Because that scritch was mine. You understand, don't you, Nera?*

"You can't be barging in like that on Chestnut," I said, stepping out of the gilded elevator behind them, into the red carpeted hall. "If you need extra scritches, you should sit and ask for them politely."

Okay, right, but look, Gurty said. *I sit, right? And your dad just ignores me. Then I say, "Hey over here," and he tells me to be quiet.*

"But Chestnut didn't do anything," I said.

Well, whatever, Chestnut doesn't like me anyway, Gurty said. *He doesn't like anyone. But he super doesn't like me. Do you think this new girl will like me? Do you think she can give me scritches?*

"I don't rightly know her," I admitted.

Gurty's eyes looked up at me from under his black brow. I always forgot he was still a puppy. Always a puppy. As if a toddler had been transformed into a massive dog once long ago, and now he still roamed the halls with four paws. I knew that wasn't where Gurty came from. Dogs arrived in the world just as people did. But dogs usually had an air of magic to them, as if they saw more than us. Even so, Gurty was a lovely reminder that after a hard night and day of guiding souls to the Station, dogs just wanted someone to throw a ball for them.

I didn't wanna bring this up in front of the others but . . . you know this girl's alive, right?

"We know she's alive," I said.

Right, right, right, Gurty nodded, taking note as if he didn't already know this. *She shouldn't have heard me, she shouldn't have followed me. It's not my fault, I'm still a good boy!*

"Yes, you are," I said. "Maybe it is no one's fault."

We arrived at my room. Gurty pushed the door open, trotted over to the bed, and positioned himself to help me gently lift the sleeping girl onto the bed. Charlie stirred. But she did not wake.

My room had a large waterwheel-shaped glass window on the furthest wall, nestled under a trapezoidal frame that made the room cozy and felt like I had my own turret. A mirror, a closet, an old goose-feather bed that I sometimes sat on but never properly used, and a thick carpet on the wooden floorboards. I'd seen this room a thousand times and yet only now did I realize the window's glass was composed of different colors.

How had I not seen that before?

Where had the memories for this room come from to begin with? The Station was made of memories, and this room had always existed, up in the higher floors where Father and I lived. It must have been a room in my father's old house, then, from before the Fire.

Alright, food time. Gurty jumped up and down, and hurdled over me and a small wooden chair before catching his leg and crashing into the wall. *Now it's food time!* he corrected himself and waited at the door for me to go out first.

"You can go, Gurty," I said. "I'm going to stay here until sunrise with Charlie."

Gurty turned his head to me, and then to the girl. *Charlie,* he said, trying out her name. He looked at the empty hallway, and then back to the room. *Well, if you're staying, I'll stay, too.*

"That's very kind, Gurty."

Gurty sat down at the edge of the bed on the floor, resting his head on the ground. I placed myself in the chair between the bed and the wagon. I watched him try to stay still. It lasted ten seconds.

He jumped up. *Okay, so while we're in here, which I'm fine with, being here with you is the greatest, I just wonder if maybe you have a ball for me to chew?*

I looked to my pocket on the left side of my dress, and because Gurty asked for a ball, a ball appeared in my pocket. I pulled out the little rubber toy and threw it in the air. He jumped with an agility that Elbee could never match with his stubby legs, then Gurty hopped into the wagon, gnawing on his new toy. *I'm set,* he said.

"For now," I said. The length of a minute must be very long when measured against a dog and his attention.

Then I'll need scritches, he agreed.

We settled in. Charlie looked peaceful, sleeping in the bed. There was a tattoo on her left wrist; just a small image of two little music notes tied together like they hung from a branch. An artifact of her life in the city, and perhaps of her missing person.

"She's pretty," I said quietly.

She smells good. Gurty sniffed.

"What do you mean?"

She smells like rain, Gurty said. *And like a really good cheeseburger. Yeah, with ketchup. People don't put ketchup on enough things, you know.*

I pet Gurty on the head. I did not know what rain smelled like, but I knew that the creases of her eyes were sunken and her brow looked worried and soft, and there was something hurt but honest about her.

The Station settled into peace. We finished our job, and now the dogs rested. I imagined by now, they were in the atrium singing together, howling and baying, and playing like dancers at a May Pole celebration. I usually watched them, but tonight Charlie pulled all my attention. Still, just because I wasn't there didn't mean the dogs wouldn't celebrate. Play bows, nipping at each other's ears, and pushing into each other with little growls. Jumping over one another. Although I sometimes danced with them, I had never felt that excitement myself. I once asked Father what it meant to be joyous, and he said, *Messy.*

Now I longed for something normal; to dance with the dogs rather than sit in a bedroom.

The door opened.

Father stood on my threshold. His shoulders were bent, his eyes even sadder than before. *We need to talk,* he said.

I tore myself away from Charlie's side and signaled Gurty to wait. I followed Father from my room, around the foot of the lighthouse with its door and stairs and bricks, and to the other side of the curved hall. The door to his private chambers was a simple wooden one, with a big lock and no knocker. He pressed his hand to the lock, and it clicked open.

Father, I didn't mean to be contrary, tonight has been so odd—

I am not here because I am upset with you, he started. I folded my hands in front of me as he opened the door and we walked into his scant chambers, my voice gone again.

He did not have a window, he did not have a bed. He only had a chaise, a mirror, a coffee table with a candle lit, a small overstuffed chair, and a wardrobe full of clothes he liked. I hadn't ever really had more than this one outfit, I realized now. But he had many bow ties, lovely vests, leather boots of all colors. And large jackets that wrapped him up like a sea captain.

Please sit, he said.

I sat on the overstuffed chair. He took my hands as he sat opposite, right on the top of the coffee table.

My Nera, he said, *you are a miracle. And I've tried to keep you safe. But I'm afraid that tonight shows how I have failed.*

What do you mean?

There is a lot about the city and the living I've tried to let you not worry about. Our job doesn't concern them. But it seems as if, perhaps, I'm not enough any longer.

Of course you are, I said.

No, darling. He sat back. *The lighthouse is my heart and my essence. And when I fail, it fails. I am tired. No, exhausted. And I am failing, so it is fading. I've held it together for over a century, and we have never had the problems we've had as of late. The Haunts crowding outside, and now a living person has breached . . . Nera, I have to set down my light and let you take up the torch.*

I stared at him, as he casually waited for me to respond.

You and I, he finally added, when I said nothing, *we . . . have had quite the adventure. But Elbee is right, we are not yet dead. We were given this chance to stand sentinel for all the others. But . . .* he broke, the ferryman slipping from his face and my father sitting there now, reaching out to me with his heart. *Nera dear, we have spoken of you taking over the lighthouse, in the past. We knew I couldn't keep the light strong forever. I believe the time has come for me to cross through the Veil and finally rest.*

I was used to endings. Every night at the Station was an ending. I saw thousands of endings, decades of endings, each sun setting and the ferry boat rocking softly into the dark.

But Father now spoke of his own ending.

In one night, everything went from steady to shaking.

As Station Master and apprentice, we didn't hurt like those who had to live. I never felt a skinned knee, never went hungry, never got caught in the rain. The flu was as real as a fairy.

We didn't have to die. But something in him . . . he needed to.

I don't understand, I said. *You could stay here forever.*

I want to rest, he said.

But why now?

This is the worst they've been since the Fire, Nera, he said.

Exactly, so why—

They will be much more than a nuisance if the lighthouse goes out. Haunts consume souls and perpetuate. Like flames. We are here to protect the souls, darling. To protect the Veil.

Maybe, before the living girl had entered our home, we could have felt minimal pain from the words we exchanged. But now this realization flickered between us, a father and a daughter, of the depth of our history. As if our shared life danced along the walls around us in the candlelight. A little girl running to the edge of the stairs, jumping like she could fly. A man catching her. There was no laughter, because those of the Underworld do not laugh. There were never tears. But there had been me and him.

The lighthouse was his heart, and he felt it wasn't enough. I wished I could show him the whole of his heart; how it had always been more than enough for me.

I will be passing over through the Veil in one year, he said. *This will give you time . . . it will give you and me time.*

I should have said, *I'll have to honor that.* I should have said, *I will help you cross over.* But what came out of my mouth was, "No you're not."

He hesitated, looked at me with a flick of his eye, and said, as if he'd forgotten himself, "Sweetheart, I can't hold on any longer. Your heart is ready for the lighthouse. Your soul is ready to lead. You—*you*—can and will protect them."

"No Papa," I said. I needed him to keep catching me, even just a bit longer. "I am your apprentice. I am not the Station Master. I am your daughter. You are my father." I wanted to say, *Who am I without you? And who are you without me? Why do you want to leave?* But those words just went unsaid.

Now seeing him stand up, his suit too big on him, his back hunched over and hand shaking in a never-ending rattle, his eyes sagging like a tired basset hound and the glow of his soul so gray and frayed . . . I could suddenly see how exhausted he was.

"You can do this," he said. "Your name is Nera: light."

"And what if I'm not enough?" I said.

"You will be."

We left his room, walked once more past the lighthouse that would now be mine.

He embraced me, and the lighthouse beamed above us, brighter than it had been moments before. When he was content, it was so much stronger. When he was tired or sad or scared or any of the few emotions we'd discovered in our home of in-between, it became so very dim.

Love, I thought. Love should be enough. Even in death, even in the Station, there is love.

I had never wished for the ability to cry, but now I wished with all my heart to show with my body how much my spirit hurt. But those outside the living world could not cry.

He said, "I shall be here for another year, as you take over being the Station Master. And by the time we must say goodbye, we will be ready."

We both knew that was a lie; we would never be ready. It had always been us in the Station, together. The world outside grew with the seasons and changed with the tides. But there are no tides in Lake Michigan; only the waves tossed about by wind and boats.

Only us and the dead, on the edge of the end.

"If I could make you stay forever, I would," I said.

He smiled. And then he realized he was smiling and speaking out loud. "That girl . . ." he muttered. The colors of the moon and stars and city lights had painted our simple world, because Charlie was here and she brought color and time and life with her.

He looked behind me, to my room's open door, as if Charlie was radioactive. *Whatever we do next,* he said, stepping backward, *we must be careful and mindful of what the Station needs. It is the bulwark that keeps the souls safe.* Then he looked to me. He softened again. *I see what a wonderful soul you are. I believe in you, my Nera.*

Then he took his leave with a small nod and a numb hand on my shoulder. He sighed and stepped down the staircase, exhausted, to return to the main portion of the Station. I felt as if my soul had been knotted and twisted around itself, discomfort and disorientation. My father was going to die.

No, I couldn't accept it. This was too much.

I returned to the room with the living woman. I waited for the pain to subside and for my mind to wander back into routine and magically comprehend what my father had just said.

It did not. The night simply continued to count its minutes.

REMNANTS

This city is alive, every minute of every morning and evening and even dead into the night. Yet, it is hard to find space to live as we wish. I wish we could hold one another on every street at every hour. I promise, we will find a way, my love.

—The journal of a young man named David Stein, 1872

5

CHARLIE

The sun blasted through a stained glass window. I heard the seagulls outside. The lake. The sunrise.

The *lake*.

Panic shot through my body. I opened my eyes. Jumped out of the bed.

I wasn't home. Dad probably hurt himself last night, didn't get sleep. Oh God, what if something happened to him?

I saw a huge black dog at the foot of the bed. *The* dog I'd seen out on the street in Chinatown.

Beyond the dog was the woman from the night before, standing by the window, admiring the blinding dawn. Like last night, she wore a long Victorian dress . . . Edwardian? Her hair was pulled back in a curled bun, the color of a redwood. Her white cheeks glowed. She looked at peace. Good for her.

She looked back at me. Her hazel eyes struck me, from beneath strong furrowed brows. She opened her mouth to say something but I cut her off.

"Where's Sam?" I demanded.

She stopped. "I don't . . . know?"

"Samantha Connor," I said. "My sister. She died six months ago. Did she pass through that black hole veil thing? Is she here in this building?"

"I'm sorry, I—"

"This is where the dead come to leave, right?"

"Yes, the dead from the city."

"So check your records." I hit the bed with my fist. "March 20, 2005. Samantha Connor. Her song brought me here. That dog was singing her song!"

The big black dog jerked awake and shook his head back and forth, groaning. *Song? Oh, yeah, the song! I don't know, I just heard it and thought it was pretty.*

If ghosts were real, if a boat could swim into a netherworld and make the lake part of the sky, if her music could rematerialize after the sheet music drowned, and if dogs could talk, then my sister could still exist.

I bolted for the door.

It wasn't locked. Surprising. I threw it open, and I shot through the hall. I flew down the first stairs I could find. Big, clunky carpeted runners led me down a turret.

Where are you? I shouted through my mind. *Samantha, get your ass out here, I'm here, I followed you, now show yourself.*

"Sam!" I begged her.

I hadn't found her in all the places live people are. So maybe I could find her here, in the ghost hotel. I tried to feel her, like an invisible thread was going to appear and drag me right to where she was. But all I could feel was the blood pumping in my ears.

Good morning! an old twang of a voice rang out. I looked down at the end of the stairs. Two dogs. One very old, shaggy and gray, and another a cocker spaniel low to the ground. The low-rider pawed at the air, like he was . . . no, he waved. Waved?! The first old dog said, *Wait a minute, are you alive?! That's not how this works, you know! Oh dear, oh dear . . .*

I ran past them.

All around me, the dead in their gray bodies. They watched me, everyone stopping and gawking. I looked into each one of their eyes. *Sam. Sam Connor. Do you know her? Sam! Sam, please! I'm sorry!*

Bark, bark, bark. Past the dizzying crowds of the dead, dogs ran down the stairs and to me, *Sam, Sam!* they shouted out, like it was a game.

I shoved through the atrium lobby I'd passed through last night. And that's when I heard it.

Her song. Unfinished but unmistakable.

Beyond the atrium and the ghosts, out the door and past the stone pillars, past the fountain. I followed it, my feet nearly flying ahead of me. And I . . .

I stopped.

Ahead of me floated a suffocating wall of static and smoke. Something worse than the void in the lake, something that wasn't supposed to be there. I had never been this close to it before. It was too close. But still far enough away. My head felt fuzzy and my eyes had trouble focusing. Where was it? What was distance? Where were we?

The impenetrable cloud licked the sides of reality with sharp, buzzing edges. It wasn't human. But something about it was human. It looked like it was made of scribbles and a thousand smoky souls melted together, all the limbs the wrong size and smashing into a blob like a bunch of torched plastic and rubber toys left out in the sun, welded, gushing into one another. The sound screeched around like the space between radio stations.

Let me in, they rasped.

I'd seen it eat souls. I had not heard it speak. It made my head pound.

"Charlie!"

That voice came from behind me, but I couldn't turn around. Was it the Victorian lady?

Let me in, the fog screeched in my head again. I stumbled back. The static lashed out at me, like there was a net between us that they struggled to reach through.

Then I saw what stopped them. The sun. A beam shone between me and the shadow of the trees where the fog was stuck.

Light.

I stepped backward, onto my side of the river of light. Then I continued backward, past the fountain and the pillars of the Station. I couldn't look away from the static.

They screeched at me.

"So you can see that, as well," the woman beside me broke their spell.

I doubled over and gasped for air, the pain receding. "Yes, I've seen it in the city. What is it?"

"Haunts," she said, touching her necklace. It looked like a little lantern. "They keep getting closer."

"Ghosts don't look like that." I jutted my finger at it. "Ghosts are just people. Why do they look like that?"

"Well," the lady said. "The Haunts are no longer people."

"How can something no longer be people?"

"There are a lot of things that aren't."

I looked to her. "Listen, bitch, that thing knows my sister's song. How? *How.*"

There was a flicker of light from above, as if this entire place lost power for a second. Like a plug pulled out of its wall socket, teetering to keep contact.

The door behind us clanged open, and I saw the ferryman with his red bow tie and a basset rush out of the door, with the big black dog behind them. They all carried lanterns. The ferryman handed the woman her own lantern. The four of them held their lights high. A rebuke.

The Haunts screeched, then vanished from sight.

But I still heard a voice. **Let me in.**

"Lanterns," the woman said. "It helps us concentrate the light. Like a sword."

"Mazel tov," I scoffed.

The ferryman stared out to the fountain. And then to me and then to the woman.

"Let me see her," I demanded, marching up to him.

"You said we would talk when she woke up." The woman directed her words to him as she followed me.

His mouth opened. He spoke in a raspy voice that sounded like he hadn't spoken to a living person in decades. The words came out with dust and cobwebs on their edges, but he was still very clear: "I don't know where your sister is."

The ferryman's desk held one name in calligraphy, settled on the edge like a nameplate. *Harosen.*

Mr. Harosen looked like the owner of a mattress store that was going out of business. All pomp and circumstance, with a deflated balloon sort of style to his weariness and number crunching. I didn't know if I should be afraid of the paperwork he might make me file, or if he needed a big overdue hug.

I could tell he was just as alive as me. But his eyes skimmed everything he saw with a morose detachment.

His daughter in the Victorian dress, whose name I learned was Nera, stood behind him and the desk like his captain of the guard. Or henchman. Whichever.

The three of us awkwardly looked to one another in this office, right off the atrium on the main floor.

"Your name," Harosen asked, not so much as a question. He spoke as if everything he said was the most important thing that anyone in history had ever said.

"Charlie," I said. "Charlie Connor." It felt like an interview.

"You're alive," he said.

"Yes?"

"How did you find us?" he said. "You can see the Station. How?"

"Okay, well, that's more than one question."

"How about you start with seeing the dead." He fidgeted with his bow tie. "I don't know many who can."

"You can." I waved my hands at him.

He narrowed his eyes. "Yes."

"So how did you get about seeing the dead?" I said. "You're, like, a live person, right?"

"We are the in-between," he declared. Like it was a *duh*.

"Cool, that didn't answer that question, but how can you see ghosts? When did it start for you?" I hadn't ever met anyone else like me.

"Charlie Connor." He folded his hands. "Let's focus on your answers first."

"My sister died," I said, feeling my neck burn. "That night, I wanted to see her. I opened my eyes and bam, there were ghosts."

I remembered the shock. The scream that came out of my mouth. The ICU suddenly crowded. Ghosts. I felt like I was going to vomit. Ghosts. Everywhere. I had a concussion, they'd go away. But they didn't go away. And no one else could see them. This weird, horrific, beautiful gift, it was only mine and I was alone.

But Harosen didn't need any of those details.

I said, "I've been looking for her, but it seems like I've run into every single dead person in the metro area except for her."

"That is how you found the Station?"

"I followed music," I said. "I crossed through the ivy on the bridge under Lake Shore Drive. And . . . I mean, it's sort of hard to miss. Even though I've never seen it before. But I can see a lot of things I couldn't see before. Or maybe this is all a psychotic break. Who knows? What a fun mystery, time will tell."

He blinked his wide eyes. "The living are not supposed to find this place. This is a crossing place for the dead."

"I don't know what to tell you, man," I said. "This weird shit's been happening for half a year, so if you have any explanations, I'd love to hear them."

He had no explanation. And I couldn't tell if he was afraid or angry, or maybe he was just used to getting the answers he sought. What the hell was he? Was he really a ferryman of the dead?

There were stories about crossing in boats. In Dad's song, he talked about Charon, this guy who looked like a skeleton with a big curved gondola. This guy was not Charon. He looked like an old Gregory Peck and his gondola looked like a Windy City Sightseeing boat.

"What music?" Nera asked.

"My sister's music," I said. "She composed songs. And there's one that she didn't finish and the big black dog was singing it. And then he *Star Trek*-teleported us from Chinatown to Lincoln Park and . . ." From the looks on their faces, there was nothing weird about a dog singing or jumping from place to place, so I just kept talking. "And then I was here. And this place was pumping out that song . . . But all I've found is you guys and more of those shadow-knifey things and . . ." I stopped. A thought I'd had before sliced through my brain, a deep cut. The things outside, they were singing the song, too, after all. I pushed the thought away. "Samantha Eleanor Connor, died March 20, 2005 . . . you say you don't know where she is but you're in charge here. Check your records."

"We don't have records," he said.

His daughter looked at me from where she stood behind him. Studiously, like an intern.

"If she came through," I said, "is she still here or would she have crossed?"

"It depends." Nera took a step forward. "Some stay for more than a night. Some go immediately. Whenever they're ready—"

"Miss Connor," Mr. Harosen interrupted. "There is a flow, a direction, of existence. We are born, we live, we die, we cross over. If your sister is dead, you cannot bring her back. So why are you here?"

I stared at him. My eyes burned. It wasn't any of his business. I didn't know him, and he was being way too direct and personal for someone who didn't know me. But someone had finally asked, and I wanted to answer.

"I didn't get to say goodbye," I said. That was the short of it. That's all they were getting. I doubted the ferryman of the dead understood the lack of resolution, the massive gap that is ripped open by an unknown, when a young woman is alive one second and then destroyed the next. She was beside me. She ran. Then she was not coming back.

Harosen, though, just asked plainly, "Why didn't you say goodbye?"

My eyes burned with fiery tears. But they didn't fall. The sounds of screams, the chaos, and she pulled her hand from mine, I should have held her tighter—

Abruptly, the memory was cut off by a chord out in the atrium. A chord I knew well. The first notes of the song that had started this whole mess to begin with.

I stood up, turned on my heels, and walked out the door. Mr. Harosen followed as well, burning under his little bow tie, stopping at the door.

"If you are here to hurt us—"

I stepped out into the atrium, into a magical palace sort of place. Everything I saw last night had been real. The epic golden staircase, so many rooms with swirling thresholds and doorframes, the colorful lights and a kaleidoscope tunnel . . . the people here, the ghosts, filling this place with their full forms dancing and singing and mingling. A mishmash of a baggage claim, a vacation, a high school graduation, and a theme park.

But what caught my eye, nearly stopped my heart, was the piano in the middle of the atrium.

A baby grand. A black Wurlitzer, the lid shut but the fallboard open and ready, black-and-white keys shining in the lantern light.

As I got closer, I saw it wasn't just any Wurlitzer. This piano had a large gash in its back leg. One diagonal line, scraped through the corner. And I knew exactly where the piano came from.

When Sammy was young and had just started piano lessons, I had been running with a toy and tripped, and the toy scuffed the leg of the piano. Mom was furious. Dad said it gave it character.

"Like the rose in *Little Prince*," he comforted her. "Now Sammy will know that with all the pianos in the world, this one is hers." And then he'd etched a rose carving into the wood, just above the high C.

I stepped forward, into the center of the atrium. I put my hand on it. It was real.

And there, on the music stand facing the bench, above the keyboard . . . I saw sheet music.

Was it—

The handwriting.

It was hers.

Dad searched the past for her. Marco searched the myths for her. I searched the city. And somewhere between all three of those, her notes sat in front of me.

"Goddamnit." I marched back to the dude's office.

"My sister's piano is in your atrium." I stepped in, jutting a finger back at the piano. "How?"

Mr. Harosen stared at me. Nera just said, "I . . . this place is made of memories, Miss Connor."

"So that is *my* memory of my sister's piano? Or was she here after all?"

Mr. Harosen said nothing.

"We . . . have many guests," Nera piped in. She stepped forward, like a manager handling a belligerent customer. "We stopped learning their names a long time ago."

"You two care for the dead and you don't bother to know their names?" I said. "Wow."

"We are trying to get to the bottom of this for both our sakes, and you are being rude," Mr. Harosen said.

"Was my sister here?"

"If your sister has passed," Nera said, "and you haven't seen her in the city, then she likely came here or she . . ." She stopped. "I'm sure she's gone through the Veil and is at peace. Can I walk you out?"

"Or she what?" I said. "Or she's one of those shadow knife things? One of the creepy fog monsters?"

Nera swallowed. Her eyes flitted to the floor.

"Is she?" I said. "What exactly is a Haunt?"

"The Haunts are an ocean of souls who drown in their hopelessness and sorrow for an unfinished life." It sounded like a recitation, like she'd studied for a test. "They're like fire, trying to destroy everything."

"Fun," I sniped. I had to snipe. Because "unfinished life" echoed in my head. Sammy was not out there. "So beyond the metaphors, what are they?"

Nera looked to the ground. "They died, and were trapped in the web of the demon." That answered nothing.

"Haunts cannot get near the lighthouse," Harosen said. "We work as a ward, keeping the lake safe and keeping them weakened in the city. If they got hold of the Station, they would level it. Chicago would fall to darkness." He grunted. "If your sister is part of the Haunts, then it's best you don't know. Go back to your life and forget about all of this until it's your time to arrive properly."

I glared at him. My body felt electric with anxiety. She couldn't be one of those monsters. Sam brought me here. She was somewhere in here, or beyond the Veil. No, she was not beyond the Veil. She was here, her music was *here*, her piano was here. I was going to see her again.

Goodbyes were more than just words to one another. Goodbye was knowing what happened, where she is now, knowing she's okay.

Telling her I was sorry.

"What. Is. A. Haunt." I demanded. Not a question.

Harosen touched his cedarwood desk with his fingertips. As if bracing himself. And then the illusion of a great fire burst out of the left side of the desktop, a small stage between his fingers. Outlines of people appeared, clawing over each other and running away from the flames. "More than a hundred years ago," he said, "I built this lighthouse to save us all from a demon who sought to destroy the city." The fire rose and spread across the length of the desk, chasing the terrified crowd. "He sparked a fire. The fire devoured many souls, turned the living and the dead into wrathful things. The Haunts, they started as those who were swallowed up in the Fire. They've since grown into a blight that roams the city."

I'd grown up in Chicago. I knew what the Chicago Fire was. But now, seeing it in front of me . . . The fire engulfed the people who fell, tripped, couldn't run fast enough. The fire grew. Smoke. Fog. And from the fog I saw more images, as if they were my own memories. A city that looked so different than the sandstone and bricks I knew. Wooden buildings. Muddy streets. People bottle-necked at the LaSalle bridge, unable to escape. The whole of the world, eradicated by hot wild flames. A tall clocktower, the bell sounded, warping and moaning and howling as it crashed to the street. And above it all, a tornado of black smoke blotted out the sky.

By the time it would finish, I knew 17,000 buildings were burned to the ground. Seventy-three miles of street eviscerated. The Great Fire had almost wiped the city off the map forever. And with this image in front of me, I now understood that those facts learned in high school were simply regurgitated by people who'd had time and distance to make sense of what had happened.

Like a recap given by a spotless reporter while people suffered behind them. Like all the spectators at the vigil for my sister. When really, it was terror. It was the end of days.

It was personal and reality-shredding.

The only question you asked yourself over and over again was, *Why. Why. Why.*

That question would never really leave you.

"We ran for the lake," Harosen said. "The living and the dead, whoever could escape the demon's grasp. But the fire and its Haunts overwhelmed us. And I had to protect us."

He then placed his palm on the right side of the desk, a small light glowing from his hand. It reached out, like a flower, and the fire screeched back, like a cat to water.

"And my magic, the light I hold, bloomed out of me and became bricks and mortar. On the banks grew this Station and its lighthouse," he said. "It shielded us, and it weakened the Haunts in the city. The demon was trapped."

The fire did not disappear. It only simmered. Always trying to whip out and destroy the light.

"The dogs retrieve the souls and keep them safe on their journey to the Station. Because the Haunts still eat the dead and multiply." Harosen waved his hands and small images of light in the shapes of the dogs charged out into the fire. "And the Haunts can't come in here or cross the light that comes from deep inside me. That is how the story has gone for over a century."

But then I saw something horrible: the light in Harosen's hands started to flicker and fade. Dimmer and dimmer. The smoke and fire on the desk licked his fingers dangerously.

Nera looked to me. "You're not the first thing that has been different. My father's lighthouse has been dimming. The Haunts crawl closer, trying to break through and consume the souls here in the Station, and maybe even the Veil itself. And now you're here. You can see why we have questions."

I felt a lump in my throat. "Great pyrotechnics. Sam's not a Haunt. Her piano is here."

But her song was in the Haunts' mouths.

Neither of them replied.

Everything about death was too complicated. A queasy feeling turned my guts.

But there was something that wasn't complicated: music. It was an old friend. And I needed to hear it.

I stormed out of the office and back into the atrium, to the piano. I sat on the wobbly wooden bench Mom bought us from Keyboard Kastle.

I lifted the lid. I was gonna make it sing. The lid-prop clicked into place, echoing through the belly. The keys were still sticky because Sammy secretly snacked while she practiced. All the notes resting where she left them. And my father's carved rose.

I pressed my fingers down.

A chord. Three notes, singing together as a family, all different but somehow they still made sense together.

Mom always thought music was math. She counted the rhythms, knew all the ways to mark time, saw it all as a formula.

Dad played his music as if it was his last chance to find hope in this world. Whenever he started feeling down, he'd grab his guitar and sing us a song about monkeys or a million dollars or the sun shining down on our freckled faces. If music existed, then magic existed. Something he could hear but not see. Sacred roots burrowing deep down into places he thought he'd lost in the war.

Sammy, she saw music as life. It wasn't hope. It wasn't math. It was pumping her arms, running faster and faster under trees as they changed in the autumn. She loved curving a minor chord in the middle of the cheery major chords. She loved to trill her fingers on the keys. She loved to slap her guitar. When she sang, she closed her eyes, she'd stick her chin up, she'd smile with her whole face.

For me? Music was my mother, my father, my sister. The sound of all the people that made my life its own original piece of art.

It was love.

Something lost had returned. The echoes in my childhood, singing out: *Welcome home.*

"Miss Connor," Harosen interrupted. He stood midway between me and his office, shaking. "We do not have answers for you. I believe it's time you left for the living again."

But then another voice cut him off; this one soft and gentle. "No. Go on."

I looked up. It was Nera. She beamed down from her spot beside me. She'd followed me. She'd looked like a staunch schoolmarm before, but now, this close, she had a reassuring calm about her. She held her stomach, her back straight.

And she smiled.

"Nera," Harosen warned her.

"Go on," she said. "Play."

6

CHARLIE

Out of my tired, rigid soul came music.

Chords that Leonard Cohen pressed into the world to remind us of partisans in France, that made Johnny Cash hurt, that twisted the pain of Billie Holiday's strange fruit. Chords played by thousands before me, all trying to put a sound to the feeling of having a soul.

I couldn't see my sister in the music, but I felt her hands on these keys. I could hear her prayers in the lifting melody. The strings and hammers inside the piano hummed an incantation that brought something out of me, unearthed something far down below my bones, something warm and forgotten. I heard our laughs, Sam's and mine, the same voice in two different bodies, us starting in the same place and branching in our own directions but still coming back to each other. We understood one another because we had grown from the same roots. Like my tattoo, two notes tied together.

Follow the roots, Sammy. Find me here.

Remember what you told me? Left hand is the foundation with its beat, the right hand is the dreamer with its melody.

I will be your beat now. You dream your way back to me.

I held the notes, like holding onto the paws of an old and loved family dog.

I let the chord hum through the atrium.

If I let the note go, the song would be over. And where do songs go when they're done?

I finally let my hands free from the keys, and looked up to Nera.

Nera wasn't Sammy. But she smiled, again.

"That," she breathed, "was beautiful."

Behind her, Mr. Harosen stared up at the light above us.

The lighthouse was nearly as bright as the sun.

Nera touched the piano, looking up at the dazzling light. "Play again?"

I played a chord.

The light swelled even more, the earlier flickering now forgotten for its own starlight.

Nera grinned.

Harosen stared at me, a breathing pair of lungs in his great glass crypt.

"Well," he said. And nothing else.

REMNANTS

there is a thing in the dark.
i do not know if it is still me.
if you can read this. please. come find me.
i can see no sunlight, although the bricks sometimes warm up in a way
that reminds me the world is still spinning.
i hear the rain pounding against the walls when the clouds gather.
i hear the thunder.
i still remember my name.
i still know names hold the story of a life.
so i know in some small way,
i am still here.

please hurry.

time doesn't stop, even for stone.
there are now cracks where i can see the sun.
it took decades for the cracks to form.
it burns in the day.
but at night, the moon comes.
and i can reach out one hand past my cage
or maybe it isn't me anymore.
all i feel is rage.
all my hand wants is to reach out,
and crack him until there is nothing left but moonlight.
i want him to feel the fear that comes from sitting alone in stone.

—the writings of a thing in the dark

7

NERA

The lighthouse should not glow for her. But why wouldn't it, when the whole world could be ignited by her eyes alone? Somehow, she'd found a way to this place, and a part of me wanted to sing, *She found a way to me.*

I looked to my father, saw his awe of the light. The lighthouse shined when he heard the music. His old heart could still thrive when he heard beautiful things from the living world.

I didn't know her at all. I only knew she could see ghosts, she could play the piano, her name was Charlie—and she was going to heal us.

Was my fascination simply because she was alive, like a flower growing through concrete?

She stood from the piano and stared up at Father, but she didn't say anything. She seemed stuck, in between wanting to shout, wanting to cry, wanting to keep playing, wanting to run.

All I knew was I couldn't say goodbye.

"Father," I called to him across the atrium. "I am to be the next Station Master, and very soon. You said so yourself, it is my job to keep the light lit. So, you must trust me."

"I do," he said, "but I see where this is going, and it is not a good idea."

"The lighthouse is lit," I said. "You can't deny that."

"Uh, guys, what the hell is going on?" Charlie tried.

"Do you trust my judgment?" I pressed him.

"Yes," he said.

"Then please, trust it?" I asked him. "If this is my mistake, it is mine to make."

If he was not happy, he did not argue or condemn. Perhaps, we both realized, this was the first time I'd asked for my voice to be heard over his. And the Station's glimmer spoke for itself.

I stepped forward and smiled at Charlie. "We would love to welcome you to the Station."

"Okay," she said slowly. "Well, I didn't come here to be your department store pianist and make muzak for your atrium. I came here for Sam."

My wave of relief washed away.

"You . . . you made the lighthouse shine," I said.

"Yeah," she said, grabbing the sheet music. "You should look into that."

"If you play the piano for us, I'll help you find your sister," I blurted.

Both she and Father stared at me.

I had just given a hasty promise without thinking it through. Perhaps it wasn't even possible to find this spirit. On the other hand, it *was* my duty to help people.

"Nera," Father warned.

"The Station must know where she went, if she went through here. I can't promise that we *will* find out what happened but . . . if you come back at night and play music and keep the lighthouse bright, then I will do everything I can to help you." I looked to Father. "While I take over, her music can help keep us safe from the Haunts."

Father did not say anything. But he slowly nodded.

He trusted me.

Charlie narrowed her eyes. "You don't know any of the names of the people that come through. They're just a massive crowd to you. Have you ever even looked into their eyes?"

That struck me. No, we had not. No names, no faces, no hands, no voices; they were just a group that needed corralling to the ferry and beyond. They came in and out of the rooms in the Station, healing and trying to let go. It was their business, not mine. I was their keeper, not their mother. Which was how I had missed Charlie last night.

"Didn't think so." Charlie stood. "I suggest you look at them. The dead are still people."

The dead are still people.

"So tell me, oh great mysterious lady." She sized me up with her arms crossed, sauntering closer to me. "If you don't even know their names, then how the hell are you going to help me?"

"You came to my Station," I said. "And I am to be the next Station Master. You're right, I don't know their names. But I do know I care."

She studied me. "You care," she said. Then she leaned over and offered me secret words under her breath. "I've got a hunch you're gonna be a better Station Master than he was. Don't prove me wrong." Then she added to everyone, "I'll be back this evening."

"Wait!" I said. If she left, she may never find her way back. "There . . . are Haunts outside!"

"Give me your fancy lantern then."

"I can't . . . it's my lantern."

"Then can I have my own lantern? The dogs get lanterns."

I'll accompany her to the bridge, Elbee said, appearing out of nowhere as if he was waiting. Charlie jumped.

"Yes," she said. "This little basset hound will accompany me to the bridge. Hear that?"

I have a name. It's Elbee.

"Elbee," Charlie corrected, "will accompany me to the bridge."

They trotted away, Elbee holding his little lantern in his mouth like a shield and sword.

"Charlie?" I said softly.

"Trust me! I'll be back!" she said. And she took off, to who knew where. A stranger still.

But something deep in my soul knew she wasn't finished here. I had to trust her, but also myself.

Father sighed, as if he was unbuttoning his vest, unclenching his jaw. He shook his head, coming to join me. "We can't look into every death, help every grieving person. We're not here for the living left behind, we're here to—"

"Papa, not every person comes here looking," I said. "She is the only one who has ever found this place. She has asked us to help her. And she is someone who can keep the light on. You wanted me to take more responsibility here, and this is me taking responsibility."

He turned to face me. He looked softer now, not as worn down. As if Charlie had brought the dust of the earth onto his face and then took it with her when she left.

"Your light shone when you heard her music," I said, holding out my hand. He said nothing. He fixed his tie and looked around the Station as if he was trying to understand it. Or maybe trying to understand himself.

Life left the Station, along with Charlie. The vibrations around the breathing girl were gone, and so we, the in-betweens, stopped breathing. It was eerily easy to stop. She had said I was alive, but how alive could I be if I could exist without breath?

I hoped I would not lose track of myself again, that I would continue to be me and not just the ferryman's daughter. Maybe before the spell wore off completely, I could grab my father and embrace him. Hold him in a tight hug and squeeze him. Just a small moment before we got caught up again in the humdrum of the day.

Whatever it is she has brought with her into this place . . . She is from the city. Father spoke without his voice. *The city is beyond what our souls should need to carry.*

I hesitated. *You created the Station,* I said.

Yes.

So before the Station, you were from the city, I said.

His origin had always been a part of the story, but now it was dimensional—the man in front of me was someone from Chicago. The light had not just appeared, the fire was not just a fire. It had all happened to him. He was a mortal once. I never knew the city, but he once had.

Father's mouth opened. And then he closed it. *What was before the Station is no longer a part of me.* He turned to leave. *Now today I will be cleaning the lamps. I will need you to check the perimeter before tonight, when the Haunts get bolder.*

I watched him walk away with his formal ceremonious air; he glided through the Station. I saw around us the ghosts that had not passed last night or the night before as they ventured out of the hotel wing. Some lined up in queues for the atrium's magical rooms, and there was a notably long line in front of a massive golden door behind one of the staircases. The glittering threshold was framed with a red curtain.

GIFT ROOM, it read above the curtain.

It was time I looked into the crowd.

8

CHARLIE

I followed Elbee past the fountain, under the bridge, and back into the land of the living. There was no grand sweeping orchestration, just a small walk across the street. Like this happened every day.

Elbee deposited me on the other side of the bridge, and then gave a nod. *See you later, Charlie.* He trotted back toward the lake, beyond the ivy.

I stood shaking on Fullerton, as if I'd been dunked into the lake and was left shivering in the wet cold.

How do you return to the world after you've stepped outside of it? There was a Station of ghosts at the edge of the city and some portal to the Underworld in the middle of Lake Michigan and now I was just . . . back? Ready to return to the everyday humdrum, pay for CTA passes and brush my teeth?

No biggie, Charlie. No problem-o, Charlie. Just keep walking. All the ghosts? Not real. Sammy? She's fine. Call her on the phone, right now. She won't answer, and her voicemail wasn't her—just the guys from *Rent* moaning: "SPEAK."

I was back with the little remnants she'd left behind.

I checked my pockets. Sammy's sheet music was gone again.

I turned around to see the Station. But I couldn't see it from this side of the bridge, just the cars whizzing past in front of a bunch of trees and seagulls.

The dead leaves scattered along the sidewalk.

The yellow taxis with their light-up Blue Man Group roof ads rolled past as the sun peeked through the alleyways.

The street sweepers hissed and the trash trucks collected.

So I was just gonna pretend I was like everyone else who didn't know about the death dogs, or what it felt like to hit the ground and lie with your heart beating as gunfire shot off too close, or that Sam's piano was in some invisible ghost ferry station.

Surviving means pretending you don't know any of that.

No one but Dad was gonna believe me.

Dad.

Oh goddamnit. Dad. I had to get home.

Sam could rest. Sam could hide.

But I didn't have that luxury.

I hated myself for thinking that, but something dark stirred in my gut. Like a thick weed, creaking out of the soil, black and ash, curling around my spine. A cancer, a shame, a hope. Death was a rest.

You found the Station.

The hissing, low voice that followed the Haunts. But it was in my head. It was in the wind.

Like I'd tuned into the wrong radio station.

Charlie.

I froze.

A fog kicked up and surrounded me like a cloud. Oh no, the Haunts were in the fog. I remembered the Polish guy. The fuzzy feeling in my head.

I stumbled backward.

I couldn't see anything. Fear smacked me in the middle of my chest. Like at the mall, watching the silhouettes from the break room in the dark . . . so much fear I thought my body was going to implode . . .

Charlie, find me in the Water Tower.

There was a sinking, terrible feeling of a void . . . but not like that Veil out in the lake. This was something dense. Something thick and dark. Like the night sky before a tornado. Like oil gurgling into the ocean.

Do you want to see your sister again? Or do you want to keep chasing ghosts?

The fog disappeared. For the second time, I found myself suddenly somewhere else in the city. On Michigan Avenue, big signs for American Girl and Hershey Café and Borders buzzing in the early dawn.

Ahead of me I saw a place I'd seen a hundred times. The Water Tower.

A landmark for Chicago—one of the few buildings to survive the Great Fire, right across the street from its sister building where one of Sam's favorite actors (the guy who played Ross in *Friends*) had opened a theater. The theater was massive and looked like a castle; the Water Tower matched, looking nothing like a suburban water tower. It was a tall, thick monument with windows and tasteful landscape lighting. A rough, fossilized stone exterior, a box foundation that rose high into what looked sort of like the lighthouse from the Station.

It wasn't supposed to be fancy. It had been built to hide a standpipe, I remember my high school history teacher telling the class on a field trip. Usually, I just saw an old building. One of those that had been built back when the city was still expanding into the swamp, trying to be innovative, the future of America. Even if it meant erasing what and who was here before, damn the cost.

The past was still here. Across the street from the Hershey Café, but still here.

This morning, the whole area was uncanny and eerie. Maybe it was because the lights were coming on all around it. Maybe it was because it was the morning after Halloween. But it was probably the fog curling around the tower's base, lapping against the big wooden doors like it was trying to break them down and couldn't. A tide that would never be strong enough.

Nobody was on the street so early in the morning. At least, no one alive. Where the living would usually tromp around taking pictures or carrying heavy shopping bags, there were only the dead. Most of the ghosts avoided the Water Tower, but as I watched, one walked through it and then came out looking like they'd escaped a spider web, the silky fog still clinging to them. Like they would never wash it off.

One time I saw a fly get caught in a web. It got out. But it crawled along the windowsill, struggling, until it finally died.

I couldn't decide if it was better the ghost had somehow escaped the Haunts' web or if it would have been better to just be eaten.

Charlie.

Fuck, that's right, it knows my name. And it said it with a guttural, out-of-breath sound in my head. Like someone who had just been socked in the stomach and couldn't find their lungs.

Charlie, come closer.

I did not come closer. "How do you know my name?"

The Haunts are my eyes, my hands, my ears.

"I guess they also make a killer transit system," I quipped, trying to hide my fear. "Real efficient way to travel."

I know you, Charlie. I know under your sharp words there is sharper pain. I know you've scoured this city for her, and instead you found the Station. But I know where your sister is. She is dead, but no one is nowhere.

I could see that the door leading into the tower was covered in a golden sheen. Light. Like the Station's lighthouse, like Harosen's hand.

"Did you snare her in your Haunts?" I asked it.

Let me out. And I'll tell you.

"Ha, yeah," I said. "You're stuck in that tower, aren't you? I don't think you're the one who gets to negotiate."

It hissed. And I heard a door rattle in the wind. I shivered. Then I realized, from the street to the buildings' cracks to the trees above, there was nothing but fog and Haunts. Their static hands, their blank, wide white eyes. Voids in the dark. Staring out, thousands from one thick cloud. All one, but made of so many.

A hand reached out for my throat. I jumped back, slipping on the sidewalk and falling on my back.

I am not here to play a child's game with you.

The Haunts circled me.

You always have so many quips and questions, but only one wish. And I can grant it. I can reunite you with your sister.

All of my insides clenched, my body burned. *Reunite.* Both a prayer answered and a curse spoken.

"Who are you?" I said. The Haunts cocked their heads.

You have one name, Charlie, but I have many names, for I am something larger than just one. But you may believe that I am truth. I am the one you can trust. I am the thing in the dark that watches and knows your shadow.

"I've gone crazy," I whispered.

You are not mad. You must remember that. Many people who hear me think they're mad. Many do not look to their own brains, their own bodies, their own lives, thinking I've made them, made them, made them. I am made in the kindling, in the rumbling of the earth. I come to those who need me. I can make no one mad. I can do nothing without your saying so.

"You're the demon that the Station Master locked away, huh?" I said it flippantly. The door slammed hard, shooting forward and back against the locks made of light.

Fuck the Station Master! You want to mock me? I am the truth! He is a coward and a liar!

I felt bile in my throat, remembering the wild flames, the bell howling as it fell . . .

The Harosens can't give you who you want, Charlie.

Who I want.

Your father will die. Your mother will never return. And Marco fades away.

No. It was a trick. It wouldn't tell me if Sam was in its web, would it? It clearly wanted out. Either she's a Haunt and he gobbles me up, or she's on the other side of the Veil and he pushes me into death. Or he has no clue where she is and he's bullshitting me.

Sam would not want me to be here. Sam would not trust this thing.

Fine. When you find yourself wanting at the Station, you come to me. In order to open a lock, you must see it. And you can see it. So open the lock. I'll fill that hole inside you. I can feel it there. And then you shall see your sister once more.

And my brain felt two things—one, the thing I was supposed to feel: disgust, fear. And two, the thing I really did feel underneath: relief, a spark of hope.

I could end this.

But down the street, by the water, while I couldn't see her, I knew Nera was there.

Nera said she'd help me.

You can't see the Station from the real world, but you can always see my tower. Because I am real, Charlie. I know the raw truth of how terribly she died.

The Haunts around me, they reached out, they touched a tree. The smoke curled around the tree, squeezing it, and they howled when nothing happened. They wanted to consume its life so bad, maybe even be alive again themselves.

"Why do you want to help me?" I said. "What's in it for you?"

I simply want to do what I was made to do. I can help those who need to raze, to rage. It would be such a relief to rage, would it not?

I stepped back. It was time to go home. "I make it a habit to *not* make deals with the Devil."

Orpheus made a deal with the Devil.

I felt cold.

I saw a live person waiting for the bus. The Haunts watched her with a hunger. Like the tree, they tried to touch her but couldn't. But oh, they wanted to. I could feel that desire so deep in them, it radiated through the air like the start of a thunderstorm.

I remembered Marco, standing on that porch beside me, drinking and looking out to nothing.

What are we going to do?

There was no we. There was only me.

I'll see you soon, Charlie.

And the fog dissipated.

9

NERA

There was a fantastic golden door in front of me, and a long line of spirits queuing outside, along the soft red wall.

There were so many rooms in the Station; why was this one so wanted?

Look into the crowd, Charlie had said.

The long snake of souls in the hall were a mass, but only if I didn't pay attention. They were individuals, they were people. And the first person in line was an old man.

He looked hungry and desperate. Still using the memory of a cane, he wore what appeared to be brown corduroy slacks, although they looked washed out in the gray scale of the dead. His bristled white face was not yet shaved for the day, and I wondered if that's how it looked when he passed or if it's how he remembered himself. His hair, though, was immaculate, thick and white and parted to one side. His eyes were large, round, not doleful like my father's. This man had his own story, his own life. One that was as rich and real as Charlie's.

I approached. He stood on the threshold, and I nodded to him as I opened the door and slipped past into the room.

He nodded back.

The room looked like the inside of a wooden cabin. Outside the frozen windowpane, I saw snow. And there were little work benches everywhere. Twinkling lights. And rolls and rolls of giftwrap and wrapping paper.

There were also boxes—white boxes with little bows on them.

I knew this room. A very long time ago, my father had brought me here and handed me a box with a little gift in it for me. A necklace with a small lit lantern on it, glowing with something cooler than fire, but still so bright.

To keep you safe, Father had said.

I now squeezed the little lantern that was around my neck, its edges round and soft, like it was made of air.

This was the Gift Room. Every soul could send one gift to a living person. My father had chosen me. The gravity of a gift suddenly hit me, my necklace feeling like a heavy anchor tethering me to my own heart. His one gift had gone to me.

All around me, souls chose their own gifts to place in boxes and send down the assembly line to the city beyond these walls. Some chose butterflies, lilacs, cardinals, rainbows, or marigolds; signs a person who was left behind may need to know that maybe those who were lost had made it safely and still existed . . . what *did* the living think of the dead?

I had seen Charlie's desperate eyes when she asked about her sister. Charlie could see the dead. But the living weren't supposed to see the dead, so the living didn't know there was anything after life. They did not know all these souls were safe.

And these souls couldn't speak to the living, but they could send one little miracle through the Gift Room, a room my father must have imagined and built with his own brilliant magic.

Every one of these souls, all of them, also had a father.

It was so much. I couldn't carry all this.

How will they know a butterfly is from me? one of the souls asked me.

I barely heard the soft ghost's voice.

Excuse me? they tried again.

I threw back all the burgeoning feelings behind me like a heavy cape. I said, with more authority than I felt I had any right to, *Sometimes, they just know. Other times, they shrug it off. We only deliver it using this chute. But we hope they all make it where they need to go.*

Why only one? another asked.

Well, you can't just go spending your whole afterlife trying to communicate, Theresa, another spirit said. *We don't belong there anymore. We gotta keep this moving.*

Moving toward the Veil, not the city. Always forward, beyond. There was no going back.

Or maybe there was, beyond the Veil. But that was not my realm.

With death, we couldn't change what had happened. But here at the Station, we could still heal what haunted the dead.

It was hard to think of us as doing any healing; once people came to us, they were dead. Their story was told. Their chapters in the city concluded and now we stood here to help them end. But looking at this room, maybe there was still peace to be found after the final chapter.

Souls still love those who are left behind, or this room wouldn't exist.

Life and Death were intricately connected.

I wondered if Charlie's sister had sent her a message. But Charlie must have been looking for messages, and she had received none. So her sister may not have even stepped foot in this room. Maybe she passed through the Station so fast she didn't need it.

Or maybe she'd never arrived at the Station at all.

The old man with the cane stepped toward me, waving to get my attention. *Could you help me, please?*

Before I could answer, there was a box in front of us on the table.

I always told my wife I'd send her a song, he said. *On the radio, if we can.*

A wedding song? I asked.

He looked at his clasped, shaking hands. *It was a song we listened to when our son got sick. Eric Clapton? We listened to it like a prayer. Can you do that? Put it on the radio?*

Songs seemed to be important. A song brought Charlie here. I remembered the feeling inside me as Charlie played the piano. Music was more than sound. A song could carry the power to beckon the living to the dead.

I looked down to the box, not exactly sure what I was supposed to do. I'd never done this before; the souls usually did it alone. But Charlie had told me to see them, *really* see them. The box sparked a little, when he spoke. It seemed as if he had it under control. Why was I here? Why did he need me?

His hand came down on mine. I couldn't feel him, and I didn't know if he could feel me. But I did sense his fear and his need to not be alone.

Our son was eleven. He got very sick at camp. She never forgave herself for sending him. But it was a fluke, what were we going to do? Keep him at home forever? He looked deflated. *If the song could come to her on her drive to the cemetery, I want her to know that this isn't the end. That . . . that I will know her, when we see each other again. That I am . . . still thinking of her, even here.* He looked around the room. *It looks like the North Pole a little, doesn't it?*

The inside of the box spun with a little light, and then I heard a guitar quietly resonate out of its contents.

I just want her to know I still know her, he said. *She was so worried about that.*

The box closed. It slid down the line, through the wall, to somewhere else, to a car radio somewhere far away from this place.

He should leave, now that the gift was sent, but I could tell he didn't want to, and I didn't want him to. I might see him on the ferry, but then he'd be gone forever. He would leave his wife behind, and his son and all the music on the radio couldn't follow him.

Everyone was a Charlie. Everyone had a Sammy.

Everyone was a Harosen. Everyone had a Nera.

What's her name? I said.

He blinked, looking up at me, his eyes meeting mine. I knew my father never looked them in the eye. *Her name is Claire. We met in college. She was so smart. And I . . . I was such a dunce. And we thought we had forever . . . She loves coasters. Not roller coasters, the little drink coasters. She collected them. I always . . . I didn't use them enough. And . . .* he took a deep breath and he gasped out the air, as if he still had lungs. *I know some souls cross on the first night. But some take longer. Do you know why I've waited this long to cross?*

No, I said honestly; I hadn't even known he had been here before today.

Because here, I still look like me, he said, touching his chest, his polo shirt with a little emblem on the pocket. It was stained with paint, like he wore his favorite shirt when he was doing hard work or creating something. *What happens to me when I cross over? Will I still be me? Will I be someone else? Will I be nothing?*

What if . . . what if when I meet Claire on the other side, we can't recognize one another because there's nothing to recognize or I've . . . or I have changed so much . . . He shook, like he needed to cry. But there were no more tears he could make.

How many people had Father and I ferried across the lake? How many gifts had this room sent into the city? And every one of them held this weight.

I looked at the long line outside. It was overwhelming. But I turned away from the line, and I reached a hand out to touch his shoulder, or rather the memory of his shoulder. He said, *I . . . I don't want to let go of this body because this is the body Claire's hands touched.*

I took him into my arms, and he collapsed into my shoulders, shoulders that were more than a memory. They had previously not seemed to be of much use, but here they were. They'd been here all this time.

He sobbed for a while, and then he said quietly, *But that's silly, isn't it? Because . . . my body is already gone. It's already done.*

It is, I said softly.

Are you dead? he asked. *Do you know if it hurts?*

I don't, I said. *But I do know you still love Claire, even here. So there must be love on the other side, too.*

But you don't know.

I don't know.

I'm not ready. I said I was ready, I'm not ready. I gotta send her another song. I gotta . . . I gotta wait for her . . . so we can cross together . . .

No one is ever ready, I said. *But I think sometimes we do things we aren't ready for, because the thing we're doing is already finished.*

He stared at the empty table. He nodded slowly. And then he said, *What?*

I . . . I flustered. *I mean to say that sometimes we have to move forward because we're sitting in an ending. There's nothing left to do here. It's okay, she'll be okay. And so will you.*

What's your name? he asked.

I stopped. We never exchanged names. I was the Station Master's daughter. They were souls.

But Charlie had a name, and she knew mine. Charlie's sister had a name, and I didn't know where she was because we hadn't learned anyone's names.

Nera, I said. *And what's yours?*

George, he said. *I hope Claire gets to keep her name when she passes through. I hope I get to remember mine. When you see her . . . will you tell her I love her? And I'm sorry about the coasters?*

Yes, I said. *Of course.*

And you'll be on the ferry tonight?

I will.

Will you stand next to me? he said.

Yes, I said.

And he left. Then another came to me. Then another. All wanting me to simply stand witness to their gifts.

A robin sent in the middle of winter to a mother from a little boy named Thomas.

The smell of lilacs sent in the night to a family struggling with the murder of their daughter named Claudine.

A book finally reappearing after being lost to storage to a granddaughter from a grandfather named Frederick, who promised her he'd get her a copy.

A flickering of the light to let a widow know it was alright to love again, sent by a young person with long jet-black hair named Theo.

One after another, all with names, all with messages of love. All with a small whisper into the waking universe, *I am still here.* One after another, looking me in the eyes and saying:

I'm scared.

If I let go of this life, it'll be real.

I want to go back, just for one more second.

I hope she knows that none of this is as scary as we thought it'd be.

Tell him I love him.

Tell him I was so tired, I had to go.

Tell her I didn't want to go.

Tell her she was my life. She was all of my life. And I would do it all over again.

Tell them I found peace.

Tell them to meet me there with stories of what they did after I left.

Tell them not to forget the Marlboros when they visit.

Tell her I wanted to apologize.

Tell him I am so proud of him.

Tell her she wasn't a bad person.

Tell him I forgive him.

Tell them hello for me, please.

There were so many names, and I hoped I could remember them all. I didn't know how I was going to hold all of this, but there was something made of grit, down deep inside, that told me this was why I was here, and this is what I was going to do.

After they all left, I also exited the room. I stood numb, feeling overwhelmed and empty, in the hallway with the red carpet.

I thought about the light in George's box. I thought about Claire, alone in her car, driving away from where his real body had been buried. The pain of leaving the person you love.

These little gifts stretched a light between two souls that couldn't be in the same place anymore.

It seemed cruel, living in a universe where we couldn't always be with the people we needed to touch.

Nera?

I turned to see a little basset looking up at me, his tail low. Elbee leaned on me, and I felt a dull blue feeling throb from his little body.

It hurts, I said, sitting down and scratching him behind his big floppy ears. *Is this why Father and I haven't asked their names before? It's too much.*

Your father would say as much, he said. He licked my hand, my face. I felt the love spread from him to me. His little blue spirit, filling me up with comfort.

He's going to die, Elbee, I said, and the words in my head were as hot as an iron. *I know,* he said.

And this grief, it's what Charlie feels. It's what they all feel. I can . . . I think I can feel grief. Is this what grief feels like?

It feels different and still the same for each person, he said. *A longing that you know will never end, and so it hurts. Something that doesn't get better, not completely.*

I thought I knew what love felt like, I covered my face with my hands, *but I am starting to understand there is . . . a lot I don't know.*

He looked up at me. *Your father says that who he was, what the city was, it no longer matters. But I was there, even before the beginning of the Station. And I can tell you, Nera, it does matter.*

Who was he back then? I dropped my hands to my side. *He doesn't talk about the time before.*

Elbee stopped for a second, and then said thoughtfully, *He was a man who cared very much. Too much, sometimes. And to understand who he is, you should know all the things he's not told you.* He looked up to me. His mouth open, not in a smile, but in a stressed pant. *Do you want to know?*

Yes, I said.

He nudged my hand. *After the ferry ride tonight, come find me. And I'll show you.*

REMNANTS

HEY KIDDO,

IT'S YOUR FIRST DAY OF
HIGH SCHOOL! WANTED TO WISH YOU
THE BEST FIRST DAY THERE CAN BE.
YOU'RE GROWING UP, AND I HOPE YOU'RE
STARTING TO SEE HOW BRIGHT YOU
SHINE. NO MATTER WHAT HAPPENS OUT
THERE IN THE WORLD, YOU'VE GOT
ALL OUR LOVE BACKING YOU UP. WE'RE
VERY PROUD OF YOU, NOW GO
KNOCK 'EM DEAD.

YOUR OLD PAPA BEAR.

—*Handwritten note from Michael Connor to his daughter,*
Charlie Connor, September 1995

10

CHARLIE

In the city, I was always in a crowd of strangers.

I took the Red Line back up north. I saw a Black girl with beautiful braided hair and buttons all over her bag, reading a dog-eared copy of *The Hobbit*. Sam's favorite. I'd found her copy in the back of the station wagon before we sold it.

I saw a dead white punk with brilliant spiky hair wearing a super cool leather vest. Sam would have loved it. She would've never worn it, but she always said she secretly wished she was cool enough to pull off punk style.

Remnants left behind.

But the Station, the Veil, they were not remnants. They were a future. I had my first non-dead end. Ha.

That hope sat in my chest and I clung to it as I stepped off the train and onto the Granville L station's platform, looking out to the rainy skyline of Edgewater. Our apartment leered at me from beyond. The big one, with "6130" written in massive and faded letters on its side. In the rain, it looked like the Tower of Terror, glowering over the rest of the buildings between it and the river.

It was a tomb.

I numbly walked down the stairs of the platform. Two blocks, past the Loyola security station, the Thai restaurant, until I stepped into 6130's maw. It was not a home. This was seventeen floors of moldy carpet, college students, divorced dads, and an assortment of people on their way to somewhere else.

What do you call a place where you live but it's not a home?

Four floors up, I found our door. But I couldn't go in. I just stood there, my keys squeezed between my knuckles and my Chucks squishing on the hall carpet. I felt sick with the overwhelming realization that I was stuck here. In this place. In this day. In this life. And the only thing waiting for me on the other side was more horror.

Someone cleared their throat.

I turned to look at the neighbor's door. In the middle of the cold brown hallway, Mr. Coleson stood glaring at me. He was old, with wrinkled dark brown skin and a bald head and a necktie. Also, he was dead. His ghost body was fuzzy, his shoes unseen and his hands gone like someone had started to sketch him out on paper with a charcoal pencil and then didn't bother to finish.

"Hi, Mr. C," I said.

Charlie, he said. *My wife got no sleep last night.*

"I'm sorry, Mr. C," I said, fumbling for my next keys. Two of them: the deadbolt and the door handle one. I hadn't gotten around to labeling them, and I really needed to. Mr. C was a talker.

Your father was up walking around, too loud, playing the television too loud, talking to himself.

"I'm sorry, Mr. C," I said again. Wrong key. Damnit.

My wife has enough going on as is, he said. *She doesn't need Michael keeping her up—*

"He's doing his best. We're all doing our best, Mr. C," I said. The deadbolt clicked open. Thank God.

I don't want to have to complain, he kept on me.

I tried my next key in the doorknob. Who was he going to complain to? No one. But I just said, "Sorry, Mr. C. You know my dad is going through it."

So is my wife, he said. His lip trembled. Maybe at some point, Mr. Coleson had been someone who could win an argument. But now he was tired and scared. So I forgot my keys for a minute.

"Is there something I can bring your wife? That will make her feel better? She doesn't have to know it's me," I said. "I can just leave it at the door."

Mr. Coleson looked at me. And then said with great certainty, *Carnations. She'll know what that means.*

"Consider it done," I said.

Mr. Coleson disappeared. For now.

The next key worked in the doorknob, because of course it did. I shoved my shoulder into the door, and I stepped into the dark apartment.

A squat living room. A kitchen to the left. Two bedrooms. Mine clearly used to be a dining room for a nice little one-bedroom, but the landlord had built a hasty wall between it and the kitchen and called it new. It didn't matter how many walls were here, it smelled like beer and sweat everywhere.

I put on a peaceful face. "Hey, Dad, you doing okay?"

Dad sat on the couch, staring at the TV near the window. Cans lined up on the side table like a senior class blocked together for a photo, three across and four deep. He wore the same robe he'd been in for a month. I couldn't get him to wash it, but when I realized there were welts on his neck, I stole the robe while he was sleeping, washed it, and returned it.

"Dad?"

"Hi, Charlie," he said, tired. My heart melted. So many things had changed about him, but his voice was the same. That hurt more, somehow. He still kept his body and his words, just hollowed out.

People can die before they're dead. Their souls give out, and their bodies keep walking. My father wasn't the one who died that day, but he didn't walk out alive, either.

For as busy as the city was, no one living or dead had come to save us. No grandparents, no old friend of Dad's from the war, certainly not Mom who fucked off to Bloomington-Normal because there was something worse than seeing ghosts and that was, I guess, seeing Dad and me.

Anyway.

You know who else sure didn't show up? Sam.

Fine, if she was mad at me for not protecting her, if she was fucking with me, okay, then don't show up for me. But she never showed up for Dad, either. And would she pass through that Veil without saying goodbye? At least to him?

He used to dress up as Santa Claus for Chrismukkah. Now he looked like the shovel man from *Home Alone,* his beard thinning, his cheeks gaunt, his entire body sunken in like he was being sucked of life. If Harosen looked tired, my father looked like he wanted to be a corpse, and his stubborn body just wouldn't let him fucking die.

I didn't want him to die. I wanted him to live again. I needed my rock.

But he had a volcano under his skin. Ready to burst, pour lava all over the floor, burn us alive. Like he had Marco.

What are we going to do?

There is no we.

That's what he'd said to Marco. Heartless. Painful.

He fears she is wiped from this world. There is no piece of her left. But if you find her, he can be saved.

The thing in the dark, in the Water Tower . . . it filled my brain and I batted it away, shaking my head and squinting my eyes. But the seed was already planted.

The night after the funeral, my dad had sat in Sammy's abandoned bedroom. Her room without her was gross, unnatural. Her paintings were everywhere, some good, all bright with color. Her clothes, soft and pastel and comfy and still smelling like her. The story of a very specific soul who had a lilt in her laughter and a soft pained secret in her sadness, who loved wearing old granny sweaters and running shorts.

Dad had held her old stuffed dog in his big, calloused hands. Like he could cobble her back together from the things she'd left behind. "She needs me," he had mumbled as I came to the door. "If I die, I can be with her again."

It hurt. But I got it. I got it way more than I should. And now an unopened moving box full of her stuff squatted in my bedroom. Another painful reminder.

The back of my neck bristled. Someone was behind me, standing on the fire escape balcony. My head snapped at the window. There, peering in, a silhouette of a person made of static pressed its hand against the glass.

Pain. Pain that felt like vomit burning my throat. I fell on the floor, hit my head, trying to hide . . .

I walked to the window. Gently, I raised my hand and I pressed it to the windowpane, just the glass between me and the Haunt. Glass, not a true solid, not a liquid, something in between that was tangible and sharp.

The city is pain. All those who jumped to the third rail. All the workers who lost their money. All the parents who lost their children. All those who lost their homes. This is not a place of starlight, and the Station pretends it is. Will it leave your family behind, or will you take what the city needs?

Sorrow flooded me like adrenaline. I pulled my hand back, gasping for air. In a blink, the Haunt was gone.
It had been my tired brain. A trick of the light.
But when I blinked again, it was back.
It just stared at me.

Go to the tower. I can help you. You will see her again.

Then, like changing the channel, the Haunt vanished again.
I stared at the window. Go to the tower. Go to her.
"Charlie?" Dad's voice sounded from the living room.
I dug my hands into my skirt pockets and forced myself from the window. "Yup!" I kicked off my Chucks in the hall and creaked across the wooden floor to sit next to him on the couch where he sat staring at the blank television.
"Did you eat?" I said. "I'm sorry I wasn't here last night."
"Are you . . . having those . . . you know . . ." Dad muttered, like he was looking through a dirty windshield. His thoughts were cataracts over his eyes.
"Flashbacks? No, I'm fine," I said. Today, the PTSD was the least of my problems.
I clicked the light on next to us. Just in case.
"No," Dad said. "Are you still seeing dead people?"
I scooted closer to the light. "Yes." Somehow my father standing as the solo believer of my superpowers did not comfort me. But drowning people cling to each other.
"Are there people here?" Dad asked.
"I thought I saw something out the window and it scared me but it's fine. Nothing's out there."
Not now they weren't.
What if the Haunt got in? I had to find a ward. A cross, a hamsa, a lighthouse—something to keep a Haunt at bay, until it didn't work anymore.
The Haunts followed me home.
I couldn't breathe in here.

Dad said nothing else. He couldn't. My rock was hollowed out.

Before this, he'd bought us a house with royalties from the songs he wrote. When we heard them on the car radio, he'd always turn it up and we'd scream the lyrics out loud. Before this, he'd write us notes in our lunches. He would be in the front row with a camera at every recital. He would make up silly songs on the spot: *"Sammy, Charlie, Sammy, Charlie, eeeee-oooo! You owe me huggos!"*

If Sammy had been the heart of our family, he had been the soul.

But now all the songs he'd written fell silent. Like waterlogged paper, blowing around the street. And I didn't know who had moved in with who, or who was protecting who. We sat on the couch, two broken people, dying next to each other.

I should text Mom. I should waste a quarter and text her and get no answer back. *He is less Dad than he is Michael, you are more Donna than you are Mom. Where did you two go?*

Or maybe I could escape to Marco's place. Help him clean up this morning after the party. "Hey, so guess what happened last night after I left?" I'd say. Yeah, that'd work out great.

Dad touched my shoulder. "We'll figure it out."

"I saw Mr. Coleson again, out in the hallway. The outside is very loud and crowded. And I . . ." I shouldn't say it. *I found her piano, Daddy.*

Dad looked at me, his softness and confusion dissipating. Like a hound with a scent. "What is it?" he said. "Did you find her?"

I couldn't. I couldn't do that to him.

So instead I said, "I found the river Styx last night." I wouldn't tell him about the Haunts. But the good parts? I could tell him the good parts.

Dad looked to me. "Oh?" he said, stiffly.

"It's the lake," I said.

"Don't breathe in when they put your head under the water," he said. "You'll forget who you are and they'll drag you down."

I nodded. "I'll keep that in mind."

"And take a song with you," he mumbled, looking at his hands. "A good one."

"She . . ." I shouldn't say anything else. Sitting in delusion with him would only hurt him. Hadn't I just gotten him to stop believing my sister was a statue at the zoo? Hadn't we just gotten through the night terrors?

But Nera promised me she would help.

I could bring music back to him.

I said quietly, "I followed a song to the edge of the lake." I hesitated. "Sammy's song." Dad stared at me. "It was playing, from a lighthouse where the ferryman guides souls across the lake. And Daddy . . ." I wanted to touch him. "I found her piano. And I'm going to find her."

His face grew gray, his blue eyes like ice that never thawed. But then his cheeks reddened, like my words struck him. And he could move and breathe once more.

"If I find her," I said. "If I know she's okay, then we'll be okay."

"Then find her." He stood, and shuffled away.

Play her song. Hear her voice. Find her. And we will have music again.

REMNANTS

somewhere in the minds of old men
there are heroes in which they used to believe.
somewhere in the bricks of the old city
there are monsters they have turned into ghost stories.

—the writings of a thing in the dark

11

NERA

She came back.

Charlie emerged against the setting sun, from under the long road's parade of lights, the bridge opening our world to her. Her hair looked like gold, her narrow shoulders and one white-knuckled hand held her backpack. Her eyes fixed straight ahead of her, firmly marching forward into the next night. She was a part of the heartbeat of the city.

Charlie came and went as she pleased, breathed in the air. How overwhelming to navigate such a big existence.

I watched her from my place between the entrance's pillars. She approached along with the dogs all around her who entered with new souls. The souls passed the fountain, and the fountain sprayed its water into their mist to return them to their bodies. It was beautiful, seeing each soul present their truest selves to the Station. Some came with canes, some without. Some were young and others saw themselves as old.

Charlie, however, was just wet and cold. She sputtered, and then shook her head to get her hair out of her face.

I touched my stomach with my hands, and the little lantern on the chain around my neck glowed. How would I look if I stepped into the real world?

I never really thought much about my body. It was taller than others, it had breasts, it was sturdy and it got me from place to place.

But to *feel* a body, that must be so much.

A low hissing made Charlie jump. I saw a flashlight in one of Charlie's hands, bright and swinging around her like she was in a fencing match with the air. I saw the Haunts behind her, in the bushes, watching with their white static eyes. They unsheathed their teeth into wide, hungry grins.

Their static fingers pressed to the stones behind Charlie, wanting to ride her shadow into the Station. But they failed, hissing backward as the lighthouse's bright beam stung them.

I stepped forward to help. I didn't pass the fountain, but I held out my lantern. "Charl—"

Aye! shouted Hermes, the brown conductor dog who kept a pocket watch around his neck like a collar. He rushed up to Elbee, who led the pack through the pillars and beyond me into the atrium. *Here she comes, Elbee! You told me to tell you when the musician's coming and now I'm telling you! She's late! Why are you late! Why is everyone late!* He gave a small howl.

"Charlie," I tried again, stepping forward. Charlie looked like she was on a mission, storming up to me.

"They followed me home, Station Lady," she said. "They keep talking to me and . . . I wanna make sure you remember our deal, because I'm not about to be stalked by Haunts for nothing. Understand? I'm not here for the creepy hocus pocus. I want to find Sam, and then I'm out."

I nodded in agreement. "Of course," I said. "I haven't forgotten." She looked scared, her grip on the flashlight quivering. "They followed you home?"

"Yeah," she said. "And I don't live alone. My dad's sick and I can't have him getting hurt by them. I've seen some mean ghosts, but I don't deal with shadow people and demons and whatever the hell else there is out there. That's not my jam and I'm not gonna do it. Understand?"

I nodded. "Keep a light on you. And we'll send a dog with you, to patrol."

"No," Charlie said. "Wait, are they even real dogs?"

That was a confusing question for me. "Yes," I said. "Dogs are real."

"They're not ghost dogs?"

"Dogs can travel in between," I said. "They're here to guide. Chestnut would be a good patroller."

"I said no."

"He's perceptive and loud and will keep your father company."

"I don't want a dog."

"Who doesn't want a dog?"

Charlie blinked. "Me."

"Well," I said. "I don't like that they followed you, and the surefire way to keep you safe is to send you with a guardian in the morning. But I'm not going to foist a dog on you."

"It kind of seems like you are."

"Alright, I'm going to foist a dog on you."

"Do you even have the authority to do that? Are you in charge or is Harosen?" Charlie asked.

"I am taking over for my father."

Charlie paused, then allowed a small turn of a smile in the corner of her mouth. A secret laugh. "Is Chestnut a nice golden retriever or something?"

"No," I said. "He's a Yorkie. And he's an asshole."

Charlie scoffed. "Great. That *would* be my dog." She walked past me into the Station.

———————————

I watched the atrium from the balcony above with Hermes. He kept checking his watch, then glaring down at the other dogs barking things at them: *Evie! The babies need to stay together, we cannot have them running around everywhere!*

Happy, I'm not going to say it again, the ferry is a mess and you're slacking tonight! Gurty! Musician to the piano! Now!

I saw Gurty escort Charlie to the piano. She sat down and opened the cover and played a song I'd never heard.

I folded my hands on my arms, my elbows on the railing. I couldn't take my eyes off her, the way her fingers glided against something so simple as wood and string to make something that transcended even this place.

Below me, my father's stark figure stood in the entrance of his office, his hands delicately rested on his doorframe. He allowed himself to listen to the music, his brow knotted. He looked up to me, then disappeared into his office. But he kept the door open.

"Were you here in the beginning?" I asked Hermes.

He came closer for a good scritch behind the ears. *Yes, from before the beginning.*

"What was Father like when he was younger?" I said.

Hermes yawned. *In what way?*

"Elbee says that who he was still matters," I said. "So who was he?"

Hermes cocked his head. *He was sad. He was full of lots of colors. And then he sort of faded away all at once.*

"My father makes a point of not learning anyone's names," I said. "He doesn't look the guests in the eye. We don't even know if Charlie's sister came through here. I cannot tell her, honestly. But he listens to her music and the lighthouse shines. I don't even know where to begin, Hermes."

Hermes perked his ears, his eyes also watching the girl. *Harosen used to learn all their names,* he said. *Before you came here, he'd learn each one of their stories. We didn't need all these rooms and nonesuch. There was the work, and that was enough. I liked it simple. You know, he stopped looking us in the eye, too.*

Charlie did not always look people in the eye. She liked to look at the ground. When someone is tired, perhaps there's just not enough in them to face anyone.

"Do you know if her sister came through?"

I take care of the schedules at night, Hermes declared very officially. *That's Elbee's job, to know who came through. He guides the humans.*

"He guides me as well." I saw the little basset, curled up in a chair on the edge of the atrium, watching Charlie warily. He lifted his head and looked up to me and Hermes. An unanswered question still dangled in the air between him and me.

Well, Hermes said. *You're a human, too, aren't you? It's his job.* He scratched behind his ear, the watch jangling around his neck. *I will say this for free. Having the girl play the piano to keep the lighthouse on? It's not sustainable. As the new Station Master, Nera, you're going to need to make changes.*

"What sorts of changes?" I asked. "Charlie told me to look into the crowd, and I'm doing that."

Hermes pointed his nose down to where Charlie was. Beside Charlie, there was an older woman, marveling at the piano like she could see the notes spilling out of it. She smiled.

Edna Meyer, Hermes said. *She's the human who's been here the longest. Staying in the hotel wing for years. She promised her daughter she'd wait, so she's waited.* He panted, his tail wagging slightly. *She's been here your whole life, and perhaps today's a good day to meet her. Hmm?*

Edna Meyer said something and Charlie Connor laughed as she played some song I did not know. The living and the dead made a stark contrast. But they shared the same spark in their eyes. They had both lived in the city.

A common depth that I could not reach.

Food was as unfamiliar as palm trees and penguins; details of another world.

While the rest of the souls stayed in the atrium, or found their way to the rooms on the first floor, Edna Meyer ventured up to the second level mezzanine. I watched her say hello to a woman whose dog wore a guiding harness, wave to two young boys, and then head on into the diner.

The diner was a small restaurant space off the main walkway that circled the balcony of the atrium. The diner had old gas lamps posted on top of a half-wall that separated the booths and black-and-white tile of the diner from the carpet of the mezzanine. Edna Meyer sat down at one of those booths and closed her eyes. A plate appeared in front of her. I kept my distance, staying on the carpet, not entering the diner space with its tile. I only observed.

Small details unfurled from her like a busy painting. Kindness painted her face, but her soft eyes held an edge of a frown. Her white hair was curled tight, pale luminescent skin showed veins underneath. With her polished fingernails, she touched her earrings nervously, and I did not realize that while I was looking at her, she could be looking at me.

Hello, Young Station Master, she said. I stumbled, but she very calmly unfolded her napkin and set it on her lap. *This diner makes you your favorite meal in the world. Mine doesn't look like much. But it's what I made my daughter and granddaughter on Sunday mornings.*

I lowered my head, clasping my hands in front of me, and stepped forward. *What is it?* I asked softly.

Bisquick pancakes with no syrup, no butter, and a cranberry juice. Edna Meyer beamed. Despite being dead, she still shook with age. So many memories she must hold, to have such a clear understanding of who she once was . . . who she still was? However the soul had related to their physicality, that's how ghosts appeared in the Station. And it looked like Edna had memorized every inch of her body just as it had been in the end.

Would you like to join me? Edna said.

I did. I walked past the half-wall, onto the black-and-white tile, and I noticed how my shoes sounded different on different surfaces. From a thump to a clack.

I sat across from her, bringing my dress in and folding my fingers together on my lap. No plate appeared for me. I hadn't expected it to.

I'm Nera, I said politely.

I know who you are, Edna said. Her voice was thick with a mix of accents from all over the world. I couldn't place them, but what a wonder, to live in so many places and have so many sounds touch your ears that you had a dialect all your own.

With no ceremony, she took a large bite of pancake. She closed her eyes and breathed in through her nose. She of course couldn't actually eat, she couldn't actually breathe, but maybe she needed to experience this and remember how good those sensations once had been.

I wanted to be sad for her; she would never actually eat this meal again. But then I realized she had at least gotten to enjoy pancakes once, whereas I had nothing in front of me.

Oh, who am I? Why thank you for asking, I'm Edna. She winked. I looked to my lap.

Sorry, yes, I said. *The dogs said you'd been here for a bit. They also said that maybe you would know things about the Station . . . my father—*

This girl your papa hired, she interrupted me, *who is playing the piano, she's not dead?*

She isn't, I said.

Edna raised her brows, in either surprise or disagreement. *Alright,* was all she gave. But then decided to add, *Well, I'm not exactly certain what's to be done for her. She should keep living, be out there enjoying her young life. The dead is for the dead, you know.* She huffed. *And that goes for you, too. I heard you talking earlier. You have a voice; use it when you can!*

"I'm sorry, it's just strange still," I said, out loud.

What's strange is having such a pretty voice and keeping it locked up. How many languages you can speak when you know the language of the dead, and you use none of them!

"Edna," I said, "Hermes said my father used to know everyone's names, and now he doesn't. Is that true?"

He's Jewish, of course he used to know all their names. Wrote them all down, too, on a big wall in the atrium. But that atrophied. Crumbled away when he stopped remembering all of them.

A big wall, with everyone's names on it.

You ever been to shul, Nera? And I stared at her. *That's what I thought. At shul, we say the names of the dead every Friday night. We pray for them. We enshrine their names on the wall outside the sanctuary. They are not forgotten. Ever. Because there is power in a name. It is the shape of who a soul is.* Then her words turned terse. *And your papa has made his own grave by forgetting that, not teaching you more than how to drive the ferry and keep the lighthouse. No wonder the light is going out. There is more to caring for the Station than driving a boat and lighting a lamp.*

I looked at the table in shame that confused me. "Today, I worked in the Gift Room. And I learned each of their names."

Don't forget them. She waggled a fork at me, her shoulders bent. *Write them down on your wall. Say them out loud every Shabbat. Even this week. This is the way.*

"What happens to someone when their name is forgotten?" I asked.

You know, Edna said, *when a name is remembered, I like to think they feel joy. When a name is forgotten, I think it's less about what happens to them, but more so what happens to* us. She took a bite of pancake. She closed her eyes, in bliss once more.

Us. She meant the humans who lived in the city. Not me, someone stuck in the misty in-between, not a dog, not a ghost, but a human.

But Edna was a ghost now, and I was not certain what I was.

Then she swallowed and said, *The dead are dead. They've lived their lives. Whatever pain came from Harosen being so cold, it's over. But what does that do to your father, night after night? To not remember them?*

Charlie's music swelled.

Now this Charlie girl, Edna prodded, *what does she matter to you and your papa?*

I didn't know what to do with my hands at a table. I decided on folding them where my plate should be. "Well, my father is leaving next year, and he's putting me in charge. There's a lot to do. Charlie is holding the light for right now, helping my father keep the Haunts away—" Edna turned from me with an *Oh* and looked very afraid. I narrowed my eyes. "You know them, Edna?"

My daughter was always afraid of the dark, she said. *And if those things ever got her . . . the Haunts, they once were human souls until a demon breathed in the smoke of their blood.*

"But the Haunts can't touch the living."

What do I know, I'm just an old lady eating pancakes. But I do know there are many things that can hurt the living. And the dead.

She said these things with caution and looked out to the atrium to watch Charlie at the piano. The new souls had started to gather for the night. Some of them arrived hand in hand with those who had waited for them. Others came with the dogs. None were alone. It was safe here.

Every culture has their own names for these sorts of shadows. Things that are on earth to cause discord and chaos. I've seen enough shadows in one lifetime for the rest of my eternity, Edna said. *It was easy, back in the camps in Poland, to get drowned in the shadows. Some people in my barracks, they said they could see the ghosts coming out of the ash. They said . . . there was one girl, she said she could see monsters consuming our light at night. She said that shadows leaked out of people toward the end. They just became walking . . . shades.*

Memories flooded Edna's eyes. *My arm was not branded like some others. They'd given up numbering how many they wanted to kill by the time I arrived in Poland. And I wonder if I had that tattoo . . . would it still be there even now? What burns and scars do we keep and which do we shed when we can? I like to think it would have disappeared as soon as I died.*

"There were Haunts in Poland?"

They come and go throughout time and the world, I suspect, Edna said. *The schmutz of the world, all that hate and fear and hurt shedding off us or consuming us, like a fire.*

"Father says a demon started the Chicago Fire and grew the Haunts," I said.

Edna nodded. *I believe it. There are pockets in this world of great good. And yes, there are some sheydim that are innocuous, not good or bad. But there are also deep pockets of sheydim whose names we do not say . . . tumah, sometimes larger, worse monsters. Shadows are cast by something, aren't they? Not all of them are human, but to be human is to feel them. They say the Fire was so vast and violent because of how much trash and wood was piled on top of each other in the city. The things that accumulate in a city's spirit can be like that, too.*

"So the city *is* as dangerous and evil as Father says," I mumbled.

Oh, it is super evil, Edna laughed, the word "super" sticking out in her thick accent. Humans lived in multiple decades. Sometimes so did their speech. *But we say, alright, it's evil. So what are we going to do now? Listen.* She moved her wrinkled hands across the table and reached for mine. I let her take them. But I couldn't feel them. Her hands had been gone for many years. *Nera, my darling, there is evil. Absolutely. I've seen it. The sheydim and the shadows, mazzikin, demons. There is death and there are things worse than death. My heart, broken in two. And then in three. And four and five. But Nera, I also held my daughter. I also saw some really lovely films and television programs. There was one night where I taught my nephew how to dance. Do I have all the answers? No. But I do know that even though the sheydim would like you to believe they're all that there is, they must work hard to blot out the sun. Because the sun is bright, Nera.*

I thought about the Haunts outside, stretching to touch the stones that led here. How many stones sat between us and them, and how long could the lighthouse hold them at bay? And was Edna right? Could they turn things in the living world?

Not yet they couldn't.

The music kept pouring in from the atrium.

"She's here to find her sister," I said quietly. "Samantha Connor. Did you ever meet her?"

Edna watched me turn to look at the atrium. *No*, she said. *I didn't. But that doesn't mean she wasn't here. I hope she made it through the Haunts, but . . . Nera, if you do find that her sister is one of them, then how will that help her?*

My mouth was empty. Edna had no answer for me, just more questions. "I don't know," I admitted.

What you should focus on, she said, *is how you* can *help her. How you can help us all.*

I could help by keeping that light on. Without that light, so many more than Samantha Connor would be in trouble. We would all be in the dark. I did not know how Charlie kept the lighthouse bright, but I knew when she played, it shone.

"The lighthouse was my father's creation, and it will be my responsibility." I watched Charlie's hands fly across the keys. The lighthouse beamed. "The Station wanted Charlie here for some reason. It called out to her with her sister's song, and it shines again when she plays music. I don't know anyone but me and my father who were alive and can see this place. And how does the lighthouse glow for her music? Is her music magical, or is there something in my father that still cares about those things?"

Hashem only knows, Edna said. *And maybe the dogs.* She laughed. *But let the lighthouse glow for her. Let your heart help her find her way. But also, perhaps she is here to help you and your papa as well.*

Edna finished her pancakes. We sat at the table, listening to Charlie's song. There was something easy and swift with her music. She grinned when she played, and so did this place, and so did I.

I saw George approach Charlie. Say something to her. She nodded, and then started a new song. George nodded along to the sound. Little trills, soft gentle notes like a hymn, or something even kinder: a hope that things will turn out alright.

"What song is that?" I asked Edna, hoping she knew.

"Tears in Heaven," Edna said.

"Eric Clapton?"

There, you got it. Edna smiled.

The song George and Claire played when they took their son to the hospital. The lighthouse beamed again.

The Station had dimmed so slowly, I hadn't realized just *how* dim it had gotten until the music played and now it was as if the glass atrium had enshrined the sun.

Charlie understood what it meant to have a song mean something.

Nera? Edna said. I looked to her. She smiled and patted my hand across the table with her thick arms and wrist and fingers, laden in bracelets and rings.

Thank you, she said, *for eating dinner with me. It was very nice to see you, speak to you. You've grown into quite a nice young lady.*

"I'm sorry I didn't say hello sooner. Father said not to get to know anyone who came through here," I said.

Edna nodded. *Well, whatever your papa says, I would love for you to come to our book recollection club at some point before you get all high and mighty, new Station Master. Would you be interested?*

I nodded.

Don't you go changing who you are, just for a job, sweetheart, Edna said. *That'll take your soul faster than any demon.*

The moon was high, and the sun was gone. I had to now fulfill my promise to George.

I also had to learn how to work the ferry's helm.

Pull this lever here, Father said, *make sure you have your concentration on the wheel. Tell it where to go. Don't lose sight of where we're headed.*

He barely looked at me, let alone all the passengers around us.

The ferry took off. I wished I could tell Father all the things Edna and I talked about. I wanted to tell him about the Gift Room, and how we needed to collect names. But all I could say was, *Tonight, I'll be by the plank when everyone crosses over. I need to see it up close.*

I didn't tell him I planned to hold George's hand. Something in my gut told me I couldn't risk being told not to.

He just nodded solemnly, and said, *Make sure you pay attention to the nose of the ferry, see how I guide it through the stars.*

As we approached the Veil, I went down to stand with George and his dog. George held my hand, and I wished that I could have given him a proper hug. If we had met in life, we could have been friends. I could have met his wife. But it was my job to meet him in his last chapter, when there was only enough time to hold his hand and not enough time to know him.

I saw his eyes wander to see two men standing side by side, holding each other tight. Two lovers, crossing together. One looked scared, as if he'd only arrived tonight, leaning into the crook of his partner's arm. His partner looked calm, as if he'd waited for ages, and he glowed so bright he kept them both alight. A lifetime's love story told in one peaceful tableau.

George was alone.

I should have waited, he said. *I'm ready, but . . . you'll remember to tell her?* George said.

Of course.

I saw George squeeze my fingers, like a frightened schoolchild. I couldn't feel it.

I always worried if I was a good enough man to go to Heaven, he said. *Now I don't even know if there is a Heaven. But I just hope . . . I just hope they let me remember her on the other side.*

The people we love, I said, *they're a part of us. No matter where we go.*

George looked at me, square in the eyes. And he said, *But respectfully . . . how would you know?*

I didn't have an answer.

I kept holding his hand.

But I said nothing else.

He let go of my hand. His bottom lip shook. He stepped onto the plank, beside his beautiful collie. He knelt and said something to her, resting his head on hers. Happy the dog took over as usual. The same ceremony I'd watched every night I could remember.

Little sparks of their own, the souls danced between the stars above and their reflection on the lake below. And then, their names and their stories and their memories and their hands . . . they all stepped through the gossamer, iridescent curtain of the end and disappeared forever.

They crossed over into the Veil, onward into the world-to-come.

Then I realized a great truth about the ferry my father had made: no one crosses alone. Everyone gets a goodbye.

But I also realized the raw, senseless end to George's story, his stepping into the unknown . . . this was not just a pretty thing, a ceremony full of lights and dogs and pomp and circumstance. It was something very human and very complicated.

And George was right . . . it was something I did not know.

12

CHARLIE

I sat back on the piano bench and stretched. Huh, my spine wasn't tired. My neck wasn't strained. I must have gotten better at posture.

The sheet music with Sam's handwriting sat on the stand ahead of me, above the keys and the little Wurlitzer logo and the carved rose.

If I took it with me, it would just disappear again.

Maybe tomorrow, I could bring some paper of my own and copy it down. But it wouldn't be in her handwriting then.

I saw Victorian Ferry Lady Nera approaching from the docks. The empty ferry returned and the atrium was scant. The moon had dipped below the big glass skylight, and the lighthouse illuminated with the fire inside. The Station looked kinda sad, but somehow it still felt peaceful.

I took my foot off the damper. I closed the lid. Grabbed the sheet music. Started off.

But Nera was on me faster than I expected. She must have hustled from the dock.

I jumped. Then forced a laugh.

"Ah," I said. "Well, it looks like the sun will be up soon enough to take its shift. Do you have good news for me? Were you able to find Sam in, like, one night, and set a new record for ghost search and rescue? Or did you just come here to kick me out, Captain of the Guard?"

Nera looked sunken, like someone had slapped her in the face.

"Oh, uh . . . are you okay?" I asked her. She clearly wasn't okay. I'd just assumed she was single-minded about her job, not as cranky as Harosen but just as flat. But now she looked past me, to the Station around us, as if it had pricked her with thorns.

"I have spent my whole life here," she said. "But I didn't . . . I knew people lived. I knew people died. I knew there were doors the spirits would go in and out of. I didn't understand . . . what was beyond the doors or that there were so many gifts or why we had a diner, a movie theater, a library—"

"A movie theater!" I said. "Thought I smelled popcorn coming from somewhere. So there's real food here? It's not like fairy food, right? Is it ghost food? Like ectoplasm or something?"

Nera paused for a second, and then she gave me some sort of expression I couldn't read. Like she'd never smiled before, and now there was a smile inside of her that didn't know how to sing out.

She bowed to me, her legs straight and her back arching down like a yoga pose.

"Uh, okay?" I said.

She stood up. "It's a play bow," she said. "Do . . . humans not . . ."

"No, not like that," I said.

"Ah," she said. "Well, when a dog wishes to engage another dog, they bow to one another. It's a hello, I'm a friend . . . I . . ." She trailed off, mortified. "Are you hungry?"

We headed to the diner. Nera pointed out every single piece of her home that she could. The velvet stairs. The golden railings. The curved hallway, leading to anything you'd ever want. The indoor park with the swings and the flowers. The room of windows. The arched ceiling. This was her *home*, but the way she guided me through the sights and sounds, it was like she was discovering them alongside me for the first time.

"This place is massive," I said. "You say it's built with memories?"

She nodded. "Yes, my father started it and the people who come through add to it. See, all of these things are to help the transition to the ferry." She hesitated. "Do . . . you think it's a kind place? I think it is."

It was clean, perfect, snug and yet spacious. The kind of place you saw in a movie or in a painting and you missed being there, even if you'd never been there and would never be able to go there. Mom used to talk about this little island she always dreamed about at night, and how when she was a kid and my grandparents were fighting, she'd take naps just so she could escape there. So many people chased finding a place like this their whole lives; happiness, peace, safety.

For me, it came too late. I wished I could trust it. But I was more like Dad, I guess. Dad didn't dream about pretty islands; he dreamt about the war. He knew what it was like to see a place like this on fire.

The music kept playing over the mall's speakers after the gunshots ran out.

I tried to imagine Sam here, the night after she died. Finding kindness in the place she'd been banished to.

But if someone died so quick, so badly, could they see the light enough to find this place?

"I just hope my sister saw it," I said, a deep weight to my voice.

The diner was a cliché 1950s diner with chrome and jukeboxes and milkshake glasses and tight cozy booths bathed in yellow light. The only thing that looked out of place was a very happy Irish setter, wearing a paper server hat and panting behind the counter.

"The dog is the one that makes the food?" I asked, taking a seat in the booth across from Nera.

"Oh," Nera said, looking at the Irish setter. "Shawny, what are you doing?"

It smells good here, he said.

"No, Shawny doesn't make the food." Nera turned back to me, before looking at the dog again. "Do not touch the food, Shawny."

Aww, Shawny said.

I tried not to laugh. "So the dogs," I said. "They're like grim reapers?"

"No, they're not grim and they don't reap," Nera said flatly, fitting herself into the booth. She was tall, with a frame like a bodybuilder. And seeing her Victorian-ghost aesthetic situated in what looked like the old burger joint set of *American Graffiti* was a fever dream. "People aren't wheat. The dogs are guardians. They find and protect souls and help guide them. You know, Cerberus, Anubis . . . Elbee."

"Gurty," I said. The big goof of a floof lay at my feet all night as I played every single song I could think of, every single movie score I'd picked out by ear in high school, every song Sam and I had half-written, sometimes just doing chords over and over again. Anything to charge up that old lighthouse. And Gurty pushed his weight up against the piano bench the whole time.

"Legend says," Nera said, "that the dogs were here long before the Station, maybe as long as the Veil has existed. And they'll be here long after."

"You have legends?"

Nera paused. "Legend is a dog."

"And he told you this?"

"Yes."

"And what does Legend say about cats?" I laughed.

"Cats do what they want," Nera said. "They're neutral about *everything*. If you get a cat on your side, though, that's some real protection. It's the rats that won't have anything to do with us."

I knew rats. I was a Chicagoan. I knew those big signs on yellow plastic paper stapled to telephone poles warning you how big and pissy they can get. Sometimes, when I passed an alleyway, I swore the rats that scurried away under the dumpsters were bigger than some dogs.

"The rats like to follow the smoke of the Haunts," Nera said.

I nodded. "I see." And I looked back at the counter. "Yeah, he's definitely eating something."

"Shawny, spit it out!" Nera said.

Aww, Shawny said again, dropping a half-chewed something. And he vanished with a little puff, paper hat and all.

"You too, Daisy," Nera said, looking to the floor.

Shawny, you blew my cover! A squeaky little voice came from under the table and a toy rat terrier darted out onto the linoleum and also poofed.

"So, I'm guessing this diner is magic somehow," I said. "What's its deal, or did you just want to take me on a nice date?"

Nera's back went straight. "I . . ." She stumbled. And in that small, very human pause, I saw that maybe she was alive after all.

"Well," Nera tried again, "Look down at your plate."

"I don't have a pl—" I looked down. "Oh." I had a plate.

Next to my empty plate was a large, cheesy deep-dish pizza, resting on a beat-up platter.

I knew exactly where it came from. I recognized the crust, flaky and buttery, or the way the plate was one of those plastic beige dishes that had been washed through a steamer too many times. Or the logo on the little paper sticker around the silverware and napkin.

I remembered this perfect day. After a long afternoon at the zoo, we'd gone up to Lou Malnati's and sat down for a meal together. We walked all the way there, the multi-street intersection glowed at sunset and bikes clicked past and it looked like a quiet little safe corner of the city. A microcosm. Bustling and breathing and the air outside the Lou Malnati's smelled like butter and dough and tomatoes and garlic.

Party of four, Michael.

"Oh, lovely," Nera said. She eyed my pizza. I wanted to snark about her getting her own, or maybe pull it closer to me so she couldn't steal it. But I was tired.

"It's pizza from Lou Malnati's," I said.

"Illuminati's?"

"Lou Mal-nati's," I said as I unwrapped the silverware and took the big serving knife from under the pizza and cut into the pie. My stomach grumbled. How did this diner know what my favorite meal was? Where had it come from? Was it alright to eat it? I didn't even care. I knew about eating pomegranates in the Underworld and all that but . . . it was deep dish.

"Ah," Nera said. "Who is Lou?"

"Some guy who started a pizza parlor," I said. "Dad told me the whole story once. I don't know it real well . . . but it's the best pizza in town. No matter what others say. Remember that. And Chicagoans are gonna say they don't like deep dish, that they know where the *real* pizza is, but no, it's all about the meaty meaty cheesy cheesy layers for me, I don't care about the gatekeepers."

Nera nodded, taking it gravely seriously.

"I didn't know the city argued over pizza," Nera said.

I raised a brow as I pulled a slice away from the platter, and I plopped the pile of cheese pie in front of me. "Wow, you really don't listen to the dead, do you?" And then I realized she had no food in front of her. "You . . . don't have anything to eat," I said.

"Well," she said, "I haven't really lived a life, so I . . . don't have a favorite meal."

There was an awkward silence.

"Well, that's fucked," I said.

"No, please," Nera said, "I don't need to. Eat!"

And something hit me in between my throat and my heart, like a shot of adrenaline. That feeling came a lot in the last year—grief and nerves. Grief, getting stuck on the way from your gut to your eyes. I swallowed it back, but it was that sort of sadness that had roots in more than one place.

Nera didn't have a favorite meal.

I did.

This wasn't just a *good* meal I had. This was the *best*.

I took my fork and knife and cut into the gooey juicy layers of cheese and sauce. The crust cracked. I stuffed it in my mouth; the hot oil and butter gushed onto my tongue and filled me up. The dough crumbled in between my teeth as the cheese melted and I remembered this.

I remembered gobbling up my first slice of deep dish so fast, Dad laughed and offered me another one while Mom said, "Slow down or you're gonna choke."

That day, Sammy and I found the statue in the back of the zoo. We saw the flamingos all standing on one leg. Dad and Sammy rented a swan boat and Mom and I crawled into one behind them and we took off into the lake and the Hancock was above us.

There was a pain inside of me, and I wanted to drown it with the taste of this meal, but I couldn't. This food came from a life I'd lost. This meal did not belong to me anymore. So now what?

"What's wrong?" Nera said.

"Nothing's wrong," I said automatically. It's a ball of fucked-up feelings, Nera, and I can't untangle it, and you sure as hell aren't gonna, either.

"It doesn't seem like nothing," Nera said. "Your favorite meal is making you sad."

I expected her words to sound like an alien observing a cow. Why do you do this thing, earthling? But instead, her words curled around me like a blanket, yearning to protect.

She genuinely cared.

I slowly set my fork down. "This is a meal from when I was a kid. One weekend, my parents took us to the zoo and then Lou Malnati's."

"And it was a good day?"

"It was a damn good day. I was happy." I hesitated. "Life didn't end up being perfect. Sam dropped out of college and when she came back, it was like she'd weighed herself against the world and came up short. She didn't know how brilliant she was . . . she struggled . . . but we struggled forward. There were more pizzas to come. We weren't done. Now my dad sits alone in the apartment all day. Sam is gone. Mom left. And Marco . . . he's not doing okay."

Nera paused. "And how are you?"

The question felt like cold water splashed on my hot face.

"I . . . it doesn't really matter how I am," I said.

"You are worried about your sister," Nera said. "Your family, your friend. But you are the one who needed this meal. You are the one here."

Nera reached across the table, like a reflex. It was as if she was reaching for my hand, to comfort me. Although we didn't touch, she was closer to me than anyone else since March.

Did I matter?

I did, to her.

"Thanks," I said. Although the words came slow, I meant it. Nera's eyes smiled at me.

I looked to my pizza. "You can eat, right?"

Nera nodded. "I can eat."

"You sure? You don't sound very sure."

"I've got a mouth, don't I?"

"Do you want a slice?"

"Oh," Nera said. And then she stared at it.

"You got a mouth, don't you?" I echoed.

"Yes, no, just . . . what if I don't like it?"

I smiled. She was really, truly worried about this. "You will," I said. "I know you will."

I took the big serving knife and divided the cheese on the edges of the slice. I lifted it. "Gimme your plate."

"Oh, I don't have a—" A plate appeared in front of her.

I plopped it down and it steamed and I waved my hands at the perfect specimen. "Ta-dah! Go on, try it."

She looked at it hesitantly before scooping it up in her hands, forgoing the fork and knife completely and chomping it up like a sandwich. Nera's eyes bulged as she put it in her mouth. "It's perfect!" she managed between bites.

Yes. It was.

She swallowed. "I've never . . . what is this?! Do all foods taste like this?"

"No," I said. "Each food tastes different."

"It's like I can see it but . . . inside? Like it's music." Nera squinted, processing. "And there are different factions of pizza? They all taste different?!"

"In Chicago, there's different factions of everything," I said. "Never put ketchup on your hot dog. Mild sauce on fried chicken. Garrett's, Brown Sugar Bakery . . ." I trailed off. "You do live in Chicago, right?"

She looked at the pizza in front of me. "I have never been in the city, no."

What?

She had never left this place.

I mean, of course, it made sense. But my God. I heard myself blurt out, "The fuck?"

Nera shrank a little, her shoulders not as straight. "I know," she said. She snuck another slice off my pizza and shoved it in her mouth.

I pushed the platter toward her. "Here," I said. "Eat however much you want. And after . . . is there a place we can see the city from the Station?"

Nera nodded, shoving more into her mouth. "Mmm-dmm-rmmm-lmmm . . ." I saw the realization slowly dawn on her face that she could not in fact speak while her mouth was full of pizza. We waited.

She swallowed. "Don't tell anyone. Not even the dogs know. But I do go up to the roof from time to time to see the city."

"Okay," I said. "Can you show me?"

13

NERA

I showed Charlie the rooftop.

Past the Station's halls and staircases, up a ladder and one precarious hole in the floor, we stood under the waning night sky full of stars and the shadow of the lighthouse tower as we faced the city. Chicago was alive and bright and all the light breathed together in a brilliant yellow glow. It all stopped where the lake was, the darkest blue. As if two worlds split but held together as close as they could.

"Father doesn't like me looking at the city," I explained to Charlie. "But I've been coming up here since I was a little girl. I don't know why, I probably shouldn't. But it's . . . so beautiful."

"Why is the Station in Lincoln Park?" she asked me. "Why not the Loop? Or the South Side?"

"The Fire ended here," I said. "My father stood on the shore right there when he stopped it. He raised his hands and shot his light out. The Station appeared. The lighthouse lit up. The clouds finally opened to rain. It was a miracle."

"Holy shit," she said. "Your dad can really do that?"

I nodded. "He's a powerful man. And I have to be as powerful as him."

I knew the skyline, but now Charlie named the shadows and lights and silver artistry of their outlines as she waved her hand in front of her like a conductor, painting the world to make sense.

"There's the Hancock, and way down there is the Sears Tower," Charlie said. "But those are just like . . . the constellations in the skyline you know? There's so much more to all this than the buildings everyone knows. There, way up there is where my dad grew up. And way down there is where my grandparents lived."

"The lights," I said, mesmerized. "What are the lights on the buildings?"

Charlie shot me a look. "You don't kn . . ." she cut herself off. I could see she was trying to not be condescending. But she wasn't, not to me. She was more in shock, I believe, at how little I must know. While I could tell her tongue was sharp, she did not stick me with words. She softly said, "Nera, those are windows. And the lights are people coming and going from the rooms inside."

I stared at the amount of windows, as numerous as the stars. Each of those was a person.

So many stories, so many souls and each one of them had a favorite food and a song they played when things got tough.

"Right below there, you can't see it from here, but it's Grant Park. And so much shit has happened in Grant Park. And they're making this new part of it, Millennium Park. We walked past, last fall, and we saw there were all these little baby trees that are gonna grow . . . and they've got this big glass statue they're working on called 'Cloud Gate.' I mean, it's really called 'the Bean' but . . . It's supposed to look like . . . well . . . like a gate to the sky."

"Like the Veil," I said.

"Yeah, well, this one is just gonna be an art installation, it's not real. Oh! There's the beach where we snuck out on New Year's when we were visiting my grandma. We watched the snow go down on Lake Shore Drive . . . oh, oh Lake Shore Drive is that long string of car lights."

"So those are cars?" I asked.

"They are," she said, side-eyeing me. "What did you think it was?"

I hesitated. "They look like lanterns," I finally said. "Or fairy lights. Making their way through the night."

I expected Charlie to laugh. But she didn't. She only studied the long string of lights, and then said, "I wish they were. That's a lot cooler."

There was a quiet between us. I held my hand out to the lights beyond. Like I could touch them. "I have helped ferry how many souls out of this city, and I still know nothing about Chicago or what it is to live there." I closed my fist, trying to catch the light in my palm. It was, of course, too far away and I was too removed.

"Charlie?"

"Hmm?"

"You asked me why you should trust me to help you find your sister," I said. "I don't know all their names. You were right. So why did you come back tonight?"

Charlie pushed her hair out of her face, perhaps a tic of nerves. Then she crossed her arms and her dark brow drew a line over her determined eyes as she kept her gaze on the lights. "Because you said you cared."

Heavy honesty between strangers. Did this mean we were becoming friends? My only friends had been the dogs. Charlie was prickly, a little intimidating, but also intriguing and so honest . . .

The wind blew. I breathed it in. Something fresh and new cascaded through me.

Charlie took my hand and squeezed it. I did not realize how cold I was until I felt her fingers on mine. I didn't remember the outside ever being cold. And now Charlie felt so warm. I looked to her. And she beamed at me, her freckles settled on her nose like a collection of wayward stars.

She had touched me. And I had felt it.

"Well," she said, "you ate deep dish tonight. That's a good start."

"What is your home like? Where do you live?"

Charlie bit her lip, and then tentatively pointed over at a cluster of buildings.

"Over there. On the North Side. You can't see it from here, because the buildings in between you and me are so tall."

"Is it beautiful?"

Charlie's hand dropped. She shook her head, her lips pursed. "It's just an old apartment. It's not like a home or anything."

I fiddled with my braid. "Well, wherever you go, there's light. You're really good at finding it."

"I wish that was true," she said.

"It is."

I saw the red and purple sunrise meet her face. A sky all its own, waking with a new day that was all hers.

"Sunrises washing over the city are gorgeous," I said. "It's as if the world is trying again."

Charlie gave a little jump. "Come see the city for yourself."

I stared at her. "Oh, no, I . . . see, I belong here, I'm—"

"Not dead," she said. "Come with me?"

To follow her out into the land of the living—I didn't even know what would happen to me if I crossed over to the city. I may dissolve in a pillar of dust. My heart may break to find that I actually am dead, or undead, or something entirely effervescent and unreal. I could be too wrong for the city.

Then I saw something else. Beyond the car's lights, on the other side of their pilgrimage, there was a cloud of fog and static. Haunts.

The fog swarmed, circling something as if it was about to dive and pounce. Then it did, shooting into the trees beyond the bridge and beyond what I could see. Charlie looked away.

"I hate the sound they make," Charlie said. "When you're closer, you can hear it when they strike and start to eat."

"What do you mean?"

"Nera, have you . . ." Charlie eyed me. I could hear a sternness and surprise in her voice. "Have you never seen Haunts eat a soul before?"

We had always been near the Station; close enough to the light to be safe.

"That's how they grow," Charlie said. "They're eating the people who don't make it to the lighthouse."

"But certainly their dogs find them? They're supposed to keep the souls safe until—"

"Not everyone wants to be found," Charlie said. "Some people hold on real hard to life."

The swarm reared back into the sky and slunk into the shadows of the streets and trees, blending into the night.

If I left and Father found out, the lighthouse could go dark. My lungs were stuck and was I even breathing and—this was all going to be mine and—if I left, I could help the people out there . . . but if the city was so wonderful could I return? Or what if it was so evil and I got hurt? Haunts and hunger, devouring the lighthouse, Father—

"Hey," Charlie said, taking my hand. "Hey, calm down. It's okay. Breathe. Look at me. Just focus on breathing."

All I could speak as the Station Master were platitudes. I lived on the edge of the city, but I was not part of its life. I had to go out. I couldn't go out.

"He'll be wondering where I am by now," I said quickly, my lungs aching. "We should go back downstairs."

She squeezed my hand. "Hey," she said. "Just stay here for a second."

"I can't, Charlie, I have to go meet him. He needs me. I have so much work to do."

She pulled me to stand beside her. And something in my stomach lit on fire, like my own lighthouse made of warm, melting glass. I'd never felt my body so electric.

"You should focus on why you're here," I said, my voice caught in my breaths. "You wish to find your sister."

Charlie seemed hit by this, woken up from a reverie. "Yes," she said. "Absolutely."

We braved the ladder once again. I followed her through the Station's labyrinth, watching the back of her head as her hair swayed in time with her pace. She hummed quietly to herself. I didn't know all the songs she sang, but I wanted to. And a deep sadness welled up inside me that I would have to wait an entire day to listen to her once again.

Charlie Connor moved through the world like a ship cutting through ice; tired and sharp and strong, but relentlessly searching for something beyond herself. How could she be so unaware of what a miracle she was? She was from the city, full of songs and buildings and pizza. I wanted to know everything about her.

I showed her to the pillars. Father was there already. "Time to go," he shooed at her, and she slapped him away.

"I guess a hundred years surrounded by dogs and dead people makes you forget your manners." Charlie peered at him, her hands clasped behind her. "'Oh, thank you, Miss Connor,'" she said in her best impression of my father, "'for all your hard work tonight.' Oh no problem, Mr. Harosen. See? Pleasantries."

"The sun is rising," he said, deadpan, "that means your hard work is finished until tomorrow night."

"Oh, I was gonna ask," Charlie said. "We . . . *I've* been seeing Haunts out in the streets fucking things up for souls who don't make it here. Is there anything I can do for them? Or anything I can do to help outside of just playing the music?"

Father paused at this, his eyes softening. "Tell them we're here," he offered sincerely. Charlie, also sincere, nodded.

"I'm glad we shared tonight, Charlie," I said.

She smiled at me. "Same, Nera. You know you're not too bad. Just don't let old Mr. Scrooge over here cramp your style too much, alright?"

"Goodbye, Miss Connor," Father grunted.

She started to walk away and then spun around in a circle, pivoting as if she had told her body to leave but then remembered something. She pulled me to her, out of Father's supposed earshot. "Hey, I have an idea. I'm gonna bring you a present, okay?"

I nodded.

"Okay," she said. "I'll smell you later." Then she turned around and muttered to herself, "Whaaat . . . why, why, what did I just say . . ."

She unceremoniously left, and I ceremoniously stayed. As it was meant to be.

Then Father returned to my side.

What did she whisper to you? Our voices left us once again.

Why did I hesitate to tell him the truth? If he knew about a present, or that we'd gone to the roof, there was something uncomfortable in him around Charlie that indicated he may not approve. Even if his lighthouse shined for her, she was still an outsider.

I had never lied to my father before, but tonight I did. *She was only saying goodnight*, I said.

Father stiffened. *Don't get mired down in the mundane things of the living. Let her play her music, and let yourself stay on your path. Now we need to clean the lamps, check the dogs' report on the streets, clean the ferry—*

Father? I said. *I have a question.*

Yes?

I didn't know how to word this. *Do bodies change temperature?* I asked.

He looked down at the ground, as if remembering something from very long ago. *I believe so*, he said. *Why?*

I almost slipped up and told him I was on the roof. But I only said, *I felt cold. Then when I touched . . . warm things . . . I was warm again. Just as warm as them. As if they'd become a part of me.*

Father grew stiff. *No, that doesn't sound like anything I know. Or anything that's real. Come now, I will go to the lighthouse and you should check the ferry.*

Father? I said. *The Haunts, if they ever breached the Station . . .*

That won't happen, Father reassured with a gentle smile. *Nera, I know that compared with shiny Charlie Connor, you see me as old and tedious. But there is wisdom in being old. I love you, you know that, yes?*

I do.

You asked me if I trusted you, he said. *Can I ask the same question? Do you trust me?*

Of course, I said.

He touched the side of his nose, and he said, *Then please, trust there is a reason we don't go to the city. And don't take gifts from her.*

He took his leave.

I wanted to follow. But—
Nera?
I turned to see a little basset looking up at me, his tail low.
Are you ready? Elbee said.

REMNANTS

mezzomermaid: hey u

mrmr80: hey ewe

mezzomermaid: baaaaa soon i get to SMOOOOOOOOCH UUUUUUU.

mrmr80: was today better?

mezzomermaid: no. i miss u.

mrmr80: u get 2 see me in 2 days!!!!!!!

mezzomermaid: i doooooooo. Hey wats ur flight # again? i wrote it down somewhere and lost it.

mrmr80: u know by flight chitown is only 2.5 hrs away from hartford. see not that far.

mrmr80: i'll just fwd my confirmation email.

mrmr80: u gonna bring me a marching band?

mezzomermaid: lol no.

mrmr80: aww.

mezzomermaid: but i'll make a sign. :P

mrmr80: i just need u. ;D

mezzomermaid: im gonna knock u to the ground with my hug.

mrmr80: i mean its been a whole month i might have bulked up by now.

mrmr80: hello?

mrmr80: u ok?

mezzomermaid: sry i'm fine . . . its just been a hard month. i'll tell u all of it wen ur here.

mrmr80: ok

mezzomermaid: maybe i can just come home w u.

mrmr80: u worked rly hard to get into yale. remember what pops said. gotta give it a year.

mrmr80: u can do this connor. i know u can. ur a badass.

mezzomermaid: im really not. not out here.

mrmr80: next time a fancy pants wants 2 call u a hick, just remind them your dad's michael connor and their parents probably played his songs at their wedding.

mezzomermaid: i do not think they will care. maybe if he was michael bolton lol.

mrmr80: ok i'll just beat em up when i get there problem solved.

mezzomermaid: lololol. but fr if i came home would you think less of me?

mrmr80: i could nvr think less of u sam.

mezzomermaid: <3

mrmr80: remember you got into YALE. ur a badass. and i love u. no matter wat happens we do it together. even if there are thousands of miles between us. ok?

mezzomermaid: ok.

mrmr80: love u.

mezzomermaid: love ewe 2.

mezzomermaid: ok so not yale news. DID U WATCH THE NEW EPISODE.

mrmr80: yes!

mezzomermaid: rly?

mrmr80: no.

mezzomermaid: CMON MARCO. ITS SEASON 6 PREMIERE. RACH AND ROSS JUST GOT MARRIED.

mrmr80: love u but hate that show.

mezzomermaid: ur such a chandler tho.

mrmr80: boooooooooo. i refuse.

mezzomermaid: booooo u! :P

mrmr80: our marriage will be better than anything on tv.

mezzomermaid: dawwwwwwwwwww. u proposing big guy?

mrmr80: oh. my proposal is gonna be bigger than an AIM.

mezzomermaid: it doesnt need to b. just tell me we're getting married and things will be ok.

mrmr80: absolutely. we will get married. things will be ok.

—AOL Instant Message Chat Log, Marco Ramirez and Sam Connor, September 1999

14

CHARLIE

To get home from the Station, it would make more sense to take the fifteen-minute bus from the zoo up to Edgewater. But I liked the train and I also liked avoiding the zoo.

But that also meant walking twenty minutes to the train on the cusp of winter through a sea of ghosts.

I hadn't told Nera about the thing in the dark, and maybe I should have. But then I might have to tell her all the things I thought, how I wished I could have the courage to just jump on the third rail—or through the Veil . . .

People couldn't be completely trusted. You had to pick and choose what you showed them about yourself.

But she had touched my hand. She had felt like a cloud, there but not there. Still, I could see the red in her cheeks, the stalwart strength of her body . . . she was no ghost.

My phone vibrated in my pocket as I walked to the train.

I jolted. Looked at it. Marco.

Without thinking it through, I flipped it open and answered. "Hey," I said, out of habit, in that singsongy way. I stopped myself. "Marco," I tried again. "What's up?"

"I was just thinking," Marco said. No formal "Hello, Charlie, how are you." Because even in the After, we had once been so close there had been no hellos or goodbyes, just picking up a conversation and putting it down. "You remember that mix CD we made her?"

"Which one?" I said, fumbling for my CTA pass in my pocket. Mixes passed between the three of us as swiftly as currency, but I was pretty sure I knew which one.

"Operation Rescue Sam," he said. "The one when we went to rescue her from Yale?"

She'd stuffed all her shit into the station wagon, told us to drive, and never looked back. We'd made a mix to raise her spirits, but also to keep her brave. Remind her of our love, of how special she was. It was a tall order for a mix, but not undoable for two pros.

"I remember," I said.

"Pops made us add 'Here Comes the Sun' at the very end."

"And I pranked her with 'Sisters' from White Christmas."

He laughed. "She *hates* that song."

"She *loves* it."

"*Sisterrrrs*," he sang. I gave a little snort. Then we were quiet. Maybe realizing we were laughing, when she wasn't here to laugh with us.

She hates that song . . . she *hated* that song. She *loved* that song. Past tense.

Maybe if we kept talking, it would bring us back. Or maybe it would just remind us how much things had changed. Then Marco could tell me to check myself into an inpatient again.

"Anyway," he said, as the train slammed and clattered about a block ahead. I pressed the phone closer to my ear. "I was just wondering if you had it, the mix."

My eyes locked on the passing train cars. Chrome, the blue circle of the CTA settled in the corners. Square windows full of people standing and gathering their things as the train slowed and stopped.

No matter how much we talked about her, we couldn't conjure her.

"Charlie?"

"Yeah, I don't know, Marco," I said. "I gotta go."

"Right," Marco said. "I . . . yeah. I'll talk to you later—"

I hung up.

I didn't know where the mix was. Sam had it. It had been a present to her. I remembered her starting that trip from Connecticut to Chicago curled up in the backseat like we'd rescued her from the island on *Lost*. But then by the time "Bohemian Rhapsody" hit, she was bouncing up and down with us, and then the musical theater portion had blasted on in and she was in heaven, doing all the voices for "One Day More" and screaming "*No!*" at Cowboy Jack when he asked her if Pulitzer and Hearst had her beat.

I kept a picture of me and Sam from that trip on my nightstand. We'd stopped in Pittsburgh for the night. Marco took the picture. We've got our arms around each other's shoulders, the same eyes smiling back in the same way. She had bright blonde hair, I had sandy hair. She was taller. I was thinner. But we were both our father's daughters.

Wouldn't it be nice to go home?

My vision blurred. I saw the rats scurrying into an alleyway ahead.

The L train left the station.

And then the train station disappeared and I realized I was blocks away. Not even on Fullerton. I could see Fullerton, behind me, the U-Haul on Clifton. Past DePaul. I spun around. A side street. Had I walked here?

I looked at my feet. My hands. I must have spaced out. Or the Haunts . . .

I was standing at our old apartment.

Another home to lose.

It was his voice. I could feel him, his tendrils flicking out from the Water Tower beyond the trees. He knew where I was.

Go home.

"Shut the fuck up," I sniffed.

This place used to be mine, but today it was a stranger.

I stood on the sidewalk looking up at our old window on the second floor. The sidewalk hadn't changed. Neither had the window. Or the bricks. Or the main door. But I didn't belong here anymore.

Endings were supposed to be something that was cued; you see the ending of the music sheet and you know it's going to be over soon. It should be soft. But this was the middle of the fucking song. I used to think, *Well but sometimes people die and it's a shock but it melts into the music and slowly makes sense* and no the fuck it does not. Death comes whenever it pleases. In the middle of dishwasher cycles, grocery lists, or watching the *Lord of the Rings* trilogy.

The day Sam died, when I was in that break room scared shitless, I'd turned to the woman who'd pulled me to safety and said, "I can't die today, we didn't get to watch the Extended Edition of *Return of the King* yet." She looked at me like I was crazy. But that's what makes a life; watching movies with your friends and your sister and singing and drinking and . . . taking it all for granted.

We were in the middle of doing so many things. And now what? I was stuck in the middle of doing a thing that was fucking gone.

I hadn't spoken to any of my friends but Marco since Sam died, not even at the Halloween party. They had all gotten weird, or they just moved on. We were an eclectic group of dreamers and artists and teachers and in this apartment, we shared joints and talked about the state of Broadway as if our opinions could shape anything. We were young.

Then everyone just sort of kept going without me.

My world had shrunk.

I wanted to hurl a rock at the window. I wanted to break it and scream, just so I still existed there. Just so there was one less thing between me and that home.

You don't stop a song in the middle of the first verse.

"Fuck," I growled, and I kicked a rock on the sidewalk.

Someone came through the door. The door did not latch behind him. Its lock sat against the frame.

I saw a wisp of fog dart through the threshold.

Go in.

"You can't affect things like this," I said. "You didn't keep that door open."

Go in.

If I went in, I would see the muddy tile. The old worn carpet. The creaking stairs. I knew where every single piece of furniture was. I knew each sound of each room. I could still feel the wobbling chair under me as I stood on my tip-toes to turn on the ceiling fan.

I needed to finally be home.

But I knew if I went any further, I'd see home was gone.

The Station Master can't give this back to you.

The voice sounded kind and honest.

The Station Master and his daughter know death, but they don't know dying. They don't deal in bodies. You know what violence means. So does this city. And so do I.

All at once, I felt something like a sharp stabbing inside me, bullets ringing out through the streets of Chicago. Fire, eating my skin alive. Starvation. Cold freezing winds. The gasping of the dying on the side of the streets underground in the Loop, grasping onto old torn coats and huddling in tents.

I was blinded by the pounding question in the cold, merciless, and sharp corners of tragedy: *why . . .*

Screams. Bullets. I clung onto her hand. More bullets. She let go. She ran. I reached out for her shirt, for her arm, but I lost her in the crowd—

"Stop," I ordered him. I forced myself to turn away. "It's not mine anymore." They were heavy words. "And you can't give it back to me."

A chill crawled up my neck like a spider. The Haunts hissed around the doorframe and curled around my wrists.

If anyone can, I can.

I found the L again. I stepped onto the train, took ahold of the pole with my hoodie wrapped over my fingers. I could still feel the Haunts' icy buzz around me.

I took a deep breath, raising my shoulders and lowering them. Trying to concentrate on not falling at the sharp turn near Sheridan. The lights always flickered at this point. Most people's cell phone calls got dropped. "Hello? Hello?" echoed through the train car. We passed Graceland Cemetery.

I looked down from the L tracks at the perfectly curated graveyard, big trees changing colors and massive mausoleums. It was full of ghosts, waving and jumping to get attention from the train car. No one but me saw them. And the train kept going forward, leaving them behind.

On the other side of the cemetery, people reconnected, the lights blared again.

Chicago was saturated with loss, beating up against the shores of the living. But we were still here.

Even if I was the only one who cared that I was alive, I was still here.

I flipped open my phone. im sorry, I texted Marco. she died bc i got to a safe place b4 i could find her.

I hovered over "send."

I shut my phone. Opened it again. Delete delete.

im sorry i had to go. hows party clnup?

Send.

There was a giggle from the side seat in front of me. Two girls, curled into each other. One had rad-looking plugs and soft brown freckles on her white cheeks, the other had big black boots and a colorful hijab framing her big smile and bright eyes. They nuzzled. God, what badasses.

I wondered how Nera's hand would feel, wrapped around mine on this train. If she was set in the present, dressed in cool clothes and had a nose piercing or her hair swooping with those side bangs . . . a satchel around her shoulder, cutting into her chest to show the outline of her bra under a soft black band tee. She could smile down at me, squeeze my hand. "Wanna see a movie?" she'd say.

It struck me. How much I realized I wanted to touch her fingers. Something in me stirred. And it was disorienting and I wasn't sure what to think of it but . . . for the first time in a long time, I imagined a future.

15

NERA

Sometimes, it is hard to trust fathers. But dogs are inherently trustworthy.

Elbee led me by many doors off the atrium, into an arched cavernous hall-way. It had torn floral wallpaper, revealing old crumbling bricks underneath. The carpet was tattered and matted. Massive sconces stippled the walls, hold-ing flickering candles whose flames seemed to be whispering smoke into the air. No other place in the Station looked like this: uncared for, frightening and bleak. Why would anyone imagine such a dreadful place?

Father cleaned the Station of dust and decay every night. But this place hadn't been touched for decades, if ever.

Elbee trotted down the hall, then turned to the brick wall. He scratched at the bricks, and they chipped away like sand. An avalanche of dust followed, cracking up the length of the wall.

As the bricks crumbled onto the carpet, I gasped. There, instead of a wall, danced the shape of a door, bright red and burning like lava. Flickering with hot fire.

Go on, Elbee said, pointing his nose to the door. *Open it.*

The last thing I wanted to do was open it. The door looked painful.

Nera, Elbee said, *he wanted this room to be forgotten. But he said if there was ever another Station Master, wait until he was gone and then show them. Well . . .* He paused, staring ahead, in a quiet sort of anger that comes from a dog sens-ing an injustice. *I'm showing it to you now.*

If he had strict instructions, we should both follow them, I said.

Elbee's big baleful eyes looked up at me. *You will be the Station Master, and he is your father. It's yours to hold. I can't tell you what to do, but I've shown you where to find your father's life before the Station.*

The door's flames curled out, licking the air in a hot whoosh. The flames turned blue.

I shouldn't open it. I should trust my father. But the way Elbee looked to me, the way this hallway did not fit the beauty of the atrium, or the diner, or the rooftop, or the lighthouse . . . something wanted to be discovered, and it was calling out for me to find it.

I touched the door. The blue flames curled in my palm to take the shape of a door handle.

After you, Station Master-to-Come. Elbee play-bowed.

I pushed the handle. My hand pressed through the door's flames. I stepped through.

I stood in a very uninspired, dusty catalogue room.

The Archive of Dead Things, Elbee explained.

Shelves upon shelves, a library with no imagination but only utilitarian storage and reluctant existence. There was no fire here; just stale air and boxes on beige metal shelves.

I followed Elbee through the rows. Boxes upon boxes. Elbee explained, *Memories of the things that had been on people when they died, archived forever. The essence of things that die with us. So if someone had items on them at the time of death, the essences could appear here.*

My father kept all this stuff? I said. *Why? If he didn't want it, why didn't he just incinerate it?*

Elbee snorted. *He would not have kept it if he could have gotten rid of it. I believe the custom was to bury it, or leave it where it appeared. But he tried to set it on fire. It wasn't his to burn, so it would not burn.* Elbee looked at the fire door. *Instead, it collects itself in a back closet. The Station is lit by your father, but not everything here is your father's. See, death existed long before your father. And it will exist after even you. So some rooms . . . some things . . . they cannot be erased. Your father has not been in this room for half a century, and he is not involved in this room's contents.*

I had said the incineration comment as a jest. I couldn't imagine Father setting anything ablaze. Father abhorred fire.

He hates the living world this much? I felt lost in the stacks of boxes.

I don't know if he hates it, Elbee said. *Fear is a lot sturdier than hate.*

Father had witnessed the city fall to fire. I ran my hand over a box. *May I?*

Elbee bowed in affection.

It had a signature scribbled on the outside: Tanika Griffin, 1997.

I opened the box to reveal a tube of lipstick. I touched it. It didn't feel like the other things in the Station. When my fingernail hit the lipstick tube, it clinked.

I felt the tapping of plastic on my fingertips. I heard it in my ears. I pulled my hand away.

I saw the rest of Tanika's things: a scribbled piece of paper, a stick of gum, lotion, and something I didn't know . . . a little folded up piece of lined paper. It was tucked into itself and had little drawings all over it. "To: Tay, From: D."

It was a letter. It wasn't mine to read; it was Tanika's.

I shut the box.

I carefully opened another, full of little reminders of a life lived.

What is that? I said, looking at an odd contraption sitting on a blue hat decorated with a red C.

Elbee looked over, definitely not tall enough to see, but then said, *Oh, that's a finger trap sitting on a baseball cap.*

A finger trap, I said. *Why would you want to trap fingers? Is it a weapon?*

It's a puzzle.

That you trap people in? That's a terrible puzzle.

The box read "Bob Wisniewski, 1986," nothing else.

The next was "Dorothy Ball, 1945": a little stuffed rabbit.

Over here. Elbee pointed his snout to a low shelf.

And there, not in a box, a big bound leather journal waited.

Then it vanished, except for a big black smudge, and a few seconds later it reappeared around the smudge. It was there, and then it wasn't, then it was there again. Like it couldn't decide if it wanted to stay or not.

Nothing else looks like this, I said.

With a little whine, Elbee said, *Nothing else* is *like this.*

I gingerly touched it. It felt light and then heavy and then not there at all and then heavy again. It was real. Then it was gone. Then it wasn't real, but it was back like a dream.

But a large black ink stain remained in the middle of the book. The smudge didn't flicker.

Is it safe? I asked.

It made it past the lighthouse, so I would suppose it's safe enough, Elbee said.

Why are you showing me this? I asked. *You said you'd tell me who my father was before the Station. Is this his?*

It will tell you who your father is, Elbee said. *He can't stand to look at it. But you . . . are not like him. At least, I hope you aren't.*

That stung in a way that only a daughter could feel humility for her father. I wanted Elbee to explain, take it back, and maybe if Father had cut this place off, I shouldn't know. Maybe Father was right and the world was not a thing I should trifle with.

We lived on the edge of the city for a reason. Death was not life.

But Father was not yet dead, and once he'd lived a life.

"If I understand my father," I said aloud, "then will I understand everything else?"

Elbee looked up at me, his big black and brown eyes wide, expectant.

I did good, he nodded, in agreement with himself, and he trotted back toward the door. *I have shown it to you, now you decide what to do with it.*

I should have just put it back on the shelf. It wasn't mine. Father always had his reasons.

But it jittered in my hands, in and out, and I saw the name inscribed on the leather.

DAVID STEIN.

David Stein lived long ago. But there must be a reason I knew his name now.

I flipped through the pages. There was beautiful handwriting in the front, and then as the journal continued, there were pictures—big inked monsters, scary shadows . . . and then something that struck me.

Ghosts. Souls.

He'd employed watercolors to make the light, the fading memories of bodies, the individual faces and the expressions of joy, horror, shock, anger. He went out of his way to find paints. He was logging them. Underneath, he'd labeled them, all of their names. *Rochelle. Sarah. Frederich. Gretel.*

David had seen the dead.

I slammed it shut and put it under my arm. Father had never hidden anything from me.

And yet.

The book flickered under my sleeve as I followed Elbee out of the archives.

––––––––

I sat on my bed, my boots kicked off and my skirt splayed out over my blankets. Elbee curled up at my feet. I stared at the journal in front of me, placed on top of the quilted patterns. It waited with a flicker. And I began to read:

I am ready to talk about the night of the Fire, while I still have my wits about me.

I was supposed to be at Simchat Torah.

So was he.

And

Then the smudge. The smudge I'd seen not flickering in and out. Like a smudge on the other side of a windowpane, unable to be wiped away, obscuring what was really there beyond the glass. A small detail of life, now a large mystery in death.

Someone in the Station must have tampered with this book. But why?

It wouldn't have been Elbee or the dogs. So that only left my father.

Why would Father want no one to read these pages?

Or maybe, why would Father never want to read these pages again?

Then scribbles continued after the absence left by the chunky, thick smudge. Just scribbles, unintelligible scribbles.

Father didn't want words to exist that told of the night of the Fire. But why? What had happened?

I turned to the beginning:

My name is David, and I am in love. I tell you because I can tell no one else.

16

NERA

My name is David, and I am in love. I tell you because I can tell no one else.

Today was my brother Abraham's wedding. And at some point, while looking at his bride, I realized this is not what I wanted. Because under the chuppah would not be Jonathon beside me.

Jonathon does not even know I love him. He believes the only thing we have in common are the dead. He and I both volunteer as shomrim. Whenever there is someone who dies, they call us to stand watch over the body until burial.

They clean the body before we arrive. Then we sit in the dark, beside it. The first time we met, I did not want him there, because I have more than one secret. I not only love Jonathon, as if that alone would not be enough for me to hide my heart forever.

So I will tell you, my little friend, my faithful journal.

I do not merely watch the body. I watch over the soul.

I can see the dead. I was born with this oddity about me. Perhaps I am lucky, perhaps I am cursed.

But the dead are not gone until you have convinced them they are dead. Jonathon was the shomer when I was not there, and I was the shomer when he was not there. So, I was alone enough to speak out loud and look the dead in the eyes. Not their bodies, but the ghost beside the body who usually raged and tried to enter the body again. I would say in calm words: "It is time to go."

Some were angry, some were violent, some were desperate and hopeless, and some were relieved and finally at peace. Some left quickly, some tried to lash out at me, some enjoyed the sound of Hashem's name and others were afraid. But in the end, they all finally left, disappearing to move along. And usually when I left after my shift, I would see a dog sitting outside, as if they too were a shomer. As if they would take over from there.

I had always seen the dead, and they could always see me. So we spoke as if it was a kibitz about the weather.

I was content being alone in my secrets. Until one night, when Jonathon was confused about when he was supposed to arrive. He came early. He heard me talking.

But he did not say anything disparaging. He only said, "Me, too."

Both of us? My heart leapt out of my chest.

"How?" I asked him. He said, "If anyone knew, you would think more people would do what it took to see them."

That was Jonathon's way of saying he did not know.

"Perhaps," I said, "it is like how some can hear higher notes, or a thunderstorm coming."

That was my way of saying I did not know.

It was as if Hashem had planned this. We were to be shomrim, we were to be friends, we were to both be one of the special silent witnesses to things outside of life.

I do not believe my teachers would agree with Hashem that falling in love with Jonathon was meant to be.

So I have not told him, or anyone.

Life continues on. Papa runs the shop. Mama watches the children. I volunteer. I study Torah. Jonathon and I stand sentinel when there is a death.

No one else sees the dead. No one else would believe in dogs who wait for you at the end of it all. And I have never heard another laugh like Jonathon's, buoyant and joyful like a duck on water.

I fear to write his name, but I cannot stop myself from doing so.

Jonathon. David. Another coincidence we must be this way. When David arrived in Saul's kingdom, Jonathon gave David his greatest cloak as if to say, "You belong here."

There are so many signs that Hashem approves. This is what life was meant for, to shine love for another as brightly as a candle in the dark.

I pray that some sort of clarity will come from all this and Jonathon will turn to me and say once again, "Me, too."

Then we will hold one another. Our bodies, warm, stitched together as if we were made to be in the same quilt. His soft hands. My rough calloused fingers threading through his. The smell of soap and fresh paper. We will both see the dead, and live our life, together.

I stared at the page, under my thumb.

Elbee sat on the edge of the bed, his eyes looking up at me from between his paws.

David and Jonathon had something to do with the Great Fire that Father stopped. And my father didn't want to just forget the Fire; he wanted to forget them, too.

Who is David? I asked. Is he my father? Did he take a new name?

Elbee raised his head. No, he said. David loved your father. Long before he was only Harosen, when he had a full name and a life.

I stared at the book. "Jonathon," I said. Out loud. "My father's name was Jonathon."

REMNANTS

—Taken from Sam Connor's notes. Footnote: "Chords for Rapunzel descent motif."

17

CHARLIE

I stopped at the flower store on Broadway and bought some carnations. I lugged the sad-looking bouquet up the stairs and set them down outside Mrs. Coleson's.

Mr. Coleson smiled from beside me.

"I'm sorry they're a little pitiful."

She'll know what they are, Mr. C said. *That's enough.*

That evening, before I headed out for the Station, I put on a coat and enjoyed the balcony.

See, Mr. Thing in the Dark? Chicago wasn't just pain. On a nice breezy November evening, I saw little trees grow through cracks in the concrete. I heard the bus drive past the alley. I saw the lights on the neighbor's balcony, right next to my own, all of our little landings splattered with potted plants and chairs, tied together by a shared fire escape. Each of us our own story, like the glowing windows I'd shown Nera and she'd been so awed by.

On the other side of my window, I could hear Dad inside, rumbling around. Then I heard the clacking and clattering of the L train. I stood in a place my sister had never seen, but she had heard that L. She had known this city.

The L was a heartbeat. A rush, a thrushing woosh, clack clack . . . there's no other city that sounds like Chicago. Sometimes, Sam would go on walks next to the Brown Line and the Red Line, just so she could hear the train roar past. When we moved into the city together, she showed me all her favorite places to take pictures under the tracks. "Little magic places no one looks," she'd said.

I gotta show Nera all this. Nera had never smelled flowers or heard traffic or . . . I gotta bring her here.

Is it beautiful where you live?

How can someone die before they've even lived? How can they know what it means to live if all they've done is shepherd the dead?

My dad continued rummaging around inside, the fridge opening, the clanking of bottles, the shuffling to the couch and the sigh as he sank into the cushions to watch TV.

I had an idea. "Ah ha ha, yes," I cackled.

I popped out of my seat, ran inside, grabbed my dad's guitar, and brought it back outside. I crossed my legs and set it on my lap.

At the Station, when I played, the lighthouse burst with fire, drawing its glow out into the night. Maybe, even in this world without ferrymen and magic, music could draw Dad out of this apartment.

I took a big breath, filling my tired lungs with new air. I closed my eyes. I cleared my throat. Steadied my shaking hand.

"*It will be okay someday . . .*" I sang his song; the one that had paid for our house, back when I was a little girl. It would come on the radio and we'd squeal and jump up and down in awe of our father. "*Though it don't look that way.*"

The notes hummed inside my chest; a gentle peace.

I heard something to my left. And I looked to the side, through the wooden lattice.

Mrs. Coleson stood on her balcony beside mine. Not saying a word. Just listening.

"*When all other promises wash away, this anthem still will play . . .*"

Then after that song, I awkwardly strummed another chord with my uncalloused and out-of-practice fingers. I sang, "*Sammy, if you can hear me, send a song on the wind. Sammy, if you are with me, let me know it's not the end. We are tired. We are giving up. We are . . .*" And I couldn't think of anything that rhymed with "up." So I let it trail off.

The spell broke.

Mrs. Coleson shuffled back inside, the screen door closing behind her.

Everyone's a critic.

No, no, I didn't know if it was because the song was too sad or too awful or if she just remembered she left the oven on. I swallowed it back. Tried to recenter myself.

Another chord I could cobble together strummed under my hands with a plunk of pain.

"*We are tired,*" I sang. "*We are searching for . . . all the places that were yours. So Sammy, if you can hear me . . . sing along.*"

Wasn't perfect. But it was a good start.

The sliding screen door opened. There was Dad. He peeked out to see me.

"Is that a new one?" he muttered.

I nodded.

He studied the guitar. "Good job, rhyming 'for' with both 'were' and 'yours.' And good melody, too."

And I felt something like light in my chest. There was hope in this hopeless place.

"Whose dog is that?" he suddenly asked.

I slowly turned to look at where he pointed.

There splooted a scraggly little dog on the edge of the stairs, panting like he'd just climbed up here. The Yorkie mix lay flat on his stomach, legs out, looking like he desperately needed an inhaler. I would have laughed if I wasn't busy trying to find my own breath.

He wore a collar just like the dogs at the Station. A big red one, sparkling leather. Dad stepped past me and went directly to him.

"Come here, little guy," he said. The dog immediately jumped to his feet and pranced to Dad's side. Dad knelt down. He looked at the collar.

"Chestnut?" he read.

I stared at Chestnut. He stared at me. No wink, no words, just stared with his little tongue sticking out.

"Dad, he belongs to somew . . . one else," I said as Dad picked him up in his arms.

Welp, if there was any part of my brain holding out that the Station was all a hallucination, that straw had been grasped at and thrown away.

Nera sent her asshole Yorkie, just like she promised. I bit back a smile. Thank you, Nera.

Dad held onto Chestnut. He hummed to the dog. "You're a sweet little pup, aren't you?"

Chestnut looked like a dog, but he did not look sweet. He looked like a Sir Didymus Muppet left in a flooded storage unit. His tongue lolled out past toothless gums, his gray eyes staring out like foggy marbles.

But the thing that struck me was my dad humming.

The Station was a weird place. It was built for the dead. But here it was, protecting us. And I remembered Nera's hand in mine, on the roof.

There was something to hold between me and her, there and here.

Dad opened the door. "Come along, Chestnut." He scratched the little guy under the collar. "We'll get you some food and see if you have a microchip or something . . . between you and me, I hope you don't."

The door shut behind them.

I was alone, on the patio, with my guitar, hearing my dad humming inside. The clattering of dishes in the cupboard. Chestnut stared out the window, on high alert.

"What's up, buddy?" I said.

Then I felt him.

I turned to see Haunts below, eyes staring up at me, like koi fish in a pond below a bridge. Waiting.

I am patient.

I narrowed my eyes. "However patient you are," I retorted, "I'm way more stubborn." Then I sang the new song out, as if it would be a shield against them. *If you can hear me, let me know you're there.*

It may have been my music. It may have been Chestnut. I don't know. Maybe I wasn't special and the Haunts were biding their time. But when I looked again, they were gone.

———————

That night, my feet pounded on the cold pavement, my arms pumping while I blasted music through my headphones, my iPod shaking up and down in my coat pocket.

I leaped through the ivy to the other side and into the world beyond. Sure enough, there was the stone path leading to the fountain and the Station.

The sun set as I caught sight of Nera waiting between the pillars, the dogs and ghosts passing by her. She steadfastly stood in their current, waiting for me.

For me.

I pulled out a wrinkled old map with cheap ink, rubbing off on my clammy hands. It was ripped from a big old road atlas of Illinois. Mom gifted it to Sammy when she first left for college.

"It won't get you all the way to Connecticut," Mom had said. "But it'll help you remember home."

I had finally opened Sammy's moving box while Dad was busy making Chestnut dinner, and her atlas was sitting on top. Sam would have thrust this thing into my arms going, "Give her a prezzie! Give it!" Sam loved presents. Even when she was a kid and had no money, she'd just wrap her own toys up and hand them to people. I hoped she would have approved.

It hurt, though. To give some part of her away. Just to open the moving box, with the scent of her wafting out casually, as if she still existed . . .

No.

I had to give this to Nera quick and cool and it was not a big deal.

I walked straight to Nera and handed her the map. "Hi. This was Sam's, and I, um, thought you might like it. It's Chicago."

Nera looked at the map like it was a holy grail. "Oh! My!" she said. "That's . . . Chicago is in here?"

"Yup." Not a big deal. Breathe, Charlie.

She tried unfolding the big page with one hand.

"Here, I can hold your lantern," I offered.

"This is fantastic." Her eyes glittered. "Charlie, thank you so much."

"Of course," I said. I wanted to add something snarky to slough off the thank-you, like, "You want any more of her junk, lemme know," but I let the discomfort dangle in between us until the alchemy of time turned it to sincerity.

Sam would be proud. She always thought I was too much of a smart-ass.

Nera folded it out, a wide, brilliant smile across her face. It showed the city better than I could from the top of the Station. "I . . . Charlie, this is beautiful. Is this where we are? This is the lake, isn't it! Which means!" She peered out at the skyline beyond. "Which means that the Sears Tower is that one," she said. "And there's the Hancock, just like you said!" She peered at the words on the grid. "What's a Starbucks?"

I patted her on the back. "We'll get to that," I said.

She stood, rigid, after I touched her. I recoiled. "I'm sorry," I offered. "I'm sorry, I didn't—"

"Do it again," she said. "But keep your hand there. I want . . ." She shook her head. "No, it's odd I don't—"

"What is it?"

Her big eyes took me in, as if she was an explorer and this was her new world. "I want to try to feel it."

"Oh-kay," I said. "I do not know what that means, but sure." I put my hand on her back again.

She gasped. "It's solid," she said. "I thought so. Do I feel solid?"

She did not. She felt like when you're sleeping and your brain tells you that you're touching something, but it just is . . . different. But she'd felt real, for an instant up on the roof . . .

I looked at the pillars, towering above us, and I took her hand. I pulled her away from under the pillars of the Station, toward the city, and she stumbled a little onto the stone path. With a giddy smile and a bounce, she squeezed my hand.

I could feel her.

Warm.

I knew she could, too.

"See?" I whispered. "Told you, you're alive."

Then it felt like neither of us wanted to let go and break this little spell we'd conjured. So, we let the warmth of our hands glow in the evening that grew colder with the sunset. The current of dogs swept past her skirt and my backpack, and we held one another with tender smiles.

Nera?

Nera jumped. Her hand slipped away. We both turned to face Harosen.

Yay.

Nera suddenly stuffed the map in her pocket. *Father, hello.*

Harosen gave me a narrow glare. *A gift, I see.*

Nera clasped her hands. *I—*

"It's just an old map," I interfered, handing the lantern back to Nera. "It doesn't have any evil diseases or curses on it and it's not a nuclear code. Literally, you could pick it up at a rest stop."

It's only some paper, Nera agreed with me.

Harosen's mouth firmly grimaced. *Nera, it's a distraction. Happy needs you at the ferry. And Charlie, you're to be at the piano.*

"Yes, of course," Nera said, rushing past him with the map still in her pocket. As she cleared him, I tried to hurry on by as well. But he took my shoulder in his grip.

He did not feel warm.

I waited for angry words. A reprimand from King Triton. But what words came clotheslined me in my throat.

"Please," he said softly, desperately, "don't let her look at you that way."

All I could say was, "What way?" I pulled back from him.

I could feel him watching me as I walked away. "She's not like you, Miss Connor," he said. "She has bigger things than one life."

I turned around and almost said something snarky. But his eyes matched my own dad's waiting for word about his daughters in the hospital. Hoping that maybe his fears would fade out for something kinder, but knowing better. His desperation was Marco's, begging my father: *What are we going to do, what are we going to do?*

That's what we all wanted, I guess: to protect each other.

I said nothing.

Before I passed the pillars, my phone buzzed. I pulled it out. Marco.

its ok. glad we r talkng again. wanna hang out this wk?

Sam would hit my arm and say, "Yes! Yes, you guys need each other! Do it!" She was never one for unsaid words.

She also was not here.

I punched the soft number buttons, moving the letters to spell out a quick message.

im working on smthng. will tell u wen i can. Send.

I flipped my phone shut and crossed into the land of the dead.

REMNANTS

—*Mix CD for road trip, Marco Ramirez and Charlie Connor,*
May 2000

18

NERA

My nights blossomed with Charlie's music. My days swelled with lessons from Father, and now Edna was teaching me more, too. Death was steady, but my life started to grow through the cracks.

Father, of course, did not know I ate pizza or that I had found David Stein's journal. Things stayed constant for him, except for his looming deadline of dying next autumn and his irritation at my map from Charlie.

I found it silly that I didn't tell him my secrets. But I worried if he knew about the rooftop or Edna's lessons, he would either put a stop to them or he would be disappointed—and I didn't know which was worse. Although I couldn't fault him. Now I'd seen the Haunts devour; the Station Master had good reason to stay strong and focused. But there also had to be a reason why a Station Master should not sit like a lone lantern in the dark. Understanding and trusting other souls, there was strength in that as well.

One night, Father showed me into the lighthouse. We climbed up the winding stairs. *Don't look directly into the lamp,* he warned me. He touched the bottom of the Fresnel lens above us; a large glass case for the light inside, looking like a ripple in water. Prisms upon prisms, magnifying my father's magic.

Now you must make sure the light is bright, the lens is clean, and there are no shadows near it. To clean the lens, you need only to reach out your hands and offer it to feel your peace and confidence in its clarity.

He did this, his hands reaching out, like a gardener tending to their quiet, beautiful garden. His hands were soft. He had nails and fingerprints. *But you must be careful with it. Protect it. Hold it close.*

I yearned to know how Jonathon had become Father. I wanted to see the in-between of his life where he had grown from a child in love on the streets of the city, to the keeper of this massive light. He did not look lonely in the glow of the mirrors around us. And yet, he looked incomplete.

Something inside him yearned to connect, no matter how much he thought differently.

You talk as if you have a shield around you, Father, and that you find comfort in it, I said, trusting him with my honesty. *But there's more to you. The light shines bright when you hear Charlie's music.*

We don't know why her music helps the light, he grumbled. He took out a cloth and wiped away his fingerprints from the glass. *A heart is something you must care for, be very aware of. A heart must only stay in your own chest, so you may protect it. You may use that heart to love, but giving it away, you put the light in danger.*

But you're giving me all your light, Father.

His eyes flashed from the mirrors to me. I saw a man who was the culmination of a story I was only now learning. He pressed his hand to his chest, then reached out to show me that there, in his palm, a little flame flittered and licked his fingers. In the flame, I saw a little girl dancing in the atrium, holding onto dogs for balance, finding her way with her first steps.

You are my daughter, he said. *You* are *my heart.*

My father taught me how to care for the light. Edna taught me to care for others. I needed both to be a strong Station Master.

I met Edna every afternoon in the library run by Stella, a border collie with a beautiful black streak that covered her muzzle and ran up her face to her mane. She had a way of looking right up at you, like a little dolphin, and seeing exactly where you wanted to go in her stacks of books.

This place was not like the Archive of Dead Things; this place was a wonder of oaken bookshelves and ladders that flew on wheels with a cascading mural on the ceiling that was a family photo of every character anyone could remember, standing in poses and interwoven in the clouds. Stella was kind enough to walk me around the shelves, telling me all her favorite stories as she pointed her nose at different spines. The memories of a thousand collections. The Monkey King, Long John Silver, the dragon and knight from Polish stories, Yoruba deities, coyotes and hares, bears and ravens, monsters from the deep, heroes from outer space.

Oh look, there's a golem up there. I do love me a good golem story. But here, my favorite, Edna said today, pulling a book off the shelf, *is this one. A book written by a girl who never found a publisher, but remembered nearly every word when she walked through here.*

Oh, oh yes, that one is very good, Stella agreed.

I should have been focusing on getting ready for tonight. I didn't understand how I was changing. But I knew I was changing, because I stood in a library with a friend.

Edna knew so much. I yearned to ask her all the questions of the universe.

Edna, can I ask you something? When we first met, you said "Shabbat," I said to her as she looked around on the wall for something she wasn't finding. *What is Shabbat?*

Edna stared at me like I'd grown three heads. *Excuse me?*

You said that you remembered the dead on Shabbat. I folded my hands, embarrassed. *So what is Shabbat? I want to do it.*

Edna scoffed. *I . . . oh Nera. No, you know what? This is fine. Any question is* welcome. *Shabbat is when we come together on the weekend. We don't work. We don't do all those things that we have to do. The only thing we have to do is be present, with each other and with Hashem.*

Edna wove stories of Sabbaths and songs for candles, songs for kiddush, songs for the dead. She promised to teach me all of them. And then she wearily asked me, *Does . . . your papa not recite kaddish out on his boat?*

I slowly shook my head.

Edna's mouth turned down.

What is kaddish? I asked her.

A prayer you say for the dead, and those left behind. It's to help them ascend, be remembered. I can teach you, if you'd like.

Of course, I said.

The dead are to be loved, looked after. And I don't know what the hell he thinks he's doing, but it's not that.

Why did he change? I asked.

Edna shook her head. *I don't know, darling. But . . . every soul is its own universe. It must be treated as such. Each life is so big, so vast, so important.*

Has he ever told you about his life before the Station?

Edna snorted a laugh. *No,* she said. *Harosen acts as if he's older than death itself. And he's not spoken to me for decades.*

If Father hadn't told me about Shabbat, what else had he not told me about? He had been *friends* with Edna? He had once looked them all in the eyes.

Edna took my wrists. She shook them. I couldn't feel her. I wished I could. *You gotta heal this place, Nera. He thinks he knows everything, but he's forgotten so much.*

I nodded. *I know.*

I did know. I knew it with a conviction as sturdy as my body. I wished I knew anything else half as well.

Now, she said, *let's learn how to say kaddish.*

———————————

Every night, I walked Charlie back to the outside. Her father waited at home, and the dogs assured me she needed to leave when the sun rose. Dogs were usually right about such things.

Let her live as much as she can, Elbee instructed me.

Father also made sure she was gone. Although as the nights passed, and he saw she wasn't going to turn me to stone, he'd just wave her off and say, "Take care, see you again soon," before retreating back inside.

One night after he left us alone, I handed her the memory of a scarf I'd knitted from all the little pieces of what people had brought with them, memories of warmth and softness, aspects that made for a good scarf. Something she could hold. She grinned and wrapped it around her face.

"Oh my God, I'm a little babushka. I love it," she said. "Thank you so much, Nera, it's a very sweet gift."

"You give me a wonderful map, I give you a scarf," I said. "One thing dogs and humans have in common: we show each other friendship by giving."

Charlie laughed, not a mocking laugh but a sweet one. "Thank you."

"Just," I added, "perhaps do not tell Father. I'd rather not upset him."

"Ha, good luck with that." She winked at me. "I'll make sure to tell him you knitted it yourself." She pushed me and I swiped to get her back. She squealed and turned on her foot and sashayed down the icy street. Sliding and slipping, zooming out of the Station's stratosphere and back to the bridge.

"I'll see you tomorrow!" she shouted back behind her.

She walked back into the land of the living without me.

And I saw the scarf disappear from around her neck.

It was not from the Gift Room. It was just a memory. The things I did here in the Station did not matter in the living world.

Time would pass for her. Time would lose meaning for me. Someday, I would look through her own archived journal, the ghost of that scarf, the memory of her hands and how she made my own hands warm and real. Someday, I would help her cross.

Station Masters lived forever until exhaustion drained them and the only adventure left was crossing through the Veil. But for Charlie, winters would stack on each other as she felt the gravity of the earth wrinkle and bend her.

We were in a pantomime, pretending we belonged to the same world.

19

CHARLIE

I smacked a very big hamsah onto our door then leaned out the window to give the Haunts the finger. "Fuck you, assholes!"

"What the fuck?!" A living gaggle of college students in the alley flipped me back.

And Marco kept texting. I haphazardly tried to answer.

Cold 2day.

Yes, Marco. It is winter. yeah super cold.

How r u

Marco, how do you think I am? Friend, she's dead. It's winter in Chicago. Life is a series of wet frozen socks and then you die. im ok. hanging in there. u?

I always thought it would suck to die during the winter, when the lake turns into ice. To know you're never gonna see another spring. That months before you were gone, you saw the sun and bare arms for the last time and didn't know it was the last time.

Sam had died in March. Right when everyone's sick of winter and there's that promise that if you just hold out a few more weeks . . .

On warmer days, the ice steamed on the lake, like the Station was on top of a cloud. When the sun dropped, I curled back onto the bench at Sam's piano.

Souls listened intently. Sometimes they joined in with memories of violins and guitars and one time a bagpipe. The bagpipe was so cool.

Then once I finished their song, like a busker asking for a tip, I pulled out my Pittsburgh picture with her and I asked them, "Have you seen my sister?"

A little question for a big prayer. Have you seen the girl who always looked the comfiest sitting in her overstuffed chair with a crocheted blanket and a mug full of tea? Have you seen the girl who melted into the piano when she played, and Marco couldn't take his eyes off her? You gotta know her, she was too big a soul to just disappear.

And yet, no one had seen her.

Sammy, can you hear me.

So why was I here?

I rocked back and forth, pressing my body into the piano like I rowed a boat upstream, cutting through the water and feeling the wind on my face.

I was here because her music was here, and so hope was here. When I sat on this bench, played these keys, heard it echo through the atrium like a hymn to the heavens . . . that is where I could feel her shadow. And maybe it was my imagination, maybe there was nothing, but this is the closest thing to home and her I had. So what was I gonna do, *not* be here?

Hours passed. Souls asked for songs they sang to their children, by their parents, at their wedding, the song they blared in the car with their friends when they were too young to drive slow. Everything from Chicago blues, classical, R&B, old Bollywood pieces, lullabies, love ballads that brought forth the smell of hairspray in my nose. And I didn't know all of the songs. But I'd find the chords and do my best. Music would glide over me, wrap me up, put together all the missing pieces again.

Frank, a young-looking soul, had requested "His Eye Is on the Sparrow." He held a certain kind of pain when he sang the words. Some people died slowly and peacefully. Others died terribly and too young.

I didn't do Frank's song justice. My hands fumbled. If only I could play the keys as well as I could sing. Jesus Christ.

I imagined Dad standing behind me. "Oh come on, kid," he'd say, "you know more chords than that. Trust if you hit a wrong note, you'll find your way out of it. There you go! Keep going, kid, keep running!"

I pressed, pressed, pressed, in a rhythm like a dragon running to the edge of a cliff to take flight. And there, in the high keys, I made that dragon soar.

"That's it, kid!" The memory of my dad laughed in my head. Like I flew a kite.

Inside the music, my family was alive. Music was more than a dirge. Joy soared from the crowd of souls that congregated to shout out for "Mambo No. 5" and "ABC" and Earth Wind & Fire and even the Macarena and the Electric Slide, and then we had a contest to see who could do "We Didn't Start the Fire" the fastest. I lost. But I mean, we all did the Macarena so maybe we all lost.

When souls sang together, joy was contagious. Even Harosen came out of his office or stood on his balcony and watched the celebration. The tomb's lighthouse lit up and the Station transformed into a party.

I imagined Sam standing there in the crook of the baby grand's belly, singing along and smiling wide.

But then when I looked, I saw someone else, past the piano's lid, dancing in the atrium's golden light. Gurty danced around her, barking, play bowing, jumping.

Nera had a smile that echoed in my chest. Like it filled me up with courage.

From the safety of my piano, I got to watch her, night in and night out. Helping the souls to the ferry. Trying to ask them their names. Stopping to thank the dogs. Little things.

I thought about her way too much.

"That was beautiful," Nera offered one night as she approached me.

I jumped, my foot slipping from the damper pedal. "Oh!" With a splat, Sam's piano silenced. "Th-thank you."

"What was that last song?"

"I just was farting around." I grabbed my coat and my backpack.

"Just 'farting' around; you do your improvisation an injustice by calling it that." Nera grinned. "It's gorgeous." Then she remembered herself and awkwardly folded her hands across her stomach. "You've been getting a lot of requests. Our ferry has been taking some of the older hotel guests now . . . Even Frank. Edna says he's been here for a *while*." She glided her hand along the wooden lid. "Music must be powerful."

"Well," I started. Yeah. It was the soundtrack to a life, wasn't it? "Everyone's got a favorite song. Back from the ferry?"

"Back from the ferry." Nera's hand fell. "I genuinely love listening to you play your music." She said her words in her alto timbre, always carefully constructed sentences that had been thought out. It sounded like a gentle caress across my cheek. *I love listening to you play your music.*

Any response I flapped out of my maw would not be smooth. I just mumbled, "Thank you." I leaned over the keyboard. "I'm glad the music is helping." I grabbed Sam's music again. Put it in the backpack again. It would disappear again. "Lots of religious songs. Lots of pop music and blues. It's an eclectic bunch."

"If the city is as big as you say," Nera said, "it would make sense for music of both life and death to be honored here. Before souls come here, everyone has their own last rites, practices, rituals, and prayers. The dogs protect, the city leads to the lake, and everyone ends up crossing over. But we all have a different way of getting here." She paused, rethinking her words. "Even the ghosts in the city who aren't ready . . . they'll find their way eventually."

I felt a lump in my throat.

She was so sure that everything would be alright.

I remembered what the thing in the dark had warned: Nera dealt in the dead. Not in the dying. Not in the living.

"Have you found anything about my sister on your end?" I asked her.

She shook her head. "No," she admitted. "I haven't. I looked in the Archive of Dead Things." Whatever that was. "It's a room where the things people died with are kept in boxes. But there's nothing there under a Sam Connor."

"That makes sense," I replied. "She didn't have anything with her when she died at the hospital. Her clothes got ripped when she went into surgery, and she dropped her tote bag when . . ." she ran. When she ran.

Mom wanted her clothes back for her to be buried in. But they were so ruined. We couldn't look at them. I don't know where they ended up. Not here, I guess.

"And you?" Nera asked. "Have you found anything?"

I looked to the little carved rose. These little details were portals to another time where she still existed. But the portals were too much like the tiny doors in Wonderland, and I had no potion to follow her.

"I keep thinking there's a reason I'm here," I admitted to her. "But I don't know how to find that reason. Do I just keep playing music? Do I go look in every room and ask every single ghost? Or maybe . . ." I hesitated.

"What?" she asked.

I looked at the keys. "What if she doesn't want to see me?"

Nera stiffened. She folded her hands again. "Why would you think that?"

It was like there was a curse in my throat. I couldn't force the words out.

My dad screaming in the hospital. *Why did you leave her? You hid without her!*

Like sharp, brash violins sawing between two notes. *Why. Did. You. Leave. Her.*

And maybe Nera saw the dread of hopelessness seep into my face. Because she extended her hand. "Hey, I had another thought. Tonight, we can look for more signs of her here in the Station, away from the piano. But . . . first, would you like to see what I've done with your map?"

20

THE JOURNAL OF DAVID STEIN

Tonight, I was the shomer for the first part of the evening. It was Rabbi Katz, and he had been ill and old for a very long time. I like the older ones most, because they don't take much convincing to leave.

I am grateful for my journal, because I can tell you the truth of my life. I love a boy. I am able to see the dead. It is not the story my father knows. But as long as someone knows it, I will be well.

Katz sat with me for a little, I think because he felt guilty that he was absolutely fine with dying.

I was ready, he tried to explain to me.

"What was your favorite part?" I asked him politely. To pass the time, but also because I always like to know what people's favorite parts were.

Of death?

"No, apologies, life."

Ah, *he said.* I enjoyed the women.

That's what most men enjoyed.

He told me not so much about his wife, but this girl he'd known toward the end of his life. Another older person in our congregation, and I suppose I have never thought about the elders dating one another like young people. He called her a girl. I knew her as a very old grandmother. Not mine, though. That would have been even more awkward than tonight was.

Soon, Jonathon came to relieve me of my shift, and I instead stayed a little longer as Katz told us about a small box of money that needed to go to his new sweetheart. We took notes, and then there was a soft scratching at the door. Through the wall itself, a small dog came.

That meant it was time.

Katz waved, his hands straight and then bent and then straight, as if he was waving to two babies, and he sauntered forward to follow the dog through the wall and away.

I am starting to think the dogs are the reapers. But when I ask Jon about it, he shrugs and says, "Sometimes there are dogs, sometimes there aren't."

For the living, we Jews have so many rules for death. But I don't understand the world of the dead. It seems that once we get a handle on how all this works, it disappears like a sunbeam in the rain. I know that death always has the same beats. The death rattle. The swelling. All of the details we can see as observers on this side of life. But then it becomes less discernible. Are there always dogs? Do the souls take the shape of a body when they emerge, do they hold onto old quirks their bodies had, are they even the same age? Sometimes the souls are so faint, they are barely a stream of light in a dark room. Other times, old folks emerge as children, children emerge as an ever-changing face like a sprite.

"It is as if you are in a dream." I tried to nail it down for Jon once, and he said:

"There is humility in not knowing everything about the world-to-come. We are to live for life, you know."

Right.

Well, humility is not necessarily a good thing or a bad thing. Sometimes, it's good to know what we are proud of, where we excel.

So I will continue to record all I find.

Another thing I have found, before I forget, are the Circlers. They are stuck in a moment. I have found some very old Circlers out on the street. Nothing bad ever befalls them, other than what is in their circle already. But maybe that makes it even more tragic; they do not deteriorate, or fade away, they just keep circling the same memory. That is, until someone can help them let go. But until then, they are stuck in a tar pit for eternity.

Maybe that's why Katz was such a surprising breath of fresh air. So many people do not want to die. Katz was ready.

Maybe death did not have to be something fearful.

After the sun came up, we should have been tired. But instead, we went to Jon's house and I met his sister and mother and father. We shared a meal. Afterward, he walked me home. In a soft moment, we embraced again. This time, I asked him, "If I were to kiss you, would I still see you in the morning?"

Then he kissed me.

The feeling of loving someone, and finally knowing they love you as well. Two pieces clicking into place. The world, finally, finally, something to trust.

21

NERA

David adored my father with all his beating heart. My father must have loved him, too. Or perhaps he hadn't. I didn't know what had gone wrong, or where David was, and especially why Father never told me about him.

I didn't know how he connected to the Fire, if he'd become a Haunt . . . or why Father wanted to forget him.

David described an embrace. My heart yearned for that, with Charlie. Our hands, they were real, just as he said, threading together like a quilt. I desired to hold her hand every minute of every night she was in the Station. Like taste on my tongue, she was solid and real in this dream that swallowed me. She was like waking up, hit by the sunlight outside.

Charlie now stood in the middle of my wooden bedroom with my handwriting all over the walls. She saw all the names I knew of those who had crossed.

David.

George.

Then the rest of their names, flooding out like the wall of a shul.

A year from now, my father's name would be on that wall, along with many more people who I wouldn't let down. Not like George.

"Oh, wow," Charlie said. "The map!"

It was tacked to my wall. Her map donned scribbled-in words and strings leading to notes. Potbelly's. Harold's. Music Box. Best Potstickers. Piece of Shit Red Line Station. Get Atomic Cake here. Riots started here. Women & Children First. Where Julia kissed Vern.

A city.

"You've been busy," Charlie said. "It's epic."

"I'm trying to look into the crowd," I said. "I may not follow you out into the city, but I can still learn from here at my post."

When I marked up the map during the day, I imagined myself walking the streets with Charlie laughing, showing me all these places and things. My heavy shoulders shed isolation. My heart danced like the parties in the Station. I belonged to something bigger than me, and it wanted me.

Charlie nodded. "You've marked all the Starbucks with question marks."

"It's all the sightings of the Starbucks and all the places it's manifested," I said.

"No, no, oh, no, there's just . . . they're all separate Starbucks, it's a chain. Like . . . there's more than one simultaneously."

"Oh." I paused. "So, there's no magic in the city?"

"I mean, no," Charlie said. "Or maybe there is, but most people can't see it. It's very, uh . . . brutal sometimes. Most people are just trying to get by and get home, so I'm sure there might be something out there. I mean I can see the ghosts . . ." Charlie gently grazed the map with her fingers. "So someday you're gonna let me take you out there, right?"

I froze again. "Oh," I said. "I don't even know if I *can* leave the Station. We never have."

"Just because you've never done something doesn't mean you can't do it," Charlie said.

"Father says the world isn't like here in the Station," I said. "People get hurt." I didn't believe the Station could heal me if I broke my body out there on the streets. I may not even be able to get home. One wrong step and . . . what would happen to the lighthouse if I died?

"Okay." Charlie narrowed her eyes. "But there's also kids playing in the park and people going on dates and music at the opera house. Nera, you live in the Station, which is built of memories. The Station reflects the city. If the Station is beautiful, then something in the city must be. Or it wouldn't look like this."

I hesitated.

Charlie grabbed my hand. "Hey, you said we'd look for evidence of Sam in the Station today, right? Then come on. Chop chop. We need to find Sam, and we need to show you a few things on the way."

We started at the diner so Charlie could orient herself. She held onto the diner's half-wall while she looked at our options around the track. "Alright, Sam, where would you go . . ."

Behind me, I saw the massive curved arch of the front window, above the four pillars. If I looked out, I saw snow, thick flakes landing along the fountain that still sprayed water even in the middle of winter.

Runa's time has come! Snow! Snow! Runa the massive Norwegian elkhound bounded past us toward the atrium. *Outta my way!* She slapped a shar-pei out of her way, like he was a tennis ball, and she flew down the stairs.

The shar-pei was fine.

"That's Runa," I explained to Charlie, who jumped a little. "She's the winter dog. Guides the others through the snow when they get lost."

"Spirit dogs get lost?" Charlie said.

Everyone gets lost in a Chicago winter at one time or another.

Edna. I turned around and she was seated in the diner area, knitting something with her plate of pancakes already finished. She winked at me. *Ah, and who is this? The famous live musician.* She chuckled to herself.

"Charlie, this is Edna Meyer," I said. Charlie nodded a "how do you do." Edna nodded back. So humans *did* bow!

We met before, dear, and Charlie, your "Bridge Over Troubled Water" was tremendous. But you spending too much time here isn't good for anyone, Edna said. *Go live your life, kid. Be free! Hashem knows I would go back to the city if I could.*

Charlie leaned over the wall. "Nera says you've been here the longest and you know a lot."

I do. But I know you're gonna ask me about this Sam Connor like you've been asking everyone. And I don't know her. If she was here, she hurried through. She your sister?

"Yes."

I'll keep my mind open for anything that rings a bell. But sometimes, people rush through to get to the Veil as fast as they can. It's nothing personal, darling. Sometimes, it's what they have to do.

But Edna wasn't saying the other part: sometimes, they didn't make it to the Station at all. I knew Charlie worried. I wished I could take that from her.

"Sam wouldn't have just left," Charlie said. But she said it like she was trying to convince herself. Maybe Sam *was* the sort of soul who would.

You remember her, don't you? Edna said. *What she looked like, how she sounded, her favorite things, perhaps something silly she said once?*

"Of course," Charlie said.

Then she still exists, Edna said. *Now I've only seen three live people set foot in this place, and all three of them are more lost than they were when they entered.* She nodded to me. I did not enjoy that commentary. *It's time for you both to scoot on out. Look at you, young and with good kneecaps. Shoo.*

"I'm not going to leave, Edna," I said.

"Yeah, Grumpy Gills won't leave," Charlie said.

Her father believes the city to be nothing but pain. And she's a chicken.

"Excuse me?" I said. "I could die, and the lighthouse—"

Or you could, you know, live, Edna said. *Perhaps, if you understand the souls more, your light could shine even brighter. Didn't think about that, did ya?*

I had not. It was such a risk.

"Edna, what did you like about the city?" Charlie asked. "One perfect day, what would you do out there?"

Edna thought for a moment, placing her knitting in her lap and scanning the tile ceiling of the diner for an answer. *Hmm. If I had my way, I would go to hear the Symphony Orchestra. Then I would grab a lovely sandwich, walk around Grant Park, and then go see a movie. There was a new theater on Diversey, right down the street from the old Golden Apple, where I would get dinner. Best pie known to man, Charlie.*

And then she waggled her eyebrows. *How about you take this young shayna madel on a hot date on the town?*

Her suggestion harbored both freedom and discomfort. Edna tutted. *Oh, right, the sun might come crashing down if you leave. And the lake will turn to lava and flood the city. Nera, there are no guarantees of safety anywhere.*

That hard knot in my throat returned, and my lungs breathed in faster than I wanted. My body panicked. I wasn't the Station Master *yet,* so the lighthouse should be fine without me, if I could sneak past my father and he didn't know—sneak past my father! What the hell was I entertaining?! The map was enough!

Charlie touched my back and rubbed it. I blinked. I felt a warmth like a red hot fire. "Breathe." Charlie comforted me. "You're all red and embarrassed."

"It's not that . . . I wouldn't want to . . . take you on a date . . ." I breathed. "It's the whole . . . well, the world . . ."

Edna winked at me. *The world is waiting,* she whispered. And she went back to her knitting.

22

CHARLIE

Our exploration led us to a large cavern with different hallowed enclaves that looked like old gilded mosques and Notre Dame. Souls bent their heads in their own corners, whispering solemnly. It was the Station's equivalent of an airport chapel.

It seemed like the room would shift into whatever people needed. A door in the back led to a private space. Other than the soft whispers of prayer, this main hub was quiet. All around us was stained glass art on the walls, with color illuminating the wood and stone.

There was no Sam in here.

"Did you ever go to Shabbat?" Nera said.

"Uh," I said, scanning the room for anything, anyone who could help. Sam liked the little free library at Temple, and she *loved* the ark's artwork of a spiraling tree. But I saw none of her remnants. "Yeah. It was more Mom and Sam's thing, I went sometimes. But we mostly just sort of had a nice evening at home and Dad played some music and Mom baked challah and then we went to bed without having to do homework."

"It sounds kind," Nera said. "Sort of like what we do here. I'm trying to learn how to incorporate more of who we were into who we are now. Father has run this place for so long, he's worn away at the edges. But I can breathe new spirit into it. I can fix this. All of this."

She looked out to the very large praying space full of very many souls.

"Do you *want* to fix it?" I asked.

Nera nodded. "If I don't," she said, "who will?"

"And when do you get to rest?"

"I don't need to," Nera said.

"I mean, if you're talking about Shabbat," I said, "you do need to. Like, Shabbat is a rule that you have to do nothing."

Nera smiled, a short, little secret of a smile. "Isn't that something."

Music, from hymns and secret hopes and old songs passed down, all echoed together like an orchestra tuning. "You're doing great," I said. "You're learning their names and being kind. And I like to think this place is supposed to remind everyone that you've done your time, it's okay to rest." I looked pointedly at her.

But she just looked at me. "And when do you rest, Charlie?"

It hit me dead center and it took me a second to recuperate. I elbowed her. "Smart-ass."

Nera laughed. Then she touched her chest. And she laughed again. And then she laughed more, and more, and it grew like a blooming lily and it made me laugh.

"What's going on?" I asked her, and she shook her head through gasps of air, and her eyes welled up with tears, happy tears, as her laugh snowballed through her body.

"I don't know, what *is . . . going on*?" she breathed, and then the laugh grabbed her again, and she doubled over. I waved an apology to the ghosts and their prayers, and turned back to Nera.

Joy was here.

I didn't want to go out into the cold again.

But maybe if she followed me, back into the Chicago winter, it wouldn't be so unbearable.

We ran our fingers across the spines of books in the Station's library. None of Sam's books were here. No dog-eared copy of *The Hobbit*, no tear-stained *Watership Down*. Not even a diary.

At the end of the long wooden shelves was a little sunroom made with wire and glass. A cozy garden party, if someone from the Victorian times had attempted to host graciously and then a punk rocker from the eighties had come in and crashed it with their décor. It was an amalgamation. Souls hovered in a circle and all spoke excitedly, holding up old copies of the same book.

"If this is a place made of memory," I whispered to Nera, "how do they all read the same book?"

"They don't," Nera said. "The copies are all their recollection of the book."

"That book club has got to be chaos," I said.

"Yes," Nera said emphatically.

Tanika, you're up.

Hey, so I was a math teacher not an English teacher, but from what I remember—

I tried to imagine Sammy here in the sunroom, gushing about Tolkien. But she wasn't here. The absence silently choked me like a piano wire.

We crossed out of the library and up the stairs and found our place in the large hotel with halls that never ended.

Back down another flight of stairs, there was an amusement park, with all the rides a person could remember, even the old ones I was sure had been outlawed by now.

We lost ourselves in these places, in this night.

I touched the wall of the curved hall, somewhere in the belly of this beautiful beast.

"If books are made of memories, if these places are made of dreams, then what are the walls and floors and ceilings made of?"

"I don't know, Father just says magic," Nera said. "And the journal doesn't have anything in it about the Station. It's all . . . from before."

"Journal?"

Nera pulled a creepy looking flickering horror prop out of her pocket. "This," she said. "A boy who knew my father in the city wrote all about ghosts, the dogs, all of it."

"Holy shit, your pockets are huge."

"They hold what I need them to hold. Focus." She held up the journal. "This place is made of all of us and what we remember. We each seem to leave a brick behind, and the Station keeps building itself."

We turned a corner, and just like the Station was depositing us back where it found us, we were on the mezzanine looking down to the atrium. And Sam's piano.

The only piece of her I could find.

"I worry that the piano isn't Sam's brick, but mine," I said. "I can't know for sure, can I?" I stopped. "Wait, maybe I've been asking the wrong question. Everyone can see that piano. Was the piano here before I was, or did it show up the night I did?"

Nera thought, her eyes cascading to the red carpet below her lace-up boots. "There has been a piano in the atrium. Sometimes it's a harp and sometimes it's a guitar. I don't know if the piano has always been Sam's piano." She looked deflated. "I am failing you," she said. "I was so asleep before all this. I should have paid attention. Then we would have found her by now. Even today, I've been so enamored with y—" She reddened. "With showing you the Station."

My breath caught in my throat, and a smile overtook me.

Then that moment was cut short by the sound of a woman sobbing in the atrium below.

Nera immediately rushed down the stairs, her skirts perfectly avoiding her boots. I followed her. It was like a dance in front of me, her greeting the spirit, actually reaching out and touching the woman's shoulders. The soul said her name was Jessamy. Jessamy sat in her wheelchair, weeping and digging her face into the dog that had guided her here.

Nera said soft things, like a mother. And I remembered the first time I saw her; cold and nearly a robot, scanning over the heads of them all and not ever, *ever* touching them. Now she held Jessamy's arm, soft and gentle, and whispered, "Can I show you something?"

I followed Nera and Jessamy to the other side of the atrium, where doors lined the wall. We entered one. There was a hall of windows.

Windows stood all up and down a dark room, siphoned off by drapes and curtains. People stepped into the small alcoves, like looking at art in a museum.

Nera led Jessamy to a window and said, "Go on."

She looked through and she gasped. *Chincoteague,* she whispered. *It's the summer I read about the ponies.*

I stood a little behind her, peering in over her shoulder.

I couldn't see what she saw. I had never seen Chincoteague. I didn't know what Chincoteague was.

But I did see a big and beautiful maple tree, reaching up to the old wooden windowpane. Beyond the tree was a backyard, rosebushes along the fence facing the street. An old wooden playground with two swings and a steel slide that got too hot in the summer.

Dad had put it together about a month before I started kindergarten.

The left swing was mine. The right swing was Sam's.

"What the hell is this," I whispered to Nera.

"Hall of Windows," Nera said. "Elbee told me it might help some folks. You look through, and you see your favorite view."

I couldn't look away. Even when Jessamy turned around and patted both me and Nera's arms. "Thank you," she said before turning back to the window.

She'd seen the sunlight one final time.

And my swing . . . Dad took down that old playground after Sam moved back in when she left Yale. I had been sad, but Sam said it was time for us to grow up. Like she'd totally forgotten about our synchronized jumping and flying that had filled most of our Julys. Something weird had changed in my sister, but she'd kept going. Things were getting better. She wasn't finished.

Well, neither am I.

Jessamy stayed there for so long, that a little French bulldog jumped into her lap and stared out the window, too. I started to wonder if I should leave or if I should wait, if I was being rude or . . . Nera was gone.

I jolted backward. I saw Nera in a little stall to the right, looking out a window of her own. Her jaw clenched. Her fists balled.

"Nera, you okay?" I stepped into her stall.

"I wanted to know which window would show for me," she said, jagged. "It's just my room from upstairs."

The only window she'd ever had.

"You're right," Nera said. "If the Station has been built with the bricks of memories from the city . . ." She narrowed her eyes at the window ahead of her. For me, the window still showed the tree and the playground. "Then the city is full of stories and films and eclectic folks and pizza. What a wonderful world."

She turned away from the window. "And I'm not a part of it."

But Nera, you deserved to be.

Nera! Elbee shouted from the atrium. Nera jumped out of her reverie and we both ran out the door and onto marble. Dogs scattered everywhere, running for the main entrance. Elbee's head stuck up to look at us, his tail straight out. *Hurry!*

I followed Nera to the pillars outside. She ran like an EMT rushing to something bloody and raw.

An old memory came back to haunt me. My flashbacks had pulled away like the tide, since finding this place. But now they swarmed in, crashing over my eyes, my ears, drowning me.

The cops shouted through the door: "Police!" We didn't believe them at first.

None of us said anything.

It was too chaotic for everything to finally be okay.

Elbee and Harosen stood at the entrance, looking out to the fountain.

They were frozen as they stared out to the scene beyond.

"What's wrong?" Nera asked.

I followed their eyes to the stone walkway.

Dogs ran around trying to set up as many lights as they could around the fountain, fighting against the dark of early morning.

Then I saw it.

A stone in the path.

It was . . . wrong. Glitching. Like a Haunt.

"This shouldn't be possible," Nera said to Harosen.

"It should not," he said. "Don't go anywhere near it."

"But if it gets to the fountain . . ."

"It will hold," he said. "The fountain is not some little rock. It's a part of the Station. The Haunts can't touch the Station."

The fountain gave form to the spirits. Just enough to help them get the help they needed without looping or bleeding out into emotions. If the fountain was infected, then what would happen?

I remembered my mom, thanking candles while she blew them out on Friday nights. "All things are alive," she said once. "All things have souls. It's why we thank the light."

The stone had been alive. And now it was something else.

23

NERA

"Don't go anywhere near it."

Father stepped forward, his arms straight out to keep me from following. He slowly approached the stone that sparked with black and white. He leaned down beside it, as if it was a small wounded bird.

The static hissed. It slowly grew, seeping and bleeding into the stone next to it.

He opened his hands. He gave a shaky breath; a breath that had not rattled in his throat for a century. And out of his old, worn palms came a faint light.

But when he pulled away, the static firmly remained.

"He didn't fix it," Charlie said.

"No," I whispered. "But he stopped it from spreading."

I pointed to the stone next to my father's hands, next to the static one. It had started to bleed gray and black and white, to be infected. But now, it was clean.

Hunched on the ground, Father beckoned me over. I knelt down beside him. "Now you try," he said.

I raised my hands above the stone.

"Think of the sun," Father said. "Think of the love you carry. And spread it to this little stone."

Think of life.

I breathed in and out. I lowered my hands.

Think of what could have been in that window. Think of deep-dish pizza and knowing all the names of the people in the lights of Chicago. Think of Charlie.

I touched the static with my bare fingers.

It healed.

No sparklers and no tired flickers. Just the soft glow of a light, like a gentle night-light, keeping imagined monsters at bay.

Edna was right. My light was stronger when I knew life.

Father stood and helped me to my feet. "It won't be enough to make sure it doesn't happen again, but it's enough to heal this."

"That was . . . amazing." I fixed my skirts, my hands shaking.

"Well," he said, "we are the Station Masters." Then the peace between us was broken as he said, "Where were you when this happened?"

Looking through a window, Father.

There was a growing list of unspoken things between Jonathon Harosen and me.

24

THE JOURNAL OF DAVID STEIN

I followed the dog tonight who came for our person. Jon did not want to. He stayed at his perch. But I had done my mitzvah, and it was time to find out exactly where the souls were taken.

They went so fast. But I kept up. We reached the edge of the lake, and they disappeared.

There is something about water. The dogs and the souls all go to the water. Escape to the water. Leave through the water. It makes sense. We wash ourselves in the mikvah. The soul needs water as much as our body does.

Jon dislikes helping the Circlers, and he refuses to help the dybbuks. He is afraid to help anything that is an echo of a human, or not human at all. There are many sorts of spirits, sheyds, perhaps angels as well. But I believe if someone is a part of this world and we have an ability to help them, we need to help them.

I break a Circler's loop by sitting with them. Let them talk in circles. Listen to them. And keep trying to point out things in the present day. Keep trying to break the circle with the words and actions you do. It will not always work, and I am trying to find a more reliable way to do it, but listening to someone has never not helped.

Jon was a little miffed with me the other day as we walked home early in the morning. I let this dead man speak to us and he went on about how he wanted to hurt his brother. He was frightening.

When the man finally left us alone, Jon said to me, "You cannot open your heart to everyone. You are going to get hurt."

"Or pleasantly surprised," I countered. "Just look at us."

Jon was unable to stop a little smile from cracking through his façade onto his cheeks. "Well not everyone is me, David. I would never attack you. Not everything we do is safe, so you have to be careful."

"I do not believe in bad souls," I said. "I believe in people who were put in bad spots." I waved my hand around to our surroundings. "Look at this place. It looks bad. But the people here, even if they do bad things, they aren't bad."

"And what if they were not people, David?" Jon said. "Those sheyds with the names we forbid saying aloud, they exist to destroy . . ."

"What is bad anyway?" I asked him.

"Alright, Rabbi David, what is bad?" Jon stopped and turned to me, amused.

I narrowed my eyes, thinking.

I gave him some sort of longwinded half-thought-out spiel, but I am uncertain. I suppose when you hurt someone else because of a selfish decision. Or when you break the covenant with Hashem because of a selfish reason. But then what is selfish?

Perhaps selfishness is doing something that will help you and hurt someone else. But if that is the case, then everything I do may be selfish. Because I love Jon.

In the night, there are ghosts. In the day, there are the ghosts of who Jon and I truly are. We do not touch hands when others are looking. But I would move the river for him, I would build the whole of the city for him from scratch, or set all of this wooden empire on fire to warm him in the winter. And he says he would do the same for me.

Though he fears someone discovering we can see the dead, he is not afraid to love me. It is a courage I admire, one of the many beautiful details that Hashem writes about him in the Book of Life that I want to memorize and never forget.

We meet when we should be at shul. We duck into barns, say we're gambling and rough housing. And then he touches me. He holds me. And suddenly so many things make sense. We are not what I expected for my life, this is not who my father wanted me to be, but it is who I am. And we are full of joy.

I am more alive than I've ever been. Let our lives sing, Jon. Let the Book of Life remember us as we are.

REMNANTS

2-22-83

Michael,

By the time you read this letter, you'll be in Los Angeles. I hope you have settled into your hotel okay. Remember, even if you don't win tomorrow, it's a really big friggin' deal you're there. Your music has touched the world and become part of the canon. And it's let us live a life that is better than we thought we'd have.

As I write this, the girls are playing your songs on their toy instruments. Sammy is singing "You're a New World" and she says it's her favorite of your songs. She doesn't know the lyrics, so she keeps singing "New World! New World!" while wiggling the guitar around. Charlie isn't singing but she has a real strong arm when it comes to those drumsticks you so graciously bought her for her birthday. Charlie hasn't told me what her favorite song is. But she seems to be into whatever Sammy's doing.

You're at the store, picking up last-minute supplies for the trip before you come home and get your suitcase and we all drive you to the airport. I am taking bets you forgot toothpaste. But I'm guessing that a Sheraton has toothpaste at a gift shop or with the concierge. You lucky duck, being in a Sheraton with an outdoor pool in February.

We are looking forward to watching you sing on TV. Sammy wants to remind you to wink at the camera. She says she will still be awake. I don't think she's going to make it that late, but she's hell-bent on trying.

I love you with all my heart, Michael. You've worked so hard for this dream. We are all rooting for you back here in Chicago. Don't fall in love with anyone while you're out there, drink responsibly, brush your teeth, and for God's sake get Pat Benatar's and John Denver's autographs.

xxoo, your three girls will be waiting at home for you.

Donna

—Typewritten letter from Donna Connor to Michael Connor, on the eve of the 25th Annual Grammy Awards

25

CHARLIE

Mom called me while I was walking up the stairs to the Fullerton platform. I almost fell off my damn step.

"What the hell." I flipped that phone open a lot faster than I wish I had, embarrassed by my desperation. "Uh, Mom?"

"Hey," she said. "I sent you something in the mail and I think it's arriving today." She did not sound like my mom. She sounded like an actor who had once played my mom, and was now tired after a very long press junket.

"Okay?" I said.

"You haven't gotten it yet, then," she said. "Go downstairs and get it. I want to explain the Metra tickets inside, they're good for whenever."

"I'm not home right now," I said.

"Okay, well give me a call back when you get home . . . wait, what are you doing not at home?"

Wasn't any of her business. "I'm working a night shift at Navy Pier," I said.

"That tourist trap?" A pause. "I can't really hear you. Where are you?"

Your mother hasn't called since summer. Now she calls. Interesting how some people believe they can come and go and nothing will change. She says it's grief. That's what she said when she left, right? Not that her two daughters always looked so similar.

"The Fullerton station," I said. "Yeah, I'll call you back, bye."

The platform rattled with trains. Down at street level, ghosts gathered to look up at the woman who could see them. And those who weren't looking, they did when I shouted out, "Hey! I can see you!"

I mean, to the point, right?

I raised my hands and waved. "There are people who want to help! Crossing is safe. The lighthouse is right over there, and if you follow the dogs you're gonna be okay."

Charlie, stop. The living don't give kindness to those they think mad.

"And you might wanna hurry up so you don't end up static, cause this demon's a little bitch."

Your tongue won't change the severity of your situation.

Then he added, maybe to all of us:

Come to me instead.

We all looked very unnerved at one another. None of us moved. Neither to the Station, nor away from his voice. Stuck in a moment. All of us.

You are not their saving grace. And they are not yours. Don't make the same mistakes others have.

`

When we were kids, Marco and Sam and I listened to Dad sing his song about King Arthur and act it out in the backyard. He had the one about Orpheus, too. Heroes. Even if most of them ended badly.

I checked the mail on the way into the apartment. There was indeed an envelope from Mom.

I tore it open faster than I should.

Heard your father threw out all his music, she said. *Found this in my things. Thought you might want it. And tickets to Normal. Come visit now that I have my apartment set up.*

I felt the little cassette tape wrapped in the Metra ticket. I pulled it out, nearly tearing my finger open on the edges of the envelope and the sharp laminated paper. There it was, *Best of Michael Connor*.

Side A: "It Will Be Okay" started us off.

Maybe I just wanted to be mad at Mom, but this felt like some kind of double whammy one-two punch in the face. "Oh, hey Charlie, now that *I'm* ready, come down here and visit *me*. Also, by the way, I'm offloading my junk onto you, so here's an old cassette I very much do not want."

She'd never seen ghosts. At first, I thought maybe she had. But she'd seen me and Dad and that was enough of a haunting for her. She'd abandoned us.

I ran up to the apartment, found my old Walkman and plugged in my headphones. Popped the tape in. Pushed the triangle play button.

Michael Connor in my ears. My dad, my real dad. A ghost in sound now, singing that it would be okay again. No matter what happened.

I'd forgotten how his voice used to lilt.

I turned off the cassette. Something in me reared up like an angry horse, kicking everything in my way.

Everything out here in the real world was tangled together and unfixable. Too much. Too much. And for what?

I yanked the headphones off.

Maybe it would be better if I just stayed at the Station and didn't come home at all.

26

NERA

The sun returned. The Haunts retreated. I didn't want to leave the stones. But Elbee insisted.

I nervously followed Elbee back through the atrium to the hall of doors. We stood at a door made of ink-stained paper, as if cut for a paper doll and waiting to be folded open. The instructions were written in elegant fountain pen strokes:

OPEN TO THE LEFT, BEST DAY.

OPEN TO THE RIGHT, WORST DAY.

The Memory Room, Elbee explained as I watched the line form outside the door.

Why would anyone want to see their worst day? I asked him.

Because sometimes it's in the pain that the souls learn the most important lessons, he said, and then he nudged me forward to stand beside the Memory Room's threshold as each person individually walked through the door.

How do they know when to visit what room? I asked.

Their dogs help them, Elbee sat on his back legs, looking thoughtful. *And sometimes they just ask the Station for what they need, and they find their way here.*

So why are we visiting this room today?

Understanding. Elbee bowed.

Each soul entered and returned moments later, usually smiling and rarely sad. Sometimes they smiled in ways I had not yet learned, the memories of full hearts still worn right on their sleeves.

It wasn't my job to be that lucky.

And you don't think this is cruel, to show me yet another crumb of life that I won't have? I said.

Elbee leaned up against my leg. *Watch and learn. Be patient. Accompany them.*

The next soul was a very old bald man named Carl with dark brown skin and a curved back. He opened the paper door to the left, and gestured inside. *Come on then,* he said.

And we entered a room made of crisp white paper. The pages on all sides, the walls, the floor, the ceiling, they filled up with ink and spilled out in different colors to create a scene that found its texture, found its sounds and sights. There was family. A big family, around a fire and a Christmas tree. And Carl smiled. He was able to set something down inside himself.

The second person, very young, had an undercut and tattoos all up their white arms. Their name was Yew, and they went in and saw a concert they'd loved. The third person, a ride through the mountains of a country I'd never seen, ending in a cemetery. The fourth, the morning after the birth of her first child.

I stood there, in the doorway, seeing her hold her baby. She cried, but she was smiling. And the world was shifting and changing around her in a way that was so big, only she could fathom the love sitting right in her arms. A baby, new life. It was a helpless bundle, a promise sent out into the world. And warmed by that love, she was able to walk out of the Memory Room.

The fifth soul to go in stopped me as I followed her in. *I don't want you coming in with me like you've been doing,* she said. She was shorter and older than me, with straight black hair and a plump round stomach, a beautiful imperfect mole on her cheek.

And then she went to open the door to the right.

That will be the worst day, I said.

Yeah. I can read. Don't follow me. I did not. The door shut behind her.

Time passed. She emerged. She solemnly muttered, *Alright.* And she stepped forward, into her brave new world.

The next person was an older woman with soft graying hair and thin wrists. Her big glasses looked up at me. *You can follow me,* she said.

We both entered. In front of her, I saw the sun rise. A brilliant, detailed memory of a ride on the bus. So many different faces, so many different eyes and mouths and hands and shoes. It looked like the Station; a mosaic of the city, from all the different corners and edges, all different neighborhoods, quietly sitting separately but still beating with the same rhythm. Closer than it felt sometimes. Further away than the bus wanted. I saw the woman, her name was Yuxi, she was younger and she was laughing with a friend in a side seat. A young, quiet girl with short black hair. They were drenched in rain. And their sneakers squished against the grid of the floor as the bus moved down the street, turned a corner, all in a quiet song.

I felt my head tilt, as Yuxi and her friend or her sister . . . the other girl . . . they laughed and spoke to each other about someone that wasn't here on the bus. I saw they had purses.

They never got off the bus. They just rode it around town, all different people climbing in and out, going to school, going to work, asking for help, singing out songs, handing out poetry, shouting drunkenly at each other, and through it all, these two women just sat beside each other laughing and looking out the window to the rain-drenched city.

Chicago was so big. I could see it, barely, through the fogged windows. It was full of people, signs and posters for things that seemed so important that week, and cars that had gone to the junkyard by now. So many different songs.

Old Yuxi turned to look at me, the two of us on the edge of this memory. *Thank you.* That was our cue to leave. But she didn't move. She just said, *I am showing you this, not for you. But for me. Do not forget me.*

Yuxi was the last. After the hall was empty, I did something I knew I really should not do, because I already knew what was going to happen.

I opened the door to the right. I walked in.

Nothing.

Just white paper with blank ink, stagnant like a pool of water.

I walked back out.

I opened the door to the left. I returned to that room.

Nothing again.

I gritted my teeth. And something roared in me that felt like it was trying to escape. It was a different sort of warmth. This heat hurt, stung the insides of my rib cage with fear and . . . anger? Rage.

I had nothing.

I didn't know how to tell him everything I'd learned.

I also didn't know when Father came looking for me. Perhaps the ferry had gone out without me. Perhaps I had missed an entire night. I was frozen outside the Memory Room, staring down the paper door. Elbee had left a while ago. I was alone, stuck.

There you are, Father said in my head.

I could see he had bags under his eyes. He patted me on the arm.

I couldn't feel it.

I tried to imagine him a young man, watching the dead, holding hands with David.

I couldn't.

I wanted to ask him why he tried to destroy David's journal. I knew there was something terrible there, and I was this close to putting my finger on it, but I didn't want to. Or maybe I did.

Nera?

Can I go outside past the fountain and the stones? I turned to him. *If I walked outside, would I turn to dust? Would I disappear? What would happen?*

Father cocked his head, one brow raised, looking at me like I'd told him I was three dogs in a dress. *We live here,* he said. *We don't belong to that world. We are of the in-between, and we cannot compromise the in-between. It's not sanitary.*

But I could. I could wear my necklace and I would be safe from the Haunts.

Father put his hand on top of mine and he squeezed my fingers. But it felt like nothing, no pressure applied, as if he was a ghost himself. *You don't need to go looking outside; you have everything you need inside of you, my little light. I hope to know, before I cross over, that you can protect yourself.*

But Charlie—

Charlie, Father said. Stuck on the word.

He said her name like it was tar in his shoe. Although she kept his light lit, although she was selfless in helping him . . . I frowned. My face moved with all these muscles as all these feelings found their way into my eyes and my mouth and my cheeks.

David had loved him.

I know about David Stein. The words came out like knives.

Finally.

I thought I would have him there. I thought he'd look hit in the face with a hot iron; his mouth hung open, grasping for words. I would see anger, fear, disgust, grief, *anything* just splash across his eyes in a split second. I waited for it.

But he just looked confused.

This is why we don't learn their names, he said. *Whoever David Stein was, he has passed on and you needn't have gotten involved.*

What?

I know you look at them now. You become too familiar with them. You eat with them and hold their hands and stand next to them while they go through doors instead of doing the job you are supposed *to be doing: ferrying them. They are dead, Nera. There's no more for them to do but to cross into the world-to-come—*

Father, stop it. He loved you, I said. He looked at me, as if he was lost and only wanted to find his way back to me. *You're not lying,* I realized.

No, Nera, what are you talking about?

Elbee showed me the Archive of Dead Things. I pulled out the journal. *This is David's.*

Father's eyes flitted over the journal, then to the door ahead of him. Then to his old boots. Then to the ceiling. Not once did he look at me. *I believe I know what this is all about,* he said.

Yes, you told Elbee not to tell me until you were gone. Why?

No, I . . . Nera, I don't know why. He said it with a shakiness to his voice; not anger, or even shame. It cut me short. *Alright, it's probably best I tell you. No harm in it I suppose. I just . . . didn't want you to worry about me.*

I stared at him.

I . . . he started. *I want you to know that I am alright, and I have always been alright. There's no need to worry.*

You're scaring me. Maybe I didn't want to know.

David, he said, *he must be the boy I used to know. And he was killed in the Fire.* He composed himself. *Come,* he said. *Follow me into the room.*

I did.

He opened the paper door to the right.

The worst day.

We entered the blank white pages. They did not stick to nothing, like they had with me.

Paint and ink swarmed the empty spaces of the room like tidal waves.

All around us. A fire. And I saw a young man, my father? He stared up at something horrific behind us.

I turned around and there, where the door had been, was a monster.

A jittering static blot of smoke and bone and ink and sinew and blood and fire. It was just a memory, but the hairs on my skin stood straight in a mortal, primal fear I'd never known. A black hole of a . . . *thing* . . . kept moving every time I blinked, every time I twitched a finger, every time I thought I knew where it was, its head moved, its legs elongated, its arms shrank or cracked at the elbow or straightened like a mannequin. It vibrated with the intensity to hunt, hurt, and feast. It yearned to rip me from the inside out. No mercy to shatter my bones, because it knew I deserved it.

A thing in the dark.

Then I heard the younger shadow of my father scream out a name. David.

Into the fire, beyond the demon, I saw a young man with brown hair, wearing a rumpled black suit, his eyes wide and bloodshot. David reached out to Jonathon . . . screaming for him.

That thing in the dark between them.

The fire made David disappear.

Then it *all* disappeared. Just a white paper room once more, like a disposable glove.

This room, Father said. *It is the only thing I can see, because it's my worst moment. My worst day. Everything else . . .* Out of an old pocket in his vest, he pulled a small wad of papers. And he said, *This is all I have, of my life before. I don't remember David. I don't remember the Fire. Because there was something so painful in what happened out in the living world, beyond the Station . . . in order to continue existing, I had to wash it away.* His hands shook. He unfolded the paper and read, *If you are reading this, you won't remember anything before stepping back into the ferry. You have drank from the lake near the Veil. And so you have forgotten who you were in life. I give you this clean slate, because of the boy you lost in the Fire. And the Station that needs your light.*

I stared at him.

Near the Veil, on the lake, he told me, *if you put your head under and let the water in, you forget.*

Father hadn't kept things from me. He didn't remember. Whatever had happened to him before had been so terrible, he had to let it leave him.

Father didn't know David; he only knew this secondhand memory of David's death.

I wanted to know why these letters didn't want me to use the Memory Room, he said. *So I did. I suppose I'm like my daughter in that way.* He touched me on the shoulder, gently. *Curious and strong-headed.*

I reached to feel his hand. Still numb. Still trapped in this in-between.

And this is your worst memory, I said. *The only memory you can see?*

Well, Father said. *I can see my happiest day as well. The day I found you.* He looked sadly to the blank paper. *That thing . . .* my father said, pointing to the white room. *That thing is the demon that caused the Fire. This thing in the dark, it reaches out, finding the worst parts of us—not only the dead, but the living as well. The dead it infects, turns them into Haunts. And the living, it possesses them, burns them. It wants only destruction.* Father was nothing but cold. I worried the lighthouse was flickering again. *It's not only the dead I've been protecting, Nera. It's all of us. The whole city. Living and dead.*

All of us.

Just like Edna had said.

Father took my hand. *Come,* he said.

He took me up to the lighthouse. We climbed the winding staircase without losing our breath. We stepped out beside the lamp, then out to the balcony. It was cold. He pointed out to the city. And there, I saw it. The scourge of a cloud, like locusts made of smoke. It reached its fingers out to the city but its center circled something near the Hancock.

The notes I wrote myself tell me the story of how I trapped the thing in the dark, he said. *But the demon doesn't only take the dead. It killed David. It set this city on fire, real fire. Like the stone, the living world can fall. The lighthouse is not only to protect the dead. I fear another fire may happen, and this time, no one will be left to rebuild. Nera,* he said, his hands rigid at his side as he turned to lock eyes with me. *Nera, I am afraid the demon may be able to return.*

The lighthouse flickered like a threat.

Not only the Haunts eating souls, but the living as well. Everyone in Chicago.

And not only the Haunts, but the demon itself.

I felt like I was going to drop through the floor and slam into the stone paths below. I stared at the smog beyond. *So . . . you are handing me this Station, knowing all this. You . . . you were just going to walk away and let me handle it?*

It's why I am handing it to you, Nera. I'm not strong enough any longer. I'm sorry. I was supposed to be enough. I . . . I gave everything to be enough.

My heart broke.

Please, forgive me, Nera, he whispered.

I took his hand and pulled him closer for an embrace; a real embrace. I wanted him to register my warmth. I wanted him to remember what it was like, to embrace another.

But he just stood there, ethereal and numb. I couldn't even feel his arms.

But I did feel something deeper. His heart, radiating out that light that had kept us safe for so long.

A warmth. A faint, but still very alive, warmth.

I tried, he said. *I tried so hard.*

He had loved David. And he loved me.

He didn't dislike Charlie. If he disliked her, the lighthouse could not shine. He was afraid of Charlie. Because whatever he had seen out in the city, the nightmares had outweighed anything else. There had been cruelty. Enough cruelty to fuel a thing from the dark.

He had taught me that light. Now it was my turn to wield it.

It had to be.

Even if it meant no one would be here with me, or come after me. If this was my forever. Or if someday, I'd find another to take my place and I'd slip away without anyone remembering me. Without any memories to see in the paper room.

He had been so alone for so long.

Something in my heart roared like its own fire.

I would die in all the ways one can, if I could not step out into the living.

Promise me, you won't leave, he begged me.

I didn't know if I could keep that promise. The city was full of Haunts, the heinous thing in the dark lurking somewhere, trapped in between the buildings and waiting, pulsing with rage to escape. But the skyscrapers' windows still glowed like stars in a galaxy. The cars still kept their pilgrimage beside the lake. Each one of those flashes of light was a life. And Charlie's life was so bright, I imagined it filling up Chicago until the light ran over into the lake.

It was all so very close.

I could live. Even if it meant I spent the rest of my existence here, for at least one day, I could live.

But still I said, *I promise.*

REMNANTS

Your father was a good man. Your mother was a kind woman. Your brother was a mensch. They are all dead by now. Your home burned in the Fire. Look forward. You were brave. You know what you're doing.

And always trust the dogs.

—Excerpt from a letter to the ferryman

27

CHARLIE

Winter gave me more night and less sun.

That meant more fun time in the Station and less depressing time in that shitty apartment.

Further from Dad, closer to Nera.

Nera needed me. "It turns out," she said, "the lighthouse isn't only protecting the dead. But it's also protecting the living in the city. Father hadn't told me everything."

"Surprise there," I muttered.

Nera screwed up her face. "He's trying, Charlie. We all are." She looked up to the lighthouse above us. "Your music is so important. I'm so glad you're here."

I was glad, too, Nera.

I wish I could have told Sam about how Nera made me feel. Nera was undeniable, and I had these feelings I'd never had before. Sam would be happy for me, I think. And when I found her, I'd tell her and . . .

In the Station, Sam's sheet music existed and even if no one could decide whose memory built the piano . . . there was a chance. And there was Nera. As soon as I stepped outside, though . . .

One morning, I grabbed my backpack and headed through the pillars. A car on the LSD backfired. Pop. Bang. The floodgates in my brain opened.

Sam ran from the popping sound. I lost her in the panic.

I could find her, or I could take cover.

The door to the break room opened. A woman with a red purse reached out her hand for me. "Come on, come on," she mouthed through the bedlam.

I took her hand. She yanked me into the dark. The door slammed.

They locked it behind me. I was the last one on the lifeboat.

We sat in the dark, screams and shadows flying past in silhouettes on the wall from the light in the door's window.

If Sam didn't find her own room, what the fuck was going to happen to her?

The door rattled.

I didn't see his face.

Just the shadow of a man in a tight cap. The way he shook as he tugged on the door so hard, I thought the hinges might crack and give. Just a millisecond, then unable to get in, he moved on. I didn't see his eyes. I didn't see his nose or his mouth. To me, he was not much more than a specter.

If the door had stayed unlocked, would he have gotten us instead of Sam and the others he found? If I hadn't hidden, could I have found her and gotten her under a desk or outside or *something*?

I didn't deserve to be in the land of the living without her.

———————

I did not go home that next morning. Instead, I asked Nera if she would like to see a movie with me. Two or three extra hours with Nera wouldn't hurt anything. Even then I knew it was a mistake, but I did it anyway. Story of my life.

The movie theater sat in the corner of this second floor-slash-mezzanine. I was slowly putting together a blueprint in my head of the Station. From what I gathered, the main floor with the atrium was huge and full of doors and the docks. The second level had a balcony and all the big set pieces like the diner, the movie theater. Above was the hotel on the third level, then above *that* was Nera and Harosen's private quarters surrounding the really tall lighthouse that jutted over all of it.

This place kept its shape but spatially made no sense. Like, for example, this was a tiny marquee with some curtains. But when we walked into the theater itself, there were multiple screening rooms and a whole-ass concession stand.

All the staples of Americana cinema that made a neighborhood theater familiar and yet unique. The scratchy eighties carpet, the walls shaking with the sound systems booming action movies. Sticky kernels stuck in the sole of my shoe.

"Is this what a movie theater is like?" Nera asked me.

"Yeah," I said. "Marco, Sam, and me, we'd go to midnight movies in a theater that looked a little smaller than this but still . . . was this." A culmination of everyone's recollections as they had walked through here. Little plastic straws sitting out on the pop fountain, a sticker-for-a-quarter dispenser—

What do you wanna see? the dog behind the counter asked. *Oh, uh Nera, listen, I can explain—*

It was Shawny.

"Shawny, why are you at the concession stand!" Nera said.

Listen, I just like food! I'm weak, Nera, I'm weak!

I laughed. "Shawny, can we watch a movie?"

"I said no more getting near the—"

We've got every film ever made! Every film in production! As long as someone here has seen enough of at least the dailies, we got it!

Milk Duds, Pop-ity Popcorn, come an' get it! Daisy jumped onto the counter, and nudged a popcorn bucket my way. I also grabbed a big cardboard cup full of pop.

"Don't encourage them," Nera said to me.

———————

We chose *Casablanca*. Nera was so excited. Seeing her tiny smile when she tasted the popcorn made me feel like maybe this was important, too. We sat in a theater all to ourselves. Her skirt somehow fit into her small, sticky seat. I sat cross-legged beside her. There was something calming about not being in here alone. She stood guard at my side to keep me safe. She could try to protect me from that deep pit in my stomach, and she would probably fail, but I still believed somehow she could.

"Comfy?" I asked her. She nodded.

"Oh, oh yes."

Then a spirit walked in, popcorn in hand. A younger woman with jet-black roots covered in some dye that now in gray scale just looked bright. It was cut off and swoop-cut to the side. Sixties badass. She wore bellbottoms, big sunglasses, and her T-shirt had a logo of a roller derby team: Chicago Westerners.

Hey, she said. *Station Master's kid and the girl at the piano. Welcome to my weekly showing of* Casablanca. Her thick southside accent stretched out "Caa-saa-bLAAN-caa" and I heard my dad in that sound.

"Sorry if we're disturbing you," Nera offered.

Nah, nah, stick around. It's a good flick. She popped some popcorn in her mouth and took a seat, her sneakers kicked up on the backrest in front of her. *I'm Red.*

"Hello, Red," Nera said.

Mom had loved this movie. Sam and I took her to see it for Mother's Day a couple of years ago. She'd come into town and we'd gone to that theater Edna mentioned off Diversey. I knew the one.

"Do you think Mom likes me?" I had asked Sam as we nervously readied for her arrival.

"Of course," Sam said. She fluffed a pillow on the couch that she had already fluffed like five times. "She's just like a cat, you know? Sometimes when things bother cats, they sort of curl inside themselves. You and me, we're like . . . bears. But she's a cat."

I wish I'd asked her what she meant by us being bears. Another answer I'd never get. "It doesn't bother you she's a cat?"

Sam shrugged. "You can't change who someone is."

Or what someone does.

Here in the Station, I felt Nera's warmth. I believed in the possibility of Sam still existing. Like any moment, Sam would be sitting next to me watching this movie, scooping out a handful of popcorn and eating it daintily from her palm. She would say, "Nera, huh? I like your boots."

And Nera would say—

Well, what'd you girls think?

I blinked. Red was staring right at me. The movie was over, and I'd missed most of it.

"Huh?" I said.

I said, what'd you girls think?

Nera waited for me to answer. But she realized we were waiting for her opinion, and she said, "Oh! I . . . feel like there's a lot I don't understand. I didn't know it was going to be that sad. But it was also happy?"

"Happy?!" I sputtered.

"The main character isn't hiding anymore," she said. "He's going to be brave and help."

There's sad and happy in every goodbye and hello, Red said. *He's just got another way of being now, you know? Anyway, I like it.* She looked at me, then to Nera, then between us. *Ah, you two are sweet. Reminds me of me and my old gal, Birdie.*

I followed Red's gaze. Our arms touched on the same little armrest. My wrist laid limp over hers, comfortable, like it had been there for centuries.

And neither of us moved away.

When the sun finished coming up, I decided to stay.

It was a quiet choice. Nera needed to see her father about something, and she told me to meet her in the front. I meandered. Back to the hall of windows. Back through the diner and the long corridors in the hotel. It was peaceful here. A nice quiet vacation, off the shoreline and in its own world. I think that's when I decided.

I stood in the atrium, daring someone to ask me why I was staying. Nera, with her lantern at the ready, was prepped to walk me out. I did not follow.

She turned to me. "Are you coming?"

"Yeah no," I said. "I'm gonna stay here."

"What? Why?"

Why should I go? I said. *There's nothing left out there.*

Nera's eyes grew wide like I'd grown a second head. I bugged my own eyes out at her and shrugged. *Okay?* I said.

"Charlie," she said, "you aren't talking out loud."

I waited for the adrenaline of fear or surprise to course through me. But I felt . . . nothing. Like I'd taken way too much NyQuil.

It was that moment where you realize your body breathes on its own, and then it immediately stops because you're aware of it, and then you're panicking because you need to force your lungs to breathe—

Oh God.

"Calm down," she said. "Breathe. Remember to breathe. In. Out." She was already shoving me to the entrance.

No no no, I said. *I told you I'm staying here.*

"You can't," she said, and her voice sounded like it was getting stuck on the jagged edges of that word: can't.

I can't.

"I'll just remember to speak in my outside voice!"

But we were at the entrance already. And she didn't want to throw me out; my sane and rational brain knew this. But my basic animal brain went: Fuck you, fuck you, you're throwing me out!

"Take me out of the city, Nera."

"Remember what you told me about the city?" she said. "It's worth experiencing. It's not all bad."

"If it's not all bad," I said, now very evicted for the day, "then why won't you come with me?"

She hesitated. Her arm dropped.

"Thought so," I said. Then I turned from her and passed the fountain.

"Charlie?" she said.

I heard her boots clacking. Then stop. I turned back around. She stood at the edge of the fountain.

"Charlie, I want you here," she said. "I just don't want you to forget to live. Please come back tonight, when the sun is down. That seems to be safer."

"It's fine. I get it, Nera." I stormed out.

Back into winter. My heart raced. My head hurt. My shoes hit the pavement. Alive. Alive. Stuck in alive.

There is an eerie sound to heavy snow. Its coat muffles, so there is no echo. Behind our apartment building was a thick two-story-long icicle hanging off the fire escape. The wind blew through the alley. The rats scattered, but still watched from behind the dumpsters.

You're right.

The thing in the dark oozed through my ears and mind.

You don't deserve to live. You didn't even see his face, and she must have. You were safe. You're alive. She is not. A life for a life, I suppose. Does Nera know how much of a coward you are?

"Shut the fuck up," I growled for the hundredth time.

The Station Master's daughter has given you nothing, just as I warned. Are you ready to ask me if I've seen her? Or do you not want to know?

That hit me. The cold dug into my bones. If she was part of the Haunts, then this thing would know. They were his tentacles.

Ask me, Charlie.

I pushed the knob and the big green metal door scraped against the concrete of the apartment complex's insides.

"I don't trust you as far as I can throw you," I muttered, storming to the stairwell.

But you trust Nera. She's done so much for you, yes? How many nights have you gone there and helped her? And how many of those nights has she found you a speck of Sam Connor? Only the half a song that brought you there, am I right? Only the piano you found. Charlie, humans are selfish. She knows as soon as you find Sam, she'll never see you again. Or worse for her, you'll join your sister. As long as you keep searching, you keep searching with her.

My floor. I burst out of the stairwell. I ran to the window that looked out to the lake from the hall. I pulled out my phone, flipped it open, raised the antenna, dialed 2, and pressed myself to the windowpane for signal.

2 is speed dial for Marco. And what is 1? 1 leads to Sam, doesn't it? The number that will never answer again. Unless you do something about it this time, Charli—

"Hello?" Marco answered almost immediately. It was morning, he should sound like he just rolled out of bed. Instead, he sounded like he hadn't gone to sleep at all. "Are you okay?"

No. "Yeah," I said. "Just . . ." what the hell do I say? "Just talk to me. Tell me something."

Marco didn't hesitate, he didn't question it. There is a shared language between the grieving. "I did laundry yesterday. I read somewhere that if you shower, do laundry, or comb your hair, your body will feel more normal. So I did. I think you should, too, if you need to."

I had not brushed my hair in a bit. But maybe I could still feel normal.

"Can I tell you good news?" I said.

"Of course."

"I'm gay."

Marco gave a laugh and an aww. Happy. I relaxed.

"Her name is—"

Then there was a crackling.

"Charlie?" he said, through the static. And the phone was dead.

I stared at it. Shaking. I caught something in the corner of my eye through the windowpane. I looked up through the glass. There, mirroring me, was a Haunt, several stories up and leaning in on the sill, its static, blank white eyes staring back through my reflection.

I stumbled back.

The voice from far away hissed so close.

How dare you two laugh.

The sun once again started to set around 4:30. I had spent my day in my room, sleeping. And finally, I gained enough momentum to stand up and look in the mirror.

Is this who Nera saw when she saw me?

I grabbed my brush and tugged it through my knotted hair. I pulled a tunic dress over some long leggings, shoved on my boots, and wrapped a coat around me. It was never any temperature in the Station; always just a straight climate that wasn't too hot, never too cold, like standing next to the lake on the last day of spring. I could take my coat off when I got there, and hopefully this little flowered tunic stretchy dress thing was cute enough.

I hadn't really thought about what I was wearing for a year. And Marco was right, it was nice.

I texted him with my charged phone, thnx 4 the tip. brushed my hair. +1 point me.

He wrote back immediately, lol glad. hey wats her name?

I typed her name out for him. Nera.

Nera, he wrote back. sounds cute.

I looked down the hall and the fake parquet floor to see Chestnut curling up with Dad on the couch, watching *The Daily Show* on TV. The audience on the TV laughed. Dad didn't. But he was watching it, not just staring at the wall. He'd gone through the steps of turning it on, picking out something he'd like, and then committing to watching it. But he wasn't eating anything. There were just a bunch of beer cans on the coffee table.

Dad muttered something as I made my way to the door through the long narrow hall. "Huh?" I said.

He snapped out of his own world for a second, stroking Chestnut between the ears. Dad said, "You brushed your hair."

"I did," I said.

He didn't say anything else. I couldn't tell if he was glad I was dressing nice, or if it worried him. If I was brushing my hair again, wearing clean clothes, and heading out with purpose, would that mean I would come back? Or would I finally disappear like everyone else?

I zipped up my coat. There was life on the other side of that bridge. I wanted to go back to the Station where I belonged, with the music . . .

You didn't find her, Charlie. You let him down.

Wasn't Chestnut supposed to shut him up?

He wasn't in here or at the window, so Chestnut must be doing his job. Or maybe Chestnut was more invested in *The Daily Show* than helping me, and what was I gonna do, throw a sock at him? Say, "Hey dog, do your job"?

> **You know I'm right. You found nothing but a song. Are you a selfish, cowardly liar, just like the rest of the living? You're going to give up because it makes you feel better.**

"I'm off," I said.

Dad looked back at me, Jon Stewart cracking jokes behind him. Chestnut was still very invested.

"What's he like?" Dad said, as if in a trance. "Charon?"

He was in this wacky world with me, where maybe we were just making the whole thing up.

"He's . . . sort of sad?" I said. Dad didn't cock his head. He didn't say anything in response. He just waited for more. "His name's Harosen. He's old. Grumpy. But like, always about to cry. Especially when he looks at Nera."

"Who's Nera?" Dad said.

Nera is brilliant, Dad. Nera is too alive to be the ferryman of the dead.

I hope, Dad, that someday she follows me here and she can be a real person in my real life.

I'd wanted to sink into her world and never return here. But I can't. So maybe she can sink into mine. We could step into the future together. When she's ready, she will come—

> **Nera says a lot and does little.**

Nera wasn't a liar, but maybe Nera was naïve? Maybe Nera believed she could do things she couldn't do.

A lot of people say they can do things, and then they give up. They don't think they're strong enough, even if they are, and they can't find their way through the path to find the end.

> **This was not a story for you and Nera. This was supposed to be about Sam. But it was always about Sam, wasn't it? You, the younger sister. He wrote a song all for her and nothing for you. He wishes you were the one who was destroyed.**

In the hospital, he'd seen me barely touched. He'd grabbed me hard by the shoulders. "Why did you leave her?" he said, too loud. "You hid without her!"

If it had been you, would Sam have searched? If it had been you, would the family be broken?

Sam wouldn't have searched, because she always ran away. Our whole lives, she needed bailing out, needed support, needed needed needed, and . . . no, that wasn't fair.

Alright, Charlie, but you'd been looking for her all this time and where was she?

My head spun.

Dad now said to me, "Is Nera the one who said she'd help you find Sammy?"

"Well," I said. "Yeah."

"Did you find her?"

I stopped. "No." And then, "Not yet."

Dad swallowed, his eyes downcast. "You know," he said, "water can be terrifying. One time, when I was in LA, I saw a tourist drive down a boat ramp and into the ocean. The whole car went under. They warn you, when you go close to the coast, to look out for undertows. They'll sweep you away and drown you, make you part of the vast unknown." He just stared at me. "What happens when you spend too much time near the river Styx?"

I clenched my jaw. I wanted to say, What do you care? If I disappeared, like her, you would still be so weighed down by her absence you would have no more room in your chest to hold mine.

"You forget," I said.

Dad nodded. "You forget. For all the time you spend near the Underworld, you forget why you're there."

It slapped me.

Dad turned back around to what was now a commercial for ShamWow. A painfully normal thing on the coastline of mythos and madness. I was failing him.

I felt my jaw ache with how much my teeth clenched.

Chestnut looked over the couch at me.

Something grabbed at my eyes, making them water. Dad could have hugged me. One of those bear hugs. I needed one. So bad.

The silence was so cutting, I wished even the thing in the dark would fill it. But no one came to my rescue.

"Daddy?" I said softly. "I wish I was enough."

Dad said nothing. A cold, soulless nothing. Those bear hugs had always felt like he would never let go, but he'd let go so quick I couldn't find my footing.

It was just me here in this room. And sometimes, people die before they're dead. Sometimes they can't be who they were. They're worse than ghosts.

They're Haunts.

I slammed the door behind me.

The snow came down, like a silent swarm of sharp knives. The quieter it fell, the colder it got. And then the wind picked up.

I saw the Haunts and the rats in the alleys, watching.

I felt him, the thing in the dark, up against my neck, curling in deep to my spinal cord, making my body shiver and buzz.

I swatted at my neck.

"Piss off back to your hole," I hissed.

The Haunts hissed back.

You keep waiting for the wrong people to save you.

The snow swirled thicker. I couldn't see the Red Line anymore, above. White blinded me, and I stepped into the alley to try to get away from the gusts off the lake. I shivered.

And I felt a stab in my skull.

I heard an engine pop.

Gunshots sound like little pops.

My entire body, frozen. I couldn't think, my heart was going to explode. Adrenaline pumped through me. My body couldn't hold me anymore. I was going to die.

But I hadn't died. And maybe that was worse.

Lying there on the floor of the mall's break room, I made peace with the idea I wouldn't be leaving. As long as it didn't hurt, I could just let go.

A void my body could not fathom nor hold, like a deep black hole in my small galaxy, sucking up everything in its path—all her songs, all her strands of hair and her laugh, and every note she had ever written for me to sing—I screamed, all of it flooding inside me. Alone. I was alone.

Stop trusting the wrong people, Charlie.

If I lay in the snow long enough, I would find my way to her. Through the Veil. Into the Haunts. Or wherever else had opened up and swallowed her.

Charlie! a voice sounded out.

I looked up. There was Runa. The big dog. Her eyes glowed bright in the snow. Like two little lanterns.

Charlie, she said, *do you need help?*

I shivered. And I grabbed onto Runa's fur.

We walked out of the alley together.

28

THE JOURNAL OF DAVID STEIN

Jon is furious with me.

Last night, the man who died was not done with his life.

He held onto me, tight, begging for my help.

He was older than us, but so much younger than most of those who passed. He was so scared. And I wanted to listen to him, I wanted to help, but he just kept getting angrier and worse and I didn't know what to do.

Jon put his hands out and shouted, "Stop it!"

Light erupted from his fingers.

I collapsed, life drained from me. I felt tired, naked, like stepping out from the water. And I gasped for air, looking up to Jon above me.

He was afraid. He looked to his hands. Then to me. Then to the ghost of the man standing behind me.

"You stay away from him," Jon warned the dead man.

With another push of light, Jon threw the ghost from the room. Far away. All night, the man did not come back.

I hope his dog found him.

"What was that?" I asked Jon. And Jon did not know. He looked to his hands.

"I . . . was scared for you," he said.

I do not know how some men see ghosts and others don't. I do not know how Jon can light up a room. But I wonder if we believe in ghosts, we may believe in light, and then we may believe in dogs and demons and like a fabric unraveling with a loose thread, we see it all.

Then it happened again on the way home. Something in me was humming with the world, open to the realms we may not see when we are not paying attention. Something sat in the corner of my eye.

It was not human. It had no body, no soul. It was more like dust, lint stuck behind furniture that you find during the spring clean before Pesach.

It ran for me.

Jon brought his light out again.

So by the end of the night, we decided to simply call it light. It could easily be called a weapon, but I will call it a light.

Light is something for protection, something in your heart that you can center yourself in. A love for a life. Some force inside, and Jon can shove it forward through his bones and out into the space of air between me and whatever schmutz I need to rid myself of.

My heart is also strong, I tried to explain to him. There is strength in letting the unknown in.

He chastises me as if I am a child. "Are you trying to lose yourself?"

I promise him I will not let someone else come into my realm.

But he closes himself off to so many who need him. He cannot even be my partner in the daylight. And I am beginning to think, I was wrong about him and his courage. Perhaps he truly is a coward.

29

NERA

I promise. I promise.

I promise, I said to Father. I promise, I *lied* to Father.

I had never not known what I was going to do next.

I walked down to the cinema and tried to distract myself with a new film. *It's a Wonderful Life.* I invited Edna and Red to meet me there.

The lights dimmed as I joined them in the theater. *Ah ha,* Edna said. *Three Jews in the audience of four for the Christmas movie.* Edna looked around. *Or maybe just two in three . . . Charlie isn't here. I suppose it's not nighttime?*

No, I said. *She spends the sunlight in the city.*

Red blurted out, *Good. She shouldn't be here in the ghost world watching old movies.*

I felt my hands ball into fists. I just wanted one moment where I didn't feel this tugging, burning worry in me. She had to live life. I had to stay here and protect the dead.

Red looked tired. She pulled out a cigarette and a lighter from her sleeve. She took in a deep sucking breath.

When she breathed out, nothing came.

I don't think you should be here either, sweetheart, Red said, looking at the cigarette that could have been a prop in a film. *A lotta people in here would give their two legs and an arm to step back in the city. What are ya doing here?*

That's absolutely right, Edna agreed, her words pressing in my head. *Nera, this river has a strong current in one direction. And the more time she spends sitting with death, the more time she gives it. You know? Same goes for you.*

I knew.

As my father continues to remind me, I said, *I have a duty here.*

Edna patted my hand. *It will be okay, sweetheart. You'll figure it out.*

What have I figured out, Edna?

Edna squeezed my hand. I wished I could feel it. *You may have only just started watching us. But we have always watched you. From when you were a little girl. He named you Nera for a reason. You are a miracle of a light. A girl who lives among the dead, a woman who will heal the city.*

He named me Nera because he found me in the winter and he was holding a lantern, I said blandly. *And I am not good at healing Charlie, so I doubt I'm going to heal the whole of Chicago. Can I please watch the film now?*

Edna studied me, then took her hand from mine to leave me be. She nodded to herself. *You are also your father's daughter. Stubborn.*

The night fell again, and I watched for Charlie to return. The snow gathered speed and blew sideways. The dogs pushed against it, leading the souls. The fountain still let out clear, unfrozen water into a mist and somehow it still transformed the ghosts, but not even the city could be seen through the haze. It was so dark.

And if I couldn't see the city, Charlie may not see the Station.

A fatigued older woman with curly hair stepped beyond the pillars, wearing a beautiful sari. She looked like she'd been crying, but the dead can't cry. She also looked out to the storm.

Are you alright? I asked her.

She looked to me. *I'm dead,* she said flatly.

I'm sorry, I said.

You didn't do it, she said. She sighed, pressing her hands on her stomach. *Now where do we go from here?*

This way. Her dog nudged her beyond me and my little lantern and the four pillars.

Did you see my children, when you came to get me? she asked her dog guide. *They looked good, didn't they.*

Oh yes, the dog said. A beautiful golden doodle.

I taught them how to dress right, she said. *I taught them how to take care of each other.*

I turned back from the warm light behind me. I looked out to the storm. I wanted to feel the cold. I wanted to step out to the fountain and be part of this storm.

Then I saw her.

Charlie held onto Runa's fur as Runa guided her blindly through the snow. Runa was bounding in the cold like a happy dog, but Charlie shivered, folding in on herself, her hair caked in white and her coat pulled over her face. I wished I could take the cold from her.

"Charlie!" I shouted out, and Runa trotted her to me, where I took her cold hand and led her in. Charlie said nothing.

The Station had become a safe haven for her, while the city seemed to be the haunted place.

But tonight felt different.

Other dogs pattered past us, all nodding a *good evening* to me, with their tongues lolling out. The smell of good food floated through the atrium. I hoped she could feel the warmth, hear the laughs. Nothing could hurt us here.

"I am so glad Runa helped you," I said. "I didn't know how bad the storm would be. I—"

"I'm not playing that piano anymore," she said, venomous. "Not until you give me my sister."

"Charlie, I'm trying."

"You promised me, Nera." Her red-rimmed eyes met mine from under her damp hair. She pulled the coat off her, snow falling to the ground and disappearing before it hit the marble. "You said you'd help me find her. And all we've done is dick around and find nothing. So come on, Station Master, show me *something*. Give me *something*. Or find someone who can!"

"Charlie, I don't know how," I said.

"You've been lying to me then."

"No, I would never."

"She's not here, is she?"

"I don't know."

"There's her piano, there's her life, but where is *she*?! Where is the rest of her song, Nera?"

"I don't know!"

"No one here knows!" She narrowed her eyes. "When the living spend too much time in the land of the dead, they forget why they went there in the first place. And you want me to forget, don't you?"

"What? N-no!"

"I wish I could trust you."

The words hit like a knife through my spirit.

"Nera?" I heard my father's voice coming down the stairs.

The lighthouse flickered.

"Of course you can trust me!" I said.

"The Haunt things." She breathed heavy between her words. "They follow me. There's one, a thing in the dark, it says it can help me . . ." She trailed off.

I felt a new sensation of my body turning against me, my spine on fire, my stomach under my fingertips clenching and twisting. I tried to digest her words. But they were too acidic.

"A thing in the dark," I muttered. "No, Charlie, that's a *demon*. My father trapped it. He wants to burn the city to the ground! You can trust me over a *literal demon!*"

Charlie bit her lip, her eyes glassy. She still could cry, because she was still alive. She looked up at me, her brow knitted, her face about to crack. "I wish I could."

The atrium rattled.

A hissing.

A shake.

Then something crawled out of the wall.

REMNANTS

break away from me.
make the world crash down around me
like broken stained glass.
a prayer you couldn't finish.
you do not deserve to cry.
you could set this right.
but that would mean the fight would begin again.
the fire would rage.
the city would fall.
but something must ignite.
i am left with nothing. you are left with less.
and once you are gone
she will feel the weight of your unfinished, broken life.
what if,
a hundred years from now,
we are all sitting in the dark,
praying to no one?

—writings from a thing in the dark

30

NERA

Static ripped the seams between two bricks above the front entrance. It shoved in and bled through, like mold. Then a long snout with two big teeth wriggled through the little space, then big eyes, scratching claws . . . a rat.

It jumped out of the wall and dove for the ground. Then another rat scraped through, then another and another—

Then they erupted in a wave.

And each brick they touched, sucked dry of light. Static.

"Elbee!" I shouted. I threw Charlie behind me as I rushed forward.

The dogs piled into the atrium, surrounding the rats. Elbee growled, flanked by Hermes and Happy. All their hackles raised along their backs. Elbee's tail went straight, and Hermes and Happy stood rigid. Elbee bared his teeth, lips wrinkling, shifting his face from a soft friend to a fierce warning.

Elbee lunged forward with a sharp, booming bark. Roo-Roo-Roo-Roo. The other dogs followed him. They jumped on the rats, their teeth snapping bones and tearing skin. Dogs of the Underworld, knowing the full extent of what it meant to guard.

But the rats fought back. Jumping too fast to follow, they didn't run away. They lunged their claws and teeth right for the dogs' eyes. The dogs charged back, then forward. They circled one another, frozen and ready to pounce again, and then one would flash forward with a screech and the other snarled and they'd lock their teeth into skin.

Runa howled from the top of the stairs and she and Stella leapt down two at a time, screaming at the rats. I saw poor Shawny with Daisy on his back rushing into the battle, Daisy screaming orders and then jumping off Shawny into the fray.

The wave of rats scattered, those who still had legs ran. Elbee did not let up, his fleet chasing the intruders out the door. Some tried to hide in the walls, but the dogs pulled them out and flung them, breaking their necks.

Father now stood on the stairs. His mouth hung open, hands still at his side. The static bricks flickered like a broken television, and blood smeared across the marble floor. This had never happened before, and he did not know what to do. *Elbee*, he said so quietly, his voice wavering.

I looked up to the light above us. It faded, almost completely out.

Then I heard a rat's scream. A dying, begging screech. It was terrible.

Pushed past the pillars! Elbee reported, shouting from outside. *But there's more! There's more!*

I ran forward, pushing Charlie back. "Stay," I pleaded. But she followed me. And through the pillars we entered the winter outside.

The snow had stopped and now the outside stood in an eerie silence.

Every stone on the ground leading up to the Station had turned to static. Only the fountain stood, surrounded by the soil of death. It was just a matter of time.

Father shot toward us and ordered, "Charlie, go play now!" And Charlie ran for the piano. She slammed her hands down on the keys and opened her mouth, singing deep and loud in a belting wave. Guilt rushed through me. She said she wasn't going to play anymore.

The lighthouse flickered.

"Please work," I begged the Station. "We have to trust her."

Then it calmed, like a child trying to breathe after a fearsome sobbing tantrum.

There had been rats in the Station.

The lighthouse glowed again. It would not hold forever. Not like this. Even now, it was scared. I was scared.

And from Father's face, I could see he was terrified.

"Nera?" Father said. "I have an assignment for you."

I felt my hand shaking. I walked down the hotel corridor. I saw an old man and an old woman walking hand in hand down the hall.

It's nice when people come together. No one should have to do this alone.

I turned down the corridor corner. The hotel was a maze of carpeted hallways leading to doors. So many people waiting to cross, not yet ready, but needing a place to heal before pressing onward. Or, like Edna, they were waiting to not be the only one here. They were waiting to cross with someone holding their hand.

Some of the corridors donned lavish carpeting. Some were threadbare. The hotel wing resembled a mishmash of all the motels and hotels remembered by those who came through. I had never seen any of them. I had seen all of them.

Ice machines, vending machines, old hand-cranked elevators, gaslights and fluorescent lights and golden dragons and bad watercolors of pastel shapes all made a home away from home.

Edna Meyer lived in a beautiful space of the hotel. Her room looked like where she stayed at the Russell Hotel in London during a trip. Her daughter and son had accompanied her on a journey back to Poland, her first time since the war. London and Poland, both places beyond my map.

It was toward the end of my life, she'd told me. *We sat in the hotel for a few days as I tried to get the gumption to cross the water and go to the continent. I'd not been back for so long, and everyone kept saying, "Mama it's changed, things are different," and I kept saying, "Things don't ever change." But then my daughter finally dragged me out of my room and we went across the street to the park. We sat there, watching people pass. Children eating popsicles. Women strolling and looking up at the changing trees. And I saw that the world . . . the world had somehow kept going.* She had paused. *Maybe things don't change, but some things not changing, that means you can't destroy everything.*

She'd gone across the Channel the next day.

I forced myself across the red carpet, beyond the crown molding of the walls, along the gold outlines, and finally to Edna's hotel room.

I didn't want to do this.

Maybe I could just skip this part, find a way in my brain to shut off and not feel anything. I'd said goodbye to so many people. But Edna was my friend.

I knocked on the door. Because I had to.

She opened the door.

Oh, hello, Nera! she said. *Come on in! Let me get you something to drink! Red was supposed to come by, but she's gone missing, I'm afraid.*

So Red had gotten word that Father was clearing the hotel out. I knew where she would be. The movie theater. But right now . . . right now, I had to be with Edna.

The living room and bed looked like the Russell, but I had a feeling the attached kitchen that did not match must have come from another apartment she'd known. She'd mentioned West Lawn. The kitchen had a lot of plants, and a little television with *Johnny Carson* playing quietly in the background as she rummaged around.

I took a seat on the blue "davenport" as she called it. She brought tea for us both.

Want to watch Charlie Brown's Halloween special with me? she offered, taking up her remote. *It's always a good one. Linus waits all night in that pumpkin patch. I know it's not the season for it, but . . . it's my favorite.*

All I wanted to do was watch television with her. I just wanted to stay here, in this hotel apartment room, and we could just hide here, forever.

But I suddenly realized she was already gone. All of the things surrounding us, they were just memories. They had already been pulled out from the city, from the world. They had already been lost. Now all there was left to do was let go.

"Father sent me to speak to you," I said.

Edna nodded. *What did your papa want? Letting you do all the dirty work now that he's retiring? Well,* she said. *I'm perfectly fine, and I don't need anything and I haven't been bothering anyone.*

"I know," I said. "It's not you, Edna. It's . . . there were rats in the atrium. The fountain is going to go dark."

Edna's cheer turned to stone. *The fountain can't go dark.*

"The Haunts are trying to break through. And if they do, Edna, all the souls here are in danger of being swallowed up. We're evacuating the hotel, because Father thinks the people who have been here longer may be at more risk. If the breach happens."

So you think I'm going to become part of that monster and you want to get rid of me. She looked so sad. So angry. She looked away from me. She set her tea down. *I see,* she said, her voice breathless and old and full of hurt.

I wish I could trust you. That's what Charlie had said, in a voice full of hurt.

"No, no no," I said. "We're afraid *for* you, not of you. I don't want anything to happen to you, Edna. I can't let anything happen to you." I turned to face her. "Edna, can I please help you cross over tonight? I'll hold your hand. We can do it together."

But you see, Nera, Edna said, *we can't do it together. Because it's not your time to go. And I'm already gone.* She looked around the apartment. *This apartment . . . I raised my granddaughter in the apartment that belongs to that kitchen. Her mother was alone in the world and needed somewhere to go, so they came here. We named her together. Just us three, living in a one-bedroom. Until my granddaughter got older, of course, and my daughter got a new place to live. But I taught her how to read here, at that little green desk over there. I taught her how to play all the board games I had. She took her first steps here. And if . . . either she or my daughter . . . show up here and I'm not . . .* Her words broke, as if she'd gotten stuck. *What will they think of me? How will they know that I . . . didn't ever want to leave . . .*

I pressed my lips together and took a breath. "Maybe, on the other side," I tried, "there are better ways to help them."

Or maybe on the other side there's nothing, she said, deadpan.

Maybe. I honestly couldn't say.

She clutched her armrests with her bare white knuckles. She looked around the room. Like it was already fading. I had expected more of a fight from her. But the spark in her was soft tonight, and it frightened me to see her give up.

I hadn't wanted her to give up.

It was such a lovely dream, she said. *Our years in the apartment. When I was little, I couldn't have imagined such a lovely dream. My . . . my family . . . when my girls were living with me, I was always so afraid I'd wake up and they'd be gone and this apartment would be gone and I'd be back in my barracks . . .* She lowered her head. *It was such a lovely dream.*

I touched her hand softly. And she looked at me.

Then she looked away, shaking more than she'd shaken before. But no tears.

I'm afraid of the monster. Her voice was so small. *I don't want to go. But I'm afraid. The monster was so big, full of smoke and bones. My mother promised I never had to see it again.*

"I can't go the whole way with you, Edna," I promised, "but I will stick by you until I literally can go no further."

———

She stood at the apartment door one last time.

She brought a suitcase of her things.

Always have a suitcase packed, she said. *That's what we all learned back then.*

We walked down the hall together. Her eyes still wandered back to her door.

When my granddaughter . . . Marcie . . . was little, she said, *she lined up all of her dolls in a row across the living room floor. And she said it was a parade. She was so happy, making them all dance and sing and making floats out of old cardboard boxes.* She smiled. *Just a dolly parade. Nothing else. Just joy.*

We went down the stairs to the atrium, past the piano where Charlie played, and joined the growing crowd filing onto the ferry. I tried not to look at Edna, because then I wouldn't be able to keep going.

And when she was in the second grade, Edna said, *she helped me paint these light-catching glass hummingbirds and we put them up on the sliding glass door that went to the porch. Just like the hummingbirds we'd seen in Colorado.*

We stepped past the red archway, to the dock. And onto the ferry. Father had rounded up the rest of the longtimers. He didn't stand with them. He stood above. Father nodded solemnly to me. I didn't nod back.

She always wanted to go to London, Edna said. *And I hope she made it.*

The ferry pulled out from the Station. Edna looked out at the city as it shrank.

There was no turning back now.

I felt as if I might not come back, either.

Edna gripped my hand. I knew there would be no more hugs from her, no more conversations. We were at the end of a long story, now reading the last page, and knowing it was worse than over: it was almost over. That space in the in-between of everything happening, and everything being a memory.

Please, I said to no one, *don't make me say goodbye.*

The ferry stopped.

Edna did not let go of my hand.

I followed her to the plank, the dogs around us, the other souls around us.

She held me tight.

And I held her.

There's no knowing when the final hug is supposed to end. It should never end. But it must.

I love you, very much, she said softly. *You remember their names, Nera. Remember all their names. And honor your own. Nera means light.*

Then Edna Meyer, along with her suitcase of memories and her parades and her London hotels and her Great Pumpkins and all the pancakes in between, glowed bright and stepped through the Veil. All I could see of her was a ripple, then nothing.

I stepped down, back onto the boat in a haze. Father scooped me near him with his arm around my shoulder. He pulled me in. And I let him.

"I warned you," he said. "It's too hard to say goodbye. So don't say hello to begin with."

But I would say hello to Edna a thousand more times even knowing it meant saying goodbye forever.

There was something in me, and it was burning up and it was coming into my head and then I felt it.

Tears.

I gave a loud sob.

Father grew rigid. He looked down at his shirt. It was wet. I had cried on him. And he looked at it like it was poisonous.

"No," he said. "What is happening?" His voice was shaking. "Nera, what is this?"

"I think . . . I'm crying, Papa," I said.

Father pulled me further away from the line going through the Veil, one by one, each one with different pairs of eyes their mother had made them, different colors of their soul that had danced to music . . . He leaned down to my face and tried to wipe away my tears like he could erase them. "We can't cry . . ." he mumbled to himself.

No, the dead can't cry.

"Oh, my Nera, do you see what all this is doing to you? Oh God—"

"We don't look them in the eyes, Father," I said.

"Because there are too many eyes to see," he said. "We have a way of surviving this, sweetheart, so this doesn't happen—"

"The way we're doing it clearly isn't working," I said.

"It has worked for a century—"

"They write them on the walls, Father," I said. "The names, the synagogues in the city have all of them memorized. And what about saying kaddish?"

Father stared at me, blankly.

"You don't remember, do you?" My breath shivered cold in my throat. My heart, it hit my ribs again.

Father said nothing.

All of it was gone. Not just David. Not just the demon. But everything.

I pointed out at the Veil, where the others now stepped into the unknown.

"They all have names, Father. They all have to be honored, and loved, not just forgotten." My voice rang with anger, and he pulled away from me.

I saw the line was very short now. And I whipped to him and said, "Her name was Edna, Father. She was waiting for her family to join her! And we should care about that!"

"Fine," Father said. "Then you make friends with all the Ednas, and you can be just like me in a hundred years."

He stormed away to turn the boat back around.

I watched him, tired, turning the helm as I pulled the plank back in and stored it on deck. I felt even sicker. Father wasn't cold; he wasn't worn away. He was empty. But rage still rose up inside me like a fire.

When the city reappeared, it was quiet. The absence of the souls was felt, even with the dogs onboard. The boat felt very big. Then we docked.

"Starbucks," I said as he stepped back into the Station. "It's a coffee shop. They serve coffee there. And there are better coffee places but for some reason everyone goes there anyway! And the person who taught me that, the person I promised to help, I can't help her because I never paid attention to the souls! If we'd known their names, we would know if Sam Connor had been here, and I wouldn't be useless!"

He looked like he was going to say something. But he didn't. He strode away.

"I am speaking to you!" I pursued. "Edna said you used to know their names! You used to watch over them, protect their bodies as their souls let go. You sang to them, you spoke to them, you loved—"

"Do not tell me what I did," Father said. "You have no idea. No journal or ghost is going to tell you who I am."

"Then *you* should tell me! Except you can't, can you?"

Then he *did* stop, and he turned around. I felt something clawing its way up through me, wanting to burst out. I felt my fingers turning to fists. All the ways a body dances with anger. And my father, so still, so emotionless, like a placid lake. "You lived in the city, Papa, before you lived here. You were in love, you were a boy, and you watched the seasons change and felt the snow and had a favorite window and a family. They all did! But you never died, you just locked yourself away! You're still alive!"

"That's what this is about." His voice was gravel. "It's about living in the city." "What?"

"As soon as we fix the lighthouse," he forced his voice through his shaking, "Charlie Connor is gone from here."

The light shuddered above, dangerously, like we'd hit choppy waters.

"You need her." I waved my hand at the lighthouse. "The Station doesn't lie, she helps your light, the music—"

"Stop. Nera. This is beyond . . . *We* don't have tears," he said. "*We* run the Station."

"Well." I stood straight. "You aren't the only one who gets a say in any of that."

But he was right, Charlie would have to leave eventually. I knew that. I'd known that.

We couldn't live here together.

The light shivered again.

He looked at it, frightened, but then looked to me. "Until I have crossed," he said, "this is still my Station. This is still my boat."

"That's not your Veil." I jutted my finger to the lake. "This is bigger than either of us!"

That's when the light gave out completely.

31

CHARLIE

The lighthouse blacked out.

I jumped up in the dark. I reached for one of the lanterns, still lit, hooked to the wall.

The wind blasted. Something outside screamed like a banshee . . . like someone had opened fire outside. A flood of fear, energy flying toward the building, running . . .

The gunshots had gone so fast, one after another, rat-tat-tat-tat-tat—I crawled up the escalator . . . where was she . . .

I hurried to the entrance of the atrium and I shone the light out into the dark. I saw a flock of newly arrived ghosts and dogs trying to run through the fountain and press forward, finding shelter in the Station. It was normal for souls to trickle in at all hours, but with the fountain in danger, things had gotten so much worse, so quickly. My breath caught in my throat.

The stranger held her hand out to me. She yanked me through the door to the break room. There were so many people who ran past. There was someone who pounded on the door after it closed, screaming, "Let me in!"

But tonight, I fought back against the fear and yelled out, "Come on, in here!"

My lantern shot through the shadows and something shrieked beyond. The dogs and souls rushed past me like a hurricane gale, and I fought through the torrent of the dead's fear and shock and grief.

In my narrow light, just beyond the fountain, I caught sight of a large, terrifying curve of a Haunt, made of black shards of glass and static, bleeding rats across the courtyard. It reared up, its mouth open, fingers long and splayed, stomach ripping to show gaping holes of nothingness. It hissed, like a snake locking in on a mouse. It jolted forward, lightning-fast, a wail whistling out of its smoke.

Toward a little ghost girl just trying to make it to the doors . . . she wasn't going to make it.

Back off! Gurty barked, rushing in between the girl and the massive Haunt. He barked again and his collar blazed like a lantern. A stream of light shot out and pierced a hole through the Haunt, and the girl took the chance to run.

The Haunt lashed out at Gurty, and the massive dog yelped. He fell to the side.

"Gurty! No!" I ran forward, my feet thinking before my brain could. I screamed out, and the Haunt looked at me. I dropped the lantern. It crashed. And we sank into darkness.

But I still kept going.

The Haunt recoiled back, then jittered forward.

I grabbed Gurty as best I could. I tried to drag him, but he was too big and heavy. I wasn't leaving him. "Hey, boy, stay with me. It's okay."

Gurty whined, scared. I curled around him.

The Haunt clawed closer. It said nothing. Just shook in and out of focus, limbs flickering then disappearing, eyes multiplying then none, a terrible chimera of the lost and gone, clawing its way through the air to us. And the bricks under its smoky path lost color, jolted, turned wrong. Like sheet music inverted, ripped up, silenced.

It reached out a hand to Gurty. I braced, pulling Gurty closer. I dug my hands and head into his fur.

Then light.

It smashed through the static, and the Haunts squealed and shot backward as if they had placed a hand on a stove.

Nera stood over us, her necklace shining bright.

"Sing," Nera begged. "Charlie, please sing."

I looked past her glow. There was Harosen, hands reached out to us by the pillars. We had to get to him.

I opened my mouth. Singing my father's lullaby to Gurty.

It will be okay someday . . . And light flew out into the world, and the Haunt shrieked and retreated. A glowing, golden sphere encased Gurty and Nera and me.

I was terrified.

The silhouette in the window. The rattling of the door.

I had been so scared. So alone. For three hours we had sat in the dark. I texted my parents, I love you. I texted Marco, is sam ok? I love you. I texted Sam, tell me you're ok. I love you.

My swan song through a small phone. I love you. I love you. I love you.

I wasn't strong enough to save anyone.

The sphere started to fade.

"Charlie, please sing!" Nera cried. The Haunt reached out. It could touch her.

I had to keep trying.

"It will be okay someday."

The Haunts stared at me with those white, empty eyes. Nera's necklace glowed. And far beyond Nera was Harosen, and the lighthouse above us splashed into the dark night, trying, failing to sputter back to life.

The demon had made the fire. The Haunts had tried to hurt the dogs. That silhouette in the window had taken Sam from me. But Nera and I, we still held onto each other. We still believed in the lighthouse.

"Though it don't look that way.

When all other promises wash away

This anthem still will play."

The light roiled forth, shoved itself out, growing to engulf the fountain and the stones and piercing through the fog. The Haunts screeched and scrambled back to the trees and the shadows.

I grabbed Gurty, big Gurty. He cried, his round black eyes bloodshot and terrified. *Oh no,* he whimpered.

"It's okay," I said. "You're okay. *Help!* Someone *help!*"

The dogs ran forward, pouring out of the Station. Harosen stopped short of the pillars. The dogs grabbed Gurty awkwardly, trying to put him on their backs, pull him up by the nape of his neck, get underneath him, and eventually they figured it out so they could all amble back to safety.

I followed, still shaking. Nera, a light still glowing from her necklace, held me. "You're alright," she whispered.

"Gurty's not."

Gurty fell on the ground at the entrance. The Station was still dark. The Haunts continued to lash out at the fountain's border, screaming ceaselessly. We might be inside. But they still persisted outside.

Gurty shivered. His leg was slashed across with a wide, black gash. There should be blood, but there was just static, like the Haunt's abyss had glommed onto him and now tore a hole in his reality.

"Just like in the Fire," Harosen whispered. "They're not only touching the dead and stones now." He looked around at the dark Station. "The light . . . the light . . ."

Oh no, oh no, oh no, Gurty said, panicking.

"It's okay, it's okay," I said. "Here, let me see." I put his head on my lap. I held him so close.

I wasn't going to leave him.

I saw my dad, looking down at me and Sammy when he tucked us in. I saw him in that hospital. The heartbreak.

"It will be okay someday," I sang, my voice quivering. "Though it don't look that way . . . when all other promises wash away . . . this one I can say . . ."

How people stay with us, even when they've gone so far away.

Nera touched my arm, listening to my song. Her fingers gripped my shoulder, solid and shaking all at once. "Oh Gurty," she whispered.

And Gurty looked down at his leg.

It was throwing out a golden glow. Just like Nera's lantern.

Just like the lighthouse, now reignited, shining weakly.

"Keep singing," Harosen said, in a voice too soft to be his.

I pulled Gurty closer. "It will be okay, it will be okay, it will be okay," I sang, just that part over and over again. "It will be okay . . ."

And Gurty nuzzled me, like the final note on a piano, where you look up and realize it's over.

His enormous eyes were so wide and full. His leg healed.

I like that song, he said.

Harosen stared at me, and then at Gurty. Then at Nera.

Elbee stepped forward. *You alright, pup?*

Gurty gingerly got up on his legs. He tested them out. *Well!* he said. *I'm better than alright! Did you see how I gave them the ol' one-two out there, Elbee? Did you?*

I did. Elbee gave a small, relieved chuckle. *Come on, kid, let's get you something to eat.*

I did it! I got them back to the Station, didn't I?

You did, Elbee said. And Gurty bounded behind him, as all the dogs tried to decide if they should disperse or . . . stare hauntedly at Mr. Harosen.

Harosen wasn't paying attention to them any longer. He was staring past the pillars.

"He's alright, Father," Nera assured him, coming to stand beside him.

But Harosen was in a daze. "Haunts aren't supposed to be able to hurt the dogs."

I stood, too. "Then how did that one slice Gurty?"

Shrieks echoed through the entrance. They sounded closer than the fountain. Outside, the ocean of Haunts rammed up against the pillars. They swirled in a furious torrent, and I could see within it, eyes, noses, hands, all out of focus. Even though the lighthouse was lit, they still tried to slam and pound their way in, fighting the assault like a terrifying, desperate mob.

It churned my stomach. Something that felt like the house when parents fought, when families broke apart, when I was at the end of a long run with my sister and I had forgotten my water bottle and she just kept running and my insides were turning to dust.

No, it wasn't my sister.

It was something worse.

It was me.

The thing in the dark felt like my insides, when Dad wouldn't look at me. When my friends stopped calling. When Mom didn't want me anymore.

Nera's arms encased me. I felt myself breathing, trying to find air in the marble halls of a dream.

The Station was not going to save me.

Nera held onto me, close.

"I'm fine," I lied.

"You're not," Nera said. "It's alright you're not. Hold onto me, Charlie."

The first person to wrap their arms around me since Sam. And with all the courage I had, I let her.

The lighthouse kept on, dimly beating out, but the sounds above it were a funnel cloud of sour notes.

Nera took one hand as she kept me close, and she yanked at her necklace.

It unclasped and sat in her hand. A little lantern on a chain. Harosen watched her, in shock, but said nothing. "This is something my father made in the Gift Room, so it will follow you wherever you go, even to the real world. It will keep you safe." She leaned in and whispered, "The demon can't talk to you anymore if you're wearing this, and if they make it into the Station tonight . . . at least you'll be safe." Her fingers brushed against the back of my neck and pressed together as she hooked the clasp under my hair. She leaned back, touching the little lantern.

"I'm sorry I haven't found her. I'm sorry you're hurting," she said.

"Stay with me?" I asked her. "I have to go play her piano now."

"Your sister's piano." Harosen stepped forward. "If you manifested your own, then maybe it would be stronger. She isn't here, Charlie. It's you."

"I didn't have a piano," I said. "She played, I sang."

"Sing then." He stood straight. "Just sing."

Sing?

My singing was never enough without Sam's piano or Dad's guitar. Singing alone was sad, like an *American Idol* contestant. Who the fuck was I, Zooey Deschanel in *Elf*?!

But even with the Haunts at the door, Nera smiled at me, so bright, so forgiving. Who was I to her? Someone worth trusting. I could tell, it wouldn't matter if I sounded good or bad, it didn't matter what I sang, because that's not what mattered to her.

Her smile wasn't for my music, or what I could do for them. It was for me.

And so the song had to be for her.

"They're going to breach the pillars. Sing!" Harosen ordered.

"Charlie." Nera softly drew to my side again. "I trust you. You can do this. You have a beautiful voice." She touched my hand. I felt it. Warm.

She wasn't gonna let go.

I thought back to my favorite song I'd written. It wasn't Sam's, it wasn't my dad's. It had made my heart fly through my chest, soar up my throat and out of my head like starlight leaking from my eyes and my ears. All of everything I hid inside me, past everyone else I carried with me, and I kept my eyes on Nera. I opened my mouth.

There it was, in my lungs, the little spark of a song. To beat against the crashing waves of the rot outside.

―――――

I sang.

It was a shaping of my throat, a shout shoved into my head, a swell that burned hotter and hotter in my chest before I let it free to burn in the air ahead, like breathing fire. It was the difference between using a matchbook and being a dragon.

This song was sad, but hopeful. It drowned out the screaming broken sounds outside. From the rise and fall of my chest, and lyrical incantations from my lips, I painted Nera's eyes, bright and wide, kind and giving, even in the night. I painted for her those steady hands. Her strong core, her brown chestnut hair that was so soft, so smooth and yet curled, pulled back in a bun. I wanted nothing more than to set it free, wild, around her shoulders. I had never met a woman like Nera before and never would again, and I was lucky enough to see her standing here, smiling at me.

I forced myself past anger, because underneath was something sturdier. Trust.

Yes, trust.

She was kindness in a world that had promised none. She was trying. Protecting. I should have realized earlier just how much I relied on her. And I felt her soft touch in my heart. She filled my lungs. And my spirit poured forth, escaping my chest and singing the unspeakable joy and goodness of Nera Harosen into the air and back into her world. To her. For her.

Above us, as I sang, the lighthouse didn't just shine.

It looked like the sky had opened to cut a path made of stars.

The lighthouse beam radiated out of the glass Station, begging to burst from its cage, as if it couldn't hold it all inside, and needed to cry its own song to the city.

The coldness, the uncertainty, it shattered and gave way to an inexplicable, undeniable familiarity. Home. I was struck with a barrage of emotions.

The anticipation of stepping behind a wall of ivy and seeing a miracle. The laughter that rolls from a silly joke only you find funny, but damn is it funny. The mutual bliss of being truly seen, no longer a mystery, even to yourself. The recognition of someone loving you not for all the people you've tried to be . . . but who you are.

I let the last note ring out under the new sun of the Station.

And before it could blast all the glass from its frame, I let that note go. I let it ring by itself, through the atrium. I let Nera hear it, hold it, memorize it.

"There you are." She smiled.

Then she gasped and held her chest. A small sob escaped, but one without tears. She laughed a little, and looked to me.

"Feel this," she said. She touched her chest again, her hand pressing against her blouse's buttons.

I rushed to her. "Are you okay?" I put my hand on her collarbone. She pressed it there. I felt her heartbeat.

"What's wrong? Talk to me, are you okay?"

And she smiled. As if she had seen her first morning. She said, "I can feel my heart."

I saw Harosen standing behind Nera. I thought he should be beaming up at that lighthouse I'd fixed for him. But he was just staring at Nera and me, like he'd just seen two bodies dumped into graves.

REMNANTS

You are alone in this lighthouse. I wish I had better news for you. Perhaps Hashem will answer your prayer and this will not always be the case. Perhaps someone else will come to help you keep the light strong. But if they don't, there's no need to grieve companionship. There is the known in loneliness. To be alone is to hold onto all your heart. It is to be in charge of your own light.

—Excerpt from a letter to the ferryman

32

NERA

The ferry had left early that night, to clear out the Station during the first attack. But we had more who had sought refuge, and so there would be a second ferry in less than a couple of hours. I was exhausted.

Weariness was new to me, but this was a place where goodbyes never ended.

I sat down next to Red in the movie theater, and she didn't look at me. She just kept watching *Casablanca*.

You here to escort me, Oh Wise Ferryman? Red said, popping some popcorn into her mouth. It wasn't real.

"Yes," I said through the dark.

Ah, Red said. *So this is the last time we see this movie together.*

And I could see for the first time since I'd known her, Red was afraid. That's why she'd hid from the earlier ferry.

"Well," I said, "let's just do what we always do. And then let's just . . . say that we'll meet up again next week. Even if we won't. Yes?"

We watched the comings and goings of people in that gray-scale bar, as we always did. Sadness slipped away into the rhythms of singing along, saying our favorite lines, and afterward when the theater lights went on, we let our minds wander to small talk, and we forgot altogether to mark the moment as an end. I didn't count the patterns on the curtains, I didn't memorize how her eyebrows curved when she smiled.

I had the courage to take it for granted.

And when it was over, it had been a very good time. The film was still a very good film. Red and I kept chatting as we headed out of the theater. "Same time next week," she said.

There were many different ways to say goodbye. Each of the people who left were unique. Grief changed its face every time I saw it.

There was a smile on Red's face, though. And on mine. We'd allowed ourselves the time.

She gave me a peace sign before she headed to the ferry and we all took off, me directing the ship. Father touched me on the back. His energy was soft, worried about me. Maybe I wasn't the only one becoming more alive.

But something heavy and hot and painful hung around my neck, even though my neck was now bare. I couldn't look at him.

The Haunts had been pushed back. But Edna was still gone.

How do I let go of my little girl, he wondered aloud, *when I see she runs into dark waters?*

I gripped the helm.

The Haunts are stewing for now, pushed back all the way to the road, he told me. *The demon is still in the tower. Soon, you will take over and there will be no need for Charlie. I hope.*

My nails dug into the wood.

He sighed in my head. A sliver of him remembering how to breathe. *When you arrived, I was no longer alone. And now I see that you don't feel as alone when you talk to them. I wish I could stay. And I wish Charlie Connor could either leave or stay forever. But sweetheart, sometimes things are the way they are, and we can't do anything more than what's been given to us. Please,* please *protect your heart.*

"And I can't even be angry with you, can I?" I suddenly snapped. "Because you're going to be gone soon, and I will forever remember how I wasted my time with you being angry. I will feel guilty, like the people who come through here." I had never wanted to learn what it meant to let go. "I don't want you to leave when we are angry."

Fine. We'll talk about all the unspoken things, then. You gave her your necklace.

It cut me, almost as deep as it seemed to cut him. He didn't look at me. He looked at his hands.

His one gift, I'd given it away.

"She . . ." needed protection from the demon, but I wasn't going to say that. Father would never let her in again. "She feared the Haunts and was overwhelmed. She needed it more than I did."

I really thought Father would snap back. But he stepped forward. He grabbed me. He hugged me.

I kept my hands on the helm. The ferry didn't need me to drive, it knew the way, but it did need me to focus. To urge it forward.

But he kept holding me in a hug he'd never given anyone else and had now given me twice tonight. I could feel the pressure of his arms. He was so cold and numb, yet he held on tight. He pretended he did not see the world, but there was still a part of him that loved it.

And though he grabbed me and held me tight, I was now taller than him, desperately wanting to be little again. When he was gone, this hug was yet another thing that would disappear from this place. All things disappear eventually.

But wouldn't they cheapen if they didn't? The suddenness, the temporary flash of life, that's what made it special. But I'd been here for how long, would be here for how much longer, and some of the sweetest, most wonderful moments seemed to stretch forever. The seasons may change, but my father never did.

What happened to someone, when they crossed? When it was my time, *if*

I got a time, would he be there on the other side, just a step away, waiting for me? Or would he be gone forever, just like the passengers feared?

Where was Edna?

Now I understood why they were so afraid.

"Edna wasn't ready to go," I said softly.

There's been so many tonight. Which one was Edna again? he said.

My jaw clenched. My body stiffened.

That was it.

He was not cold. He was lost. I pitied him.

And I would not become him.

He loved me, but the world he offered wasn't enough anymore.

Charlie waited pacing on the docks when I returned from the lake. Father left us alone, walking past and busying himself with the dogs.

"Grab the lanterns," he said, "we need to repair and heal the front entrance."

Charlie reached out her hand, but it wasn't to take mine. There was something in her palm.

A rock.

"My mom left after we buried Sam," Charlie said. "But in those days between the death and the funeral, she was a star. She went into go-mode, super mom. At the funeral, we stood over Sam's . . ." She trailed off for a second, and then she took my hand and placed the rock in my own fingers. She clasped them around the little thing. "We each put a rock on her gravestone. Mom said it's something we do. We Jews, she said, we remember."

"That's what Edna said, too," I mumbled.

"I thought you might want to remember her in a way she'd like," Charlie said.

I looked at the dock. It sat under the red arch, the ferry settled next to the planks of wood. Beyond, there was the space the ferry left through. But it wasn't for people or dogs without a boat.

With rock in hand, I walked down the dock, past the ferry and the arch, to the back brick wall of the Station. I put my hand out. I touched the bricks.

We've spent so much time together, and we've never really spoken until tonight, I said softly to the Station. *I don't know if anyone has ever spoken to you at all. So this may be silly, but could you maybe make me my own little walkway so I may see the lake and the sky and the stars?*

The bricks moved out of the way, an arched threshold magically appearing. Beyond the end of the Station was a new covered stairway, made of polished marble and stone, wrapping its way up around the Station, like beautiful architectural ivy. Past its railing, I could see the waves and the stars.

"How did you do that?" Charlie said in awe, pulling her coat out from under her arm and putting it on.

I looked to her. "I'm the Station Master," I said.

We stepped out onto the staircase, up the stairs, and onto a little viewing platform that curved along the lavish sculpted railing. A little brick half-circle at the end of the path, just for us.

"Hold my hand," I said. She did.

I felt the rock in one palm, and in the other was Charlie's hand wrapped in her coat sleeve.

The lake sang its soft lullaby underneath us. And I didn't know how to say goodbye. There were too many things I wanted to tell Edna. If we had a thousand more years to speak, we would not have run out of words.

I bit my lip. I held the rock up. "Thank you," I whispered.

And I set the rock on the railing. Charlie squeezed my hand. Although there were only two of us, and Edna said we needed ten, we whispered kaddish together, a prayer we both knew. Like magic. Then:

"May her memory be a blessing," Charlie said quietly.

Good words.

She would have liked them.

Thank you, Edna. For seeing me. For loving me. For helping me see who I could be.

I was going to help Charlie find her sister. Then, I would follow Charlie out of this Station.

REMNANTS

I know someday if you are kind,
And I can find the perfect rhymes,
The two of us won't be alone,
I'll make your world my home.

—*Lyrics from "You're a New World" by Michael Connor, Copyright 1982*

33

CHARLIE

In the peace of the Station, my body slowly remembered to forget my fear. There was this calmness, watching the water with Nera beside me. Like that time Sam and Marco and I all got high and we just laid on our backs in the graveyard and stared up at the sky. Relief.

When the sun came, maybe I wouldn't go home. Whatever home was.

"Charlie?" Nera said, standing next to me on this balcony.

Yeah? I said.

Nera's mouth turned to a thin line. "Charlie, out loud," she said.

"Oh," I said. "Yeah. Right . . . the sun isn't up yet, though."

Nera pointed to the bricks in the wall surrounding the arch. She touched them. "You were right, about what you said," she offered. "When you said I didn't uphold my promise. We acted like we have all the time in the world, and I'm afraid we don't."

"I was angry," I said.

"You were right," she repeated. "But I think I figured something out. I can speak to the Station. I asked for it to hold on, during the attack tonight. I asked it for this balcony. It can hear me." Nera's eyes glowed in excitement, as if she'd finally cracked an impossible math problem. She took my hands, shaking. "Charlie, you said if I can't find Sam, find someone who can. Well. We can ask the Station if Sam was here."

She stepped down, touched the outer wall of the Station, and closed her eyes. Her hand went *through* the wall.

She pushed forward. Her whole arm disappeared into the bricks.

I went to the wall. I touched it. I pushed my own hand through. Like Jell-O.

But I wasn't afraid. It wasn't scary, it was more like . . . it was embracing me. A heartbeat around my fingers.

And I heard Sam's song again. I felt the vibrations of music on my fingertips. I stepped forward.

"Charli—"

But I was now through the wall.

And in a place full of light. Blue, green, yellow, the bright glare that can bounce off a wet road right into your eyes while you're trying to drive, the perfect bioluminescence of the cave worms I saw in Arizona on our road trip to Disneyland, the glitter in a lip gloss my sister had worn on her first day of fourth grade.

I was home. I could feel it. The smell of freshly cleaned carpet and laundry, the crinkling of birthday wrapping paper, the smell of my mom's turkey meat-loaf on a Thursday night.

Nera came in after me. And we stood in the liminal space of the wall.

"What the hell is this Station?" I felt tears against the corners of my eyes.

Nera swallowed, and she took my hand. "I don't know the whole answer to that." She put her other hand up to something that was cobwebbed with shadow, a small fleck of static on its insides. She rubbed it away. And all was light again. "But I know it's something worth protecting," she said, delivering the words like the Queen of Troy looking out at her kingdom.

Suddenly from far beyond the two of us, I heard a quiet sound. A laugh. A piano tinkling. And I stepped forward, further into the blues and greens.

There was my house.

Then it rippled. The colors and shapes from a photograph I knew well, us standing in Pittsburgh together. Glowing like it was projected in the air, fuzzy and a memory I could see in my head but . . . a ghost. It was a ghost. I heard us laughing, right after Marco had taken that picture.

There was the Northridge Mall, a mall that was still safe and only held good memories. My sister and me and Marco walking through it in high school, laughing and sipping our big fountain drinks.

I saw myself. Not critically, not how I saw myself in the mirror, but maybe the way someone who loved me could see. Kindness, joy, laughter, brilliance . . . a mercy toward myself that I had never felt.

Then a ripple. And I heard my sister's song.

I took a breath that filled me up. "Nera, I don't understand this, but I can hear her music. Does that mean she was here or not?!"

And the music surrounded us. Something swirled around my hand. And then into my hair and my ears like starlight in a song on my father's strings.

The world was going to be okay, it told me.

I was loved, it told me. Maybe with this, I could hear her finished song. Maybe I could still see her smile.

I stepped forward. "Sammy? Are you there?"

Just more music. No Sammy. No face, no hands, no voice, no forgiveness, no absolution.

Nera took my hand. "The Station has been trying to tell you something since the beginning, but we need a clear answer." She smiled. "I have an idea."

———————————

Back in the Station proper, we stood in the abandoned atrium. Nera ushered me to another wall. There were the doors, all leading to different rooms.

"Uh," I said. "Do I pick one?"

"No, give me a moment." Nera fixed her skirt. "I'm going to build one for you."

She put her hand out in a plea. "Come on, old friend," she whispered to the Station. "Give me a room to heal this soul. It can become a part of this place forever, if you wish."

There was a pause. As if she was listening to something very hard to hear.

"I need a room that will answer questions," she explained to the Station.

And the wall shifted under her hands.

Nera looked as if she took every curious urge, all the questions she'd ever had, and she gave them to the Station. Nera wanted to understand everything.

And with that hope in her heart, a door settled into place: paneled, bright blue, the paint still wet.

Then Nera looked to me. "Go ahead . . . if you like."

I opened the door, expecting the blue to come off on my hands. It did not. It just held that good squishy feel of new fresh color.

Inside was a blank white room.

"This is the Question Room," she said. She took my hand and walked me to the middle of the white. "You can ask one question. Just one. And it's the only one you'll ever get, as long as your soul exists, living or dead or beyond. And you'll get an answer to that question. So I thought you could ask about Sammy."

I felt joy and sadness all at once. "Thank you," I managed. "Please stay with me."

She nodded. "Always."

I turned to face the room.

One question.

How could I word one question to find all the answers? *Is my sister okay? Is she part of the Haunts now? Did she cross through the Veil? Will I see her again?*

All of those were yes/no questions.

It needed to be something that would require more than one word.

I rubbed my fingers against my wrist, the two notes tied together, and I thought.

What happened to my sister's soul? Is she a Haunt? Did she get lost in the city? Does she just not exist any longer? Did she make it here, leave the memory of her song, and step into the Veil? Can she forgive me?

I stood there in silence, cradling the question in my heart like a little bird, as it fluttered inside me with broken wings.

Why did it have to happen?

After she fell to the ground, after the bedlam clattering through the tile hall-ways thinned out and the cleaning crew came, the coroner bagged the dead, took them to the cold, suffocating truck. But Sammy had a chance, they said. A chance, not a promise. She went to the hospital. And then after, my father gave all his tears to her, leaning over her with his heart shattering.

Why did the world have to be so cruel? Why did he have to hurt? After all that, what happened to my sister's soul?

What happened to all of us?

I always held this thought that if I just kept looking for her, if I just kept staring ghosts in the eyes and I kept seeing into the corners of reality and its façade, I could find her. That there was someone left to find. On the cold shitty nights where Dad talked to himself in his sleep, in the mornings where I missed my mother, the parties where Marco drank himself sick, and the missed holidays we all pretended died along with Sammy. We were drifting in a useless, senseless pain, and yet I still believed that she was there. *There.* The proverbial somewhere far away behind a Veil or high up in the clouds or in a new world I'd never seen but would maybe meet her in. Decades from now, I would hold her again. I would sing with her again. I would tell her I was sorry, I would scream at her, I would scream *with* her. The warmth of the spring wasn't dead, it was going to come back, and even though the dead of winter had no proof, there was the eternal promise that the world would turn green again.

Does Sam forgive me for losing her that day?

And by asking one question, I could find hope that she still existed. I could know, for the rest of my life, that she was in the new world and waiting. She wasn't gone, she'd just gone earlier than the rest of us.

But in asking for absolution, that meant no more possibility. There would be the answer, the *one* answer to the *one* question. And if that answer was painful . . .

What if she is part of the static outside?

What if even the Station didn't know where she'd gone?

What if her soul was broken along with her body? Was it too terrible of a death to survive any part of it?

And now that I could ask, my heart wouldn't allow my voice to speak.

I needed her to exist.

Just for a little while longer.

I turned to look at Nera. She was waiting for me, so patiently. Always there.

"I can't," I said, my voice cracking. Something fluttered against my ribs, my throat. I felt stuck.

Nera gave one small nod. "It will be alright."

But I didn't know what to do. Was there another question I could ask? Maybe a yes or no would make more sense.

I knew one thing: if Sammy went through the Veil, she wasn't in danger in the city. I would know where she was. I would know she was okay. Maybe I didn't want to know all the details.

I turned to face the room.

"Did my sister cross through the Veil?" I asked before I could change my mind.

34

CHARLIE

Nera faded as the room blurred in a tornado of color.

Then stars, of all different shades, all different sizes. They rushed past me. And I felt a sense of peace.

I saw a faint outline, like a washed-out photograph. My sister. Her straight blonde hair down to her shoulders. Her oversized hoodie, her slouched stance that always made her seem so cool. The memory of a beautiful song that had once been heard.

Yes, something whispered in my head.

I felt relief. I felt joy.

I felt like I'd made a terrible mistake.

The room turned to white again. Sam was gone.

Nera returned to vision.

My body shook.

"I asked the wrong question," I whispered.

Nera touched my arm and led me out of the room. When we were gone, she asked, "What question was the right question?"

"What happened to my sister's soul," I muttered. "Or if she had anything to say to me, or if she . . . I want to know . . . and I . . . all I know is she went through the Veil."

Nera squeezed my arm and we sat against the wall as I tried to breathe through my hyperventilating lungs, up and down, in and out, too fast. I gritted my teeth to keep the tears in. I was so tired of crying.

"Charlie," Nera said. "This is good news. It's what we wanted. We know she's not a Haunt. We know she's not *like* the Haunts. She's not in the hotel here, she's . . . where she needs to be."

"No," I snapped. "No, she *needs* to be here with *me*." The tears came. "I want to see my sister!"

Nera held me.

We sat there for a long time.

She didn't tell me we needed to get going. She didn't uncomfortably shift and sigh. She just held me. As if she had nothing else in the world to do but to hold me. She didn't run away, she didn't catch herself up in her own thoughts, she held me. And I let her.

I let her.

I heaved a sob. "It hurts, I'm full of so much stuff and it hurts."

"I know," Nera said. "Let it out."

"It's too much, I can't—"

"Tell me about her," Nera said. "Not her death. Tell me about her life." Something no one had asked. Everyone had either known Sammy or wanted to ignore that Sammy existed. Except for the news reporters, who just wanted to hear how great she was, how tragic her death was.

So I gripped Nera's hand. And I said, "She pulled the sides of the buns off her cheeseburgers." Nera gave a small laugh. "Because she wanted to wrap it around her fries. Especially if there was cheese in between the bun pieces."

"Why not just put the fries on the burger?" Nera said.

"I don't know," I said. "I just . . ." I was just sad that a small fact about my sister's fingers peeling away at McDonald's Quarter Pounders would be lost as she dissipated from the present. So I said, "She loved Koosh balls. She was afraid to go out on the grass without her shoes because once she got stabbed by a stick. But her biggest fear was that the scorpions at the zoo would get loose. Her favorite place in the world was on the shaggy carpet in the den at our parents' house, and the zoo . . . minus the scorpions. She liked to put *every fucking song* in C-sharp minor and it pissed me off because holy shit whyyy. She secretly collected dolls, not the ugly dolls, and not like ironically. She liked them because one of our grandmas had said she'd never had them when she was little because she was so poor. So Sammy, she collected them so Gramma could come over and play with them without suspicion. When Mom tried to put a limit on our pop intake, she cut little holes in the bottoms of the cans and sucked the pop out and Mom thought she was getting cheated by the grocery store."

Each word blossomed in the air, like painted pictures, like it was a part of the Station itself, and the world seemed to glow a little brighter. The Station seemed to be more detailed, more tangible, and Nera's hands grew warmer.

It was as if she was becoming more alive. Or maybe Sammy was, too.

Maybe I was.

I didn't know what it meant, but it felt like Sammy hadn't gone through the Veil at all. It felt like she was still with me. And I didn't have to say goodbye.

"Thank you," I said softly. And Nera squeezed me hard.

"You don't have to thank me," she said.

"You had so many other things to do tonight."

"No," she said. "No, you are the only thing, Charlie."

And there was a quiet between us.

"I didn't tell you how she died," I said.

I felt my whole body burn. My eyes blurred. My skin was like paper, shredded so easily by blades and bullets and anyone could be behind me.

"You don't have to," she said.

I thought about it so much. I needed to let it out. But to let it out would mean to trust her to hold it.

I had given her the truth of my hot fury, and the wisecracks. But I could tell her about Dad with his fucking couch and fucking silence. How he made us stand out by that fucking statue in the zoo when he found out I could see ghosts. It was Sammy's favorite statue, so we kept waiting for her to appear and she didn't.

I could tell Nera about all that. And maybe I needed to tell her.

"Do you want to go sit in my room for a little bit?" Nera said.

I followed her on autopilot.

I walked up the stairs.

Did Nera know how dark it had gotten inside me? I had tried to go to a support group, just once. Some random guy named Kyle said, "It's one of those days, where the waves recede and the sky comes out. And you remember what it's like to breathe. You know what I mean?"

And I'd realized I did not.

"No," I said. "My waves don't recede, Kyle."

They should have.

I was broken.

Even Marco could see the sky long enough to brush his hair more than once.

I would never heal, not outside the Station. I would live in this throbbing ache, like wisdom teeth scraping against jawbones. Never enough room. Never enough space. Just slowly rotting.

Nera led me up golden stairs to her bedroom on the edge of the lighthouse. She opened her door, a circular wooden thing that looked like a hobbit had built a pirate ship. We entered, and the stained glass window had grown floor to ceiling and looked out to the lake. In the morning, it would throw color everywhere. And her wall, with the memorial. The names. The map. It was all Nera.

I sat down on the quilted bed. Nera sat beside me.

"You can rest," she said.

And it was everything inside of me that told me, begged me, to let her stay. I didn't want her to leave. And I didn't want to go.

She didn't ask for anything. She just sat there, her hand on my hand.

"I'm gonna say its name." I forced it out of me. "My sister was one of the people killed in the Southwell Mall shooting." I heard it finally pry free from my mouth. It had become an impersonal label rattled off by people recording history. Southwell had just been the mall down the street from our parents' house. Now Anderson Cooper knew it. In this larger-than-life event, my very real sister got snared.

Nera looked at me. "Killed."

Then I said, "I'm sorry, I'm sorry, it's a lot, we don't need to—"

"If you don't *want* to," Nera said, "then we can sit here. But if you want to tell me, then I'm listening."

"All you do is listen to me," I sniffed.

"Because you are wonderful to listen to," she said. "You sing beautiful songs to heal the darkness. You tell me very emphatically which pizza to eat. You look adorable wrapped in a scarf. And your heart is so big, it's carrying your sister inside."

I hesitated. "Are you sure you want to hear?"

"Yes," Nera said. And she opened her mouth to say something and then didn't.

"What is it?" I said, nervous.

Nera laughed a little laugh. "I just . . . I was thinking one of my thoughts."

"Tell me."

"I just . . . I was going to say, Yes, I am sure I want to hear. Because with the songs and the scarves, with the pizza . . . with *life* . . . comes death. It's all part of being . . . a person." She looked at me, expecting me to . . . roll my eyes? But I just touched her arm.

"You should talk more," I said.

"I'm working on it."

I looked at the stained glass window, then the list of names. I said hoarsely, "She was more than just a dead girl. I feel like her whole essence, it got shrunk down to this one thing. She had a whole life and the death was just a little part of it. And why the fuck does death have to be so big?"

She said nothing. I charged on.

"The mall's out in the suburbs. There was a shooter." There was an uncomfortable gravity in those words. "He was a . . . I don't know, some sort of Nazi fuck. He . . . he had diaries full of Columbine clippings. He'd been planning it. Because it's like the Haunts, isn't it? One person does a thing, then it grows and it grows and this guy is gonna bleed into the next guy." I swallowed back bile. I stopped, nauseous. If I said anything more about him, I was going to hurl.

Nera squeezed my hand and turned to look at me. She was still dressed in her coat. She had her old-school boots on. Her soft oval face with those full cheeks and kind, round hazel eyes. There was a softness that I didn't deserve. And I could see her so clearly, sitting beside my tired body. Her curling hair, flyaways out of place in her messy bun. Her flushed skin. She was alive, she was here, she knew me, and she wasn't leaving.

"She was killed," I said. "Murdered. But I was fine. When it all started, she ran and I couldn't keep up . . . I lost her . . . I found shelter. She didn't. The medics came, too late, not until after the cops had secured the entire mall, they said, and it was a clusterfuck."

It was a while before I said anything else. Then I said, "I fucking hate him. He was a monster and I want nothing to do with him in my head. But I keep seeing him, coming into sight, charging forward like the world was his and he had all the right to do it. And I didn't believe in evil before I saw him, I didn't think that this feeling of . . . of adrenaline getting stuck in my chest . . ." I trailed off. "Do murderers come through the Station?"

Nera nodded. "They do."

"How can you forgive them?"

"I can't forgive them," Nera said. "It's not my place to try to forgive them. My job is to get them to the ferry."

"How can you show them all this beautiful stuff? If I saw him here," I said, "I'd fucking drown him in the lake."

"He's already hurt his soul," Nera said, "you don't have to hurt yours, too."

"He already fucked up my soul!" I said. "How can you say that? He's a fucking monster."

Nera squeezed my hand. "I'm sorry," she said. "I don't know. It's not fair. But I know you wouldn't drown anyone. You're not him."

"Okay, then who am I, Nera?" I sputtered. "I don't know who I am anymore! I used to! I was gonna be a teacher. I loved theater. I was funny. I had this strength in me, right down to my bones. That feeling like you can go forever and always have enough energy. And I could keep my thoughts strung together. I could tuck myself in at night."

"You are still those things," she said.

"No," I said. "No, I'm not. A week after it happened, I knew something was wrong. I couldn't fix my fucking blankets to fucking go on the bed right. It was too much energy, to make sure they were spread out, all stacked in an order, all comfortable and safe to climb into. I broke down sobbing because I was broken." Because I now lived in a world where men walked into your peripheral and opened fire, where ghosts were real.

There was a void at the end of the world, and I still needed to fold blankets. My sister was dead, and I still needed to trust that any loud bang in a hallway wasn't out to kill someone.

"Mom always gave Dad a hard time after he came back from the war. Whenever Dad tried to talk about it, Mom would roll her eyes. And so us kids learned to roll our eyes. And he learned to be quiet, and then he learned to laugh loud. And then one day . . . it just all came crashing down on top of him, didn't it?"

The words kept spilling out, faster.

"But he can't see the ghosts, even though bad things happened to him, too. Why can no one else see them?"

"Perhaps when we no longer sit inside our life," Nera said, "we have our own ghosts. He has ghosts, too, even if they aren't like yours."

"How did he keep going? How can I remember how to be a living human when there is a veil torn open and the truth is spilling out? And all the while, the world goes on and it expects you to be the same person you were before. So I try, I try to be who I was. To hold my own. But who I was is dead, and I'm not coming back."

Marco was the only one who understood. He'd known Charlie before, and he knew me now. And still he called me. He was trying to get through it, figure out who we were in this new world. And I had been no help.

What would happen to Marco if I didn't go home? What had happened to Marco in the last few months? I was here, and he was out there, alone. Before all this, we leaned on each other. The first few weeks, we kept leaning. It was easier. That's why it hurt when he couldn't see or believe in my ghosts.

"That night that the blanket incident happened . . . Marco came in and he fixed the blankets for me. And I sobbed and he held me and then he sobbed and I tried to hold him but the weight . . . the weight was too much for me. And I want to be there for him and I can't. I just can't. And my brain won't work the way I want it to. My eyes see things I don't want to see. I can't get myself back to who I need to be."

My eyes burned and my nose wouldn't stop running, but if I didn't say everything now . . .

"And I can keep talking about all of this, but it's not gonna change anything. The man with the gun, the ghosts, the sounds, the fear, Nera, the blood." I shook. "They tell you to close your eyes while you are being evacuated. So you don't see it all. But I wanted to find her. I . . . I never stopped looking. Sometimes, I think maybe I never left that mall at all. I'm still searching for her and reliving it all over again."

A pause. To breathe.

"I needed her to know I was sorry. For hiding before I could find her."

Nera's eyes glided to mine, wide and pained. "Oh, Charlie," she whispered.

"I tried giving myself dates. 'On her birthday I will leave it all behind. That's the milestone. Now I heal.' It didn't work. Because there's no healing, is there? It's chronic. All you can do is figure out who you are now, in the After."

I loosed a deep sob. Nera held me. I shivered into a scream. She still held me. To have someone stay with you, in the dark. Finally, I was not alone.

"I wanted to see her again. I wanted to know she was okay. To just have a fucking conversation, to . . . tell her I was sorry and I loved her. That she had all this good in her."

"It's not your fault," Nera said.

I said nothing.

"But I know I wasn't there," Nera added. "I haven't lived through it like your family has. Perhaps it would be healing to tell Marco?" Nera stroked my arm. "Tell him because he's still here."

I hadn't. Panic and shame rose. *There is no we.*

"And perhaps," Nera said, "you can tell yourself those things as well. I see all the good in you. You are not only your grief."

I snorted.

"For a start, you can still belt out a beautiful song when you haven't been shown much beauty."

"And I like pizza . . . and honestly, I like cheeseburgers, too."

"Your doodles are all over your shoes."

"Yeah." I looked down at my shoes. "Yeah, they're called Chuck Taylors and I named them Chuck."

"You wanted to be a teacher."

"And I'm a lesbian."

There was a silence. The truth was finally out there in the ether. Somewhere hanging between us, between life and death, night and morning, and I couldn't take it back.

I didn't want to.

Finally, to Nera, I had given those words the life I needed them to have. And she squeezed my hand with a small smile.

"I know that word. You say it like it's dangerous," she said. "When really, it's one of the greatest words you've ever said."

We were a very small flicker of light in a very dark night. But it was enough to stay in my body, to keep crying, to keep trying to explain, to keep letting her hold me. One more moment, then another. That's how we would lay here.

I turned around and I curled up and let her lay down beside me and hold me. She said nothing. She just held me.

And I cried for my father and my mother and I howled for my sister and I clenched my fists for Marco and I gritted my teeth for all the dead I'd met along the way and finally . . . *finally* . . . I cried for me.

And through it, there was Nera and her embrace. Between us, her lantern around my neck glowed, lighting up this little room of names and maps. We were a lighthouse.

35

NERA

Charlie was more than her grief.
I was more than my father's plans.
It was time to go.

36

NERA

We stood at the front of the Station, looking at the cleaned-up bricks, the fountain covered in snow, still working. The dogs milled around, making sure all the patches were taken care of. The lighthouse flickered, but the sun slowly rose behind us, straight up through glassy water, a loud ceremony of light.

The new day had come, even without the people who were left in yesterday. Life resetting itself.

Maybe a sunrise was all those people who disappeared last night telling us from beyond that it was okay to keep going. A signal fire to show us they weren't extinguished.

I made sure we were outside before the sun got too high, making certain that all the worlds living and dead saw that Charlie had no intention of staying. I needed the world to never take away her voice again. Charlie breathed in the crisp air. I saw the lantern still hung around her neck.

"Please, Charlie, promise me you won't let the thing in the dark inside your head," I said. "I know it's hard. But I . . ." The words left me. "Please don't take the necklace off," I managed.

I looked out to the fountain. The furthest I'd ever walked away from the Station.

I wanted to know what would happen if . . .

"The lighthouse is safe, with the sun so bright," I said. "I have a day."

Charlie looked over to me, her eyes wide. "What now?"

I looked to my boots below my skirt, touching the newly mended bricks. If I *did* turn to dust, then that would mean the Station would be left without me. But it would still have Father.

The bricks felt warm under my soles. A reassurance. Go, the Station seemed to be saying. I didn't know why or how, but my heart told me, the same way my heart loved the sunrise.

I needed to listen to my body. I needed to have faith.

I hoped that's what the Station was saying. My heart pounded, and my brain was telling me this was a selfish, terrible mistake.

But I had to.

"The lighthouse will be mine," I said. "And to keep it bright, I must be a better Station Master than my father. This means understanding the things I don't yet understand. So. I'm going to cross. I'm going to spend a day in the city, if you'll guide me."

Charlie's face exploded with a great big grin. She jumped on her toes. "Fuck yes! Let's do this!"

"There is a chance I cannot cross," I said. "I've never tried. If I dematerialize, if I turn to dust or, I don't know, am thrown into oblivion or something . . . I don't want you to see. So, I will meet you on the other side of the bridge. Just walk to the bridge, don't watch me, and then wait on the other side. Alright?"

"Okay, so I don't love this," Charlie said.

"Neither do I." I took a deep breath. I was risking everything. This was so foolish. But there was the city, so close. "There is one thing, before you go."

"What?"

"If something terrible goes wrong—"

"What?"

"I mean, if this is the last chance I have to experience . . . will you kiss me, Charlie?"

37

CHARLIE

To kiss her on the cheek, on the lips, all over, bathe in Nera the way we now bathed in sunlight. I leaned in.

She leaned on me, too.

She enveloped me.

Here was someone who wanted me, with the same weight that I wanted her.

I wanted to know her, to really know her. To be ten years down the road from now, have her memorized as if our bodies were a house where we'd grown old together. Her smile, her heart, her hands. Our minds holding all the treasures and souvenirs we'd collected over the decade, all the places we'd seen, all the times we'd made each other laugh with something silly that no one else would understand . . . I didn't just want to hold her. I wanted to see all the people she would become. So I brought my lips to hers.

38

NERA

A first kiss. To do something for the first time that has been written into the history of humans for so long, like an old song that we've passed down. *I know the concept of love. I know what a kiss is. I know that when two people press their lips together, something sparks between them and it is meaningful.* But to truly be in this moment, not with a concept of a person, a concept of my heart, but Charlie, Charlie Connor, in my arms . . . my own body radiating with the deep pulsing rush of finally physically belonging somewhere . . .

I was not prepared for how fully and completely I would awaken when my lips touched hers. The longing in me. I could drink in this want forever and never be filled. But then I had to breathe. I summoned the strength to pull away.

"Go back into the city." I promised her, "I'm ready to find you there."

"Just one day?" Charlie asked, breathlessly.

"I'm concerned what will happen if we're not back by nightfall, if the Haunts . . . but, please, show me Chicago. It will have to be enough for me to understand."

I will follow you, Charlie.

I held her in my arms. Like I could protect her. And maybe I could.

The sun scattered on the lake. The stars disappeared. Life began again.

39

CHARLIE

Nera Harosen practically glowed in front of me, a beacon of courage and kindness. Her fire melted my freezing heart. She folded her strong arms, looking down with deep, hopeful concentration as a plan seemed to sketch itself out in the air ahead of her. Behind her, the sun rose.

I wondered if she knew how badass she was.

I touched her arm. She squeezed my hand and put it over her heart.

"Okay," I said. "I'll uh . . . I'll meet you across the street. The other side of the bridge."

And she kissed me again. She held me close, like she really saw me, like she could protect me from the world. And even if she couldn't, I didn't care, I just wanted her to hold me.

A new beginning in the middle of winter.

"Alright, alright," she laughed. "Go, go! I'll be along soon, Father can't see us."

I started my walk. All I wanted to do was look back. If this was the last time I saw Nera . . . no, I needed to believe.

I needed to know not everyone disappears.

REMNANTS

With the dead and the unknown, I have learned the universe is large and unfathomable. I have seen fear, felt forgiveness, tied a thousand others' memories to my own recollections like the cords of a tallit. I have spoken to the dogs who have crossed the lake and they painted me a picture in words of a massive void at the end of the world.

Journal, there is no miracle, no prayer, nothing else in this land and beyond, that shows me proof of Hashem more than Jon's lips. The rabbis have taught me this is against the Talmud. But Hashem has taught me more.

To not love Jon is to lose my soul, and every soul is a universe. So let our kiss not be sin, but the holiest of mitzvot.

—Excerpt from the journal of David Stein

40

NERA

All I needed to do was step forward.

The large moments of a life, I was finding, were lonely ones. I was afraid to move forward and unable to stay. Father would hate me, if he found out. But I would be back. If I didn't turn to dust.

What would it feel like, to die?

What if I didn't turn to dust, and instead I walked out into the world and my body broke under a car's tire? Pain that I could not take back. I did not understand what lay before me, and perhaps this was too much. It was not worth the risk of losing the next Station Master.

But Edna had said I was alive. Charlie said I was alive. The Station urged me on. I had to believe what I felt in my heart.

A soft wet nose nudged my hand.

Gurty leaned against me. *You don't have to go alone,* he said. *I'll come, too.*

"You don't have to, friend," I said.

I know, but you are *my friend, and so I will.* Gurty panted, giving a small furry smile. *Us dogs will tend to the Station while you're gone. And Hermes says he will pay attention to Harosen's whereabouts, keep him busy. Elbee just said good luck, don't die.*

"Thanks, Elbee."

And I want to come. I was very brave against the Haunts, did you see?

"I did see. You were a very good dog," I said.

Gurty's ears quirked up. *Me?!*

"Yes. You know your way around this whole city. You go out every evening, and you protect people. I'm people, so can you protect me? I don't have my necklace anymore, and I'm a little scared."

Gurty's eyes got big. He sat down on his back legs. He smiled with a pant. *You love me!*

"Of course I do, Gurty," I said.

Well, I like to hear that every day! Gurty wagged his tail against the brick. It did not make a sound, and I wished it would thunk-thunk-thunk. *I love you too, Nera! And you've never been outside, so this will be extra special!* Gurty said. He arched his neck down so he looked like a scheming vulture. Then he jumped on me with happy yips, catapulting up to his back legs to get hugs. *Oh boy oh boy oh boy. Wait . . . does Charlie love me, too?*

"I'm pretty sure you're her favorite," I said.

WHAT! Gurty gasped.

I laughed, but it was cut short by a hissing in the shadows. Gurty's collar glowed.

They're out there, Gurty said, *but I'm here, Nera. And I love you, too.*

"Do you think it'll hurt? Going past the fountain and the bridge?" I said.

I dunno, Gurty said. *But I've learned a thing or two about courage lately, and I'll tell you that sometimes the things that need the most courage are usually the most ill-advised things you could ever think to do that could end very bad. I mean, very bad. That's why you have to be brave, because, wow it could be a mistake.*

"Thanks, Gurty."

But if it was a mistake, then why did it feel like I was going home?

To go out into the world.

The curdling feeling in my stomach of staying the rest of my eternity in the Station . . . it didn't used to make me feel like this. It was all I'd known, my entire world. But now the universe had opened up, and I was an astronaut. How could I say no?

Gurty bumped me from behind, and I patted him on the head. He looked powerful in the brightening dawn, black and curly and very large. He was more of a bear than a dog.

I've done this before, remember? he said, as if he was explaining this to himself, trying to convince himself. *You're not my first soul I've guarded in the city!*

There was terror in me. There was excitement in me. I felt like I was about to step into a meadow with no cover. Is this what going into a haunted house felt like?

Take the step, Nera! he pushed me. *Beyond the fountain is the whole world!*

"My body is more afraid than it's ever been," I admitted to him.

So, I stepped forward, past the fountain.

The furthest I'd ever gone.

I didn't turn to dust.

I thought about all the stories I'd read in the library where the women stepped out of line from the magic and their heads fell off or they shifted into stone statues. But nothing happened. Actually, my body felt like it shed something, a cloak of numbness, a weight I hadn't known I was carrying.

Color. So much color, everywhere, even in the snow. And the details! Sharpness and clarity of separate glinting snowflakes, the grains in the brick, all of it sturdy and solid. It was as if I had been looking at watercolors all my life, only to discover photographs.

There was fresh air, and my lungs breathed in like they realized they existed for the first time. It stung.

I felt the cold wind on my fingertips. I felt the aches in my ankles. I slipped and Gurty caught me.

"It's slippery," I said. "It's slippery! That's what slippery is!"

Gurty pushed me forward.

Another step. I felt blood hot in my cheeks. I felt my underarms get so warm. I felt my toes get so cold. How could one body feel so many things in one moment?!

I took another step.

My lungs hurt when I breathed in the air too fast, it was too cold.

I took another step.

How many years had I sat in the Station?

Then I was far beyond the fountain.

I stood there, staring at my feet. Then I turned around, holding onto Gurty, to look back at the Station.

I'd never seen it from this angle before.

It was gigantic. It was shifting. A bright glowing dome with big pillars, softly humming with an otherworldly glow.

The lighthouse did not go out. It just stood there, unfazed.

Father didn't know.

Hopefully it stayed that way until I returned. Maybe I should stay . . .

I turned my back on the Station.

I took another step.

I saw the Haunts watching from the alleyway ahead. I glared at them, one hand clinging to Gurty's fur and the other pressed to my collarbone to find . . . nothing. I had given Charlie my lantern.

I was now out here, as alive and unarmed as any other soul.

I closed my eyes. I imagined a soft light around me, another necklace around my neck . . . I opened my eyes, and no such thing existed.

This was not my Station, but instead a city that I couldn't speak to.

There was a prickling on the back of my neck as we headed down the soggy concrete street toward the bridge. It was as if someone was following us . . . or many someones. But every time I turned around, there was no one.

The streetlights clicked off as the sun came up. I took in the bridge, and the cars above.

I allowed myself to smile.

But then my cheeks hurt. They stung, like there were needles in the air. I gasped and held onto Gurty. "I can feel the Haunts, on my cheeks," I whispered.

What do you mean? Gurty said, looking around.

"It stings," I said. "My skin feels like it's breaking apart."

Gurty looked to his paws, then around and said, *I think you're just cold, friend.*

Cold! This wasn't cold. Cold was the rooftop. This was uninhabitable.

I touched my cheeks. They immediately felt warmer, flushed, and that made my blood cramp.

"Who the hell would live in this weather?!" I laughed. "This hurts!"

It hurt. I was hurt. I was *hurting*. Present tense. I was living. *Living*. Not a memory. Not someone else's recollection. Not a dream. This was my experience, my cold cheeks, *my life*.

I gave a little howl. Gurty jumped back and forth, excited. *Oh, good, it's time to play!* he said, and I tussled his head and ran for the bridge. Gurty ran after me, jumping in the air to try to knock me down. I pushed him away and laughed, running faster and faster.

I'd never had space to run.

I tried to remember being a little girl, trying to run, but I only ran in circles.

With endless time, what was the sweetness of a moment?

And I could have been a child forever. It was only when I saw my father getting tired that I grew up. How long had I been grown up? How long since I'd run?

My lungs hurt.

And I realized I could not run forever, not out here.

I gulped in chilly air, and my insides froze with stabbing pain. I doubled over and let out a terrible cough. I kneeled on the concrete. Gurty ran ahead, and then stopped short.

The bridge. The final portal to Chicago.

Are you ready, Nera? he said.

I stood. Charlie was on the other side of that bridge. That's what mattered.

I walked forward. Under the loud cars with their dimming lights, past the dead ivy, and then out to the other side.

The city.

A long street that disappeared into the buildings beyond. Big, bright traffic lights. A park on either side.

The grass in the park, it looked dead. Wasn't this supposed to be green? No, of course not, it was winter, and things grew white in the winter. Snow.

The snow was already melting on the edges of the street, drawling along the gutters in big brown oily puddles.

Like the Veil.

"Death," I said. "No, dying," I corrected. "Things still hurt out here. They haven't died yet."

To be in the world of the perpetually dying instead of the world of the dead. What would it be like to walk about the living world, knowing every single thing you saw, heard, touched would someday degrade, melt, chip away, die?

And while this was the living world, I still saw the wisps of the dead. Not in corporeal form, their soul attached to a grayscale container to enjoy the Station with. Instead, some were orbs, some were whispers, some were looping in one action. They were like an old film of memories over the city's present. Different clothing, different technology. There was so much death.

This park is really lovely in the spring, Gurty said, sitting down next to me and nuzzling me with his warm fur. I realized I was frozen on the sidewalk, nervous to walk out of the shadow of the bridge and to where Charlie must be waiting. *It gets all green and pretty. Some of the trees even have flowers and they smell so good. And that's the thing about living and dying,* Gurty said, lying down on his stomach. *Things die in the winter. But they always come back. Not the same things, different leaves and different flowers and all. But the same.*

I sniffed, coughing again. I knelt down next to him and I petted Gurty quietly.

I know, Gurty said. *I'm not half as air-headed as Harosen thinks I am.*

I snorted. "Oh my lord, Gurty, no one thinks that."

Well, Chestnut does, Gurty said.

I put my forehead to his. I breathed in the cold air. He pressed against me.

"Thank you for coming, Gurty," I said.

You're welcome, he said. *Charlie's coming to meet you. I'll hang back, keep watch. You enjoy yourself, okay? A day is just a day, but wow can a day be something cool.*

That stony feeling came back around my ankles. I checked behind me, where the bridge opened to where I'd come from. But there was no lighthouse, no Station . . . I knew it was still there, waiting for me to return.

This day would affect the living world.

So it held more weight than anything I'd done in the Station.

Then I saw her, Charlie shivering and walking toward us with her hood up against her ears. She was smiling. A small soul in a big wide world, unafraid and looking at nothing but me.

"Hello," I said.

REMNANTS

—Photos of Lincoln Park Zoo, by Sam Connor, Fall 2004

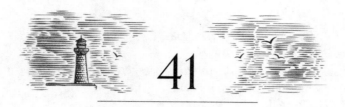

41

CHARLIE

I looked to Nera, alive and without magic. She looked so cold. She shivered like the Little Mermaid pulled onto land.

"You're here," I muttered. You're real.

"Remember, I have to be back by evening." Her teeth chattered together.

I rubbed her arms, pulled out some extra mittens, handed them to her. "Jump up and down."

She laughed as she did so. "No, it's fantastic. It's all-consuming, the cold."

"Babe, the winter's fancy and all but you're gonna get sick if we don't get you inside somewhere. Look at you."

Nera smiled. A real smile. She wasn't something I saw in between closing and opening my eyes. She wasn't a half-remembered melody. She was here. She was *here*. We could see the world together, we could take on these streets and trains and lines of music together.

The city vibrated in a way it hadn't ever before. Because she was now in the city. And she needed no lantern to make the world shine.

"Charlie," she shivered, "I really do have to be back by evening."

"I heard you, yeah yeah," I said, because it wasn't evening. And anything felt possible. Maybe she would just stay. We would never let go of one another. "Your dress is all wet. Do you . . . well, you wanna go to my apartment and get some new clothes?"

I gave her my coat. I could handle the cold in my hoodie long enough to keep her safe. Together, we walked out of the park, then to the street and the L train. To see Nera, the ghostkeeper of Chicago, sitting on the train in absolute frenzied surprise, was so wonderful to watch. She touched the pole, the seat, the plastic window; all the small things I loved about this city, she saw beauty and brilliance in the mundane as well. And it wasn't silly to her, to feel how amazing the shitty little seat fabric felt against your fingers. How the train screeched and squealed around corners. How every time the doors opened, a gust of fresh winter wind would blow in, bringing forward new strangers to meet for the first time.

She saw and loved it all. Even the backs of the brick buildings we passed inspired awe in her, covered in graffiti and rusted fire escapes.

When we got to Granville, she looked down off the platform onto the street below and said, "There are so many distances, so many ways to be above and below. The city has built on top of itself."

"It has," I confirmed.

"And not just after the Fire," she said. "It kept doing it." She shook her head. "It's got so much dirt on it."

"Well, it's not a magic castle that cleans itself," I said. "We're all busy. And tired. And the snow turns to muddy slush pretty fast."

"Ah." She grinned. "It is real, and I love it."

"Ha, well, if you love dirt and grime, wait until you see my apartment, you're gonna super love it." I wiggled my eyebrows, trying to make her laugh.

Then the bust of a dead man in a WWII uniform brushed between us. I couldn't see his feet, just the fuzzy image of his brass and his scared eyes. Nera saw him, too. And I didn't feel so alone.

"Where do you think he's going?" Nera asked.

"Well, there used to be a resort down the street from here, back in the forties?"

"A resort!"

"Like you said, the city has built on top of itself," I explained. "Stories on stories, lives on lives."

"I didn't know there were so many out here, not following the dogs, not wanting to cross or ask for help," Nera said. "No wonder the Haunts are so numerous, if they have all this to feed on."

Where before there would have been a worry that maybe Sam was one of them, I realized now I could breathe easy. She was safe. She wasn't here anymore.

We headed down the stairs. It was Nera's second real staircase, so we took it a little slower.

But she stopped halfway down the stairs and looked around. "Where is the elevator?" she said.

"It's over there," I said, pointing to the scratched-up plastic and steel box that smelled like a sewer. Nera stared at it.

"Just one?" she said. "Do all the stations just have one?"

"Well," I said, "some of them don't have any."

Nera stared at me. "But . . . how do people get up and down if they can't use the stairs?"

"They don't," I said. "Not everything is like your Station."

She was quiet. "That needs to change," she finally said, like she was making notes on a checklist, and she kept gingerly walking down the stairs.

I explained each of the shops as we headed up the street.

"I cannot believe," she said, "every single box has a label, every single window has a crack or a smudge and a story, and . . . is this too much? Am I being too much?"

Nera, I *wanted* too much of you.

"No, no," I said. "You're right, when a place has been around here long enough, it gets little breaks in the brick and stuff. Like, back over in my old neighborhood . . . they were redoing the street and my shoe got sucked into the mud and then they paved it over with cement. And in my old house . . ." I wanted to tell her the story of my house. My parents bought it when my dad came back from the war and finally made some money from his songs. It was wooden, Tudorstyle. It smelled like lilacs and leather and old dusty wood and beer and plastic Barbie dolls fresh out of the box.

I wanted to show her my heart, my real life, my real home, my family, complete and alive.

I trailed off, trying to swallow all the things I felt, because I didn't want to ruin today. I needed today to be happy and perfect, I needed to be normal. Nera was in the world and I had to be in the world for her. I wanted to show her all the things we'd both find fascinating. I wanted her to know there had been more to me than this sadness.

Nera stopped me, like she could read my mind. "Charlie?" she said. "Don't put on a mask for me. Whatever this day brings, whatever you bring to the table, it all still brings you."

I felt a little teary. I wanted to snark. But I didn't. I just nodded.

Thank you for the carnations! Mr. C sounded as we came to my door. Nera smiled at him. And he looked to her. *Who's this?*

"I'm Nera!" she said. "It's wonderful to meet you."

Mr. C jumped back. *Another one of you live girls can see me!*

Yeah, she was very much alive.

I opened the door to the apartment and cult-followed songwriter and retired father Michael Connor was sitting on the couch. We just stared at each other like two shipwreck survivors washing up on a beach.

Nera came out from behind me.

The apartment was stale. But now I saw it through her eyes. She stepped forward, looking around, no judgment, just some sort of reverence.

The places of dirt and dust where we make our nests, they hold so much of our oxygen. Was this a home now?

"This is where you live," she said. "These walls get to see you every day." She smiled. "They're lucky, to hold you."

Dad stared at her.

"Dad," I said, "this is Nera Harosen."

Dad, in the Before, would have hugged her. But now he just sat with Chestnut sleeping on his lap, his eyes unfocused like he was looking at us through fogged-over cellophane.

"Hello," Nera waved. "It's good to meet you, Mr. Connor."

Dad turned his head slowly. "Uh," he said, looking down to Chestnut. "This is my dog, Chestnut."

"We've me—" I elbowed Nera. "What a beautiful little dog."

"Nera needs some more comfortable clothes," I said. "She's a lot taller than I am. Can we raid your closet?"

Dad nodded.

"Perfect," I said, shuffling to his bedroom door. "Let's get you some real clothes, ya big lug."

I just wanted to get out of here and get back to adventure. This was a time suck, and Nera only had until the sunset. But Nera didn't follow me. She just stood, stiff, in the hallway, "Er, I have to use the bathroom," she said, trying not to be giddy about it. I laughed and she slowly turned to look into the bathroom. In a daze, she walked in and shut the door behind her. "Oh my God," she whispered to herself.

"Okay, I'll . . . grab something for you," I said, entering the dark cavern of my father's room.

As I touched his closet, the bedroom door creaked open more to show Dad standing there on the threshold. He stared with big raccoon eyes, smelling like Budweiser and tomato soup.

A wave of anger reared inside me. Because I also saw the ghost of who *should* be standing there. Someone Nera would love. Someone who would love Nera. Two of my favorite people, finally crossing paths and creating a nebula of fantastic souls. But no, I lived with his shell, and no matter how I tried to pretend like this was okay, it was not okay.

"Can I help you?" I managed.

Dad drew nearer. "So you're moving on?" he said.

I stopped, my hands on the plastic hangers. I felt sick.

"No," I said honestly. "I'm not. I'm just adding."

Two people who used to be in conspiracy together now afraid of what the other might say.

He was afraid, wasn't he? That was the look in his eye. Not a fury, but a fear.

"I like girls," I said dumbly.

Dad didn't say anything.

I didn't know if he didn't understand or if he didn't care. I knew where his brain was. It wasn't with me.

"Nera helped me find out what happened to Sammy," I offered him.

"We know what happened to Sammy," Dad said.

"No, I mean . . . what happened after . . . Nera works for Charon, remember?" I said. "Sammy's music brought me to her. Dad, I found out that Sammy crossed through the Veil. She's safe. She's not here anymore."

"So you're letting her go." I felt the words stab me.

"Dad, she's gone," I said. "She's safe."

"The Veil is a door that leads to a place." He moved his hand in the air like he was building the sentence in front of him. A musician speaking in rhythm. "She's not here. So she's there. Have you seen the Veil? Do you know where it is?"

"Yes, but—"

"Then go get her, Charlie," he urged. "I'll go get her. *We'll* go get her."

What.

"Dad, it's not that easy."

"We need to make things right," he said. "You can't give up on your *sister.*"

That last word echoed through my soul.

He waited for an answer. And I couldn't give him one.

Would I bring her back to the living? Could I even do such a thing? There were stories about dogs at the gates, Charon in his ferry . . . there were also stories about bringing people back to the land of the living.

Maybe I could. Or maybe he was as hurt and confused as me, and this was a terrible idea.

"Like Orpheus," I said, "your song."

Did he not remember how that story ended?

But stories can change.

He touched my shoulder. For a second, I could feel him in there, in that shell. And he said, "You're a good kid."

Then he walked away. Back to the couch.

You're a good kid.

Words my father would have said back when. A phrase that was familiar. But was it a reflex of a dying body, or had he come to the surface for just a second?

This bedroom was too dark.

I grabbed one of his old band tees and some jeans, along with a belt and his old army boots, and I walked back out to the hall.

I held up the clothes while I kicked the bedroom door shut, both with my foot and in my mind as I stuffed away any feelings I had about his words.

So, you're letting her go?

Nera opened the bathroom door. I held up the clothes for her to see.

"Hope you like the Beatles," I said.

———

She tucked the black logo tee into her faded blue jeans that she in turn tucked into the army boots. She clunked around in them, and I guess decided that they fit well enough. She had let her hair all the way down, flowing to her waist, and I handed her a hair tie. "Just in case," I said. "Always gotta have a hair tie, just in case."

She braided her hair down one shoulder, flipping it in front of her.

Her curved, full face. Her chestnut hair. Her strong arms, her piercing eyes . . . she towered over me as she stared at herself in the mirror.

"You look . . ." I started. She looked like she finally belonged, like she was finally alive. A ghost brought back to the world. A woman who was allowed to breathe. Allowed to be with me in this place.

"Like me," she said. "I look like me."

Turns out not sleeping for decades will mean that you need to take a nap before lunch. I let her sleep on the inside part of my bed, next to the wall. I sat next to her, keeping watch. After a while, I lay down, gazing at her breathing in and out, her hair moving ever so slightly. I pushed it out of her face.

Nera opened her eyes, blearily.

"I . . . what happened?" she said. "I was . . . we were on the train, and you turned into a chicken? Are you alright? How did you turn into a chicken! How was I completely alright with it?!"

I stared at her. "Nera, you were dreaming."

Nera blinked. "Dreaming?" she said, like she was finding out she'd had a heart attack. "No, to be dreaming you have to sleep and . . . I was sleeping?!"

I touched her hand. "Nera . . . you really have never slept before?"

Groggily, Nera focused on my hand. "Your hand is warm. And so is mine. Is my hand warm?"

I nodded.

"My body is warm," she said. "I slept. I . . ." She sat up, tears in her eyes. "I'm real."

I smiled a little. "You always have been," I said.

"But was I alive?" she said. "Have I ever been alive? *Really* awake and alive? In order to sleep you have to really be awake, don't you?" There was something humming inside her. She said the word "alive" so forcefully, like a violin jumping in a song about old Irish hills and the green of places I'd never seen, places *she'd* never seen, all the places she could *now* see and walk into the world and discover for herself. And she laughed a little. "Charlie," she said, "kiss me."

"What? I . . . don't think . . ."

"You don't want to? We already have."

"I know but now we're out here."

"So, the one in the Station didn't count?"

"Oh God, no, it counted," I said. "But this is your first foray into the living world and I'm not gonna just let you smooch the first person you—"

"You think I want you because you're 'the first person' I—?" Nera said. "You think I'm that naïve? That you mean so little?"

"I—"

"No, Charlie," Nera said. "I want to kiss you because you're you. Now please." And then she added, "But only if you want to. I'm sorry, I—"

I kissed her. Deep. Desperate.

She shuddered. She moaned. Then she kissed me back, leaning in close, grabbing the back of my head, twining her fingers through my hair and cradling me in her arms. She enveloped me. Her hair fell gently against my face. And my entire body felt like it was melting into hers.

She let go.

In a daze, I leaned back. It was so much more than at the Station. I could feel her, all of her. "Jesus Christ," I muttered.

Nera stared at me, her entire body shaking. She touched her thigh, and looked down. And then looked to me. She laughed. She laughed and hugged herself and then leaned over and kissed me on the cheek. "I'm alive, Charlie," she said. "I'm fucking alive."

"Mr. Coleson next door," Nera said as we lay on my bed, the way that people do when time means nothing and they keep telling themselves they need to get up but they never find the moment where they actually do. It just becomes a liminal forever, two people on a mattress, their heads propped up on soft pillows and their legs hiding under blankets.

"What about Mr. Coleson?" I said.

"He said something about carnations?"

"Oh, yeah, he wanted me to bring his wife carnations," I said. "His wife lives next door and he won't go anywhere or with any dog until he knows she's okay."

"And you did that? You helped her?"

"Yeah, it was no big."

"It may be a small kindness, but it meant the world to them," Nera said. Then she looked to my ceiling in thought. "He must be strong indeed, not to be losing his mind or found by the Haunts." She bit her lip. "Edna had me read this book about Gehenna—"

"Jewish Hell," I snorted.

Nera touched a little thread that had come undone from my comforter blanket. "We don't know what's on the other side, no more than anyone else. But no, Gehenna isn't Hell. According to the stories, it has a large lake made of fire."

"Definitely not Hell then," I snarked.

"Except in the story of Hell," Nera put her finger on my nose, "the lake of fire is seen as a bad thing. But Edna didn't see it that way. She said it's a challenge. To make us stronger. It's not necessarily a punishment. It's like . . . how people go for long jogs that hurt to make their legs stronger."

"Gehenna has a lake that's a Bowflex?"

"Sure," Nera said, uncertain. "But there are other parts of the spirit world. Not a lake, but an abyss. And whatever form it takes, it's always the same thing: destruction." Nera took a shaky breath, still learning how to breathe through nerves. "And in between are the lost souls. The Haunts. And demons . . ." She hesitated. "I wonder if it's all a lot closer than we think it is. If that abyss has anything to do with the demon that started the Chicago Fire."

I felt a little sick. The demon. She had never met the thing in the dark. The idea that all those lost people hadn't meant to get lost, but maybe sometimes being lost was better than struggling to be found.

"That is confusing," I said. "What the fuck are demons and ghosts doing here in Chicago? It's not the other side of the Veil."

"I don't know all the answers," Nera admitted. "But like I said, there may be more magic all around us that most just don't take the time to see. I don't know if anyone truly would understand it; it seems to be layers upon layers . . . like the city itself."

"Well, Hell being here on earth doesn't sound too wacky." I snorted again. "It very much is."

"As I said, *not* Hell," Nera corrected. "The world-to-come. I am saying it must be closer to the world-that-is than we thought." She looked down at my hand. "This place is not Hell. If the living world was that bad, no one would be afraid to leave it." That made me feel a way, deep in the pit of my stomach. "Mr. Coleson and the many ghosts we can see, they would be running for the lighthouse as soon as they died." She hesitated and then said, "And it wouldn't feel so right to be here."

Her eyes flicked up at me. Like she was going to say something sweeter, something that would fucking break me as soon as she was gone again.

"The clock's ticking." I rubbed my eyes. "We should get up."

"I could spend all my time right here with you and be happy," she said.

"I'm not the world." I forced myself to untangle from her. "You're here to see the world."

42

NERA

The world was a gift. I only had one day, but that would be enough. This moment was mine, this moment was *ours*, and if I never saw the city again, I would hold onto these memories every single second moving forward. I would have a window to see, food to taste, a person to miss.

We walked down the street, a park to our right. Sounds bombarded me. I wondered, if Chicago were a song, what instrument would play it? So I asked Charlie what she thought.

"I think some people would say drums, because of the L and the jackhammers and the shouting," Charlie said.

"But you?"

Charlie cleared her throat. Her hands painted the air around her as she answered: "A clarinet. Wise, wooden, a wind breathing a truth that is sad and calm and steady. At least, that's what the city would be right now. With you here."

Charlie Connor spoke with her heart on her tongue, and I fell hard for her words.

She shrugged. "Either that or like an electric guitar with the whammy bar." She let a laugh slip out. But then she chewed the inside of her cheek, turning around to look at the skyline past the rocks and the lake. "But I'm not the city. There are lots of Chicagoans, and each one sees Chicago from a different angle. So each person you'd ask, you'd get a new answer every time."

I took her hand. She squeezed.

Charlie led me, like her own sort of ferryman through the living. We walked in the cold, back to the Granville station, then got off at Belmont. We kept walking, surrounded by brownstones and people hurrying by with their faces half-covered by polyester coats and knitted caps. Each one of them in such a hurry, hiding their thoughts in the back of their head.

I gazed above us. Bare trees on one side, the tops of houses and apartments on the other, and in between, the gray sky so bright I couldn't look long enough to make out the clouds. The sky had become one massive fog.

I watched some children build a snowman, their bodies rolling and packing snow. No flickering. Where were their souls? I was so used to seeing them. They must have souls in there. Although there were wisps of ghosts all around them, some watching them play and some trying to play with them and some just staring out into nothing . . . these live children were so solid, so in motion, always moving forward, buoyed by the present.

Each one of these children would eventually die, like the ones around them they couldn't see. But today, they played in the snow.

We crossed the street, an odd little intersection with multiple lights and multiple directions like a spoke on a wheel. It wasn't clean like the ones I'd seen in the movies. I gripped Charlie's hand harder.

We went into the restaurant on the corner. Immediately, an aroma of pizza hit me in my face. I could smell it. It filled my head. My mouth watered. It *really watered*.

"Who . . . is that?" I said, pointing to the multiple pictures on the walls, all the walls, of a particular man playing basketball.

"Oh," she said. "That's Michael Jordan."

Of course. Michael Jordan. So many people had come through with memories of him. He was somewhere in my map, a name listed like a vocabulary word in a word bank, near the United Center. But here he was . . . in a pizza shop?

"What does he have to do with pizza?" I said.

"I don't have a clue," Charlie said. "But this is the place. Lou Malnati's."

We were seated. The jeans were . . . freeing. I could balance in these heavy big boots easier than my old heeled boots. No one looked at me oddly, no one regarded me. No one knew who I was. And strangely enough, with the amount of food and bustling and music and live bodies, there were barely any ghosts. Just one, a very flustered woman who kept floating in and out of the kitchen door, her feathered hat the most vivid thing I could see. She didn't look at me.

"I'm so used to being the Station Master's daughter." I gave a small chuckle. "But no one here cares."

"No one here knows there's a Station," she said. "I mean, I don't know about that woman, but no one *alive* knows."

"But they surely know they're going to die," I said.

Charlie nodded, and then nervously looked around. "Yeah, but no one really wants to believe it."

"Believe it?! They think they're going to live forever?"

"No." Charlie scrunched her face up, looking at her menu. It was laminated in little pockets with cloth on the edges. "But no one wants to think about it while they're living."

"So, they just think that every day they get to sit here and eat pizza and build snowmen?" I asked. "They're just walking around with a cloud over their eyes?"

"Nera." Charlie tried to direct me. "You have one day here, before you go back. Would you want to spend the whole day thinking about how you're returning at sunset, or would you like to pretend we have forever?"

I thought of me and Red, watching *Casablanca* in the early hours, pretending *we* had forever. It wasn't any different here.

"No one talks about death," Charlie said.

"That must be very lonely, for you," I said.

Charlie looked at me over the menu, sizing up my words. Then slowly, she nodded. "It is."

We ordered Lou Malnati's pizza. The memory of Lou Malnati's was one thing, a recollection of a pizza. The actual pizza, this one particular pizza that had never existed before the ingredients were mixed together in the last hour in the kitchen and would never exist again after we consumed it . . . this one specific pizza had chunks of cheese in places, burn marks on the crusts on specific slices. I picked up a knife and fork, heavy in my hand . . . I sliced through the gobs of cheese. I stuffed it in my mouth and I felt a stinging scream on my tongue.

"ACK!" I spit it out. Everyone turned to look at me. I felt warm, but not the good sort of warm.

"You burn your tongue?" Charlie grabbed an ice cube from her drink and handed it to me. "Put that on the spot that hurts, quick."

I did so. Freezing cold. My tongue numbed. It sizzled back to normal.

"You can blow on your pizza to make it cooler." Charlie explained chemistry to me. I gave a small smile. Eating was harder than the memory of eating, but Charlie knew how to put ice on a burn. I felt safe.

I let it sit for a minute, and then I couldn't wait any longer. I blew on it, as Charlie said, and I stuffed it in my mouth between my teeth. Cheese, gooey, sharp, soft. Tangy tomatoes smashed into sauce, bread with butter—how to explain a pizza. It made me feel full, it filled my mouth with a new world of thought. I chewed down on it, and it pressed against my gums. I shivered.

It wasn't perfect, so it was so much better than the memory in the diner. There would never be another pizza like this again, and there never had been one like this before.

Charlie dug into her lunch. Like she'd eaten a thousand times before and would eat a thousand more times.

She would have so many days without me.

I supposed Charlie was right, it was sad to not pretend we'd live forever.

What was the point of a pizza, when it all ended at the Veil? We didn't get to take pizza with us.

Well, in that macabre way of thinking, what was the point of anything? What was the point of seeing Charlie, as beautiful as she was?

There was so much more to Chicago than the lights I'd seen from the Station's roof. There were details. There were voices. There were faces.

This is why death was so sad. Because it was a goodbye to all this.

I sat in the warmth of the shop. After all the pizza was gone, we ordered as many different drinks as I wanted. Pop, water, milk, hot cocoa . . . I felt the hot cocoa on my lips. Chocolate. I always thought it would taste more like nuts, or bark; did bark have a taste? But this was milky, with sugar, and so warm in my throat. I felt the different pieces of my insides as the cocoa scorched its way down my throat and into my stomach.

There was a world outside my body. There was also a world inside. Not just light and a soul, but bones, muscles, a heart, a stomach, a brain, eyes. I had been gifted these things and they weren't anyone else's but mine. They weren't Father's, they weren't the Station's. They were mine.

I sipped my cocoa more. When the cocoa was done, I scooted it over and brought a tea I had also ordered closer to me. Three of five orders.

I looked at Charlie across from me. She looked sad.

"What's the matter?" I asked. She sighed.

"I told Dad that I'd found the Station," she admitted. "And he says I . . . should go get Sammy. Bring her back."

There was something new in my stomach, a knot, a stone. "Oh no," I said. "Charlie, things don't work that way."

"Okay, we don't know that." She leaned in. "We don't know how *any* of this works. You said so yourself. Remember when we walked through the wall? How are you and your father living in a dream your whole life, never sleeping, never eating? How do the dogs talk?"

"There are things that are made of dreams and then there are things that are going against the tide," I said.

"There's no tide in the lake," she said. "Well, maybe the lake makes weird new things happen."

"Charlie," I said softly. "Charlie, she passed away. She doesn't have a body any longer. Just as we can't stop growing, we can't stop—"

"Your father stopped growing," she argued. "And if we went through the Veil, maybe we could bring Edna back, we could find them all and—"

"Charlie, please. You know that no matter what you do, you can't heal your father. He—"

"She's my fucking sister, Nera," she snapped. "If I can bring her back, then I will."

It was a statement that she did not need my approval for. It was a truth. A fact. But it didn't matter how much Charlie wanted it, she wouldn't survive the Veil. It wasn't for us yet.

I took her hand.

"Your hands are chapped," she sniffed. "Are you alright?"

I gave a sad little laugh. "Yes," I said. "The cold cracks skin. But it's a part of all this, isn't it? The pain?" I looked in her big brown eyes. And I said, "I can't help you bring your sister back to the living, Charlie. I just can't. I don't know everything, but in my gut, I believe that the ferry and the Veil and the lake, all of it, is to bring us peace in the right direction. If she's passed through the Veil, which she has, it's where she needs to—" Charlie let go of my hand. "Anger is a part of grief," I said. "It's alright. You can be angry. Denial is as well. You can't just hold onto the music. There's dissonance in it, too. Charlie—"

"Where she needs to be," she sniffed again. "I told you, she needs to be *here*."

And something welled up inside her. I saw it in her eyes. Tears, right there, waiting to fall. But she wouldn't let them fall anymore.

"Charlie?" I said, quiet. "She *isn't* here." She said nothing. I took a deep breath. I plucked a sugar packet and put it on the table between us. "This is us, in this life, who we are in this moment."

I opened the sugar packet, and I put it in my tea, like Charlie had just showed me how to do.

I swirled it around.

"Then we pass on, and we become something else. You can't ask a ghost to keep on doing the small life they had before. Not when they belong to something much larger now."

"And what about us?" Charlie asked. "What about the living, we're just abandoned?"

I pursed my lips. "Maybe when they pass on, they're still here. Just in a different way. Maybe it's like the Station—they're in the walls and the music and the light and the memories. But as much as you want to put the sugar back in its packet . . . you can't. It's already moved onto the next thing it was supposed to do. It would be cruel to take out every single little grain, try to dry them off, piece them back together, shove them back into the ripped package . . . pretend things were okay. When to the sugar, things were already okay."

Charlie held her head, like it hurt. "There was so much she hadn't done, so many things we were supposed to do. She wasn't ready. *We* aren't ready."

"If you go after her," I said, "if you pass through that Veil, you will die, too. You will not be able to be put back together. I don't want to see you disappear, Charlie. And I know that if your father was well, he wouldn't want that, either."

She looked down at her cocoa. "My dad wasn't always . . . he didn't always look like the walking dead. He was a real great dad."

I nodded. "Just because someone is lost doesn't mean they don't exist," I said. "He's still there. He's just not the person you knew. Maybe, we learn to love people in all their iterations."

"Okay." She scooted up in her seat. "So lemme ask you this. Brain cancer people. People who lose themselves before they die. People who every part of them gets eaten away. What happens then? They just loop? They just go be part of the Haunts?"

I shook my head. "No. The Haunts are poisoned by the Fire, by whatever is leaking out into the city by that . . . demon." She looked away from me. I looked to my hands. "Someone who is sick in life, that's their body. And yes, it might become imprinted on their soul, but . . . the mind? It's a tool. It's not the person. And even the Haunts, I still believe they are themselves, under all that muck and fear. You're always you, even when you don't feel yourself."

That was easy to say for someone who had never suffered. I knew that. And from Charlie's expression, I knew she knew as well. She leaned forward and the lantern necklace slipped out from her shirt.

"My sister was ripped open just like your sugar packet," she said. "And I'm supposed to be hunky dory with that. Where's the justice? Where's the peace?"

"I don't know," I said. "I just have to believe that it works out. That things are bigger than we see."

"How?"

I paused for a moment, then shrugged. "Because of the way laundry smells, when we walked past that vent on the street on the way back to your home. That is something both tangible and wonderful and exists just as much as the bad things. Because of hot cocoa and how your dad still has a big heart. And Charlie, I want to try greasy fries at a greasy diner in Belmont. I want to try this Harold's chicken people keep talking about. This day and, the way the sun keeps coming up and going down, and . . . sitting here with you?" I said hopefully. "Because even in a world with the Haunts, Mr. Coleson still waits for his wife."

She narrowed her eyes. "So Sam being murdered is fine because laundry smells good?"

I wished I had something better to say. Perhaps if I was someone else, if I was smarter, then I would. It did sound silly; offensive, even.

George's eyes looking me over before he crossed, that disappointment shivered down my spine.

"For someone who says she doesn't know all the answers, you sure talk like you do," she said.

"I'm sorry," I said, my face getting hot. "I should learn to feel more comfortable saying that I don't know."

"What about us who don't get ripped open?" she asked. "What about us who are still stuck here?"

I squeezed her hand. Just like she'd squeezed mine. I wanted to hold her.

"I hope," I said, "that life isn't about being stuck. There are things that hurt, but also healing. There is constant motion. And while you aren't the same as you were in the beginning, you are still you. You . . . persevere."

"I get what you're saying," she said quietly. "I . . . just hope to God you're right."

And I wished we could see ourselves with the love we felt for this city around us.

To have thousands of days. To see the sun come up and go down from different buildings and parks, thousands of times. To meet every single one of these living people, to see them not just in their graduations through the Veil but in the little mundane moments of a Sunday afternoon. Sit next to one on the train. Let someone cut in line. Share a meal with them. Overhear a phone call about a relative they had time to catch up with, talk groceries, ask about the weather. To be completely cocooned in the illusion of routine.

What a privilege, to believe this would last forever.

I had recently learned that a symphony is heard for only minutes. There are too many instruments and notes to understand and love each one. Even to remember them all. Still, there will always be the sound of the music, coalescing and weaving itself into our spirits.

This day was a symphony, and I wanted to memorize every sound.

43

CHARLIE

The city became a poem that I needed to curate into eight stolen hours for someone who had never read poetry but had only heard of it.

There were so many things I wanted to show you, Nera. And if I was Ferris Bueller, I could have.

The Museum of Science and Industry's massive gaping atrium that looked so much like the Station's.

The Art Institute where I could show her my favorite painting, the one with the girl singing to the sunrise, looking just like Nera must have looked when she was younger.

I could show her my favorite street in the Back of the Yards. I could show her that little spot on 47th, on the bridge over the ugly-ass highway, with a little hole cut in the chain-link fence so you could see the Sears Tower perfectly. I didn't know who cut that hole, but it had been there for a few years. It would be one glorious little detail of the city in the afternoon on this cold December day.

But instead, we ended up at the grocery store.

We walked into Dominick's, giggling over her confusion at the revolving door, and I pointed out my favorite cashier who looked exactly like Don Knotts. He waved, and I pointed out his tie, which had Don Knotts's face emblazoned on it.

"This is a grocery store," Nera said. When we passed the produce, the song from *Singin' in the Rain* hummed through the speakers and the sprinklers turned on and washed the vegetables in their shelves.

Nera jumped, and then she laughed.

"I should be taking you somewhere cultured." I laughed, too. "Not a Dominick's."

"No," she said. "This is . . . magical." She put her hand in the water. "This is like something we'd have at the Station."

"Have you seen *Singin' in the Rain*?"

She nodded. "Red showed it to me, a double feature with *Casablanca* when she was trying to teach me film history," she said. Then Nera sang "Good Mornin'" to me, and I showed her the upstairs. The smell of the gritty bathroom permeated down the stairwell, but she ran up to see if she could find a window to look out of.

"You know there are more sights to see than the grocery store," I said, joining her.

The lake could follow us all the way up and down the face of this city. The pigeons, the library, the smell of piss and coffee beans and pork and gasoline all mixing together to slide across fresh snow as commuters slipped their way through ice patches and big ugly puddles.

We got on the train.

She wanted to ride above the streets, see the backyards of strangers. Turn the corner on the Brown Line and see the perfect snapshot of the skyline right before Sheridan.

Death's daughter stood in awe of a new perspective of the city. "It's like a dream," she said softly.

She pulled me close, hugging me with her arm. I fit into the groove of her curves, and it was warm. It was home.

Then we went past Graceland Cemetery, where everyone lost their signals and I looked out to see all the dead in the graveyard waving up at us, trying to get our attention again. Nera waved back.

And I smiled.

We went to Grant Park. She forced someone to take a picture of us in front of the big Buckingham Fountain.

"Nera." I sprinted after her as she ran down the walkway. "You know we're never going to see that stranger again, right? We aren't getting a copy of our picture and they'll probably just erase it."

"They won't." Nera spun around. "And even if we don't have it, that picture will exist. We now have a photograph together."

I didn't understand, but I followed her past the lines of baseball fields down to the Hilton, and back through the southern side of the park.

Still the sounds echoed through the streets of those who had been here before. *The whole world is watching, the whole world is watching.* I didn't like to come down to Grant Park usually, because of how many things had happened there. Riots, murders, uprising, revolution, brutality, concerts . . . just the layers upon layers of festivals were enough. Even now, a Looper was marching a half-circle, his top half holding a blurry unreadable sign. But with Nera beside me, it felt manageable.

Nera breathed in. "The park smells like . . . what does this smell like?"

I took in a deep breath. My lungs hurt. "Diesel," I said. "Cigarettes. The lake's clear cold air."

"What does it smell like in summer?" she asked.

I tried to think of the last time I'd been in Grant Park in the summer. "Flowers," I said. "Food. Sunblock. But still diesel and cigarettes."

She nodded. "I wish I could see it in the summer."

Then our bus came.

On the bus was a baby, alive and healthy and screaming in its mother's arms. Nera couldn't look away.

We glided past McCormick Place. The growing construction of the South Loop. We got off the bus past Chinatown. We ate ice cream in the freezing cold. We explored the streets, all different, with so many years of memory and history, and for all the reasons my mother had to leave this place, I had to stay here. Chicago was a quick, breathy feeling between phrases, a clipping along keys to hit every single note in a glissando. It was fast, it was hard, but it was beautiful.

The day was getting short. We went to return to Fullerton in a cab.

"You'll have to come back when it's warm," I said as I looked away from the face of my flip phone. 3:34. "You were talking about summer, but . . . When the city is in spring, it comes alive. The first day of spring, everyone blooms. They come out of their doorways, all the restaurants spill onto the sidewalks. Everyone takes off early from work and school, the windows open, and people look at one another. It's the best day in the city."

Nera smiled. "On the first day of spring," she said, "I'll come back."

And I leaned into her.

It was a calculated risk. Even here in Chicago, outside of Andersonville and Boys Town, it was an act of bravery to hold her hand. She didn't know this. And I didn't want to worry her. So I squeezed her fingers. And she leaned in for a kiss.

I let her kiss me. And my eyes shifted uncomfortably to see if the cabbie saw us.

Maybe I was overreacting.

We stopped in traffic. Suddenly, Nera pulled away. "The zoo!" she said. "There's the zoo!" She opened the door and was gone. I fumbled some cash to the driver, then I followed, making sure my wallet stayed in my coat pocket and my feet didn't tumble down the side of the street.

The sun was still up, but it was evening and the holiday lights had already begun. Whole symphonies of Christmas music played through the speakers, as light-up trees danced alongside little LED animations of penguins. One Christmas in a string of Christmases, pictures being taken on disposable and digital cameras, children who would grow up and pass on and this place would be a memory one day.

But today was today. And it was ours.

We walked past the statue that had been Sammy's favorite. The one that I had checked so early on, but found nothing. Dad had insisted Sam would be there. But now there was just me and Nera, looking up at the beautiful fairy sprinkling flower's dew on sleeping children who dreamt of boats on magic waters.

Nera stared at it. "Land of Nod," she said. "What's the Land of Nod?"

"I guess it's a statue about where you live," I said. I touched one of the sleeping children's cheeks. "I haven't been here since right after Sam died . . . she loved this statue. But . . . I'm okay, being here with you now."

Maybe this place could be happy again.

I watched Nera laugh as she saw the little light-up, LED-animated penguins slip and slide all over the Christmas display, then I showed her the real penguins and she lost her damn mind.

"Look at these!" she said, waddling beside the fogged-up, scratched-up glass. "They are perfect, how have these been across the street from me this entire time?!"

"Ellos son mi animal favorito!" a little boy squealed beside her, and without skipping a beat she squealed back: "¡Yo también!"

Nera. Brilliant, beautiful, penguin-loving Nera.

We sat in that little alcove, warm under a glowing heater. She kissed me again. It was less scary, here with the penguins hopping around.

Ahead of us, standing beside the plexiglass and holding hands, were two old women with their hands entwined. With no fear. Only joy.

"No one ever tells you about the penguins," Nera said. "They're, I guess, worried about bigger things. But . . ." She looked to the little waddly pack in front of us. "But I was missing so much."

So was I.

I kissed her a little fiercer.

And somewhere in that space, in this place with her, I started to feel myself come back to life. I wasn't just Sammy's sister, or my father's daughter, or the child my mother left, or Marco's friend . . . I was me. The kid who liked penguins and hot cocoa, the one who had come to the city to be a teacher and who was trying to find the music on the piano using chords learned on a beat-up guitar. I claimed my own chapped hands, my split ends, my beating heart, my life. *My life.* I was *alive* and so was she, and the whole city seemed to wrap around us like a blanket, enveloping us in its lights and its car horns and its Christmas music.

Maybe she was right. Maybe she wasn't. Maybe the Veil ate us alive. Maybe the Veil was just a door to something better. It didn't matter. Because here, right now, life included Nera Harosen. And that was worth the rest.

We all were more than grief.

"I only have a little more time," she breathed, looking at the setting sun. "I have to go back soon . . ."

She couldn't go back. I couldn't let her go. I held her, she held me, and the thought of my hands never touching her like this again . . . she could not go back to that cage she wasn't supposed to even know yet.

This was only the beginning and she said there had to be an ending.

Nera looked out to the sky, and she said, "There's still a little time. A few hours?"

Not even that.

I wanted to pretend we had all the time.

I wanted to walk down the street with her at night, go see a movie, show her the top of the Sears Tower, the Christkindlmarket in Daley Plaza, the beautiful parks in the south, baseball stadiums, all the places beyond this one city . . . the world. Everything I couldn't fit into one day. Everyone else had lifetimes, and it wasn't fair.

"Let's go back to your bed," she said quietly.

I gawked at her. What did that mean?

"If we hurry," she said, "we can get to Edgewater and I can find my way back before the night gets . . . too dark."

We were kidding ourselves. And I wanted to say we should turn back to the Station right then. But then I wouldn't have held you, Nera. We wouldn't have had what came next.

I'd been to Nera's room. It was much nicer than mine. In the Station, her room was a soft loft made of pillows, like an attic that had been built to be a comfortable reading nook. It had been a magical shire of just Nera, a nest of her smells and sights and I had never wanted to leave.

I wondered if that's how she saw my dark cramped cave.

Seeing her touch the photographs on my drywall. Taking in the air that was a mix of my deodorant, my shitty perfume, the incense I'd lit for a ghost that needed help—that smokey scent had never really gotten aired out.

"It's a shrine," she whispered.

Much better word than shire. Shires were safe. Shrines were holy.

I looked to her, in her tucked-in tee. And she looked nervous.

I also was very nervous.

It was silent in the apartment. Dad and Chestnut were out, Chestnut's leash missing from the hook by the door. It was peaceful, just me and her, in this room. There was so much space between us, but I knew it wouldn't be hard to cross that ocean and kiss her again. With her, it was easy. Something about the way she moved with me, the way she smiled down at me.

She was someone who was as close to my heart as my own voice.

"So, what do we do now?" she said, and she pulled her brown hair out of her braid. It fell across her shoulders, down her back, so far down. And I felt my insides come alive.

"Oh, wow," I said.

"This is . . . I'm not exactly certain how this works," she said.

My pelvis ached with want. I felt like I was going to melt. She didn't know, but this . . . was also new to me.

I had never told anyone. The boys I'd forced myself to have crushes on in middle school, the arduous conversations with my sister about who I wanted to go to the dance with or what celebrity was cute. I would feel sick. Girls were pretty, yes. Girls were someone I'd like to hug, or watch a good movie with, or snuggle into on a cold winter night before getting up and having hot cocoa together . . . I wanted to hold someone. I wanted someone to hold me. I wanted to be loved. And anything less than that, or something that was just physical . . . I didn't want it.

But that's not what teenagers think about. Or kids in college. No one wanted to think about the future; no one really believed in a future. It was just live for today, feel good today. But I wanted to feel good with only one person, my one person, and that made me a freak.

The shame came back, looking at Nera. My roommate telling me that if I kept holding out, then I was going to be alone forever. That I should go have fun. That I should let that nice boy next door ride me like a . . . whatever. And I had sat the rest of the night on my bed, staring at my wall, wondering what was wrong with me that the thought of sex with a random person made me feel sick.

But this night, Nera—this wasn't a girl next door. This wasn't a boy in my English class. This was Nera. And this person was a place that fit me. A home.

I had always been a fool to love a woman I'd never met.

And now here she was. I knew her. It wasn't just sex, it was a homecoming.

I then realized Nera had been standing there with her hair down with no verbal input for too long. I had said nothing and she looked like she was going to cry.

"I'm sorry," she said. "I shouldn't have been so forward."

"No, no, no, Nera." I rushed to her. I took her arms in my hands, pulling her closer to me. "No, Nera, that's not it. I gotta . . . tell you . . . something, okay? So, look, I try to act all badass and all like I somehow have *anything* figured out. I'm cool, I wear Chucks and I play piano, ooh . . . but, Nera, you're my first kiss. And this is gonna be my first . . . you know." I took a deep breath. "I know I'm too old for this shit—"

She stared at me. Like she'd found relief in me, like she was in awe of me and would continue to be in awe. She said, "W-what? But you've been out in the world, you're gorgeous, you—"

"I didn't ever want to kiss anyone," I said.

She blinked. "I . . ."

"I'm weird, I know," I said. "I know. But I was . . . I didn't want to kiss anyone until I found someone I absolutely wanted to kiss. And I've been told that's childish, I get it. But Nera . . . I . . ." I didn't even know how to explain myself to her. I barely understood me, and I *lived in here with me.* "I'm not . . . like other people, I've learned. I like girls. And I don't want to just date around. I know other people want to, and that's great! I just don't want to. And I feel like I'm going to have a panic attack whenever I . . . whenever I was gonna be pushed into doing anything . . . I just don't think like that, there's something broken in me, and most of the time I'd rather share a pizza than—"

She placed her hand in mine. And she rubbed my wrist with her thumb.

"You're not broken," she said. And she put her other hand on my cheek. "You don't have to be anyone but yourself. Because it's you I want to be here with." And then she said, "It's my first time, too, obviously. And if you don't want to do anything—"

"I want you to hold me close," I said with all the honesty I held in my heart.

She pulled me in, by the waist, and I looked up at her, this picturesque, solid woman, and her hair cascaded down her rosy cheeks and I died inside her big eyes and perfect nose and . . .

I kissed her nose, her forehead, her lips.

She fell back on the bed. I fell on top of her. The warmth of her body, the fact that she was here and taking up space and I could touch her. I could feel every inch of her. I could wrap my fingers around her wrists and I could press my stomach to hers and I could lean down to her breasts and trace her arm, her shoulder with my fingers . . .

I wanted to cry. Because finally, my body relaxed.

"Please touch me," she said.

And I didn't think anymore.

I just felt her, our souls pressing into each other's chests, my hands holding her breasts through the thick clothing. "This shirt needs to come off, please," I told her. Our spirits were too big for these small bodies.

We laughed and giggled while she tried to teach me how to unhook her underclothes. But it didn't have to be perfect, it didn't have to be timed to a weird sexy soundtrack. It was just us. Then she was there, her broad shoulders, her soft skin, thick stomach and hips, her curved ass, and I couldn't fathom how I was staring at someone so beautiful.

And that someone wanted me, too.

I wondered if there had been other lives where we'd done this exact same thing. Hundreds of years of finding each other, holding each other . . . even if not, this had been a scene that had played out between so many people. Love.

It was real.

The best dreams, the lightest hearts. It was like playing the piano, using things I could touch to create and feel something untouchable. But goddamn could I touch her; I felt her curves under my palms. I felt the soft heat in between her legs.

A violin, a clarinet, the swelling of strings and woodwinds whistling above, the low bellow of a bass, a cello gliding along the bottom of the staff, the pressing of a damper pedal, as I felt our hips press into each other, her leg between mine, her fingers inside me, pressing parts of my soul, finding and carrying something deeper than anyone else had ever discovered, lending me her warmth to bloom open like a belting, strong contralto at the end of a musical I never finished, but wanted to so badly.

We were the same song. No longer wrapped in instruments. We were only sound.

We were music.

44

NERA

I'm not exactly certain why an unfinished song brought Charlie to the Station. I could have easily gone through my existence never seeing another living soul. Let alone holding her. Yet here she was, curled into me. Our bodies looked like they were from the same era, but my garments were so different, had *been* so different when I was wearing them . . . now they were all strewn on the floor as if we were both time travelers from different worlds. Her cotton polyester T-shirt and jeans with my bodice with her sports bra and my stockings and her mismatched rainbow socks and the Beatles shirt she had loaned me, the space between a costume and a future I could really have.

It was a miracle we found each other. I cradled her head in the crook of my arm, her breath hitting my bare breast, and I didn't want to move ever again. I wanted to stay in this space, with her, and never press her away. It didn't matter if my body felt heavy, if my neck cramped; I belonged to her now.

She was sleeping, and I could see her skin and bones, her ribs poking out from above her stomach. She was so small. She had made herself so small. And I didn't know if it was because she thought she was too big for this world, or if she forgot to eat after her sister died, but I hoped she was okay.

She'd told me about running and never stopping. How fast her sister would run, and how she could never catch up with her. I had the same feeling about Charlie.

I couldn't ask her to stay with me; she couldn't. My Station never changed; it never ran anywhere. It was at the end of a story, and hers had only just begun. If I tried to keep her, it would be a trap. I knew in my heart that was true.

But if I kept chasing her, if I ran away from the endings, right into this new beginning . . .

Could I ever leave for good?

In the library, I read about astronauts who traveled to space. After so many days away from the world, they returned and their muscles were weak and their entire physiology had transformed, because their bodies believed they were no longer in need of the planet but instead had to survive in the stars.

I still hadn't known a sunburned summer day, running out of water, getting older faster than you wanted to. I'd never had an infection, a broken heart, a boring Sunday afternoon with the dread of a Monday morning.

I had spent my entire life in space, never knowing gravity. Could I even survive in this world?

My place was with Charlie, I knew that for a fact. If Charlie wasn't going to be there, I would have to be here. Somehow.

My arm ached. Then I couldn't feel it. But not like at the Station, it was as if there was blood pumping and nerves tingling and—

I felt sick, all of a sudden. A swath of emotions and physical pains that I had never felt. I jerked away from Charlie and held my stomach. What was this wretched feeling—no, *feelings*—so many senses and pricks and stretches and tingles and . . .

I sat up.

Was I dying?

I couldn't be dying. I hadn't chosen to die.

But out here, it was not a choice.

Charlie stirred. "Nera?"

I didn't say anything.

"Nera, you okay?"

Her city wasn't mine. My world wasn't hers. This was never going to work.

"I can't feel my arm," I panicked. "That's never happened before. I believe it may be broken?"

"I think it just fell asleep . . . you've never had an arm fall asleep before?" Charlie said. "Wow, your place really is magic."

"You radiate the world off you," I said. "You make me part of your world."

"It's yours, too. I don't think it's me making you alive, you're just alive," Charlie touched my arm gently. "Wait for a minute and your arm will be fine again."

And it was. I reveled in the brilliant sensation of blood and life pulsing back into it, like it was waking up and yawning and laughing with tears.

Joy, that's what it was. That joy may come with eventual death and pain and loss outside of my control. But to stay by her, to drink chocolate and see penguins, I would make that bargain.

My stomach settled, so I laid back down, and I held her again.

Life. *L'chaim.* A Shabbat evening, a Sunday afternoon, the whole week, all the seasons, no picking and choosing. I had spent my life in the station of goodbyes. And here was my first hello.

My one precious day, and it was ending.

The sun had completely disappeared. I worried I was late, but I couldn't get out of the bed.

I held her hands and squeezed them tight. "I don't want to go back," I whispered. "And I can't ask you to stay there forever with me. You are to grow older, I'm to stay the same. You can't live your entire life in the nighttime, Charlie. Especially now that you know where your sister is."

Charlie touched my cheek—my hot, rosy cheek—and I felt my heartbeat.

"Then stay here," Charlie said softly.

But I couldn't. I wanted to, Charlie, I wanted to more than anything. The idea of walking back through the pillars into the atrium, I felt like I would suffocate. Stale air, identical days, with only the promise of the same walls I'd memorized.

Out here, there was Charlie.

There was *me*.

What could my life look like? If I were to stay here, the feeling of cotton against my stomach, hugging me around my waist and grounding me like a soft lasso in this bed, my socks warm, my fingers grabbing at the bars on L trains and unfinished crusts on burnt pieces of pizza. A thousand meals, all different.

The sun coming up and down, over and over, until I lost count. Hot days, burning my skin. Cold days, making my nose go numb. Making friends with people I didn't know yet, and they would be smiling with all their lives ahead of them, not just memories and dreams to sustain them as they grasped onto their only song. And we would have days where we laughed and never thought about the Station.

I could see all the cities, the entire world. All those windows, they could be something I saw with my own eyes. I could take a breath, open my eyes, open the curtains, and there would be the Alps. The curved mountains of the Hunan province, a koala, the waters of Nam Lowe. Venice. Glaciers in Alaska and beaches in Hawai'i. All the towers, all the ruins, all the hopes for the future.

It would end, yes; someday it would end, and I wouldn't get to choose when I crossed over. It would come for me in a quiet whisper on a Wednesday morning, when the world was still asleep and I was barely awake. Or maybe it would charge toward me with fury, pain, and injustice. I would leave behind my clothes, the smell of my body, strands of hair . . . but I would have existed.

I would have lived.

But I couldn't.

"Your life is real, Charlie," I said. "Mine isn't."

She gave me a balmy smile as the streetlights shone through the slats in her window blinds. "Follow me."

We dressed and walked out onto the balcony. It was beautiful, the moon starting to show in twilight above and all the people I'd not met yet sitting on their balconies with bottles of beer muttering and laughing amongst themselves. Like it wasn't the middle of winter.

This could all be ours.

"There is possibility out here," she said. "In the Station, it's over. It was hard and scary but you're here now and . . . you are real, Nera. So, stay with me."

The lighthouse . . . my father . . . the sun had already gone down . . .

What if I just stayed another minute?

I couldn't chance it.

It wasn't fair.

"Will you walk me back?" I asked her.

Her face fell.

"I'm sorry," I said.

She took my hand. "Alright."

We grabbed our coats and opened the door, just as Mr. Connor and Chestnut came up the stairwell, Chestnut on a little leash, pretending to look grumpy but also looking quite content and sleepy.

Mr. C watched us from the top of the stairs.

"Good evening, Mr. C," I said to Charlie's father and to Mr. Coleson.

Evenin', Mr. C said.

"Good evening," Charlie's father muttered.

"You took him on a walk?" I said to Chestnut.

"I did," Charlie's father said. "It . . . was a long walk." He looked to Charlie. "You headin' out?"

"I'll be home in the morning," Charlie assured him.

Charlie's father looked away, something doleful in his eyes. "Maybe we can talk when you get back."

"I'd like that," Charlie agreed.

"Good to meet you," Charlie's father said to me.

He walked past me, and I felt words pressing on the back of my teeth. None of us were dead yet, and what we did still mattered.

You didn't mean to hurt her, but you did. Can't you see how wondrous your daughter is?

But the moment passed. He went inside and shut the door.

We returned outside, which was something I had known for only a day. It was not enough, and I had been wrong to ever think it could be.

I could still feel Charlie around me, our bodies pulsing together like a giant star's fire. I could feel the hot chocolate cascading down my throat.

There was more to me than I could see. There were multitudes I couldn't touch. I was so much more than I had been allowed to know.

45

CHARLIE

Could I please have a home that wasn't taken from me?

Could one thing in my life be fucking stable?

In Nera's arms, I didn't feel alone.

I remembered my childhood home and standing inside it for the last time. It was silent and empty, the spots on the carpet still showing the radioactive silhouettes of our furniture that hadn't been moved for decades. I felt stabbed, kneeling down in the middle of the living room and holding myself. I memorized the windows, the fireplace, and I understood how nothing would stay. I understood that ghosts didn't need to be dead; ghosts could be the sounds of the years that would never repeat. Sammy didn't know the last time she was here that she would never return. I don't know which of us was the lucky one.

Probably neither.

But now, holding Nera's hand, her hair nuzzling against my cheek as she enveloped me from behind, rocking back and forth and swinging me around . . . now I saw ten thousand more days with the woman who didn't even have one to give.

"Stay with me," I whispered. "Please. Please."

And she held me closer.

"No," I pressed. "Promise. You'll stay."

She looked out to the city lights now turning on, the streetlights flickering above. And she looked at it like she would never see it again. Her eyes glassy with tears.

"It's beautiful," she said. "I would never get sick of it." She tucked a lock of my hair behind my ear. "Perhaps there's a way. Maybe we can steal more days."

Suddenly, the streetlights popped to black.

It was too dark out.

The air got colder. The hairs on the back of my neck stood on end. And behind her, I saw the smoke, swirling, coming closer.

"Get down!" I shoved her out of the way. The smoke and static shot past us.

The Haunt's souls shrieked and turned around.

Nera's mouth gaped open, her face as gray as the shifting mass of the Haunts. She looked petrified. "The Station."

The cloud of screeching voices and hollow mouths and hollow eyes spiraled around us. With the sun down, they broke free of the shadows between buildings. Haunts reigned. I looked through the park, down Fullerton . . . all filling with what looked like fog.

"No." I started to run. Nera followed. My lantern necklace glowed out into the fog. They couldn't touch me as long as I wore the necklace. And as long as Nera was beside me, nothing in the world could hurt me.

But that didn't mean that other things couldn't be hurt.

It took too long, but we crossed under the bridge.

And my heart stopped as Nera gave out a low howl.

The fountain. It was static. Murdered.

The cops told us when we walked out to close our eyes, touch the shoulder of the person in front of us. But I didn't. I saw everything.

Everything but her.

Gurty ran behind us, always only a few paces away. And he yipped, in pain. *Oh oh oh,* he whispered.

The Station loomed above our small shadows, less like a cathedral and more like an infested mausoleum. It was cracking. Rats hissed up its sides, their eyes red. The lighthouse's mirrors distorted. The light not only dimmed, but warbled in the air, in ways that light should not move.

We were too late.

I felt a pit in my stomach. Everything falls. Everything ends. Even the Station.

I'd gone back to the spot where they said they found her. There was a morbid hole to fill, and I thought maybe her ghost would be there. But she wasn't. I couldn't save her now, it was too late.

"I have to get to the piano," was all I could say.

Nera and I grabbed each other's hands. And with the same fear, we shot forward, toward the fountain and the fog.

The first thing my father said to me in the hospital, "Why did you leave her?" And my mother's eyes pierced through me. She agreed. It was my fault.

46

NERA

Before Charlie, time was uncounted. Then this past day, every minute was recorded in my memory, every hour having to be enough to last forever.

Now, in this moment of rushing to the Station, I felt time in a new way: a guttural, horrific moment I wanted to escape.

I wanted to tear away from it and sprint so fast into the future that this memory would starve, and be forgotten. But even as it happened, I knew I would always remember this night. It would carve itself into my heart.

As we ran ahead, as the Haunts hissed and shrieked at the fountain, as the fog got thicker, we lost our way. I held her closer. "Charlie, you must sing here and now. We're not going to get as far as the piano." She was so small in my arms, curling her head into my breast, shivering. "Sing, Charlie, please!"

She sang into my chest, and it vibrated, and I was the only one who could hear her. I worried it wouldn't be enough.

But it was. The lighthouse throbbed in yellow. I saw my father in the distance, raging, his glowing hands shoving off as many Haunts as he could, with Elbee fighting along. But I felt a warmth in my heart, stoked by Charlie's words.

I knew that Father couldn't hear Charlie.

I knew that Father couldn't see us yet.

I knew that Charlie wasn't in the Station, wasn't close enough to the lighthouse for her music to echo through the atrium.

No one but me could hear her beautiful voice.

Yet the Station sighed peace.

The fountain froze, half static half alive. The souls sizzled in between lights and bodies, like a broken television screen. The lighthouse beamed.

Then I realized the light wasn't just a constant stream, and it wasn't warped. It was a steady beat—a heartbeat.

My heartbeat.

The lighthouse thrummed above.

The fog retreated.

"Oh," Charlie said. "Oh my God, that's beautiful."

The moment sank in like poison, as if it had turned all the veins in my skin a sickly gray. The moment became a scream in my head. And as my heart beat faster, the Station fluttered in light. The fog paused behind us.

It was *my light*.

Beautiful? Was it? It meant I was tethered to this place. It meant I was just as responsible as my father. The lighthouse wasn't him any longer, or him healed by Charlie's music, or even something in Charlie herself. It never had been.

It was me.

I was never leaving here again.

47

NERA

The moments that came after were a fevered blur. My heart raced. I tried to stay calm to keep the Station calm. Had anyone else discovered this? Had my father known? When had it happened?

Father gazed out past the fountain from his spot in between the pillars. He saw Gurty, and then me and Charlie. His expression turned as stony as the fountain.

I knew what this meant. Like gravity I would go to him, and even with the whole world out there, I realized that I would never belong, that no matter where I went, what I wanted, how hard I tried, my story would end here.

"They won't hurt you now," I said. "I'm back. And I'll keep the lighthouse going."

"Nera, come with me, we don't have to—" Charlie started.

"Charlie." I kept my voice steady. But nothing else could come from my mouth. I was done.

She stared at me, and tears filled my eyes and it stung like nothing else. "Charlie," I forced myself, "it wasn't your music that kept the lighthouse lit. Charlie, it was my love for your music. It was how much I . . . loved you."

Charlie stepped back. "No."

"I have to stay here."

"No." Charlie shook her head and grabbed me in a panic. "Nera, it's not yours. It's your father's."

"Not anymore," I said. "I don't know when or how it happened, but . . . it's mine now."

"We don't know that."

The lighthouse flickered. I closed my eyes. It steadied as I squeezed Charlie's hand. "I can't live in the city with you." My voice was so hoarse and small. "Knowing you are in the city, and I am keeping you safe . . . that will be enough for me to keep the light shining for you."

Charlie touched my face as my necklace glowed bright across her chest. Haunts circled the perimeter of the Station, waiting for me to slip up.

She said through gritted teeth, "You promised more days."

"I didn't know," I choked the words out. "Please, Charlie, I can save the light. But I need you to be safe. Go to the city. Find your father. Promise you'll keep the necklace on."

"Of course, but why are you talking like I'll never see you again?" Her fingers clawed into my arms, like a wind was trying to pull her away. "Just because you know how to keep the light bright now, I'm no good to you? I'm not leaving you!"

"Oh, Charlie," I managed. "You're never going to leave me. Ever."

I had seen every part of her. I knew what it felt like for her to brush her fingers through my hair. A thousand years from now, it would still be worth everything.

"Go, Charlie, please," I begged her. It was getting darker. "Now, while I can still save the Station and you can still run."

"I'm coming back," she sobbed. "I'll stay safe, but I'm coming back."

But she couldn't. Shouldn't. Because she knew where Sam was now. Because she had a whole life to live. Because even if I could steal a few more nights with her, her voice would turn to a ghost as soon as she stayed too long. She would need to keep moving forward. And I would be here. Always here.

"Please," I begged her. "Please don't." I said it kindly. And I hoped she heard my kindness. "The Haunts will always be at the Station, and so will death. Please live, Charlie."

She turned away. She would not look back behind her. But I kept my fists clenched. I kept my hope alive. I had to.

If this was a goodbye, let her know I meant my word. Let her see the Station shine.

I loved her.

The lighthouse glowed brighter than so many nights before. Not as bright as it did when she sang in the atrium that night, but it would light her way home, to Edgewater.

Goodbye is something I understood. Goodbye was Edna, goodbye was Red, goodbye was all those people named on my wall. But this was something different. She would still exist, in the city. I would still exist, only a stone's throw away.

It had all been a fantasy to begin with, the idea that the sun and the night would rise at the same time and find a place to call their own. I saw the life we could build together unravel, the further she ran.

We would have rented an apartment, somewhere on the South Side. We would go to the store and pick out cheap furniture. I'd take walks early in the morning under the green canopy, day breaking through the leaves. We would have found an overpriced place to have a ceremony, fuss too much over what our dresses would look like, although they all looked the same to her. We would have cut cake, gone on a long trip to a place in the woods far away, and we'd discover a diner that was perfect. Maybe it wasn't actually perfect, but we would be so hungry it would taste like the best thing on the planet. For years, we'd talk about the food we had there. We'd buy a house and watch the trees grow in the backyard, curling in between the chain-link fences. We'd forget to mow the grass. We'd snuggle together under cotton sheets. We'd grow old.

Then Charlie was gone, and so was everything else.

I could hear Father stepping closer to me. "Nera, tell me you didn't go out into the—"

"It would have been a home," I declared. "Not the Station. Not a goodbye." I felt sick. "We would have had a home, all ours, where I could just live." The lighthouse flickered. "But you knew, didn't you?" I said, low, trying to keep my breath, keep my light. The lighthouse hummed. "You knew the lighthouse was mine now."

"I didn't know." Father frantically rushed forward. "I've told you all I know. I had a suspicion last night, but I . . ." He trailed off. I froze. Father had never known everything. This was so much bigger than one man, and he'd been keeping it as well as he could.

He was not enough. He couldn't protect me. He didn't know anything anymore.

I closed my eyes. I hadn't known how tears burned. I gritted my teeth. So many bones to grind, in my fingers, in my jaw, my skull throbbing.

"But," he said, "I can make it better. I can. Come with me."

A glimmer of hope latched onto me. There must be something in his letters. Maybe he knew how to keep Charlie safe here, or maybe a way I could spend my days in the city . . .

So, I turned and walked with Father. We stepped through the static into the quaking Station. I looked up at the dome. It was still there. But right now, it didn't seem like home. More like a beautiful snare. A promise I'd never chosen to make.

I followed Father into his office.

48

THE JOURNAL OF DAVID STEIN

There are things that are not human in the in-between spaces of this world.

I have seen them. Things that chitter from the alleyways, things that protect the few remaining trees and mourn the loss of the bears that used to be here. Pure joy. Pure grief. And then some things that sit like dust and grime, schmutz, soot to the earth. All the energy of those in the city, a kindling for a great fire that only needs to be struck with a match to ignite. The poor going hungry, the rich not ever quenching their thirst. The Council of the Three Fires that lost the war were thrown out, replaced with no remorse by white wooden houses. Us Jews, the Black neighborhoods, the Irish, all trying to hold on to the stress of dreaming that tomorrow might be better.

Humans, we make something other than light. A fog, a smoke, sizzling like the fires that the city fights this summer.

I see the light, I do. Humans with light coming from their hands, or their hearts, or their eyes. In love and joy.

I also see the smoke, the gray mist, hissing from their mouths . . .

I see it land and settle on the uneven ground.

Chicago will someday be something even greater. But right now, it is not sure what to be.

"If you let it all in," Jon tells me, "you will go mad."

"Some things are not for us to know," Jon tells me.

Jon tells me, "You don't believe in bad souls. Do you believe in bad things?"

Bad things, schmutz, a gathering of people's fog. Soot on our souls and on the ground like dust we leave behind.

We wash our hands to rid ourselves of it. But where does it go?

The soot will be in our world forever, won't it?

What if I could clean it? Like we helped the souls?

In the beginning, Hashem created light and monsters so closely to each other.

"Someday," Jon said, "there will be something that you let in, and we both get burned. Because if you go into the dark, so do I."

How do I stay so joyous when I see such destruction?

Sometimes, I see the soot catch fire in men's souls.

The city fights it.

I do not know what is happening, the blurred lines between the spirit realm and the physical, the souls and the living . . . they are not so clear to me now. Where does reality end and the dreams begin? Is it the demons that start the fires? Or is it the weather like everyone says?

Perhaps it is the people who built this city out of wood. The people who set us in these houses one by one to suffocate on top of one another.

Perhaps it is the firemen who can never do enough.

Perhaps there are no demons, no angels, no magical dogs. There is only us. And we do not want to hold that culpability when the world burns. So we delude ourselves.

Jon holds me at night, when we sneak off to the barn down the street after everyone has fallen asleep. We do not go home. We simply sit in the hay, surrounded by cows and horses, and Jon holds me.

"Tell me who you are," he says to me.

"I'm David," I tell him.

"Write it down, in your journal, when I am not here to remind you."

I am David, and I wish I could just be in this realm. I wish I did not see the dead, did not feel the pain of the city. I wish I was still sane. I wish I could do that for Jon.

I am the son of a tailor. Our family came from Germany. I am in love with a boy that I can never hold in the daylight.

Maybe it is only in dreams that we will be happy, and that is why I cannot stand to think about three-piece suits and shul and my mother's laundry and the living world. Maybe with the possibility of a larger world, Jon and I stand a chance.

49

CHARLIE

Please live, Charlie.

My spirit shattered into a thousand pieces when she let go. My heart stopped beating. My guts wanted to come up, my feet begged me to follow her. But I couldn't. I just marched away, back under the bridge. And now she was gone.

Because all things end.

Every day ends. Every note ends. Every life ends. Every single joy was fleeting and a trick to keep moving forward. For what?

I had seen what my life could have blossomed into. Only to stand here alone on the cold icy sidewalk, looking out to the end of the world and the black of the lake. She was a ghost after all. My one person was a lie. I wanted to stay with her.

Please don't. Please live.

She was gone. With no mercy, no apologies, just gone. And the city kept on.

I meant to go home. My feet were pointed north, in the right direction. I would have never lied to Nera. I would have told her where I would end up that night, if I had known.

I wasn't going to go back to the Station.

It hit me, even before I got to the L train, the cold chill of the Haunts. It was near the zoo.

My feet took me to the statue again.

I stood there, looking up at something my sister thought was magic. But statues weren't magic. And music wasn't magic. This place would never be happy again. I was nothing. I was powerless.

And then the text came.

call me now plz, Marco said.

There are some texts that you can feel in the palm of your hand. They are more than just a string of words. They are the whole person on the other side, reaching out, clamping around your wrist, trying to pull themselves up. A lifeline.

I needed to talk to him, too.

I stared up at the fairy on the statue. Leaning down to the little girl and little boy preparing to cross into the Land of Nod. And I dialed his number.

"Sa . . . Charlie?" he said.

It cut right through my lungs.

"Marco?" I said, as if I'd not heard it.

"Charlie, are you okay? I haven't . . . heard from you . . ." and he trailed off.

"I've been busy," I said.

"Are you mad at me?"

"Of course not." Yes. I was *now*. Sa-Charlie. Sa-Charlie. I'd lost Nera and now Marco's little tides had pushed back in and the water was drowning him. Grief was no straight line. But it was supposed to get better. When did it ever fucking get better?

"If you're not mad at me, then what the fuck, Charlie?"

I couldn't tell him. How could I tell him? He didn't want to hear anyway, he wanted me to listen. Sometimes people ask you how you are, what's going on with you, and they just want to tell you their own answers to their own questions.

And if I did tell him, *Marco, I fell in love with a woman who lives with ghosts and I can't ever hold her in bed at night.*

And if I did tell him, *Marco, I had a chance to ask the universe what happened to Sam, and I fucked it up.*

I never saw her.

It's all over.

There's no way to fix this.

Nera told me to live, but she doesn't get to live.

The Haunts crept closer, coming out from behind the statue.

They were waiting for the inevitable. They weren't asking a question. They already knew the answer. But they were wrong.

This statue, it didn't belong to them. I did not belong to them.

Marco, my dad wants me to go bring Sam back. I can't.

There was one thing he would understand. That we both knew now. Losing someone you loved to the Station.

The Veil is a door to a place.

But she can't come here. She can't follow you.

But . . .

My brain was scattered. My heart was tired.

"Marco," I said. "You remember when you brought up Orpheus?"

"Yeah."

"Do you remember how Orpheus even gets a chance to save his wife?" His silence meant no, I guessed. "He makes a deal with the Devil. That's the only person who can help him."

"Alright?"

"Not Persephone. Not Cerberus. Not even the ferryman. Just Hades."

"Okay?" he said. "Charlie, I . . . I called because I gotta tell you something." I wasn't listening, but I felt my lips whisper, "What is it?"

"I'm not okay," he said. "I just gotta talk about her or something. No one talks about her. No one says her name."

Oh, he'd said her name more than enough for me tonight.

"And," he said, "and I'm just thinking about like . . . we're so young, we have so much more life to go . . ."

"We're not that young."

"We are," he said. "I'm only twenty-six. When you look at the amount of time we had her, and the amount of time we won't have her . . . it's not fucking fair, Sammy."

I paused. "Marco, are you drunk?"

"Yes."

"Marco, are you safe?"

He gave a small, exasperated cry. I heard my own pain in that cry. Being ripped from your own heart, seeing it crumble to dust in front of you. Feeling that hole. "There's so much weight, and none of us can carry it. What the fuck are we gonna do, Sammy? What are we gonna do?"

There is no we, I heard my dad say in my memory.

There was no we, was there? Not anymore. Sam had been the glue. And here I was fucking around on the precipice of the Underworld, when the Veil was right there . . .

I didn't want to.

I really did not want to.

But Nera couldn't help anymore. Harosen was useless.

Dad and Marco were drowning. Mom was gone. There should have been justice. Sam's fucking song should have been finished.

And now Nera was just another story that would never get to end. It hadn't even been able to really start.

I wanted to say goodbye. I wanted to know if she was okay.

But maybe, what I really wanted all along, was to not be alone anymore.

I started walking south.

REMNANTS

—*A sheet of music, 3/19/05, by Sam Connor*

50

CHARLIE

There was no music in me tonight.

The Water Tower was silent as I approached, walking through a sea of Haunts.

There were so many more of them.

We all crowded at the Water Tower. I took off the lantern necklace.

You've returned.

"Yeah," I said flatly. "You said you could reunite me with my sister. Tell me how."

Let go. Let go of this world, of this terrible pain you carry for everyone. You know where your sister is. You know what you must do. You've known.

I did.

"And why do I need you for that?" I said. "I can go throw myself into the Veil without your help."

Will you though?

A silence between us.

"What are you gonna do, push me?" I scoffed. "I'm good, thank you."

I can take away your pain. I can make it mine. I can let you remember her, help you find her, have a friend that will never ever lie to you, Charlie. You will not be alone in the journey you must take. I know the way. And I will hold your hand as you cross the Veil. All you have to do is say yes.

Say yes.

He said we'd be reunited. He didn't say we'd be able to return.

Did it matter?

I felt the glowing necklace in my hand. It matched his glowing door.

Could the living see this light? They couldn't see the Haunts, and they couldn't see the lighthouse, so no, of course they couldn't. They didn't see the door imbued with starshine. They didn't see Nera perform miracles.

If I left, then Nera would be alone.

But if I didn't leave, would Nera . . . *could* Nera . . . ever leave the Station? Of course she wouldn't.

I can free Nera from her prison, as well.

That struck me. I remembered Nera's panicked eyes, looking up at the lighthouse that tethered her.

"You're a liar," I said.

I am many things, and nothing but the truth. All you have to do is trust me, Charlie. Look at me, let me in. And we'll all go home.

If this was Sam, standing before him . . . no, strike that, Sam wouldn't have even come down here. When she saw something sketchy, she didn't fuck with it. Right, she would just run off without thinking, away from the gunshots. Not take any precautions, not even look for a place to hide, a way out. Just run, Sam. Then it'll disappear. Then you don't have to worry about Dad or Mom. Then fuck Marco, right, Sam?

Of course she'd just jumped through the Veil without saying goodbye, sending us a gift, doing *anything*.

Fuck you, Sam.

I stepped forward. I reached out my hand. "Please," I said, "I don't want to be alone anymore." And I opened the door.

A blinding pain in my eyes. I barely saw the door's light disappear.

I did not die.

But I felt something **cold** and awful **slither** into my chest.

The lantern necklace seared my palm. I had to throw it down, shattering it on the pavement.

The worst part about all this?

I liked how it felt.

The syrupy wriggling feeling of giving in. Of slipping away.

Slipping **away**.

I remembered Nera waiting for me at the entrance to the atrium.

I had promised her I wouldn't take off the lantern.

How could I forget that promise under the weight of all this other shit?!

"No," I said, and I pulled away.

But it was too late.

I saw the thing in the dark, a monster, writhing and hissing right in my face, behind my eyes.

But then he was gone.

And I was alone again.

The door, the Water Tower, all fine and untouched.

Nothing had happened.

Which was worse? If he'd kept his word? Or if he disappeared and left me alone? Where had he gone?

My blood froze.

This fucking city with all its goddamn ghosts. The skyscrapers were too high. The streets too trashed. The lake too fucking cold.

I shook my hand. I went to pick the necklace up. But it was just pieces.

I was so tired.

I felt a sick roiling in my arms, in my gut. When was the last time I drank water? I looked to the world. Dizzy.

Sam. She should have been here.

Dad. He didn't care if I lived or died.

I could flay myself open and bleed for the morning crowd and no one would give a fuck.

I used to be someone worth loving, and now I was a waste.

I stopped. No, this was how it had felt months ago, before the Station and Nera. No, something was wrong—

Trust me.

I looked to my hands.

To the shadows where the pain looped and I lost myself and I needed nothing else. Just pain. Just biting down on a cut on the side of my mouth. A burst of hurt that eclipsed everything.

It filled me up.

It filled me up.

It filled me up.

Grief. Grief, stuck like broken glass shards in memories all across my life, like a machine gun had blown out my windows, had raised hell and left me riddled with holes. Me and Sam on our bikes at the Fourth of July party when we moved to the nice house, *bang.* Sam and me wading into the creek down the street, mud between our toes, her laughing that she was a hobbit hiding from the ringwraiths, *bang.* Me walking with her to school on my first day of first grade, grabbing her backpack and zipping it all the way because she'd forgotten to, *bang.* The lake, us sitting on her car hood, next to the lake, leaning into one another, *bang.* The Taco Bell down from Wrigley Field where me and Sam and Marco all drunkenly stumbled in way too late and begged for cinnamon twists, and Marco laughed and kissed Sam for the first time, or at least the first time I'd seen them, *bang.* Her freckles, her laugh that sang like her piano did. Her raspberrying every time she didn't like one of my ideas. Her exclaiming, "By George!" when she did like one of my ideas. Gone. All gone.

Splattered with blood. Finished.

All the things to come, all the words **unwritten** and notes **unplayed**, the **end** of a scale, the final note, **gone**. DC al Coda with no end. Just a missed cue to turn a page. Sam would not marry. We would not grow old. I would not be an aunt to her children. There were no children. There was no future. There was nothing left for her to do.

I screamed out, the pain, the voice I couldn't use when Dad screamed in the hospital. A ghost of that grief roared through my lungs, up my throat, through my ears, into my brain. I had looked everywhere, but it hadn't mattered. Sammy was gone.

Nera was gone.

fucking gone.

And the world was **irreparably broken** for it.

destroy it.

I wanted to destroy it all. I wanted to **eviscerate** everything and reach into the unknown and take her back myself. She was ours, and she wasn't finished, and this was not fair and . . .

It **filled me up.**

There was no more light glowing from my chest. Just a black smoke from my hands. I drunkenly gave a small chuckle. I **wasn't alone.**

i would never be alone again.

let go of the light, charlie.

stop being afraid of the dark.

REMNANTS

i can feel all their souls, all the truth they keep pushing back
keep the sadness at bay, all is fine, is it?
i give them the freedom to be who they are, to see the world
for the shit-stain it is.
we all have been fucked, we all have been forgotten,
and so let us rage.
a mourning father sits in this girl's apartment, the door now open.
i've felt him, even from afar,
but now i am free.
i breathe into him. and a thousand others.
i live through them.
and now i will burn through them.

—the writings of a thing in the dark

51

NERA

Father opened the door to his office; it had not changed in decades. There was frosted glass on the door, the cedar desk in the middle of the room. Father still wore his vest, a bow tie, suspenders.

Nothing had changed. But I was different, dressed in my borrowed T-shirt, my jeans, and the boots that felt like weights.

Father went to the cabinet where he kept his most important things. He opened it, and out came a little box.

Sit down, please, he said.

I did not.

Please, he begged me. *Sit.*

"Just tell me how to fix this," I said.

He didn't sit behind the desk. He came to me and put the box on the desk in front of us. He opened it. There was a stack of papers with his handwriting, and a small glass bottle with a cork stopper with water slushing inside, as if he'd trapped a small ocean. He gave a shuddering breath, trying not to feel the weight of his own fear.

"What is that?" I asked.

I hoped when the lighthouse finally passed from my hands to yours, you would find joy in its safety, he said. *As I did.*

"I don't want it," I said.

Why did you go out there, into the world? he asked me. He grasped at my bare arm, a desperation leaking from him.

I looked to him. "Because I belong there."

You are willing to abandon your post for a woman you barely know, he said.

"Abandon my post," I said. "You've *shackled* me to the post!" I felt dizzy, angry, spinning in my fury. The lighthouse didn't simply flicker; it sputtered. And I felt something like fear in the pit of my stomach. "This was never my choice!"

You are the next ferryman, he said. *Only you, my little light, could be trusted to keep the travelers to the world-to-come safe. And you have the gift of safety! Out there is nothing but fires and Haunts, and here we have everything, anything. This place is a dream.*

"It *is* a dream," I said. "That's all it is. And you're just a dreamer. What do you know about the world out there? Who are you to tell me what I want?!" The floor cracked. The Station wavered. I tried to breathe. "It should have been mine. Everything I saw out there, it should have been mine."

A crack in the wall. It severed his perfect, pristine office. It frightened me.

I brought my breath back to normal. I would keep the Station lit for her. No matter how it hurt.

I once was human, too, Father said. *I was alive. Just as you are.*

"You still *are* alive."

He pressed on. *But I found a way to keep myself steady and keep the lighthouse shining for the city.*

He raised up the little bottle.

Then I understood.

He held a delusion of control over something he could not fathom. I could see now, how much of a lion he was not. He was a house cat, caught up in the shadows he saw outside a window. He didn't comprehend any of this. But he had made doors, walls, little boxes in little cabinets.

"You still have the water from the lake," I said.

The myths, he said, *they tell of shedding your old skins when you cross over. Rivers that can make you let go. So you can live again. I was attached to that world, and it hurt so much. I let it go, Nera. And when you arrived, I never wanted you to go out, to hurt as I did, to tether yourself to something outside of the lighthouse. But . . . we can fix this, sweetheart.*

I stared at him. "You want me to . . . to forget her?"

I am giving you the answer of how to make it easier. He didn't hand me the bottle. He held it in his hands, wanting me to take it. *I would help you remember all the things you needed to remember. We still have half a year. We can salvage this and make things the way they were. Content. Safe. Stable.*

A void opened where my stomach used to be. All the hard work from the past months, all over again. Every door, rediscovered. Every soul forgotten and every name scratched out. Edna's suitcase. Yuxi's memory of the bus. And Charlie playing Sam's piano.

Snowflakes. Penguins. Burnt food. Sugar packets. They were now a part of me.

He wanted to erase *me.*

"No," I said.

This way you can be happy.

"I wasn't happy," I said. "I didn't even know what it meant to be happy. Charlie is what keeps my light going."

Until she doesn't, he said. *You will stay here. She will go out there. You will hold onto the light. She will live, dance around, travel, move forward with the world. She will find someone, or she will change for the worse, and one day, she will die. Then you will know what true grief is, Nera. And when you recognize her, when you write her name down on your little wall, it will break you. And how can the lighthouse survive a night like that?*

I swallowed.

He was right.

But still, he was so very wrong.

"No," I said.

Nera—

"You drank this water," I said. "But your job was to love them. All of them."

We live on the edge of the end, he said. *We don't have that luxury.*

"I have to go find her," I breathed. I started for the door.

Father's eyes narrowed. His body went slack.

The ending isn't in your hands, Nera, he said. *You will either lose each other in life or in death. Ends are inevitable.*

"I don't get an end!" I roared at him. "You pulled me out of the story!"

I spared you, and I am trying to spare you now.

"You have no right to spare me!" I held my chest. "I want to live!"

Father's eyes glinted in the fire. *You are alive now,* he said. *More alive than you've ever been. And are you happy?*

I stopped. And I looked at my shaking hands. I felt my body pulsing with nerves, adrenaline, fury, grief, despair. Tears.

Oh God.

Then a terrible tremor. A sound like a tornado. I'd heard it in the memories of those who had died in storms. Something too close to outrun. Something too fast to see coming. It was already here.

"What is that?" I whispered.

We ran to the roof, up and up.

There, out in the city, bedlam raged.

52

NERA

The city filled with smoke. The fog from the alleys had climbed out and wrung the neck of the city's glow. The air was sick, polluted. And I heard the people. I heard them screaming. I saw cars on the LSD crashing into one another. Little fires.

A loud shrieking. Not just the dead. But the living.

It's too late, Father whispered. *The dead have seeped into the living. The Haunts have grabbed the city.*

"No," I said. Charlie.

I ran back into the Station. My poor, withering Station, rumbling like it knew what was coming. The cracks spread like varicose veins. The red carpet bled its color onto the walls and down the stairs, losing track of its edges, melting . . .

I ran down the shaking stairs. The lanterns and the dogs' collars extinguished, until the only light was from above, my weak little lighthouse beating out against the dark.

"Gurty!" I shouted out. "Elbee! Help me! We have to get Charlie!"

But there she was already.

A stark answer to a prayer. Just standing there in the atrium, the light above cresting her hair and pressing shadows against her brow . . .

She was alive. She was here. Oh, thank God.

The dogs parted for her.

I ran across the atrium to grab her and hug her tight.

"You scared me." I choked back my fear. "The whole city is about to burn. Are you alright?"

But Charlie didn't return my embrace. She was stiff and cold, like a corpse. There was a disgust on her lips like she'd tasted mine and recoiled.

"Charlie?" I whispered.

"I didn't make it home," she said. "Sorry about that." Her eyes were big. Out of focus. And there was a buzzing electricity around her, followed by a dead void. Over and over again, like she was darting between two temperatures, two colors, two songs.

I said, "Charlie, look at me, what happened out there?"

Charlie looked past me, to my father. Father was stopped short on the atrium staircase. Staring in horror at her shoes.

I looked down.

The ground she stood on was completely static.

A void.

"Nera, get away from her," my father whispered.

I couldn't. I held onto her, like I could take the shadow away. I couldn't. She had tethered it tight. It had grown on her like mold, stretching out from her fingertips, through her own shadow.

"Charlie—" I started.

"You're a goddamn liar, Harosen," Charlie barked at Father. She pushed away from me. "This is all your fault. And you know that. You know what you did, you piece of shit. And now you're passing it on to her to fix."

Father shook his head. "I don't know what you want, but leave her alone."

"Leave her alone?!" Charlie rasped. Father trembled. "Does she know what a horrific fucker you really are?!"

"Father?" I asked. "What is happening?"

"Nera," Father said. "She's been taken by the Haunts. We have to get her out of the Station. Now."

Charlie stormed past me, closer to Father. "He's outside, Harosen," she said. "I let him out. I let him out, and he knows what you are. There's just one more thing to do, and nothing will be able to protect you anymore."

Father said nothing. I could see in his eyes the same overwhelmed exhaustion that had plagued him all this time. He had forgotten not only what his life had been, but who he had been.

"You really don't remember." Her eyes narrowed at him.

"I'm sorry," he said.

She raised her hand, upward to the lighthouse.

"No you're not," she said.

And she screamed.

The world shook inside me.

"Charlie, stop," I said, charging forward. "Don't break the lighthouse, please."

"Nera," Charlie said slowly. She turned to me, her whole body moving with her head. As if she were a doll. "I don't have to break the lighthouse. I only have to break you." Then she winked at me. "You gave her power over your heart, stupid girl."

My heart tremored. The lighthouse flickered.

"Charlie, don't!" I begged her.

"It's not your fault, Nera," Father rasped, desperate. "It's not your fault."

I was too alive now, to not feel my body shaking, to not feel my heart break. Everything inside of me crumbled.

She spun back around, as if she was drunk. She raised her own hand and dug her fingernails deep into her skin, until the blood came. She howled out in pain.

"Stop hurting her!" I screamed.

"I am her," Charlie said. "And I am also those who are banging down the door. I am the city. And soon, *he* will come and we will all be him." And she laughed. "We are here now, Nera. And we can say you will never see her again without us."

"Charlie, please come back to me," I said.

She held out her hand to me. She opened her fingers. There, in too many pieces, was my lantern necklace, shattered.

53

CHARLIE

Ghost stories never really have an ending. Just a lingering malevolence, an unknown fear of what fucking horror will still be here tomorrow. Ghost stories end with a scream, with a scratching on a door, with a threat.

In my head, I saw a thousand deaths. Drowning, cars, blood, fire. So much fire.

Then, there was no I. There was only seeing through the eyes of the city, all the pain and the memories. All the memories. And he breaks free of the light. And he is coming.

We are coming. Because we have waited here too long to believe anyone is coming to save us.

Fuck the world.

The thing in the dark cradled Charlie in his mind, hissing from the city. **This is how we break the light.**

Charlie threw the shards of the lantern necklace at Nera's feet. The glass, the wax, the chain. Destroyed.

"Charlie's gone," Charlie's mouth said. "She did not love you enough to stay."

Nera's eyes grew large.

And above her, the lighthouse died.

Smoke, like the world had blown it out.

The earth shook.

54

NERA

The Station crumbled around us, a dream disturbed and shaken awake. From Charlie spilled static, the mist, bursting into the atrium and curling around the walls and banister, pulling everything down as it pushed itself upward into the sky. The windows shattered inward, like a sinking ship crushed under the weight of an ocean. The pillars fell. The entire Station cracked and capsized around us.

A million memories falling apart, ground to dust.

Suddenly, night surrounded us, a stark unforgiving frozen dark.

The Station was gone.

Then the silence was pierced by the sound of an explosion in the city. Another fire.

A tidal wave of smoke raged closer, past the bridge, engulfing the fountain, uncannily so, too fast.

Out stepped a bleak, black void, the size of a man.

I grabbed Charlie and the shattered pieces of the lantern necklace from the soot and ran, the dogs rushing on my heels. "Father!" I screamed, "Father, where are you?"

Father grabbed me from behind in his weak arms, and we fumbled through the dust to find the threshold of the ruin. We were buried in a cloud, facing a wintry night ahead.

Charlie was so limp in my arms, as if she didn't care to move anymore. I kept her upright, dragging us forward with my father.

Out in the darkness, I could hear the Haunts shriek, the rats' claws scurry and scrape. I saw their smoke and static. And like the dead rising from Tartarus, the plagued souls rushed at us.

But Father didn't move.

He let them wash over us.

Charlie breathed them in like they were clean air after nearly drowning. I held her closer. But the sea of Haunts nearly washed her out of my hands.

"Charlie!" I wrapped her in my arms. "Charlie, please, wake up . . ."

A hissing behind me. A rotting stench. I turned to look. And there, dragging himself across the threshold of the broken pillars, was a corpse.

In the middle of decaying. Never finished.

A man, dressed in once-nice black clothes that clung and fused to his bloated skin. His eyes glazed over, his jaw slack and gaunt, emaciated and bursting with fluid under the surface, all at once, uneven like a rotting cloth.

The fire burned behind him in the city.

I couldn't find my breath. I felt something in my stomach threaten to come up. I clung to Charlie harder.

The walking rot stared at me, then his eyes slid to see my father. The corpse raised his hand, one finger, thick and green. And a voice came from his rattling ribs, as if his lungs were made of bones.

"**You fucking traitor,**" he grated.

I took the chain from my ruined necklace in one hand. "Papa!" I shouted out. I threw it to him. He caught it. And the body laughed. How was this thing not dead? Or was it dead?

"**Papa,**" the thing said. "**So this is Nera. The girl who fears my Haunts, who loved my Charlie.**"

My skin crawled. He knew my name, knew *all* of us. He had been watching, even from his prison.

His eyes darted to me. "**He had a whole life, did he?**" he said. "**Was it a good life? A life worth all this?**" He shoved the word *this* out of his raw, rigid throat with vitriol. He waved his hands at the rampaging mist around us; the dust of the Station, clumping together.

"I'm sorry," my father said. "Whatever you are, whatever I did, I don't remember."

The corpse glared, running his hand through patches of burnt brown hair. "**I was not worth remembering, was I?**"

"My father drank from near the Veil," I tried to explain to him. "He doesn't remember anymore, I'm sorry—"

"Don't speak to it, Nera," Father said, jumping in front of me. "Angel of Destruction, I beg you to—"

"**Angel of Destruction,**" the corpse rasped. "**Not my true name, unfortunately for you. And I am so much more than a name. I am all of us.**" I clung to Charlie harder. She was so heavy. "**Your great love is here, Jon,**" the corpse said, his rotted palm hitting his chest as if he was going to cry but couldn't. "**Right where you left him.**"

David.

The corpse, dressed in a black suit, burn marks all along its arms and neck was alive, but anything but alive.

"The boy died in the Fire," Father said. "The demon was trapped."

And the demon looked to Father through David's white clouded eyes, face slack. Somewhere behind the inhuman horror on his face, I could recognize something I'd felt. Betrayal.

"**You really did forget,**" he rasped.

I stepped out from behind my father. David's body looked to me. Lost. And I nodded. "Tell me, what happened?"

"**Your father trapped the demon,**" he said. "**He certainly did. In a fucking body.**

And neither of us have peace. Although, Jonathon, it looks as if you have found peace in your prison." He looked at me, with those white marbles. "This Station is made of memories. So find his memories, Daughter of the Station Master. Find who your father really is."

"I know who my father is," I said.

"And you know who we are as well," he growled. "You've been reading our own memories."

As if summoned by the bristling words of the undying, dust spun around me. The dust settled and coalesced into the shape of the journal and the chain of the necklace Father had made me. The journal and the chain fused, transformed into one brick, just like the thousands that had made up the Station's walls.

David's unresting body jerked beside me now, and the demon took the brick in his bloated fingers. He held it out to me.

"Take it," he demanded. "Take it, Nera."

Gurty walked to me and gently slid Charlie onto his back and safely down to the ground where he curled around her. I faced the body of the eternally dying man.

I took the brick in my hands. It curled around my fingers and wrists, and climbed into my eyes . . . all around me, the dust dissipated into another night, so close to where we stood and so far away in time.

The present disappeared.

55

NERA

To live long enough was to lose.

His entire life was marked by only twenty years.

Too young, too soon, he was trapped.

That night, they were supposed to be at shul. They did not go. And usually when they did not go, it was because they held each other in secret, tucked away in the haystacks of a barn or under the sheets of one of their bedrooms while the rest of the family was out. But tonight, it was different.

David had a burning need inside of him. Jonathon was frozen in fear.

The summer had been too hot. Too dry. Little fires had sparked everywhere. David had spent the time chasing ghosts, trying to stop Circlers, opening his mind to as far as he could sense. He knew the dogs' names now. He knew all the souls went to the lake. He had even learned how to navigate some other plane in his dreams, where he swore he could speak to people no one else could see and those who had already passed or things that weren't even human. Was he going mad? Or was he only hitting the ceiling to crash through to a much larger sky?

David's journal had grown and grown over the years, as they had grown from boys into men. David always closed his eyes, his body stiffening, when he tapped into something sinister. Like he was channeling something invisible and malevolent. He would scribble down more information. He kept it with him in a satchel that I could see at his side as he led Jonathon through the Chicago night.

"It spoke to me, while I slept," David said. "It whispered out that it needs our help."

"I cannot do this anymore," Jonathon said. "Why can't we just be here on this earth? David, why won't you just be alive, with me?"

Because others suffered, and it was his duty to help the dead cross. If he had these abilities, how could he turn away? How could he live his one little life after knowing the universe was more vast than the night sky?

Jonathon followed David through the streets and alleys, the little ramshackle farms and shanty shacks surrounding their muddy path.

The hot night burned David's neck as he found the barn he'd seen in his dream. Just a glimpse, of a man with one leg standing across the road. A rowdy raucous party next door. The little barn, he would go in and find animals and the thing that had called out to him, curled in the corner like a lost child.

Help.

David stepped forward and touched the barn. They'd been here before. David and Jonathon knew this barn.

Maybe that's why it was in his dream. Maybe all of this really was fantasy.

He felt dizzy. Maybe it was the tobacco smoke of the streets or the smell of animals. Or maybe a strong spirit was near.

"David?" Jonathon said.

David entered.

There, in the barn, was smoke. A shadow. Fog. Static.

I knew what it was.

I tried to pull myself out from David, but I couldn't. I was stuck in this memory, almost like that memory I had glimpsed after walking through a door. But this was thicker and more potent than anything behind any door. I couldn't leave. Neither could David.

David knew this might be the end.

A memory swam behind his eyes. Jonathon and David sharing an apple, reading a pamphlet on the half-raised streets of Chicago. They were laughing.

Maybe that was David's happiest day.

"Please don't go," I whispered.

But David couldn't hear me. We stepped forward.

"Please," Jonathon said behind David. "Please David, let's go."

Help.

The static pleaded, in the voice of a child. The barn animals were unbothered. The static shifted forms, looking like a rooster one moment, then a human, then a beast, then back to a human. For one moment, it looked like it may be an angel under all that static.

David outstretched his hand, palm up. "I'm here," he said. "What's your name?"

Your kind does not say it aloud.

"My name is David," he said.

"David, if people don't say its name, it means it's too dangerous," Jonathon warned. But David saw the good in everyone and everything. He was willing to trust. I could hear their conversation, as memories remember words, slow sounds and syllables that bring meaning to the forefront. Words stuck out that lashed like a whip. Other words were forgotten. Jonathon said that maybe David was living too much for the afterlife. That maybe they needed to step back to what they were supposed to be doing: studying, living, loving.

David's eyes had gone blank. He was no longer listening to Jonathon, because he'd already heard it and decided it was bullshit. And he said, "If you tell me one more time to pretend this isn't real, I'll never speak to you again."

"That's not what I'm saying—"

"This is real," David said. "I'm not mad. It's in pain, can't you feel how starved it is? And we have to help everyone, Jonathon. You may not trust the world, but can you trust me?"

And Jonathon got quiet.

David tried to remember what they had been like, before he dove too far. He remembered when they were younger, and Jonathon would laugh and they would sing all the same songs, both on pitch, both holding the other deep into the night. They spoke of how they were soulmates, must have known each other a thousand times before, how their hands fit perfectly together.

David remembered that before (when had it changed?), Jonathon had allowed David to see him laugh.

Now Jonathon had to follow him into alleys full of muck to even see his face.

And yet, even tonight, Jonathon stepped forward. And he said, "Yes, I can trust you. I can *love* you."

"If you love me," David said, "can you love the world?"

Jonathon, with all the courage he had, nodded his head.

So David reached out both hands to the static.

"What do you need from me?" David said.

I need you to let me in.

"No," I said. "No, don't do it."

But we were already opening our arms. Our heart. His whole soul, with no fortress around what he wanted to give the world.

It ate him alive.

The static curled around David. David gasped. And the mist flew into him. It sank into his pores, under his fingernails, into his eyes.

The demon used David to set a fire in the barn. He smashed his lantern in the straw.

Fire.

This memory of fire pushed everything inside me to escape, as if my bones were trying to evacuate my body. It was so hot I couldn't breathe, I couldn't think, it burned around me. The barn. The street. The houses. Everything.

David struggling, screaming, singing to get the static off him. Jonathon pressed against him, and the fire flew into the air and the demon screeched. Bright light from Jonathon's hands had forced the demon away from David. David was free, but the damage had just begun.

The thing in the dark howled at them, shot into the fleeing folk around them. A plague. Everyone breathing it in.

I looked up, as if looking through a glass into a diorama, trying to move my eyes in this fixed moving photograph. A tornado made of fire. Ash and black in the sky.

A large bell on one of the buildings across the bridge sounded with a massive roar. Then it rang, warbling, falling, crashing. Silence following echoes. The fire devoured downtown. It jumped the river.

Screaming. Begging. Horses rushing through the mud, people howling out names. And I could see the dead, too. Rising. Catching in the smoke, suffocating, turning to static.

The Haunts multiplied.

The demon and its tentacles seeped into eyes, shoved bodies into open graves to be eaten by the fire.

The whole city burned.

David and Jonathon followed the flames, trying to help, trying to push out the light from their hearts and scream at the demon to stop him, but the fire was stuck in their throats. David was desperate, I could feel his sweat, his adrenaline shooting through his fingers that had nothing to hold, nothing they could do to make this right.

Then I saw, in the blaze, a stone wonder that had not burned. The Water Tower.

"Jon!" David said. "Please, follow me!"

The memory skipped to David and Jonathon, holding hands, outside the open door of the tower.

"We trap it in the tower!" David said. "We lure it in, you use your light to bind it! It won't be able to spread any further."

"It won't work!"

"It will work! You're strong enough!"

"How are we going to get him in the tower?"

David's mouth turned to a firm line. I knew that look from my own Charlie. Stubbornness. "Me," he said. "He reached out to me, so I'll lure him in."

"No."

"I won't let him in."

"You already have!" Jon said. But time was running out.

"Trust me," David said.

And they kissed. An embrace of souls.

David ran inside the tower, screaming for the thing in the dark. It shot into the belly of the brick monument. David rushed back outside. "Now!" he screamed, and Jonathon shot his light, his eyes never leaving David.

David reached out for him, and Jonathon grasped for his hand. Between the two of them, nothing was impossible. He pulled David close to him, but . . .

David tugged back. He was snared by the demon.

"No," David whispered, under the raging fire and the screeching Haunts.

The world went silent in Jonathon's ears.

As I watched the thing in the dark's tar-black figure crawl up David's spine, down his legs, pulling him back into the tower, I wanted to believe that my father did not let go of David's hand.

But I knew my father. There were too many risks for Jonathon Harosen.

He let go.

The demon shoved itself back into David and they both stumbled backward into the tower.

And Jonathon Harosen did nothing. He did not shove the demon out. He locked the demon in. The doors slammed shut around both it and David. David screamed in the smoke and the fog and the static, and then Jonathon couldn't hear him any longer. Jonathon was only left facing a Water Tower that needed light to secure it. So he did, weeping as he created a prison to last for all time. I remembered, from my father's stories, what happened next. People ran for the lake, and those who couldn't run fast enough jumped into the open graves in the cemetery that used to be where the zoo now was. The Haunts ate them alive.

The others, who made it to the lake . . . Father was one of them. Father was surrounded by both the living and the dead, hiding from the Fire and the Haunts.

He saw the dogs, like a hymn, coming to collect the souls that had been killed and ferry them across the lake.

The lake would be safe. He would make sure of it.

He raised his hands. It started to rain. It was over. The fire died out. The Station rose.

But David didn't see any of that. His memories were then just black. A shaking hand trying to pull his journal from his satchel and bloodstained eyes trying to read his words through static and darkness. Trying to find a way out. But he was trapped. A body with a soul cannot turn to ash. A soul trapped in a body cannot leave.

David imagined Jonathon would go to the lake. He gave out a scream through the static. But he was alone.

Then one day, there was a light through the crack. A possibility that Jonathon had returned.

The thing in the dark sent out more Haunts.

And he found the Station. He found the lighthouse.

They could go no further.

They were all trapped.

Life always ends. There is always a goodbye.

But David's life had never ended. And grief never ends. It spills into the next day, into the next year, the next story. David and the demon, a thing in the dark, spilling out, consuming itself and the city.

And Jonathon had saved himself, in more ways than one. Because he'd let go of David's hand. And then he'd let go of his memory.

Their words of love, a pact between two souls, broken.

56

NERA

My father trapped the demon with David in the Water Tower, surrounded by light.

The demon now took the brick from me. And he threw it on the ground. **"Your father . . ."** he said. **"He betrayed me. He betrayed all of us."**

He waved his broken arms in a jerking motion to the sea of Haunts flowing out of the city like a dam had broken. Then I realized, they weren't touching the dogs. They weren't touching Father. Or me. Or whatever was left of the Station.

They were going to the lake.

"That doesn't make sense," I breathed. "The Station is gone. They should be devouring all of us, the city—"

Unless they didn't want the city.

David and the thing inside him smiled at me. **"Oh no,"** they crooned. **"You seem to have lost her."**

I looked to Gurty. Gurty stumbled, looking around frantically. Where was Charlie? *Charlie!* he shouted out. *Charlie, I found the ball . . .*

Where was she?!

All the Haunts were going to the lake; they skimmed across the waters, screeching and begging and praying.

I ran.

But not into the city.

I ran to the docks behind us, to the lake.

She was gone.

The Station was rubble. The ferry was missing.

I held my breath, waiting for it to change. Willing time to go backward. It didn't.

I stared out to the black lake. If there were stars tonight, they were obscured by the wall of souls rushing for the Veil, a constant funnel of panicking voices as they flew past me, catching my hair in their wind.

Now that the lighthouse was gone, they could pass freely.

"Oh no," I said softly, as Elbee rushed to meet me.

Nera, what are you doing? Elbee said.

"They didn't want to destroy us," I said. "They didn't want to hurt my father. They just wanted to go home, and they couldn't."

I turned and looked at my father and the monster he'd kept at bay for so long that they both had decayed.

A hot rage was in my throat.

"The Haunts weren't the thing in the dark. He hurt them, twisted them . . ." I said. "They didn't want the city. They didn't want the Station. They just wanted to break free and cross and they couldn't . . . just like David . . . and all because of my father." I held my aching chest. "I've felt heartbreak," I whispered. "I've felt joy. What is this that I'm feeling now?"

Finally understanding, Elbee said, *and sometimes understanding hurts.*

Death wasn't my father's decision, to hold in his hands.

Then I saw the corpse's white eyes turn to look at me. A sickening head tilt. He said, "**Oh child. You'll know real pain soon enough.**"

Charlie.

The ferry was gone.

It hadn't dissolved or broken; she'd taken the ferry.

"She's heading to the Veil," I realized.

"**The Harosens don't care who turns to dust, as long as they keep their light,**" the demon prodded.

The thing in the dark spoke through David's body, a horrible sound. After a century of being intertwined, it must be hard to not sound the same. David had spent more time with the dark than he had Father. That wasn't fair.

But my pity dried up when the thing in the dark mused, "**Now you'll have nothing. You truly are your father's daughter.**"

"What did you do to her?" I demanded.

"**She's already gone. She will walk into death.**"

The thing fed off David's pain. It would feed off the hopelessness that would grow inside me like a black flame if Charlie crossed. Because the thing in the dark didn't want to cross. It wanted bedlam. It wanted terror.

But this was still a ground of dreams. This earth was still covered in the bricks and dust of memories. And I still felt my heart, a love as bright as a lighthouse.

I closed my eyes and tried to picture a boat, and when I opened my eyes, I saw a small wooden rowboat with two oars. I jumped in.

"Nera!" Father said weakly from across the ruins.

Father may have given up on David, but I was not my father.

"**Go on, little Nera,**" the thing in the dark cackled.

Nera, no, Elbee refuted me, and I sat down on the bench. I grabbed the oars. *You can't just row your way to the afterlife.*

"Fucking watch me," I said.

Elbee whined. Then, *I'm coming with you!* Elbee jumped in the boat. It rocked, and we shoved off.

I left my father in the ashen bricks of his memories, with the shadow he'd created.

REMNANTS

Samantha Eleanor Connor was born on July 11, 1979. She loved composing music and was a regular on the Chicago open mic scene. She also had an ear for musicals and loved the theatre and any other art she could get her hands on. Her friends and family will remember her in joy. Sam is survived by her father Michael Connor, her mother Donna Connor, her sister Charlotte Connor, and her loving fiancé and best friend Marco Ramirez. Donations can be made in lieu of flowers to the Amelia's Home Women's Shelter, where Sam volunteered in their music therapy program.

—Obituary, March 2005

57

CHARLIE

In my body stands an I and a he. A we. We anchor the ferry near the Veil.

Death is to be done alone, but Charlie is not alone.

Charlie and his tether inside her, something so much bigger and stronger than one little girl stuck in a thunderstorm. They, whoever they were now, stood on the plank facing the Veil, in a fugue state.

"Dad is still alive," Charlie said peacefully. "The city will take care of him. He'll be here soon."

"Yes, he can take care of himself right now," it said through her mouth. **"We just need to find Sammy. Just as I promised."**

Their voices came from the same place, as if Charlie was playing dolls with herself, acting out a scene secretly in the corner of her bedroom. All of the people she'd been—a child, a teenager, a teacher, all of them—intermingling with all the things they now were.

Who was this inside her?

I am you, I have always been you.

That didn't sound right.

I am your friend, here to help, just as I promised.

Was this even real?

And who was she really? Was there even a Charlie anymore?

"In order for you to make it," they said together, "you must let go of who you were. Charlie is of the past. What comes next is something else."

She always wondered how it would happen, if she would be shot like Sammy. Or get sick like her grandpa. Or maybe she would just asphyxiate in her sleep and drift away in a nightmare about traffic.

She did not think it would be as easy as taking one step through a door.

It didn't hurt. Everything up to this point had hurt.

The Veil consumed her, vibrating her body. The eerie smoke of her friend kept her from pulling apart, and so her body went with her over the threshold into the unknown. The thing in the dark held on as long as it could in this Veil, but then she saw the black tar of the demon pull away from her skin. Like she was oozing out poison.

"What are you doing . . ." It was me. Just me. My friend was leaving me, retreating back to the living world.

I can't follow you. But you are brave. You are enough. You can find her. I've gotten you this far.

"I'm not supposed to step through alive."

I protected you. Keep going. For her.

I was just a woman. As I traveled through the Veil, I wasn't even that. The boat dissipated, no longer needed. I was wind. I was shadow. I was stars.

Stars.

Then I stepped out of the Veil and to the other side. That world-to-come.

There was nothing but the ferry sitting in black glass. My body banged inside like it was repelling the new world. Bodies were not supposed to be here. Allergic reaction, sepsis, the—

I panicked, my breath gasping for air like I was drowning. I felt my body growing tired. I looked down at the tar water. Faces screamed up from below me. Singing a deep, guttural song.

One I didn't recognize but had feared all my life.

"I'm not dead," I tried to explain. I gave out a loud wail. "I'm not dead!" I screamed at the Underworld. "I'm not dead!"

I saw ahead, the shore. I saw the Haunts, no longer Haunts. They had shed their static, too. They were healing.

But I was stuck in this boat. I had to follow them, find Sammy, find peace. I stepped out, onto the black glass, and my feet sank like I'd walked into quicksand. If I kept moving, I could make it.

But the music, which wasn't music but a throng of notes, something missing from it . . . no beginning, middle, or end . . . what a treat to be able to sink down and not *have* to be alive.

My heart slowed.

For . . . her? Oh my God. Nera's heart. The lighthouse.

It was a trick. A fucking trick. The thing in the dark had sent me to my death to break Nera. *For her.*

"Stop! Stop!" I screamed out. But my voice grew mute. *Stop! Let me back!*

But there was no point in fighting. A sudden and sharp peace dragged over my body and into my soul.

Now all there was left to do was sink.

58

NERA

The lights of Chicago disappeared behind Elbee and me as we rowed into the dark.

The lake was inky black. The stars still shone, but they seemed more like holes in the side of a great beast, bleeding out light, crying out, and about to fade.

Elbee looked forward, as the boat rocked in a muted wave.

The Veil floated just ahead, shimmering and waiting. Anchored, beside the Veil, the ferry bobbed in the water like a dead body. Empty, its lights were dark.

"Charlie!" I shouted out. I scrambled my oars to sit my little boat beside the ferry. I secured my rope to its aft ladder and pulled myself up the hull of the ferry. I rushed to the nose where the plank was still set by the Veil. The Veil hummed. The plank thunked under my boots. I spun around.

"She's not here," I said, turning to Elbee. "Where is she?"

Elbee came to the edge of the plank, but he said nothing. This place that was usually bustling with souls was abandoned.

"Where is she," I whispered, haunted, my skin cold. "Elbee, tell me, what did she do?!"

Elbee looked to the Veil. *She went through,* he said. *She took her body with her.*

I looked to the Veil. "How," I choked.

She may still be alive, if she has her body with her. For now, Elbee said. *For now,* Elbee repeated. *But the living are not supposed to go through. She won't survive long enough to return.*

I stepped closer to the Veil, its rainbow oil like foam on top of a dying pond. Winter, hushed to a vibration against my hand.

Nera, wait, Elbee commanded. I started forward. *Nera, no! Don't!*

"She said it when we first met," I said. "She said I was acclimated. I've lived my whole life between living and dead. I can go through and not get stuck. I can do this."

Even if you can take your body, if you stay too long, you won't make it back, you'll die, this is sui—

"And if *she* doesn't make it back?!" I snapped.

That's not how this works!

"Damn how it works!" I said. "If my father can curse the city with his Station for a hundred years, I can mar the afterlife with my body for a night."

I'm coming, Charlie.

I stood on the plank, my new black boots firmly at the edge. I peered out to the Veil. It hummed at me. But it didn't sound like music; it sounded like a growl in the back of a dog's throat: don't get closer.

Elbee ran to cut me off, but the water rocked and he stumbled. *The living don't come back. They never do. And you're alive.*

"I'm the Station Master," I said.

I stepped through.

The gossamer, iridescent curtain passed over my skin. It felt like that moment when Charlie and I had been exploring the city, just hours ago, and we ran to catch the train. I threw my arm in between the doors. I thought it would hurt. It did not. The doors stopped, catching my hand, making it so the train could not move without us. Then Charlie clawed open the doors and we jumped inside, catching our breath.

But now Charlie was not here to help. Now, a cold nothing pressed against me. A humming so thick it numbed my skin. But I kept on. It pushed back and I pushed forward and I wanted to retch. I fell onto the other side.

My chest hit the wood of a plank. I held onto it, gripping it as my only life-line. And the smell hit me hard. Cold, stale, stinging, like bleach.

I craned my neck up from the floor to see I was on the ferry; the same ferry as on the other side. But everything was different here. It was a dream of black and stars, the ferry's edges outlined in blue, the shadows barely sketched in, like an unfinished painting. The stars surrounded us as if we'd fallen into the sky.

There was Elbee on the plank right next to me, looking down at me.

"I didn't ask you to come with me." I got to my feet and charged forward.

I was here already, Elbee said. *Dogs are on both sides.*

So everyone who had passed through before me, they had been greeted by friends. They hadn't been alone. "How?"

You aren't supposed to understand, Elbee said. *You were never supposed to be on this side, not until it was your time. Nera, what have you done?*

I jumped up to the second deck. I was going to drive this thing ahead, away from the Veil, until I found her.

Wait, he said. *Wait. Wait!*

Beside the ferry floated a small rowboat, looking just like mine. But it was made of blue smoke. I looked to Elbee.

Elbee sighed. *She didn't take the ferry. Because this ferry doesn't move. It's only a reflection of what's on the other side. Like a mirror. But the further away you get from the Veil, the less of that world is here.*

"So the rowboat will disappear, too," I said.

Eventually, he said. *But you've created it so I hope it . . . stays longer.*

"And what happens when it goes away?" I said. "What is she using to travel?"

He put his paw out on the water. A small ripple jumped from his step, widening and scattering the stars. I stepped forward.

No, he barked. *No, Nera. Don't touch it.*

I saw something in the water. Something moved.

That's why we have to hurry, he said. *Get in the rowboat.*

I stepped into the boat. I found the memory of the oars, outlined in blue. I held them in my hands, although it barely felt like they were there. A pantomime of life, I started to row.

I had to pretend there were still things to sense. It smelled like bleach. It looked like the lake. It sounded like winter. No, it sounded silent. It was silent. I—

The further we get, he said, *the less you'll see. Your mind is going to try to make sense of it. Don't, because it will just make you lose your wits and then lose yourself. We aren't in a place you are supposed to know yet.*

"Is this still the lake?" I said. "Is this all there is of the afterlife?"

No, Elbee said. *This is still the lake. The shore on the other side is the beginning of the After, the world-to-come. But you won't make it that far. And neither will she.*

"Worst case scenario, we die," I said.

That's a terrible scenario, it's not your time, Elbee said. *But no, it's not the worst thing that could happen, Nera.*

The water trilled, like a big snake was underneath us.

I was afraid.

No, I couldn't be.

I shoved forward.

There was nothing out there to answer me back. There was nothing that would bring her back to me.

Suddenly I looked down into the starry waters. I saw bodies all around us, bobbing right under the surface. Perhaps they were people who jumped from the boat. I couldn't tell if they were corpses or still alive. They looked stuck, in a tight loop for as long as they'd been in the water.

Elbee shivered beside me. *They're people who got scared and fell in.*

"But the ferry takes everyone who is ready," I said. "So you're telling me not everyone from the Station made it to the afterlife?"

Those aren't the dead, Elbee said. *They're the living who went after the dead. We're not the first ones to try this. And if we fail, Nera? You and Charlie will be stuck down there, too. Trapped.*

My eyes couldn't look away from them. Each one of their faces, stuck in pain and shock, in heartbreak, their brows creased like they were in the middle of crying out. Their mouths open in a prayer that didn't end, that maybe hadn't even started . . . did I look like that now?

I grabbed the oars, and I plunged them into the waters. The bodies shifted away from the oars, like they were made of water. Like they were liquid, and they reshaped into faces and arms and legs as soon as my oar passed through them. Not alive, not dead.

Elbee was afraid. I was not. It was eerie, but there was also a sad comfort to it. So many people broke out of the boundaries of life to climb their way here, all because they loved each other.

I was stuck. I'd made a rash choice that ended in something worse than death. I'd stepped off the map too early. Neither of us were ever coming home.

No.

I couldn't drown like them. I had to keep going. I wouldn't give up. I needed to remember that while the world around me was for the dead, I still lived.

So did Charlie.

I pushed forward, the spirits simmering like fog coming off the lake as we kept going.

Elbee shivered again. He gnawed at his paws, nervous. He looked like he was going to cry.

"Hey, my good boy," I said, nodding him over so he could sit next to me. "It will be alright. I promise. You've guided me so far. Please let me guide us now."

Elbee put his weight on me. He was not afraid for himself. He'd lived in the in-between. He'd been here before. He was afraid for me.

Music rose from below. From the bodies.

All these different songs, all these loops of verses and choruses; they all sang.

It filled my ears. Loud. Pulled at me. Join in. What would my song be? What were all the songs they sang? Where had they learned all of them? Were they prayers? Were they lullabies? Were they lost here forever? Maybe I could find their voices, follow their songs, save them—

Elbee pulled me back as my foot left the boat.

I shivered and sat back down, picking up the oars again.

Don't listen to them, Elbee said.

There was something ahead.

A shivering, thin darkness like ink spilling through the air, coming closer, skimming across the water. I hadn't even realized I was moving.

"This place is supposed to be kind," I said.

Elbee breathed in and out. *Just because something is frightening does not mean it's to be avoided. Nightmares are dreams, too.*

Like things in the dark.

Stay on the boat, Elbee said. *You are not ready for these tests, Nera.*

Neither was Charlie.

After the ink spilled around us, I could barely feel the boat. The oars were gone. The stars were gone. There was only me and Elbee, and the world fell away.

59

NERA

I forced myself to see through the nothing. A lake was not an ocean; it had another side. There was an ending.

So finally, I saw a shore.

It looked nothing like the banks of Lake Michigan; it was white, and I could not tell if that was light reflecting off it, or perhaps snow, or perhaps just very clear white sand. Above, the sky offered not only stars, but the night danced in pulsing waves of green and red and blue and purple.

The end was not an end; it was only a new beginning, splashed in new things to see, brilliant lands to explore, beyond beyond beyond . . .

My eyes blurred. I was not supposed to see this yet. I squinted, and my vision weakened. It was as if everything was a chalk drawing and a rain had come.

But I could still see souls. The souls that had been the Haunts were now just colorful lights that slowly drifted from the water's edge into the unknown land beyond the shore. Seeds blown from a dandelion, onward.

Then I saw her. Through the ink and the light, I saw Charlie.

She was not on the shore, there was still time. But her colors slowly faded, spilling out of her and into the murk below.

"Charlie!" I screamed out. "Charlie! Please!"

I didn't know if I even had a voice anymore. We had been here too long. If there was nothing in this space, then how could sound carry? But she turned around, and she saw me.

But those eyes, they were too calm. She understood what was going on. It was as if she had made a decision. Her mouth was a firm line, but her body was so relaxed. She sank into the blurry waters.

"No," I said. "Charlie, you have to come back with me."

She said nothing.

I saw no static. The demon wasn't here. She was only herself.

I should have known, because between the music and the smiles and the beautiful day in the city and the precious nights in the Station . . . she had been sinking. I should have held her tighter, maybe then we wouldn't be here at the end.

It would never end. Not really.

"Charlie." I tried to remember I had a voice. "Charlie," I said her name again. "Charlie, please," I begged her. "It's not time to go."

Why do I get to live and they don't? Charlie finally offered. Her voice repeating in my head like a fading echo. *Why do I get to live and she doesn't?* She sounded like a ghost.

And here at the edge of the world, I looked for an answer inside myself. I was the Station Master; I had spent my entire life in death. I had seen all the souls that passed from Chicago to this place I couldn't fathom . . . why did we get to live and they didn't?

"I don't know," is all I could offer.

Charlie's colors disappeared.

"Don't sink," I begged her. "Come back with me. We're not done yet."

He said he would stay with me, all the way through, Charlie shivered. *But I can't feel him anymore.* She sank further. *The Station . . . it hurt him. It hurt the Haunts . . .*

"I'm sorry my father kept them from this place," I pleaded. "I was taught they wanted the Station, when it was only in their way. They deserve to continue on." I looked to the universe around us. "But please, please give me Charlie back. It's not her turn."

No one was there but Charlie and me. The stars above said nothing.

Nera, Charlie said. *We are going to find Sammy. The thing in the dark promised me.*

"No," I felt my words, thin, soft, nearly broken. "Charlie, your sister wouldn't want this. You're still alive."

I'm already late, Charlie muttered.

"If your sister, wherever she is out here, remembers what it's like to be alive, she would *never* ask you to stay here!"

She would! Charlie shouted. *She needed me! And I should have gotten us both home!*

I tried to step forward, but I couldn't. I was stuck in my space. I reached out a hand. "Charlie, it's not your fault. Now please . . . please let *me* get us both home."

Home, she mumbled. Then she looked calm again, a little lost. *Nera, look, we're somewhere we can't see. We're not . . . there . . . anymore . . .* and she drifted, sinking deeper.

She was nearly gone, into the fading ink. All that made Charlie who she was, sank into the cold humming waters. Her music, her freckles, her accent that was formed in the city and dipped in sticky sarcasm. The pizza, the statue at the zoo, the penguins . . .

And me, I would fade, too. I had only just stepped out but it had been a glorious adventure. I had so much life inside me, and now what was the future but this void? What was the future without her? Without her music? I could only hear the humming below us. I could only feel it pulling me—

Her music.

I closed my eyes.

I remembered that song she shouted into the atrium. The words that were nothing more than vowels.

One of those brilliant days in the library, I'd asked Edna, *How does everyone remember all the words to every song?*

Well, Edna had taught me, *in shul, when we don't know the words or can't remember them, we just sing out with no words. What is important is the prayer in the song.*

So, I wrapped my lips around an "ah."

I shouldn't be here.

I started to sing.

I shouldn't be here.

I don't know if I had ever sung, and my singing sounded more like warbling. And I didn't know what to do. And all of this wasn't going to work. And I was unraveling.

I burned and drowned in ice and nothingness, all at once.

"Charlie, please," I begged her.

I felt something glow inside me.

I stared at my hands. I gasped. There was light in this place with nothing. But my necklace was gone . . .

Elbee nudged me. I saw in his eyes a reflection of light.

Me. *I* was the light.

I closed my eyes.

I sang out.

The music below had no words. But I had words and a melody. I had a beginning of a song. I had notes, not just sound. I was not ready to be just sound. I was still a part of the symphony of life.

So then I sang to Charlie: *"When all other promises wash away, this one I can say."*

I shone, as bright as a lighthouse.

"We'll find our way someday. It will be okay someday."

The words slowly became *las* and *das* and *leis,* like one of Edna's old prayers sung on Shabbat. But I kept singing. Until they became new words. *"I am here. I am here. I am here."* The melody moved forward.

The world around us, the water swirled out colors from the black. Ripples of blue. Then ripples of red. Then ripples of gold.

The inky water glowed, turning into constellations. I felt the warmth I'd felt in the Station. I heard laughter, I smelled pancakes, the harsh accents in the words, *I am here.* I knew that accent.

It was the voice of Edna Meyer, somewhere deep in my mind, beyond my ears.

Then the smell of lilacs . . . I'd never smelled them, but I knew . . . *I knew* . . . they were lilacs . . . George.

A well pressed suit. A sticky popcorn floor of a movie theater. It filled me up with memories.

In the light, I think I heard other voices.

And then a piano playing, unlike any other, even more skilled than Charlie. That couldn't be real. There was no one else here . . .

But they were. Small stars, twirling down from the black sky, building a bridge one by one . . .

I let out a breath. "Sammy?"

The music filled me up.

The world on the other side of the Veil wasn't somewhere new. It was where we were. She had been here all along.

They *all* had.

They were the stars.

"Charlie!" I laughed. "Charlie, follow the stars!"

Charlie stopped sinking. She looked up to the stars, their light shining in her dull eyes.

The netherworld could close in on me again. I could feel my soul trying to pound against bones and ribs and a heart. It was hopeless after all. I was going to disintegrate.

I had never really lived, so how was I going to be dead? Had I lived enough to know what either meant? Best to just sink, at least we'd be together.

I felt Elbee tugging at me.

Keep singing, Elbee demanded of me. *Turn around and keep your light. Sing her a bridge home, Nera.*

I turned on my heels, the black glass below filling with light. Filling with a path back to the Veil, and the city.

If she was going to make it home, I had to keep walking.

"They never went away, Charlie," I said, the music rising between us. "They were with us. They are here. *We* are here."

I couldn't see her anymore. She was supposed to be behind me, but I couldn't look back. I needed to focus to create the path, and I needed to trust that she would follow me. I needed to find our way home.

I sang louder. "Please," I said, "This is our song. *You* are my song."

I heard a small voice; one that was hers. I knew it was hers . . . it *had* to be hers.

In this terrible place, I felt a soft hand in mine.

Something solid, something real.

Keep walking, Elbee said. *Don't turn back.*

But I was tired of being afraid, of feeling alone. There was strength in walking side by side, a courageous trust in looking one another in the eye.

I turned around, and there she was in this nightmare, holding my hand. Between us was a light, and below us a bridge of uncountable stars.

She gripped my hand, harder. Her quiet voice, barely a whisper, kept singing. "We are here, take me home."

I was not my father. I would not let go.

We kept walking, and I never took my eyes off her. Sometimes she stopped singing, but it was me and her and we kept believing the other would sing when we couldn't.

And I knew how this story always ended. My father, losing David. Charlie, losing Sammy. There is so much loss, every damned day, so many people torn apart by the void or by each other or by a darkness that we can't seem to understand why it even exists.

But today, we don't lose each other.

Someday.

But not today.

In the world where there is the night, there are also stars.

And no one survives on their own.

We are here, the song rang and rippled the Veil ahead.

We stepped through the shining unknown, together, and back into life.

60

DAVID STEIN

when we were young, it seemed as if we had the whole story ahead to write.
i learned from you, how to read, you truly loved words and poetry
and i said if i were to not be a shomer, i may be a poet
although you would always be the one who should be.
we were young boys with all of chicago growing along with us.
awkward, stumbling, trying to find the right words
sometimes in peace, always at odds, wondering
what we should be built from.
steel, like philadelphia.
brick, like new york.
cement, like minneapolis.
clay, like denver.
no, wood. and we burned. we burned so bright all together.
and i wish we were made of sterner stuff.

now we are dying old men,
between the lake and the city that grew without us,
no, despite us.

you don't remember any of this.
and the only person who ever listens is the thing you trapped in here with me,
it and i were both the thing in the dark.
we were made of memories and rot,
shuffled away.
and now in the open.
you and i were never to look at one another again,
as you orchestrated it.
i have to believe that if you did remember,
if you did still know me,
you would still love me.

in the end, it doesn't matter.
my life was not yours.
as much as i wanted it to be.

behind us two men, comes a light.
has the lighthouse returned?
no, it is your daughter.
bright dust of the station swirling around her,
carrying charlie in her arms.
i stand over you, my rotting hands covered in your blood.
but you refuse to die.
we are an abscess, the two of us.
bursting on the ground where your station once stood.
so you can still bleed.

your daughter comes to me.
she stands above you. stares me down.
she is singing, you can hear it,
and if i'd had a daughter who sang like that,
i would have never stopped listening.
the entire grounds are singing.
the dogs surround us.
there is a light, like the one you chained away,
but this one is so much kinder
than either of ours.
it makes the city glow.

61

JONATHON HAROSEN

Harosen remembered when Nera arrived on the lake, a freezing winter night. She was nearly dead. The dogs suggested Harosen make her warm. She started to cry, clinging onto his beard, holding him as close as a baby can.

She used to run in circles for days, and he would watch her.

When had she grown up?

"It is time for you to go," Nera's voice sounded, loud, her eyes even shone as she looked to the thing in the dark and the boy entwined.

The thing laughed. It rasped: "Little woman—"

"I know your name," she said.

The thing in the dark looked afraid through human eyes. "No one knows my name! I am ancient and much more than a human—"

"Not yours, you shit," Nera interrupted him. "David. I know your name."

The body stalled, stuck somewhere between shock and hope and fear.

"David Stein," Nera boomed. "You are not the thing in the dark. I know who you are. You loved my father. I know what that feels like, to love someone. It means you were kind and you were brave, even when it was hard. You must let the thing in the dark go, David. You are so much more."

They stared at Nera.

David was trapped. Harosen understood. He'd seen the memory just as Nera had.

It had not been fair. Harosen had felt how much the boy named Jonathon had loved David. And what a beautiful life they could have had, if David had followed him out of that barn before . . .

If Harosen had been brave enough to not let go.

David's bloody knuckles dropped to the side. And he wavered.

"You have to go now, David," Nera said. "The demon can only follow you so far through the Veil. But I've seen it, he doesn't cross over. You deserve to go home."

"We are one and the same," the demon rasped.

"David is so much more. That demon can't love," Nera said. "It can only destroy. So, you have to leave it behind, David."

There was a hesitation.

"I will find someone else, I will always survive," the thing in the dark whispered through David's lips.

"It might," Nera said. "But so will I. So will the dogs. So will the stars."

David's body looked at the choir of stars behind her, with white, fogged eyes. And he closed those eyes.

"David," he said, softly, in the voice he had left.

Harosen watched as Gurty came to stand by his side. David's body dropped. And David's soul kept standing, a static black and white, a fog wrapped around him like a cloak.

Gurty howled, and the thing in the dark hissed, peeling away from David's ghost. The demon whispered to Nera.

You will die someday. And I never will. There will always be another
fire. So in the end, I'll win.

"Will you?" Nera said.

The choir behind her sounded louder and louder. Harosen saw David join in the song.

When the sun rose over the edge of the lake, the demon had disappeared. For now.

Harosen saw Elbee come to his side.

It was time.

He closed his eyes. He let go of his body. He was so very tired.

———————

Harosen wished he could remember David.

He imagined they had met when they were young boys, walking out of shul after a long Saturday morning of Torah study. David could have handed him a candy he snuck from somewhere. Harosen ate it. And in the language of young boys, that meant they were now bonded for the summer.

The summer had passed, the season had come, and they still walked down the street together.

They both had deserved kindness. And guilt choked Harosen.

Harosen wondered, as David stood on the nose of the ferry, not touching him, but standing close . . . he wondered if on the other side, there would be something like peace between them.

It felt so early to end their story, and yet so late.

Then came the Veil. Nera dropped the anchor on the ferry.

I wasn't supposed to leave until next autumn, he said.

"I know," Nera said, as the plank reached out to the Veil all on its own.

David looked, enraptured at the Veil ahead. Then scared.

Harosen held his daughter's hand.

I wish, he said, *those days between us, just you and me, I wish I'd known they weren't forever.*

Nera nodded. And her strong façade cracked. No longer the Station Master, but his little girl.

"But if you'd thought about how they'd end," Nera said, "maybe then they would have been sadder."

What does it matter, if we're sad now? Harosen wished he could still cry. But the dead can't cry, they can only melt into the wind.

"I'll see you on the other side," Nera said.

Harosen grabbed her with everything he had left. An embrace from somewhere other than arms. Somewhere deeper.

Don't stay too long, Harosen whispered. *But don't come too early.* He paused. *And remember, the dogs need—*

"I know," Nera said. Then he saw, she was crying. "I love you, Papa."

He pressed his finger against her tears. He wiped them away. But they did not move.

I love you, Nera, he said. *I always have. I always will.*

Then it was time.

David and Harosen stepped to the plank. There was a question of who would go first, unspoken between them. But Harosen offered his hand. David didn't take it.

But he did study it.

I am . . . so sorry, Harosen whispered. David looked to him. *I don't want to believe I was that boy who hurt you. I wish I could have made your life beautiful.*

David shook his head. *I am not ready to forgive you,* he said.

Harosen nodded. *It was beautiful, wasn't it? Before the Fire . . . we were something beautiful.*

Quietly, David agreed. *We were.*

As they passed through the Veil, they couldn't even see the city behind them; the one that had burned in their fire and had shone with their light. It had felt so big, and now there were just the gentle waves of the lake as Harosen turned around to see his daughter one more time.

He should have—

62

CHARLIE

The morning after days that change our lives, our brains usually haven't caught up.

I just sat there, on the concrete slab where the Station had once been. If there even had been a Station. The dust had blown away. When Nera returned without Harosen, she immediately started talking to Elbee and the other dogs, but they didn't raise the Station back up.

They all stood at the edge of the lake, looking out to the sunrise, as if something had been freed.

Gurty came to sit beside me. *You're still alive,* he told me, just in case I didn't know.

Maybe I didn't believe it yet.

You don't have to say anything, Gurty said. *I know you're tired. I'm tired, too.* He looked at the lake. *Nera says she's going to get you home, somewhere warm.*

"The Station," I said, "—*your* home . . . I'm so sorry."

Sometimes, Gurty said, *it's okay to knock things down. Sometimes.* He eyed me. *Not all the time. You really need to be more careful, you could knock yourself down! Or a small child . . .*

He curled around me, and the winter couldn't touch me. He was so warm.

I'm gonna miss you, Charlie, Gurty whispered, a goodbye I didn't know was coming. He knew something I didn't. And when Nera came to sit beside me, our legs high above the rocks of the lake, I could tell she also knew.

"We're not rebuilding it," Nera said. "The dogs did this job just fine without my father. His pillars and his perimeters . . ." Nera shook her head, and I saw the pieces of the lantern necklace in her hand. She let them disappear. Like she'd wiped them from a painting. "We don't need magic hidden behind doors and fountains to be kind, to know who we are, to watch the world . . . Mr. Coleson got carnations for his wife because someone was there to help him. It still happens, even without us."

I shivered, resting my head on Gurty. Nera didn't touch me. She didn't even look at me.

"I'm s-sorry . . ." I tried.

"So the dogs will take their place again," Nera said, "and I'm to go out into the world."

I felt my heart jump a little. I raised a shivering hand, to touch hers. She pulled her empty hands away. And then, after a minute of shock between us, she took my hand in hers. She said, "But I'm going out into the world alone. And so should you."

"I c-can't . . ."

"You can, Charlie." Nera fixed her gaze on me. She was so alive, so warm. I felt so pale, so done. "You have to. Because you're still here. You're you. And now you get to live for you." She put her other hand over mine, cupping my shaking fingers in her embrace. "And I need to live for me."

"Nera . . ."

"But you said that you would show me spring in Chicago," Nera said. "So . . . if you find yourself . . . if I find myself . . . then maybe we can find each other on the first day of spring. When the cafés open up and everyone takes off work early. Remember?"

I nodded, my teeth chattering.

"I can't promise it will be this spring," Nera said. "But if there ever is a year the day comes around, and you want to find me, go to the statue at the zoo. The one with the woman with wings. I'll meet you there."

"Where are you going until then?" I managed.

Nera gave a small smile. "Everywhere."

"And where will I go?" I said.

She took my head in her hands, and she pressed her forehead to mine. She was so warm. "That's the exciting part." And then she whispered. "I don't know, but wherever you go, she'll be there. And so will I. Because we love you."

I fell asleep in her arms one last time.

They said it was a gas leak, slithering from the Water Tower on Michigan Avenue all the way up to Belmont and all the way down to UIC. A few explosions, a few deaths, but nothing as catastrophic as it could have been.

Nothing like the Chicago Fire.

Dad didn't remember anything much about that day. Chestnut had gone missing for a few hours, and I worried he might never come home. But when he did, his red collar was gone, as if to make way for Dad to pick a new one out for him.

I asked him where he'd been, and he just barked. No wink. No telltale signs that it all hadn't been a dream.

Dad bought him a collar. Dad asked me if I'd found Sammy. I bit my lip. "No, but I'm right here, Dad."

And I turned away from him to go back into my room.

A lot of the city was siphoned off and under construction while they checked for leaks. It meant the CTA was terrible and I couldn't go a lot of places on foot.

So I rented a car, and I drove out of the city. I drove past the suburbs. I kept driving, until I hit the Mississippi River. Hours away, surrounded by hills and dead fields, I looked over into Iowa, still in a haze that I'd taken the whole afternoon to come here.

How would I explain this moving forward? When anyone would ask my life story, how would I tell them that once I talked to dogs, stepped through walls, almost sank into the Underworld . . . and loved the magical girl who shone like a lighthouse?

Sammy still wasn't here. And Nera was gone.

I knew as the months would pass, the rough edges of the impossible would smooth out into explanations. It was a mass delusion between two grieving family members; my father had rubbed off on me with his hallucinations. Or maybe this gas leak had been happening since the fall, and it caused some sort of delirium in me. Maybe I just lost my mind, because that was the only way to move forward, in some sort of insanity.

I sucked in a breath.

I looked around.

Then I realized there were no ghosts.

They'd not been on or around the interstate where they'd died. The street outside my apartment had been empty. Mr. Coleson hadn't said anything to me when I left home. He wasn't even there.

I felt tears tip over onto my cheeks. I sobbed.

It was over. It was done.

The haunting had ended.

But without the ghosts staring back at me, how did I know they were there? Without the Station, without Chestnut's collar, or Nera or Sammy's music . . . how did I know it was all real?

It was too easy to believe there was an afterlife, that everything could get tied up with a bow.

I drove back to Chicago. I drove under the bridge. I sat there, staring at the concrete slab that used to be the Station. It was not there. Even when the sun set, it did not appear.

I had no more tears to give.

So I drove to Marco's.

I found him, held him, let him cry and let him see me cry.

"What are we gonna do?" he sobbed.

"I don't know," I said. But we sat together in the dark of his apartment. And for now, that was enough.

He clutched onto me, like I was a life raft. "I'm so glad you're here. I thought you hated me."

"I never ever hated you," I said. "It was all my fault."

"What?" he said. "Charlie, it was not your fault."

Words I needed to hear and didn't quite believe. But I wanted to believe, so bad.

I had missed my friend.

"She loved you so much, Marco," I whispered. "We all love you."

It seemed those were the words he needed.

63

CHARLIE

I waited in a daze through the rest of winter.

Then the first day of spring came. And I ran to the statue. I waited all day. And she did not come.

I sat there, broken.

Another year came. The first day of spring again. Nera did not appear.

I was in love with a dream.

The next year, I moved out of the apartment. I told Dad I would see him at Chrismukkah. I told him to talk to Marco.

I took a train to Normal, to visit the address my mother had texted me. We met at a diner, one that had a big papier-mâché mascot statue outside. We sat in the hot summer weather on the patio, eating ice cream. I told her I was moving to Minneapolis for a little bit. Something new. I told her a lot of things. I held out for a good ending, an apology or an explanation. I gave her all of me, but she didn't have enough trust in me or maybe in herself to reciprocate.

I couldn't save her. And she couldn't save me.

"Why did you leave me?" I finally asked her.

She blinked. "Honey, you're a grown woman. You'd moved out. You were living your own life. And besides, I'll never leave you, I'm your mom."

As we headed for our cars, I said I loved her. Complication between us. But it wasn't the end. Because we were still here.

"I love you, too, Charlie."

Marco helped me move. When he saw Dad again, he said nothing. But Dad looked to him. And Dad said, "Hey, kid."

So Marco said, "Hey, Pops."

They didn't embrace or talk about what had happened. But they both carried my boxes down the stairs to the U-Haul. Dad patted him on the back as I drove away.

Like Nera said, we wouldn't be the same. But we'd still be here.

Marco came to visit me in Minnesota when his work allowed him. That first summer, we explored the city and walked above Minnehaha Falls. We both knew she would have loved it. But we, us there in the present, we *did* love it. And there was a peace in that.

There was no Station along the Mississippi River that cut through Minne-apolis. Or if there was, I couldn't see it.

By the next fall, I was working at a nonprofit as a club director for their after-school program. Every day I carried the memory of what happened with me. It never disappeared, but it melted into my story. Maybe not entirely a de-lusion, not entirely fiction. Still, no one would understand. But I was starting to understand a little more. I made a trip back to Chicago for the spring.

Another year without Nera at the statue.

And yet, I still couldn't believe I'd made her up. Someone who was kind, warm, who loved me.

Grief is made of absence. In order to miss something, it needed to have been there to begin with.

Sammy existed. Nera, she existed. Because I could not still love them if they'd never been there. And in that way, my grief was their ghosts. Proof that once, they'd lived, and once, they'd loved me.

That would never be enough, but maybe it was something I could learn to hold.

Marco and I went to Lou Malnati's when I visited the following spring. Nera was not there, but he was and so was Dad. I saw my old friend and my father laugh for the first time in a long time. Without guilt, we told stories about Sammy, saying her name out loud. And we told stories about what we'd done the last few months. She was still there with us, but we were also here. Charlie, party of three.

When I looked out at the lake, from my taxi on the LSD, I only saw blue water, people running up and down the new bike path near the shore, and some sailboats. The only dogs I saw were the ones catching frisbees and taking walks. They were still made of magic, but today they were busy playing with their favorite souls.

When I got home to Minneapolis, I started to take more walks around the parks in town. I danced in the kitchen, I ordered too much takeout, I forgot what day the trash was picked up, I bought a car and stuck too many bumper stickers on it because I was that bitch. I bought a keyboard.

I paid movers to hike the keyboard down the stairs to my garden apart-ment. I plugged in headphones. I couldn't conclude Sammy's song. It remained unfinished. I didn't know what she had planned for it, and I wasn't going to rewrite her notes with my handwriting.

So, one cold winter night, five years after my sister was killed in the South-well Mall shooting, I sat down and wrote my own song.

64

NERA

Today, the L train platforms turned off their heater lamps. I saw people holding their coats over their arms as they timidly checked to see if the weather was kind enough to not freeze them in a T-shirt. And it was. For the first time in a long time, it was.

The Brown Line curved around Sheridan and up to the North Side. People laughed with each other, all smelling that new grass smell that they'd dragged in on their green-stained shoes. We passed above on the tracks and I looked down through the blooming flowers.

She'd been right; the cafés were spilling out onto the street like clockwork. The wilderness came out of hibernation behind brick walls and glass windows. Folding French doors finally yawned open, chains rattling off stacked chairs. Windows lifted in the apartments above the stores, people leaned out to feel the clean air like they'd not breathed for months. A variety of music echoed from inside their homes out into the city, mingling with one another in a grand cacophony of lively sound. Each individual story, each person sitting alone in the windows or in their cars with the windows rolled down, or on the stoops with their radios . . . they were all a symphony, together.

I gave a small wry smile to myself.

"Doors open on the left at Fullerton," the train warned me.

I pulled my bag close to me and shuffled through the crowd. I was so much taller than most people here, and I squeezed my body out onto the platform. I wondered if she would recognize me, in jeans with a pink carabiner and a cami under a black jacket, big army boots like the ones she'd let me borrow years ago. I'd worn those out, and somewhere around Peru I had to get something a little sturdier.

Here I was, worrying if she would recognize me, when it had been years I'd kept her waiting. How could I believe she was going to be there at all?

The trees along the street bloomed open with green. The brownstones sat in rows, newly planted flowers catching the light through the canopy above, their petals illuminated as they swayed in the soft wind.

Gurty had been right about the park.

It was enormous, it was perfect. This was something I never thought I would see. But here it was, the Hancock reaching out from the trees, beyond the bridge and the garden. Music played from an old upright piano outside the conservatory. It must have been there for an art installation.

I looked to see who was playing. Was it her?

No, it was a boy in a beanie hat, working his way up and down the octaves in abrasive arpeggios. She would never.

"Don't lose hope," I muttered to myself. I'd gotten very good at talking to myself. "You told her the statue, not the park."

And what if she wasn't there?

I kept walking. A woman played the Beatles on her guitar, busking from the curb at the entrance to the zoo. The animals, the people, the workers, all their hearts beating and all their voices raising in that symphony I'd missed: Chicago accents, familiar words, sounding out in exhaustion or joy but always taking for granted these days would last forever.

Maybe today was different and nothing was taken for granted, because everyone had just lived through another winter. They knew that tomorrow might be another cold day, because it wasn't yet May. So today was a day for the zoo. Today was a day for the sun.

I turned at the big cat complex.

I walked through the hedges, behind the buildings.

The sun seared my eyes as the statue came into sight. I held my hand up to my temple, squinting, holding my breath.

And I smiled.

THIS BOOK IS IN MEMORY OF

Dorothy

Wil

Tracy

Vivian "Red"

Bob

Sarah

Joy

Seth

Leonard

Julia

Daisy

John

Letta

Victor

Lin

Barbara

Carolyn

Roxane

Heidi

James

Robin

Kitty

and Bea

May their memory be a blessing.

ACKNOWLEDGMENTS

Every single book that I write is for my wife and soulmate, Jessie. Without Jessie, this book doesn't exist. From the cookie deliveries to the late-night brainstorms to breathing life into a beautiful Station Master I couldn't let go of. I love you. I hope I keep getting chances to write stories to tell you that.

This book also doesn't exist without the incomparable and legendary Lindsey Hall, and the wonderfully sharp and kind Aislyn Fredsall. Thank you to my agent, Stevie Finegan, for coming along on this ride with me. And to the entire team at Tor: Jocelyn Bright, Sarah Reidy, Emily Honer, Emily Mlynek, Eileen Lawrence, Angie Rao, Shreya Gupta, Heather Saunders, Rafal Gibek, Jeff LaSala, Jim Kapp, Michelle Foytek, Alex Cameron, Lizzy Hosty, Erin Robinson, Alexa Best, Will Hinton, Claire Eddy, Lucille Rettino, Sarah Walker, Ed Chapman, and Devi Pillai. It takes an unbelievable amount of work to create the book you're holding. And across the pond I owe thanks to Sophie Robinson, Grace Barber, Melissa Bond, Holly Sheldrake, Charlotte Williams, Lucy Doncaster, Siobhan Hooper, Stuart Dwyer, Poppy Morris, and Mia Lioni. Thanks also to my sensitivity readers K.S. Dunigan and Michele Kirichanskaya.

Thank you to Cecilia Poon for being the earliest reader beyond Lindsey and Jess, and giving your insight on end-of-life care and death. Always a thank you to Jen Finstrom, who always welcomes me back to Chicago with pizza and a story. Thank you to Heather Styka for your insight on the 2000s Chicago music scene. Thank you to Ariel O'Donnell for their Grief Café. A big thank-you to Rabbi Joey Glick for taking the time out of a busy schedule to talk shomrim and sheydim with me. One more thank-you to Jess and my father Dave for donating their handwriting to Charlie and Michael respectively in the Remnants. And also a thank-you to Katherine Applegate, who was my E.B. White and wrote my "best friend books." I got to meet you while I was in the revision process for this book, and it was such a blessing.

Thank you to Mom and Dad, Gramma and Bob, Wil and Bry and Mike and Dani and the multitudes of people who raised me up and taught me what a life should look like. And a big thank-you to Patrick Schley, for following me out to Lake Michigan multiple times to look at the stars and speak about those we'd lost at such a young age.

Thank you to John Wiswell, Sarah Pinsker, Seanan McGuire, Travis Baldree, Ronnie Virdi, Julia Vee, Emily Jane, Emma Mieko Candon, Mia Tsai, Jen St. Jude, Yume Kitasei, Elisa Stone Leahy, Jenna Miller, and all the amazing writers who have believed in me and lifted me up. And a special thank-you to Ryka Aoki, for being a mentor, a friend, and a beacon of light as bright as the stars you write poetry about.

A massive thank-you to my medical team at HealthPartners for making sure I got through this manuscript and who kept me alive through some scary moments.

I also want to take a second to apologize to rats in general. Rats are actually very awesome. One of my favorite students would remind me on a weekly basis that rats and weasels get a bad rap, and they deserve only kindness. I promise my next book will have a kind rat, who is given all the good things in life. Adopt a rat, please.

I also want to thank our old house in the middle of that city park. We had to sell it and leave it behind in the middle of writing this manuscript, due to painful legislation and choices made by the state of Nebraska. May the mulberry tree still grow, may the sun still rise over the garden, may that beautiful state someday be for everyone.

And thank you to the city of Minneapolis and the state of Minnesota, for giving my family a safe place to flee when our home was no longer safe.

Finally, all of the love to the dogs who have loved us to hell and back. Specifically, Tobias, Paddington, Stitch, Sugar, Winks, Happy, Stella, Runa, Hermes, Penny, Roo, Evie, Ember, and Daisy. May you have all the treats, all the scritches, and then maybe just one more treat, if you please.

ABOUT THE AUTHOR

Caulene Hudson-Pace

J.R. DAWSON (she/they) is the Golden Crown Literary Award–winning author of *The First Bright Thing*. Her shorter works can be found in places such as *F&SF, Lightspeed*, and Rich Horton's Year's Best. Dawson currently lives in Minnesota with her loving wife. She teaches at Drexel University's MFA program for creative writing, and fills her free time with keeping her three chaotic dogs out of trouble.

jrdawsonwriter.com

@jrdawsonwriter